Starbound

Tess Barnett

ALSO BY TESS BARNETT

Tales of the Tuath Dé
Those Words I Dread
Because You Needed Me
To Keep You Near

Devil's Gamble

Domesticated: A Short Story Collection
In collaboration with Michelle Kay

AS T.S. BARNETT

The Beast of Birmingham
Under the Devil's Wing
Into the Bear's Den
Down the Endless Road

The Left-Hand Path
Mentor
Runaway
Prodigy

A Soul's Worth

Starbound

Tess Barnett

Pensacola, FL

Cover Art by Jasmine Monterroso
kikissh.com

His Princely Delicates
An Imprint of Corvid House Publishing
Fantasy and Science Fiction Gay Romance Novels

Pensacola, FL
http://www.hisprincelydelicates.com

ACKNOWLEDGMENTS

Thank you so much to all of the readers, fans, and friends who have made this crazy ride so much fun.

1

Elijah had made a mistake.

Omicron was a dirty, crowded station made of creaking metal and flickering neon that stained the cramped corridors in strobing, garish colors. Humans and aliens shouldered by each other in the claustrophobic walkways, overlapping voices jeering or shouting in a wordless buzz that drowned out any other noise. A few people somehow slept in storefronts or alleys, unbothered by the endless shuffle of feet that passed them by. Elijah dodged a pedestrian and almost tripped over a pair of legs, but he didn't stop to listen to the angry protest that followed after him. He just ran.

This wasn't what he had imagined when he had snuck off of his boring farm colony of Dhat-Badan. This wasn't why he had left his family behind without goodbyes. He hadn't run away from one pointless life just to waste away in a piece of crap station like this, where the closest thing to a room for rent had been a flattened mat on one of a dozen recessed bunks in an open room, each one looking like the lice came at no extra charge. This was just being trapped in a different place. Elijah had left home to have an adventure. To see the galaxy.

So he guessed he was going to let a stranger have sex with him.

· · ◆ · ·

Elijah puffed out a breath as he lifted the metal crate in his arms, shifting his grip to settle the weight before moving up the ramp into the cargo hold. The unfamiliar ship had landed on Dhat-Badan just that morning, and the colony Administrator had tasked Elijah and two other young men with loading up the crates it was meant to pick up. Even the average interior of the heavy, aging cargo ship was exciting to Elijah. It was something new. New things didn't happen on Dhat-Badan. People didn't leave. New people didn't come. The very air of the colony was closed off, filtered, and recycled. The inhabitants of the farming colony lived under a protective dome, shielding them from the volatile air of the planet around them while the thumping generators outside did their hundred years' worth of terraforming work. Every ship that came through had to be depressurized and scrubbed before entering their manufactured atmosphere.

But this ship didn't belong to the regular rotation of Federation vessels. It hadn't been sent just to collect grain and cheese for the research station. That meant it wasn't going *to* the research station.

Elijah set down his crate and lingered near the wall until the other boys disappeared back down the ramp, then he crouched down behind the row they'd created and edged just far enough to peek back toward the doors. The Administrator was standing at the bottom of the metal cargo ramp with a clipboard in his hand, talking quite closely with a man Elijah had never seen before. He'd greeted the Administrator with an air of authority and called out orders to a surly-looking man who'd arrived on the ship with him, so Elijah assumed he was the vessel's captain.

The man was tall and lithe, his dirty blond hair hanging down to his shoulders in waves decorated with tiny silver beads and pinned out of his face by a simple metal clip on one side. He wore rough-looking brown pants with a thick belt and military-style lace-up boots, and a sleeveless dark blue shirt that didn't even try to hide the heavy pistol strapped to his hip. When he tilted his head to check the manifest the Administrator offered him, Elijah spotted the glint of a few piercings in his left ear, and the patient cross of his arms flexed the lean muscles underneath his heavily tattooed skin. A dark shadow of a beard covered his jaw and chin, broken by a nasty scar on the right side of his face that cut through both lips. It did little to hide his easy smile. Even at this distance, Elijah could see the striking paleness of the man's eyes. He looked...really cool, if Elijah was honest.

Elijah managed to hide between the crates while the ship was closed up, and he wished there was a window to look out of as he felt the engines roar to life and the craft leave behind the surface of his colony. He felt a pang of guilt at the thought of his mother finding the hastily-scrawled note he'd left behind, but it was quickly overtaken by the excited tension in his stomach. He was actually leaving. He was finally, actually leaving.

Just when he'd almost had time to calm down enough to settle back against the crates and wait to see where his unknowing ride was taking him, he'd heard a grunt of annoyance behind him. He hadn't even had time to turn around before a massive fist connected with his head, and he didn't need a window to see stars.

Elijah had awoken in a different, smaller room with a low ceiling and exposed pipes, handcuffed to a bed and wearing only his underwear. He panicked, jerking against his leather bonds and kicking his way toward the headboard, but he froze when he noticed the lean figure of the ship's captain sitting placidly in a nearby chair. The man's feet were propped up on the edge of the bed, coat hung over the back of the chair and hands laced across his lap, and those white-blue eyes watched him with a slyness mirrored by the small smile on his lips.

"What the hell's going on?" Elijah asked, edging backward to put as much distance between them as he could. "Why am I naked?"

"Had to make sure you weren't hiding anything. Sorry; Park took the sweet rolls you had in your bag. They're his favorite."

Elijah pressed his lips into a thin line to keep his breathing steady. He'd been caught. He hadn't thought far enough ahead to consider what might happen to him if he actually got caught.

"What's your name, kid?" the captain said, interrupting Elijah's racing thoughts.

"Elijah," he answered. "Bennett. Elijah Bennett." Should he have given a fake name? Would that matter? Were they going to send him straight back home, the same way a Federation ship would have? He grimaced in anticipation, but the captain only stared at him with a slight lift of his eyebrows.

"And what makes you think you get to stow away on my ship, Elijah?"

"Please don't take me back," Elijah gushed before he could stop himself. "I won't be any trouble. I'll work. I can't stay there anymore.

The captain didn't answer right away. He tapped one thumb on the back of his opposite hand, working his jaw as he considered the boy's plea. "Well, we have a rule about stowaways on this ship, Elijah. They have to earn their keep, or they get spaced."

Elijah's heart almost stopped. He swallowed down his panic in a hard gulp. "I can earn my keep. I can. I swear."

"Now, wait 'til you hear it all." He watched the boy with a grim look on his face. "There's just one way to earn room and board on my ship, and that's with your body."

"With...with my body? What does that mean?"

"It means if you want to stay breathing and not die jettisoned into the vast blackness of space like a farmboy-sized bit of garbage, you owe me for the air you're taking up. And I take payment in sex."

Elijah hesitated, shifting uncomfortably on the bed. He was suddenly keenly aware of his state of undress. "You're joking. You can't do that. You can't just—"

The captain sat up in his chair and reached across his small table to press a button on an attached intercom. "Hey Park," he called before releasing the button.

A buzz sounded from the intercom, followed by a slightly crackly voice. "Yeah, Cap?"

"What do we do with stowaways on my ship?"

"We fuck 'em, Cap."

"Thanks, Park."

"You got it."

The intercom buzzed again as it disconnected, and the captain relaxed back into his seat, smiling across at Elijah's horrified face. The boy glanced from the door to his handcuffed wrist, hoping in vain for some kind of escape. The cuff was tight and secure, and even if he could have gotten free, where would he go? He was in space. There was no escaping this ship without the captain's say so. This couldn't be happening. He couldn't just let this person—but if his choice was to die otherwise, what choice did he have? His heart seemed to be

4

working its way up into his throat. If this person was going to "take payment" from him, did that mean that Elijah would have to...be a receiver? Oh god. His only sex experience at all had been a few times with a girl from his colony that he'd seen for a while, but that had not remotely prepared him for getting used as payment by a cargo ship's captain.

He opened his mouth to reply, but his voice didn't quite manage to make it out.

The captain broke the silence with a loud, barking laugh. He dropped his feet from the bed and doubled over laughing, one hand giving his thigh a solid slap. He was still grinning when he raised his head. "Should see the look on your face, kid."

Elijah shook his head slightly as if that would clear it. He finally half-whispered, "What?"

"I ain't some kind of monster. I'm not gonna space some kid who snuck on board a ship and didn't even think to bring a weapon with him. It'd be like putting down a lop-eared bunny."

"Wait. So...you're not going to make me pay you with my body?"

The captain settled back into his seat and tilted his head, a slow smile quirking one corner of his lips and causing a tiny jump in Elijah's stomach. There was something almost pleasantly unsettling about the way the other man looked at him. The captain's voice was a little lower now. "Disappointed?"

· ● ◆ ● ·

Elijah spent the next day roped to one of the support beams in the cargo hold. The one called Park, a lanky Korean man with a slightly limping walk, brought him a tray of food at some point. Then they docked at Omicron, and the captain half tossed him onto the catwalk leading away from the ship.

"Don't let me catch you on here again, kid," he said, "or I won't be so nice. Now fuck off."

Elijah had wandered the station with only a single change of clothes in his small knapsack and a few credits on his chip. He was bumped this way and that by the moving crowd, and everywhere people shouted. He got caught staring at an insalar, an alien race entirely made up of slender, silver-skinned humanoid men, and almost got in a fight when the alien's companion spotted him. Elijah didn't pretend to understand how a race of only male aliens worked.

Everywhere he asked for work, he was turned away, and seeing the miserable state of the beds for rent had been the final straw. He couldn't stay here. The station didn't even have windows.

So now he ran back to the docks, hoping and praying that the ship that brought him there hadn't left yet. The dented hull of the bulky cargo ship still sitting in its dock was the most beautiful thing he'd ever seen, and he sighed with relief as he rounded the corner of the catwalk to close the last distance between him and it. He skidded to a stop at the door of the gangway connecting the ship to the dock and pressed the call button on the intercom. When that got no response, he banged on the door with the side of his fist until the speaker crackled to life.

"We paid our fees already," Park's voice barked. "Get the hell out of here, Karnak."

"It's me!" Elijah said in a rush. "It's me. I want to talk to the Captain."

"Didn't he tell you not to come back? What do you need him for?"

Elijah started to answer, then shut his mouth again. He didn't need to tell everyone in the world what he planned to do. "I'll tell him that."

The intercom clicked off, and for a few moments Elijah thought he'd been hung up on and turned away, but then the speaker buzzed again, and the captain's drawling voice came through. "What do you want, kid? I'm fresh out of good deeds today."

Elijah could feel the heat rising in his cheeks already. What the hell was he doing? He squeezed his eyes shut for a moment and snorted out a steeling breath. He was getting himself off of this piece of shit station—that's what he was doing. "Can I talk to you? I mean...really talk to you. Not through this."

"Fuck's sake," the other man spat, and the speaker went silent again. Elijah waited with his fingers fidgeting at his knapsack until the door hissed and slid open. The captain stood in the enclosed gangway with his arms folded, lifting one hand to beckon the boy to speak.

"What's going on, kid?"

Elijah chewed his bottom lip and took a deep breath as though it would make his next words any easier. "I want to come on your ship," he said, not quite sounding as firm as he hoped.

"Well I want a million credits and a pony, son," the captain sighed, hip cocking to one side as he shifted his weight.

"What if I pay my way?"

The man hesitated, and Elijah noticed the slight narrowing of his eyes. "We ain't a taxi service. And you're broke anyhow."

Elijah stepped a little closer to him to meet his gaze. "I mean...what if I *pay* my *way*."

The captain's eyebrows lifted, and the cross of his arms loosened in surprise. "What's that, now?"

"You weren't joking about wanting to sleep with me, right? So I'll do it." He hoped the other man didn't notice him swallowing down the anxious lump in his throat. "Let me come on your ship, and I'll work. I'll do my part on the crew, and I'll...let you do what you want. With me."

The blond's mouth twitched down into a frown. Elijah stood silently while the captain studied him, scanning his face for any sign of a trick. Finally, he shook his head. "You don't know what you're saying, kid."

"I do," Elijah insisted. "I'm not a kid." He sighed and raked his fingers through his dark hair. "Look, I don't have anything. I came out here on my own because I wanted to do more than spend every day on that colony doing exactly the same thing over and over until I die. If I stay here, I'm just as trapped. I don't care about the sex—it's just sex. It's the only thing I have to offer right now, and you seemed interested. So I'll do it if it means you'll take me with you."

The captain let out a slow breath through his nose, and he gave the boy another brief look up and down. Then he tilted his head back toward the ship's door behind him.

"Come inside."

2

Elijah stood inside the captain's cabin once again, but this time he wasn't being ushered out by the burly First Officer who had knocked him out in the cargo bay. He turned to face the captain as the cabin door closed and locked behind him, and he waited with his heart pounding against his ribs while the blond lingered near the door, hands on his hips and a frown on his face.

"Here's the deal," he said, glancing up to make sure he had Elijah's full attention. "I'm not interested in pressuring innocent farm boys—it ain't a turn on, you feel me?" He paused. "But I'd be lying if I said I didn't like the look of you."

Elijah squirmed slightly under the other man's gaze. "I know what I'm doing," he said, but the captain shook his head.

"I really don't think you do. You don't understand what you're offering me. So here's what's gonna happen. You say stop—it stops. Anytime, understand? You aren't enjoying yourself—it stops." He gave a sigh, rubbing one hand over the back of his neck and letting his gaze fall to the floor. "I don't much like the idea of keeping a private whore on board. So if you want a ride on this rig so bad, then maybe I can do a...mutually beneficial relationship. You know what I'm saying?"

"I'm...not sure. What's the difference?"

"I'm saying I ain't some creep who's gonna keep on just using somebody who's not enjoying themselves. Are you even attracted to men?"

Elijah shifted on his feet. "I mean—" He hesitated, heat blooming in his chest at a memory of the young man his father had hired for some extra work back on his colony, working beside him in the barn, stripped of his shirt and glistening with sweat. He'd felt the same tightness in his stomach that he felt with the captain's eyes on him, but acting on it hadn't been an option. He had been older than Elijah and happily in a relationship with a woman—though that hadn't kept the image of the other man's muscles moving under the skin of his back out of Elijah's mind. He swallowed and tried again, forcing his voice up through his throat. "I don't have a lot of experience period, so, you know, I don't know that I...*don't* like it."

The older man huffed and scanned the boy in front of him again. He frowned a little and snorted out his next breath, fingers drumming on his hips. "How old are you, Elijah?"

"I'm twenty."

"Fuck," the captain laughed. He paused to let out one more sigh, and then he seemed to make a decision, and he looked up to meet Elijah's eyes as he moved closer. Elijah didn't retreat even when the other man drew near enough to touch him. The captain's hand settled lightly on the boy's waist, and he leaned in so close that the soft scruff on his jaw brushed the younger man's dark cheek. His breath washed over Elijah's ear, steady and warm, and the boy's next exhale was just a little unsteady. Elijah tensed under the light touch of the captain's fingertips brushing over his belt and under the hem of his shirt. As soon as that soft heat touched his skin, Elijah's breath hitched in his throat, and he couldn't see it, but he felt the subtle shift in the other man's cheek that suggested a smile.

"Well all right then," the captain murmured with an amused chuckle. He leaned an inch closer and dropped his voice to speak into the boy's ear. "Take your shirt off, Elijah."

Elijah did as he was told, tugging his shirt up by the back of his collar and over his head without complaint.

"And your pants."

The boy fumbled with his belt buckle under the scrutinizing eye of the older man, managing to unfasten it after an awkward moment or two. He toed off his boots and tugged off his pants and socks in one pull, finally standing mostly nude in front of the captain's light eyes. He shifted awkwardly and tried to breathe slowly to calm the rolling of his stomach, but it didn't seem to help very much. The blond's faint smirk as he raked his eyes slowly up the boy's body sent a jolt straight through him. He wasn't shy about his body, but his skin prickled with goosebumps in the cool air of the cabin. The captain reached out for him again, fingertips caressing his flat stomach with a touch of admiration. The older man looked pale against Elijah's brown skin, sharpening the contrast between them—the captain fair and calm and watching him with icy grey eyes, and Elijah dark-eyed and subtly trembling.

"Get on the bed," the captain said, gently urging Elijah backward with a press of his fingertips.

The boy obeyed. He sat back onto the mattress and scooted toward the railing that made up the headboard, struggling to keep his breath steady as the other man crawled forward to kneel in front of him. The captain had barely touched him. Elijah didn't even know this person, didn't even know his name—but he already felt a stronger stirring of arousal deep in his belly than he ever had with any of the girls back on his colony. The blond's hands slid up Elijah's calves to his knees and lingered there with a light touch.

"Spread your legs for me, Elijah."

The words vibrated up Elijah's spine, and he let his knees fall open to allow the other man's fingertips to brush further up his thighs. Every touch sent a shudder through his skin, and his whole body felt hot under the blond's intense gaze. He sucked in a harsh breath as the captain's caress traveled up his stomach and torso. His hands were strong and slender, his movements patient and agonizingly slow. His thumbs ran over the soft edges of Elijah's hipbones near the waistband of his underwear, tantalizingly close to dipping underneath. Elijah's gaze was locked onto the older man's pale hands against him, and his breath left him as those long fingers fastened onto his hips. The captain's whole demeanor had changed—before, he seemed laid-back and smiling, but now he tugged Elijah down by his thighs so that the boy straddled his hips, and he looked like a predator. Elijah couldn't help the startled yelp he made at the sudden movement, and he felt his face flush as he realized his erection had begun to strain against the fabric of his underwear.

"That's it," the older man murmured with a soft hum of approval, wetting his lips as he inspected the lean torso of the squirming boy beneath him. His hands trailed up Elijah's sides, and he bent over him, tongue laving slowly over one dark nipple. Elijah hissed in a shaky breath and felt his back arch into the heat of the caress. He saw the captain's smirking lips for a moment before his mouth closed over Elijah's nipple again, and the boy let out a faint whine that startled him. The sensation was new and intense and brought a wave of heat across his skin. The older man's arm slid around his waist to pull him closer, shifting him so that he could better reach to run his tongue over his other nipple.

Elijah did his best not to lose himself to the touch, but his head was swimming. He gripped the sheets at his sides and forced himself to release them. He didn't know what he should be doing with them. Should he keep them out of the way? Should he be touching the man over him? Did the blond *want* him to touch him?

The captain gave Elijah's nipple one more soft bite and released him, tracing his fingertips up the boy's sides to his wrists as though he could sense his anxiety. He urged Elijah's hands upward and closed his fingers around the railing at the head of the bed, then leaned close to the boy's ear.

"Hold on there," he murmured. "Don't let go."

Elijah gripped the rails tightly as the captain sat back on his heels again. He felt even more exposed, displaying himself this way, but the blond's heated gaze sent a thrill through him that he couldn't quite name. The older man finally let his hand flatten over Elijah's aching erection, the pressure drawing a grateful sigh out of him. His breath quickened as he watched the captain's fingers closing around him over his underwear, moving in slow, purposeful strokes. Elijah bit his lip to keep from bucking against the touch, and his heart skipped as he finally looked into the other man's face and found those predator's eyes locked onto his own.

"Do you like that, Elijah?"

The boy didn't have the breath to answer, so he only nodded.

"You aren't just saying that, are you, Elijah?" His voice was low and deep, and it made the boy's stomach feel hot. He stopped the movement of his hand, so Elijah shook his head in a mild panic. The blond squeezed him tightly and seemed satisfied by the gasp he gave. He curled over the younger man again and gave one nipple a sharp bite, his thumb rubbing firmly over the weeping slit at the tip of his dick through his underwear.

Elijah's next breath turned into a gasping moan so loud that he knew his face burned red in embarrassment. He fought to control his heart, but every thumping beat threatened to bruise his ribs from the inside. He'd never responded this way before. It was only a handjob— why was his breath so frantic?

"Do you want more?" The blond's words cut through the fog clouding Elijah's mind, and the boy nodded without hesitation. "Ask me," the captain whispered.

Elijah's brow furrowed in frustrated confusion as he panted out, "What?"

He stopped his touch, just letting the weight of his hand rest against the dark-skinned boy's twitching cock. "Ask me for more," he said evenly.

Elijah lifted his hips in an attempt to press into the other man's hand, but the blond kept his distance and tutted a soft scolding at him. Elijah shut his eyes for a moment before he could meet the blond's gaze. "I want...more," he finally said, not minding how pleading he sounded.

"Good boy."

The praise shot a bolt of heat directly into Elijah's belly that was immediately overshadowed by the chill of the air on his bare dick as the captain pulled his underwear down his hips and exposed him completely. He wrapped strong fingers around him and stroked him skin to skin, his teeth and tongue thoroughly abusing one of the boy's reddened nipples before moving on to the other. He pressed the thumb of his other hand into the tender skin just behind his balls, causing Elijah's hips to jerk and his hands to clamp tighter around the railing at the head of the bed. His mouth fell open to let in his gasping whine. He'd never been touched there before—it was sparking and intimate and flushed him with an all new kind of heat. The tension built in the younger man's belly quicker than it ever had before, and just as he was on the verge of bursting, the blond's hand vanished from him. A string of whimpers fell from Elijah's lips, but the other man refused to give in, only watching the boy's dark eyes until his breath slowed and his skin stopped shivering. Then he took him back into his hand, stroking him hard and fast into panting again.

He built him up and pulled away over and over again, edging him closer and closer to climax with every touch and causing deeper groans with every abrupt halt. His free hand laid against Elijah's stomach to feel the tremors and gasping breaths his squeezes caused. It was torture—the pauses and fingertip-light touches were almost painful, they were so teasing—but it never crossed Elijah's mind to ask the other man to stop. He only wanted more.

When Elijah was finally reduced to a shuddering wreck on the mattress, a sheen of sweat on his brow, his back arching sharply and the muscles in his arms straining from gripping the railing so tightly, the older man's fingertips brushed him slowly from base to tip with a feather-light touch. Elijah almost sobbed in frustration. The captain didn't grip him again, only ran his fingers up him at an agonizing pace. By the third caress, Elijah's hips bucked uncontrollably.

"That's right," the blond whispered. "Come for me, Elijah."

He stroked the younger man once more, and Elijah exploded. His vision darkened, and his body tensed, spilling pulses of semen onto his own stomach without the other man even touching him anymore. When the last wave subsided, he collapsed back to the mattress, gasping for breath and shutting his eyes against the spots in his vision. He barely noticed the shifting weight as the captain moved from the bed, but he opened his eyes again at the touch of a soft towel cleaning the cooling liquid from his belly. The blond above him tugged the rumpled blanket up around him and leaned up to gently pry his still clamped fingers from the headboard bars.

Elijah just stared up at him, his brain barely functioning well enough to form whole thoughts, let alone words. That wasn't sex. Wasn't he supposed to be the one paying? How did he end up getting a handjob? And how the hell had this man blinded him with ecstasy using only his hands?

The man gave his head a light pat, a faint rumbling chuckle in his throat as he touched the boy's dark hair. "Settle in, Elijah," he murmured. "I think this is going to work out just fine."

3

Elijah didn't quite fall asleep, but in the silence following the departure of the ship's captain, he laid under the stranger's blanket and stared up at the ceiling, flexing his fingers to ease the tension out of them. What had just happened? That was most definitely not what he had expected when he'd decided to make his offer to the captain. It hadn't seemed like a payment at all. In fact, he was more than a little embarrassed about how much he'd enjoyed himself. The teasing had been excruciating—actually painful—but he hadn't wanted to stop. Pain and pleasure were supposed to be separate, weren't they? Maybe he'd just been too overwhelmed by being with another man for the first time. He didn't know what had come over him—but something about the way the older man had gently commanded him had set his blood on fire. That felt dangerous.

When he finally felt like he could move his legs, he pushed the blanket aside and swung them over the edge of the mattress. He gathered up his clothes—minus his underwear, which, he realized with a flush of heat, were more than a bit damp. He tucked those away in his knapsack to wash later and dressed himself in a hurry, opening the sliding door to the cabin as soon as he was finished lacing up his boots. The door gave a low groan as it slid open, and Elijah found himself standing in the entrance to a cramped mess hall that went suddenly silent at his appearance. Five pairs of eyes were on him—the crew sat at a long table with dirty plates and empty coffee cups in front of them, watching him silently. Elijah got the distinct impression that he was interrupting. He automatically sought out the captain, but he was notably absent. The blond might have warned him that his quarters let out directly into the mess hall.

"Uh. Hey," he offered, attempting to smile in the face of their stares. The First Officer who had knocked him out, a massive man with a shaved head and a sour face, was scowling at him like he thought Elijah might rob the place. None of the crew members answered his greeting. The only woman there took a long drink from her mug without moving her eyes from him. The sound of the door creaking shut behind Elijah was so loud in the awkward silence that it startled him. He shifted on his feet and put his hands in his pockets to keep them from fidgeting. "Uh. The captain said—"

The man called Park interrupted him. "You found out what happens to stowaways, didn't ya?"

Elijah's face burned red as half of the table burst into laughter. The surly First Officer kept frowning, and an older man at the end of the table smiled faintly down at his coffee cup, but Park, the woman, and a young man with a mess of curly hair all seemed to find great joy in Elijah's embarrassment. Park leaned his elbows on the table to speak again.

"Make some tough choices today, kiddo?"

The woman snorted. "You do what you gotta do for three hots and a cot in this world, huh?" She smirked up at Elijah as she set down her cup. "Or did you bring that skill set with you from your dairy farm?"

"I—"

Park cut Elijah off before he could respond. "You leave behind a vacancy at that podunk little colony?"

"Don't be an idiot, Park," the woman said. "They still have the cows."

Elijah's shyness melted into irritation, and he frowned. "I'm not—"

This time it was the heavy thunk and hiss of the door across the room that stopped him from answering. The blond captain appeared in the doorway, leaning into the room with one forearm on the edge of the open frame. He'd tied his hair up into a messy bun at the back of his head, and a few of the metal beads clicked softly together as he moved. He glanced briefly at Elijah, but his thin frown was focused on his crew, who had quieted in his presence.

"Y'all are awful chatty for a bunch of assholes who are supposed to be prepping my ship," he said.

Park's teasing grin had faded; now he gestured to Elijah with an air of grudging exasperation. "What the hell is this, Cap?"

"New cabin boy," he answered simply.

The woman laughed. "You're kidding, right?"

Park shook his head with a sigh. "Since when do we pick up strays?"

The captain lifted his eyebrows meaningfully at the other man. "You gonna complain about an extra set of hands next time the actuator on that water pump acts up again?"

"The hell does this farm boy know about water pumps?"

The boy with the untamed curls shifted in his seat, drawing his feet up onto the chair and wrapping his arms around his knees to reach his coffee cup. "He's a spy," he said in a sing-song voice, and the captain sighed.

"He's not a spy. Who the hell would spy on us?"

Park gave a snort. "Oh, I dunno, Cap—literally any Federation stooges from any of the stops we make?"

The blond frowned at him, but Elijah spoke up before the conversation could go on. "Why would the Federation care about you?" Every set of eyes in the room was on him again, but no one answered. "You guys are just a shipping vessel, aren't you?"

Park stared at the captain, lifting his hand toward Elijah as though the boy's words illustrated the point he'd been making, and he let it drop back to the table with a thump.

"Spy," the younger man hissed again, but the captain's finger pointing a warning at him made him take a drink from his cup instead of continuing.

The captain sighed through his nose and frowned, watching Elijah's face. "We are a shipping vessel," he said. "We just don't always ship legal things. Sometimes we ship things that are decidedly *il*legal. Does that bother you?"

Elijah hesitated. "What kind of illegal things?"

"The kind that stays in closed crates that don't get opened by nosy parkers," he answered firmly. "It's none of our business what kind.

We just get paid. If you can't deal with that, there's still time to let you off here. Your choice."

Elijah swallowed and searched the other man's eyes for any sign of the gentle teasing he'd seen back in his cabin, but it was missing. It was extremely awkward to be standing in the mess hall talking business with someone—a man who was going to be his superior—who had been biting his nipples and jerking him off earlier that day. But the decision itself wasn't difficult. It was a shipping job. Elijah could do a shipping job if it meant getting to see the galaxy. He would have stayed home if he hadn't been prepared to take any risks.

"I can deal with it," he said.

"See?" the captain answered immediately, returning his attention to his crew. "He can deal with it. Now y'all get your asses where they're supposed to be. Brooks, I want this old girl starside in thirty minutes, you hear?"

"Yes, Captain," the woman answered, already getting out of her seat.

"Harper, you help her get unhitched."

"Yes, Captain," came the reply from the curly-haired boy. Elijah named them again in his head as they exited the room in an attempt to keep his new crew's names straight.

"And Park, if that pressor's not calibrated by the time we get to Tadmor, I'm gonna have your ass. Go on, now."

Park gave a little sigh of resignation but lifted two fingers to his forehead in a quick salute. "You got it, Cap."

He filed out with the First Officer behind him, the large man's narrow eyes not leaving Elijah's face until he was out of sight completely. The older man kept his seat at the table, and the captain watched Elijah in silence for a moment. The boy stood up a little straighter and nodded at him.

"Tell me where you need me, Captain."

A tiny smirk tugged at one corner of the blond's lips. "Cabin boys clean the kitchen." He reached out and gave Elijah's cheek a pat so solid that the boy almost lost his footing, then he let himself out and finally allowed the door to shut.

Elijah was left alone with the man at the table, who gave a soft chuckle in the quiet room. He was a broad-shouldered black man who looked to be in his early forties, with a short beard and a button-down shirt with the sleeves rolled up his thick forearms. He rose from his seat and had half of the crew's abandoned plates gathered up before Elijah realized what he was doing and rushed around the table to help him.

The man smiled kindly at him. "What's your name, son?"

"Elijah."

"Nice to meet you, Elijah. You can call me Davies. I'm the medic on this boat, and the one frequently left to clean up after the rest of my lovely crewmates." He paused with his stack of dishes by the sink and glanced over his shoulder at Elijah's arms full of coffee cups. "Wash, or dry?"

"Oh, I'll—I'll wash. You don't have to help." The man waved away his protest, so Elijah approached the kitchen sink and ran the water, scrubbing out the mugs one after the other and handing them off to be dried.

"Don't let these guys give you too much shit," Davies said after a minute or two. "We're all here for different reasons. I just hope you aren't being taken advantage of."

Elijah couldn't quite meet his eyes. After what had happened in the captain's cabin, he certainly didn't feel like he'd been exploited, but he wasn't keen to explain himself to this man. "Don't worry about me," he said. "Thanks."

"Well, all right." Davies stowed the cups back in their rows in the wire rack along the back of the kitchen counter and took the first plate as Elijah handed it to him.

Elijah chewed his lip for a moment before speaking again. "But is he...a good person? The captain, I mean."

Davies glanced at him out of the corner of his eye as he wiped the water from a clean plate. "That depends on how you define 'good.'"

"Aside from the smuggling. You know, is he the sort of person that's...good to work under?"

"I wouldn't be here if he wasn't. He runs a tight ship, but that's what keeps us going. He does what needs to be done and takes care of his crew. If you can adjust to a life on board a ship, there are worse ones to be on."

Elijah nodded and passed the man another plate. "Thanks."

The two of them finished the dishes in companionable quiet, and once Davies left Elijah to his devices, the boy looked around at the empty room. He took a quick, deep breath. He wanted to earn his place here. And cabin boys cleaned the kitchen. It certainly looked like it needed it—smears of old, half-wiped up coffee stained the counter, and the table felt a little sticky. Even the metal chairs needed a bit of prompting to move from their gummed-in place on the floor. He found a bucket and a few rags under the sink and set about scrubbing down the counters, the cabinet doors, and the table. Halfway through, he heard the pilot's voice over the intercom warning the crew that they were about to disembark, and a minute later, he felt the hum of the engine under his feet and a few bumps as the ship disengaged from the dock. He forced himself to finish his work, and he stood near the door with reddened, wrinkly hands and the front of his pants soaked in soapy water, but the kitchen was spotless.

Elijah checked one of the doors that *didn't* lead back into the captain's cabin and found only a pantry, so he checked another and found himself on the bridge. He did a quick count—one, two, three doors in the mess, and one opening to a ladder down to the deck below. This layout was going to take some getting used to.

A pair of seats blocked his view of the huge window making up the front of the bridge, and as he moved around them, the sky seemed to open up in front of him. He was vaguely aware of the pilot and the captain watching him as he stepped down the short set of stairs into the cockpit area where they both sat, the woman with her hands on the controls and the captain lounging with one leg slung over the arm of his co-pilot's chair, but he looked straight ahead at the thick glass separating him from the emptiness outside.

He walked slowly, as if he might be sucked out if he approached too fast. They had left the station behind, so only blackness filled the window, and Elijah reached out a tentative hand to touch the cool glass. He could spy a few distant, flickering stars, but the vastness of the space beyond overwhelmed him.

The captain gave a low chuckle behind him. "There ain't a whole lot to see just now," he said. "You ought to wait 'til we hit the FTL gate."

Elijah didn't answer him right away. He inched closer to the glass so that his nose almost touched it. "No," he said softly. "It's...really beautiful like this. It's so *black*. There's just...nothing."

She snorted. "That's why they call it 'space,' kid."

Elijah smiled faintly despite her jab, and when he finally glanced over his shoulder, he caught the captain's pale eyes on him, watching him with a soft look on his face. The blond didn't say anything, but his look still made Elijah's cheeks burn. He hoped it didn't show. "So where are we going?" he asked to break the tension he suspected only he felt. "You said we're going to Tadmor? That's in Gamma Cephei, isn't it?"

"Yeah," the captain answered, his eyebrows lifting a little as though impressed by the boy's knowledge. "Just the next stop. It's a crappy planet; nothing interesting."

Elijah couldn't help his excitement from curling his lips into a smile. "I bet you're wrong."

The woman feigned gagging from the pilot seat. "Ugh. I can't take this childlike enthusiasm. Tone it down, will you?"

The captain gestured to Elijah to get his attention before he could answer, and he pointed over the boy's shoulder toward the window. Elijah turned to look and actually let out a quiet laugh as the FTL gate came into view. A short line of ships waited their turn to pass through the massive center of the rotating cylinder. The ring of metal was covered in bright lights that shone off of the long solar panels sprouting from its back in a fanned circle, and signs floated in place nearby, multicolored neon letters meant to entice travelers to exciting destinations on the other side of the gate. Some of them were written in English, but some of them were words that Elijah had no hope of recognizing. There were ads for vacation spots, shops, and even a casino. Elijah plastered himself against the glass to try to get a better look as a ship ahead of them took its turn, disappearing into the center of the gate. A flash sparked from inside, and a second later, a trail of dust and light shot from the opposite end of the ring as the ship was fired off toward its target.

"We're going through that?" he asked, and the captain's voice replied.

"Yep."

"How does it work?"

"You're asking the wrong person, kid. All I know is it takes us from Rosette to Gamma Cep in a day instead of six years."

Elijah turned toward the pilot as though she might have a better answer, but she barely glanced at him before returning her focus to the control panel in front of her.

"You want a science lesson, kid, you can get on the net. I'm trying to fly this rig. Go bug somebody else."

Elijah sighed, having to satisfy himself with watching from the window while their ship slowly moved closer and closer to the gate. When they were finally next in line, he pressed himself against the glass again, not willing to miss a single moment. The comm gave a squeak of static as the pilot connected to the gate controller.

"Gate NGC 2244, this is ICV-P Chimera, registration number D801-dash-5, requesting passage to Gamma Cephei A."

A moment passed, and then a man's voice sounded from the other end of the comm. "Confirmed Chimera, you are cleared for travel. Proceed through the gate."

Elijah watched the lights around the rim of the gate until they disappeared beyond the barriers of his window. Inside the gate was somehow darker, and it felt a little claustrophobic even in their relatively small ship. Almost before Elijah could blink, there was a snap in his ears and a near-blinding flash of light, and then they were in black space again. He paused before looking over his shoulder, hands still on the glass.

"What just happened?"

"We're in the gate. Speeding along. When we come out, we'll be at Gamma Cep, and then it's just three days to Tadmor."

"So what happens in the meantime? Is there something I should be doing?"

The blond tilted his head curiously. "Have you slept since we dropped you on Omicron?"

"Uh. I guess not."

"Then you should probably do that. We're going to be traveling for some time. I know you're used to living on a planet, so don't lose track of time just because there's no sun to remind you when to go to bed."

Elijah paused, letting his fingers finally slip from the window as he turned to face the captain directly. "Where, uh...where do I sleep?"

The pilot shot a sidelong smirk at the blond. "Yeah, Captain; where should he sleep?"

He frowned at her as he stood from his seat. "Come on, kid."

Elijah couldn't make his feet work. He wanted to know if he would be staying in the captain's cabin so that he could "pay" him whenever he wanted, but at the same time, he didn't want to ask. He wouldn't want that, would he? To be sleeping in the bed where he already had a very indecent memory? He stuffed his hands in his pockets as they walked and tried not to imagine those icy eyes looking down at him, those lightly calloused hands running over his stomach and wrapping around his dick. He definitely wouldn't want to be staying somewhere where he'd be at the captain's mercy, where whenever the older man wanted, he could just take him, use his body—

The captain whistled at him from the back of the bridge, one hand already on the ladder leading to the lower deck. "You deaf?"

Elijah scurried forward, flushed with embarrassment and a growing tightness in his stomach. He waited until the captain was halfway down the ladder to the lower deck before starting down himself. He glanced around as he dropped to the deck and saw only a long corridor with a few doors along one side.

The ship definitely looked old. Elijah had seen the inside of some of the Federation ships that came to his colony to collect their outgoing shipments, and they'd been all sleek lines and holographic touchscreens. This hallway was square and bleak, with visible rivets at regular intervals along the corridor. Elijah's steps echoed from the metal floor as he followed the captain down. The ship creaked here and there, but it seemed clean and well-maintained despite the thick pipes along the ceiling and the worn ladders leading from deck to deck. The Federation ships had elevators, but these were more like accessible manholes. This ship was a bit of a junker.

Elijah frowned a little as the captain stopped in front of him. He didn't know the whole layout of the ship yet, but being on a completely different level had certainly answered his question about sharing space with the handsome blond.

The captain turned to look at him. "We don't have a lot of space on board, but there's a spare bunk here at the end." He paused, seeming to notice the subtle furrow in the boy's brow. "Did you think you were staying with me?"

Elijah's gut clenched. "I just didn't know—"

"Did you *want* to stay with me?" The blond stepped forward with a smirk on his lips, forcing Elijah to retreat back to the wall to keep any distance between them. "Was your little imagination running wild?"

Elijah couldn't meet his gaze. He swallowed hard as the captain's hand moved to rest against the wall near him and wet his lips to stall a moment more. "I did...offer to pay you," he said in a low voice. "But what happened before...it didn't really seem like *me* paying *you*."

The captain gave a low chuckle and leaned in close to murmur near the boy's ear, "Because I didn't fuck you?"

Elijah tried to nod with as little movement as possible, and he caught the smirk on the other man's lips so close to his cheek.

"Don't you worry," he purred. "I have lots of plans for you, Elijah. Get some sleep." He hit the button to open the door beside the boy and brushed a fingertip along his jaw as he moved by him on his way back toward the bridge.

Elijah took a slow, shaky breath with his back against the wall and squeezed his eyes shut for a moment before forcing himself to turn into the room. It was more like a closet than a bunk, really, and it looked like it had been unoccupied for some time. But the cot beside the wall looked comfortable, at least. Elijah pressed the switch for the light and let the door close behind him. This was home now, he guessed.

4

Elijah laid in his little cot with his hands laced on his stomach, unable to close his eyes. The soft rumble of the ships engine thrummed through his body, a reflection of the excited thumping in his chest. Everything that had happened to him between leaving his colony and now seemed like a dream—he'd either been locked in a tiny hold, left to wander a filthy, dangerous station on his own, or been reduced to a babbling mess in a stranger's bed. Now he was a real member of a shipping crew. At least, he was pretty sure he was. On a probationary period, at least. He hoped. It hadn't had time to really hit him.

But now the reality of his situation was setting in, and sleep seemed like an impossibility. He was in *space*. He wouldn't have to wake up at dawn to go out and haul open the barn doors or rake out the stalls—in fact, there wasn't even going to be a dawn to wake up *at*. Whatever sun they happened to be closest to wasn't going to be rising or setting to him. When he did wake up, he could just go and have a cup of coffee and see what the day had in store. He would actually not have every single moment of his day laid out for him before he even opened his eyes. That vibration in the air was an interstellar engine, not his father snoring in the next room. The lack of noise overall was disconcerting in itself. With a family as large as his, peace and quiet was in short supply. He couldn't hear any of the other people on the ship—they were too far away. The silence was a little oppressive.

Elijah stared up at the ceiling for a few minutes more before he gave up and pushed the blanket away from him. He scooped his clothes up from the floor and was out the door before he'd finished putting his shirt on. He walked the quiet corridors, sensing from the still, hollow way his barefoot steps lightly tapped in the hall that the rest of the crew had settled in to sleep. He'd heard doors outside hissing open and shut as he laid still and tried to sleep, so he suspected the rest of the crew's rooms were on the same level as his own, but they were all silent now. He crept down the corridor, passing the ladder up to the command deck, the gangway airlock, and a sturdier ladder that led down through the floor. He'd been forced up this ladder before, when he was being kicked out—so that way must have led to the cargo bay.

He pressed his hands against the metal door at the end of the hall and stood on tiptoe to peer through the narrow slit of a window, but he could only see a small atrium and some more doors. Elijah pressed the button on the wall and winced at the noise the door made as it opened, then quickly slipped inside. He found the med bay, which he scanned but happily left alone, and a large room with a couple of toilet stalls and a row of communal shower heads. The last door adjacent to the med bay opened to a small room, where a single worn sofa with holes in the cushions sat underneath a large grate on the wall.

Elijah tilted his head and approached hesitantly, giving a single glance back over his shoulder as if he might get in trouble if he was caught existing in this room. A nearby table supported a vid screen that only showed static when he tried to turn it on. He peered at the thick grate, trying to discern its purpose, and discovered a small button at the edge. He pressed it without thinking, and the grate slid open with a quiet whirr, disappearing into the ship's walls to reveal a long, smooth pane of glass. With a broad smile on his lips, he knelt backwards on the cushions, sat back on his heels, and looked out onto the vast, empty blackness the ship floated through faster than he could imagine. Stars glinted in the darkness, and he could make out a few massive spheres of distant color.

Even if he lived for a thousand years, he'd never be able to visit them all. But he was here. He was away from Dhat-Badan. He was going to use every day he had to see as many of those stars as he could.

"Should have known you'd find this place before long."

The low voice startled Elijah almost off of his seat, causing him to grab for the creaky arm of the couch to keep from hitting the floor. When he caught himself, he froze at the sight of the captain in the doorway.

"Did you need me for something?" he asked, not sure in the slightest how he was supposed to act around this man. The captain seemed to be all business around the crew, but when it had been just the two of them in the corridor earlier, he'd seemed anything but businesslike.

The blond shook his head and moved to stand at the end of the sofa, leaning his shoulder against the edge of the window with his arms crossed over his chest. "You're just in my spot."

"Your spot?"

He nodded toward the stars beyond the glass as though he didn't need to explain any further. Elijah smiled faintly and situated himself closer to the far end of the couch in case the captain wanted to sit down, but he stayed standing with his gaze out the window. They stayed silent for a while, both watching the blackness outside.

"So," the captain spoke up to break the silence, "what was so bad about your little colony that you were willing to give up your virtue for a ride?"

Elijah snorted softly and leaned forward against the back of the couch to get a little closer to the glass. "You saw it there. It's a farm. All we do is grow corn and wheat and process it for the people who live on the research station orbiting the planet. We raise cows so they can have milk and cheese. Our whole lives are spent providing for people we'll never meet. I don't even know what they're researching up there. I'm in the third generation of people living on that colony. My grandpa was one of the first people to make the trip from Earth to live under that dome, and *he* probably didn't even know what that station is really for. He and my grandma just raised cows. My dad and mom just raise cows. My brothers raise cows. You see where I'm going with this?"

The blond glanced sidelong at him with a faint, amused smile on his lips. "I think I'm getting the gist."

"There are less than four hundred people in my colony," Elijah went on. "There are only about twenty people close to my age. Twelve of them are girls, and four of them are engaged already. One of those eight girls is my first cousin. So a grand total of seven people make up my dating pool and my marriage prospects—and I really ought to be married already, if you ask my mom. Seven girls and four guys left, counting me. And you'd better believe those girls are getting just as much pressure from their parents to get married. It's a delicate balance to maintain the population, you know?" He shook his head. "The other guys take advantage sometimes, acting like they get to have their pick, so they string the girls along until they make up their minds. It's gross."

"That's not what you wanted, then? To get married?"

"I'm not against getting married, I guess, but I don't like the idea of basically having the choice made for me. I've known all those girls since I was a kid. If I was going to love one of them, I figure I would know it already, and I don't. So I'd end up marrying someone I'm not in love with just because they were there. That's no way to live. And plus, I've already seen every square inch of that colony a hundred times over." He looked over at the blond and gave a defenseless shrug. "The galaxy is huge—how can I just let it sit out there and not even try to see any of it?"

The captain listened patiently with his gaze on the boy's dark eyes, his fingertips drumming once on the bicep of his folded arm. "You've got an explorer's spirit, huh?"

Elijah flushed at the realization that he'd just spent the last several minutes talking about nothing but himself. He broke eye contact with the other man and squeezed his hands between his knees as he sat back on his heels again, hiding his embarrassment with a soft chuckle. "I don't know what kind of spirit I've got," he said in a softer voice. "But I know I wasn't going to find out back on Dhat-Badan."

"Lots of people come out on ships like this hoping they'll find themselves," the captain said. "Or at least hoping they'll find their rich selves," he added with a soft laugh.

"I wouldn't complain about that either," Elijah agreed. "But as long as I can keep moving, I guess I'm doing okay." He peeked back over at the blond. "Why did you come out here?"

"I didn't. I was born on a ship a lot like this one. Been traveling ever since."

"You were born on a ship? Were your parents—" He paused. "I don't know if I'm supposed to use the word *smuggler.*"

The captain gave a soft laugh. "Maybe not in polite society, but that I ain't, so it's fine. They just worked on a cargo ship. I wanted to retire richer than that. So, I saved every credit they passed my way, did jobs here and there at the stops we made, and got this beauty for cheap." He patted the ship's hull affectionately. "Park and I worked hard to make her the rig she is today. And that's the story of me," he added as he looked back out the window, his faint smile replaced by a stern frown. Elijah suspected he was embarrassed to talk about himself, too.

"You want to settle down someday?"

"Eyeball deep in money," the blond answered. "Hopefully still with all my limbs. 'Til then, I'll just keep going from place to place and doing what I like."

"That sounds amazing."

"The life has ups and downs, like everything else. You'll see. I can see why some people go for the quiet farming life, too. I bet nobody on your colony ever gets chased by corsairs."

"What's a corsair?"

"Pirate. They're not so much trouble if you stay away from the sectors they're known to rove in, but we've had our share of scrapes."

Elijah nodded. "I'd rather risk it than stay back on my farm for the rest of my life, I think."

"Lucky you," the captain chuckled, "since you're here already."

The boy smiled. "I guess I haven't...thanked you. For not shooting me out an air lock. And for letting me stay."

"You'll earn your keep, kid; make no mistake." The blond pushed away from the window with a wry smile. "One way or another. Now try to get some sleep."

Elijah watched him saunter back through the exit and heard the mess hall door hiss behind him. He couldn't quite decide if that tension in his stomach was anxiety or anticipation, but he sat for a while longer with his elbows on the back of the couch to push the worry from his mind with visions of stardust.

· · ◆ · ·

After a bit more late-night exploring, Elijah finally had a nice, long sleep on his new cot—he hadn't realized how exhausted he was. When he woke up, he had a small breakfast of rehydrated scrambled eggs, then nabbed a spare rag from the kitchen and wiped the cobwebs from his room, but he didn't really have any belongings to organize. He still needed to find a place to wash his clothes.

He gathered up his spare set of clothes and made for the communal shower at the other end of the crew deck, hoping to at least be able to clean his body, if not his clothing. As soon as he was inside, he could hear water running beyond the half-wall partition between the showers and the row of lockers. He almost turned around and left straight away in the hope of returning when the room was empty, but he knew that whoever was in there must have heard the door. It would be even more awkward to leave now—and he should get used to sharing sooner rather than later, he guessed. It wasn't very much different from showering under constant threat of one of his brothers barging in on him, anyway.

He laid his change of clothes on the long bench in front of the lockers. There were more lockers than crew, so he peeked quickly through doors until he found one that was empty and laid his toothbrush inside. It looked lonely in there all by itself, but he didn't really have anything else. He hadn't exactly had a lot of time to plan his escape, and grabbing soap had been the least of his concerns.

Elijah stripped down, determined not to make the situation awkward, and stepped into the tiled space. The First Officer's massive back faced him as he moved to the farthest shower head, and Elijah kept his eyes straight ahead of him while he creaked open the faucet and let the cool water run over his chest. He didn't want to look. Now that Elijah had...*confirmed* that he was, in fact, attracted to other men, the whole situation had the potential to be awkward for more than the simple reason of being naked. He frowned at the wall as he scrubbed himself as clean as just water could make him. Better to just have a shower and try not to think about how embarrassing an erection would be, since that was pretty much a surefire way to summon one.

He risked a peek over his shoulder at the larger man when he heard the other shower head turn off and found the other man's eyes meeting his own. The boy froze under the glare, feeling as though the First Officer was boring holes through him, but as the older man stalked away to dry and dress himself, Elijah let out a sigh of relief. Not only had the First Officer not murdered him, a possibility the boy hadn't entirely written off yet, but Elijah hadn't felt even the littlest stirring in his belly that he got when the captain looked at him. That was a good thing, right? Good that only the blond's eyes on him made his face flush and his heart race—

Elijah slapped his cheeks with cold water and huffed himself into concentrating only on washing. He was here to make himself useful to the crew. So he rinsed off, scrubbed his clothes clean, and dressed in his spare set in a purposeful hurry. He was sure there would be work for him to do.

In the mess, he busied himself with prepping coffee for the crew and making sure the kitchen was clean after a few late-night raids on the pantry—including his own. The others hadn't yet made an appearance in the mess hall, but he had to edge past the First Officer on his way out, wary under the large man's scowl. He paused when he heard a quiet grunt and looked back to see the man staring at him just a little bit less accusingly.

"Thanks for the coffee," he grumbled, giving a small nod, and Elijah smiled at him before leaving him to his morning caffeine.

He tried to get a look out the large windows in the bridge, maybe help the pilot fly if she could show him how, but she kicked him out almost immediately, insisting that he make himself useful somewhere. He stood in the now-empty mess hall outside the heavy doors and sighed. The kitchen was clean, and the captain's cabin was still locked—how was he supposed to be useful if he hadn't been given any orders?

He made his way down to the engine room and found Park waist-deep in an open compartment on the wall, only his bottom half visible under the propped-open cover. Something made a sudden clanging noise, and Park swore as he reappeared from the depths of the open recess.

"Fuckin' thing," he muttered, dropping his spanner to the floor in disgust. He jumped as he spotted Elijah out of the corner of his eye and scoffed out another curse. "Don't just stand around starin' at people, kid. What are you doing in here?"

"I thought I'd see if you needed any help. We have a while before we get to Tadmor, and I can't just sit around and do nothing. I want to work."

"Thought you did all your 'work' in Cap's quarters."

"He's got to rest sometime," Elijah shot back.

Park's eyebrows lifted in surprise, and then he barked a single laugh. He waved Elijah over and gestured to the open compartment. "Don't suppose you know anything about shield collators."

Elijah did not, in fact, know anything about shield collators. He did his best to help, handing Park the tools he requested and leaning deep into the compartment to reach things the slightly shorter man couldn't, but after the fourth time he pulled the wrong wire and caused an awful grinding noise from the machinery, the engineer practically shoved him back toward the exit.

"Go scrub some floors somewhere or something, god damn," Park snapped. "Maybe next time I'll let you hold the fuckin' flashlight."

"I was just trying to—"

"Fuck off, kid; you've helped enough for one day."

Elijah frowned, huffing out a frustrated breath through his nose, but he hit the button to open the door into the corridor without further complaint. Park leaned back into the open compartment, his muttering echoing in the small chamber. He guessed he would have to cross "mechanic" off his short list of potential responsibilities on board. The hiss of the door sliding shut behind him sounded like one last insult to his usefulness. He didn't know how to fly, he couldn't fix starship engines, and he was certainly not knowledgeable enough to help in the med bay. He could pass out bandages, maybe.

With a sigh, he returned to his little closet bunk and sat down on his cot, rubbing both hands over his face and pausing with his chin in his hands and his elbows on his knees. He'd just come out on his own, demanding a place on board the ship and imagining that determination and a longing for adventure would be enough to get him by in the world outside his tiny colony. What had he thought would happen? He gave a soft groan and let his hands drop loosely between his knees. Maybe there was a traveling dairy farm ship somewhere he could find himself a spot on. He could deliver fresh milk to the people of the galaxy. That was probably all the adventure he was cut out for.

His mother probably cried when she found his note. He'd scribbled it out hastily the morning he'd gotten the call from the Administrator to help load cargo onto the unfamiliar ship. He'd talked about wasting his life, needing more, and wanting to get away from the repetition and the lack of choice he had in how he lived and what his future would be. He'd asked her to forgive him, to say goodbye to his father and brothers for him, and he'd promised to get in touch with her when he could—but he didn't even know how. He'd have to ask the pilot, probably, and get mocked for needing to call his mommy after three days away from home.

Elijah gave his cheeks a couple of invigorating slaps and rose to his feet. He couldn't just sit and mope. Moping wasn't going to make him any more useful. He could always learn new skills—and in the meantime, he would contribute how he could. If that meant starting from the bottom, so be it. He'd be a cabin boy.

The trip to Tadmor was going to take another three days, and Elijah spent the better part of the first day with a bucket and a mop that he'd had to pick cobwebs off of before he could even start. He started at one end of the ship and worked his way toward the bridge, scrubbing away who knew how many months of grime and dust from the corridors. He almost strained his back reaching upward to clean the grit from the air vents and the upper corners of the hallways, but it was worth it to look behind him and see at least a little bit of shining metal instead of the dull, rusty bulkheads he'd started with.

When he had made it past the engine room, the med bay, and the armory, he turned the corner into the corridor outside the mess hall and almost slopped his mop over the captain's boot. The blond smirked down at Elijah as he half-stumbled backward to avoid soaking the other man.

"You're energetic."

"I got kicked out of everywhere that's doing more complicated work than this," Elijah grumbled. "But I want to do my part."

"Well, I can't remember the last time Chimera got a proper wipe-down, so she's probably thanking you."

Elijah leaned on the handle of his mop, grateful for the pause. "So what's Tadmor like?"

"It's nothing special. It's a stop. Kind of a shithole, actually."

Elijah dropped his gaze to the floor. The captain was so casual about the idea of traveling to different planets that he felt embarrassed to be so excited himself. "I...guess you've been all over, haven't you? Growing up on a ship, and all."

The blond shrugged and leaned one shoulder against the wall. "I don't know that anybody's been 'all over.' But I've seen my share, I reckon. No shortage of stories."

Elijah smiled. "I'd like to hear them sometime."

The captain paused as though the boy's answer surprised him, and a few beats of silence passed between them before Elijah coughed awkwardly.

"So we're not getting there for days, right? Do you have any orders for me?"

"Not that I can say on deck," the captain chuckled, and Elijah squeezed the metal mop handle, unable to pull his gaze from the other man's quiet stare.

"That's...also my job, isn't it?"

The blond's eyes narrowed slightly, just for a moment, and he shifted his weight to one foot and rested his hand on his hip. "We shouldn't discuss it here," he said in a lower voice. "But I do have words for you about that."

Elijah hoped the little jump in his stomach didn't show on his face. "Words, or...commands?"

"Now, now." The captain moved to step past him, a faint smile on his lips. "You'll regret it if you tease me, kid. Come find me in my cabin at about 1700, hear?"

"Yes, Captain."

"Thatta boy. Now finish scrubbing this deck, and don't forget to have something to eat."

"Yes, Captain." Elijah watched him turn the corner, his eyes on the beads that dangled from his tangled bun to brush the back of his neck. To keep his mind from wandering and his body from embarrassing him, he returned his attention to his mopping and cleaned with more vigor than before, wiping away any traces of filth he could find as if he could wipe the dirty images from his mind, as well. The cramped hallways of the Chimera practically gleamed by the time he was finished, but he didn't have as much luck with the other.

5

Elijah spent so much time cleaning that by the time 1700 drew close, he had to rush to stow the mop and bucket in the mess before drifting full speed around the corner that led to the captain's cabin. He knocked on the door and tried to catch his breath while he waited for it to open. When the blond captain appeared in the doorway, he tilted his head at Elijah and glanced over his shoulder at the digital clock built into the nightstand.

"By the skin of your teeth, kid."

"Sorry, Captain. Just trying to finish cleaning up."

He took a step back to allow Elijah past him, seeming to accept this answer, and locked the door once he was inside.

Elijah stood near the bed, the cuffs he'd been strapped to not long before still visible at the edges of the mattress. The memory of being cuffed to the captain's bed in his underwear after he'd been caught suddenly seemed to make his stomach clench, so he focused on the blue eyes looking across at him from the door—not that they were much better.

"So, uh," he started, bouncing his fists awkwardly against his thighs, "you said you had...words for me?"

"A few. Take a seat, Elijah," he said, his voice taking on the same deep, soft quality it had the last time they were alone in this room. He did as he was told without lifting his gaze, his heart pounding too hard for him to make himself meet the other man's eyes. It hadn't escaped his notice that now that they were in private, he was "Elijah" instead of "kid." The captain settled into the chair across from him, keeping a bit of distance between them that Elijah was grateful for.

Elijah felt exposed under the other man's silent gaze even fully dressed. He knew that he was gripping the edge of the mattress noticeably tight, but he couldn't seem to relax his hands. He was nervous. This was nervous, right? It definitely wasn't anticipation. He definitely wasn't remembering those long fingers wrapped around his dick and that scarred mouth on his nipple.

"Relax. You're here for talking. We need to lay some groundwork, Elijah," the captain said quietly. "If you liked what happened last time. Did you like it?"

Elijah realized that he'd been staring at the blond's slender fingers laced in his lap, and he snapped his eyes back up to the man's face. "I...did," he admitted in a slightly rough voice.

The captain's smile was slow and seemed deliberately for the purpose of making Elijah's breath catch. "I'm glad," he said. "Now, here's the thing if you want to continue. I like what I like, and what I like is very specific. What I like is when the people I'm with do *exactly* as they're told. Maybe that means undressing while I watch. Maybe it means you get on your knees and suck my cock when I tell you to. Maybe it means you let me tie you up, bend you over, and spank you."

Elijah's eyes widened over the course of the explanation, until he knew that he was staring like an idiot. "Uh," he started, then wet his lips before trying again. "Is that...something you're likely to actually ask me to do?"

"Absolutely," he answered. He tilted his head just slightly, like he was trying to gauge Elijah's reaction. "The thing I like best is to bring the one I'm with right to the brink of what they can stand. Pain and pleasure are very similar things, Elijah." He lifted his thumbs to spread his hands without unlacing his fingers. "The other side of the coin is that you set the limits. You tell me what you're comfortable with, and I don't do anything that you're not. Does that sound fair?"

The boy shifted his weight on the soft mattress, twisting a fold in the sheets with his fingers. "This is...going a lot differently from what I imagined."

"What did you imagine?"

"I mean, I guess I thought...that you'd have sex with me? You know...normally."

"What's normal?"

Elijah laughed softly. "I don't know," he admitted. "But not getting tied up and spanked, probably, right?"

The blond shrugged. "It's normal to me. It could be normal to you. And you can always stop me whenever you want. It's my job to make sure that you enjoy yourself and don't get hurt—well," he stopped himself with a chuckle, "not *really* hurt. Just enough. Does this all sound like something you'd like to do?"

"I...I don't know."

"You're not a virgin, are you?"

"No," Elijah answered, just a touch defensively. "But sneaking off with a girl after a bonfire is a whole lot different from agreeing to...whatever this is."

The captain watched him in silence for a few beats, and the boy couldn't help feeling like he was being evaluated. "I talked about laying groundwork before. That's important. So, if it's all right with you, I'd like to have the unsexy talk now, so that we don't have to do it in the middle of other, sexier things."

"I feel like this is somehow going to be even more awkward than actually doing this stuff."

"It's only awkward if you let it be. I want you to feel comfortable with me if we're going to do this—you're putting a lot of trust in me, and I aim to deserve it. So, I need to know what your limits are."

Elijah shifted on the bed, all too aware of the memory of the blond's hands on his skin. "I don't...I mean, how do I know what they are if I've never done this before?"

"Well, this here is the first step." The captain reached behind him for his tablet, brushed the screen with his fingertip to wake it up, then handed it to Elijah.

The screen showed a simple text list on a blank page, and as the boy's eyes scanned the words, his mouth fell open in disbelief. This was a list of sexual acts—some Elijah had heard of, some he wouldn't have considered sexual before this, and others he was going to need definitions for. He felt heat rising up his neck and into his cheeks as he read things like "anal rimming," "punishment," "spreader bars," "humiliation," "confinement," "collar and leash," and "bruises." He wet his lips and tried to swallow through the desert his throat had suddenly become.

"Uh," he began in a hoarse voice, then paused to give a small cough and try again. "I don't, uh...I don't know what all of this stuff is. What's...what's the difference between 'suspension' and...is it 'shibari?' They both say 'bondage.'"

"Well, one is just what it sounds like. Shibari is...more decorative. Lots of knots, keeping you in poses, but not usually anything too strenuous."

"Oh. Okay. And, uh...I've never even heard of a 'violet wand.'"

"It's a toy, sort of. More like a tool. Low current, high voltage electricity wherever you want it."

Elijah paled. "I don't—I don't think I want it anywhere." The soft laugh that came from the man in front of him relaxed his shoulders slightly, and he smiled as he lifted his eyes to meet the captain's face. "Some of this stuff is crazy."

"It's just a list of potentials. Tried to include everything I could think of, just in case you had some secret kink you'd be too scared to mention."

"Well we can safely skip all these...body fluids. I don't want to pee on anybody and I definitely don't want to be peed on."

"We're on the same page, then."

"Good," Elijah laughed. He hesitated, a flush creeping back up his face, and glanced back down at the screen. "But um. This, uh. Swallow—swallowing semen," he managed to get out, "I...I think that one's okay."

The blond visibly tensed in his chair, but he forced himself to relax just as quickly, watching the boy with calm, intent blue eyes. "You think so, huh?"

Elijah anxiously ran his thumb along the narrow edge of the tablet in his hand as he looked up at the blond. His heart was racing, but it wasn't as awkward a conversation as he thought it would be. As nervous as some of the terms on the list made him, he couldn't help the thoughts bubbling just under the surface of his inexperienced, embarrassed brain—imaginings that forced him to remind himself that the captain said he hadn't come to his cabin tonight for more than a talk. Neither of them spoke for a few beats, but the tension in the room was too much for Elijah to bear.

"So," he started, just to break the silence, "if this is just everything you could think of, how much of it do you...actually *want* to do?"

"However much you can take," the captain answered evenly, and Elijah struggled not to grip the tablet too tightly. "But you don't have to answer everything right away. In fact," he said, giving a short, pensive hum as he rose from his seat with an easy, predatorial grace, "I want you to do something for me." He stepped close to Elijah and leaned one hand on the bed beside him so that he could reach the cabinet above the headboard. Elijah straightened slightly at how close the blond drew to him. His shoulder was almost brushing Elijah's sleeve, and the faint smell of his sweat filled the boy's nostrils, drawing him back to the memory of the other man bent over him, hands on his stomach as he stroked him to completion. This wasn't helping.

Elijah peeked over his shoulder in time to see the blond stand up again, now with a small, clear plastic bottle in one hand that he knew right away was lubricant. In his other hand was a black, palm-sized object that Elijah didn't recognize. It was made up of one larger, slightly curved and undulating cylinder, with two narrow arms spiraling from the base and ending in small orbs. The captain held both items out to him, and Elijah automatically set the tablet aside to accept them.

"I want you to take those back to your bunk with you," the captain said, his hand reaching out to slip his fingers through the dark hair at the nape of the younger man's neck, "and I want you to put that toy inside of you. You've never had anyone touch your ass before, have you?"

Elijah fought desperately to keep his stomach from climbing up into his throat. "No," he answered.

"I didn't think so. I want you to try it. If you don't like it, just tell me so. If you do like it..." the blond trailed off, bending down to let his scruffy cheek touch the younger man's smooth one as he murmured, "Then I'll have a whole new way to make you come for me." He straightened again with that predatory smirk on his lips and brushed his thumb over the tender skin just behind Elijah's ear. "Do you think you can do that for me, Elijah?"

"You mean in my—by myself?" He looked up into the captain's pale eyes and shivered at the hunger he saw there.

"Will you do it?"

The boy closed his hands over the borrowed objects and nodded despite the deafening sound of his own blood in his ears. "Yes, Captain," he barely heard himself whisper, and the blond let the tiniest of sighs escape his lips as he finally removed his hand from the younger man.

"I expect a full report in the morning."

· • ◆ • ·

Elijah returned to his room as quickly as he could, though he slowed his swift walk to a casual stride when he turned a corner and saw Harper coming from the opposite direction. He did his best to make eye contact with him and to smile in a way that the wary young man wouldn't find suspicious, but from the narrow side-eye Harper gave him, he suspected he didn't do a very good job. He was just thankful that the items the captain had loaned him were small enough to fit in his pockets. He could just imagine what Park would say if he'd caught Elijah in the hallway with what was clearly a dildo and some lube.

How had this become his life?

He hid the embarrassing objects under his pillow, pressing down on it more than once to make sure they were completely covered, then moved back toward the door. It was much too early to be locking himself in his bunk and masturbating.

But the rest of the evening went by impossibly slowly. Elijah ate a light supper in the mess hall, uncomfortably aware of the captain's eyes on him from the other end of the table while Park and Harper argued about engine output versus powering jamming systems. When the crew dispersed, Elijah gathered up the dishes and cups, washed and dried them, and put everything away, but neither the chatter of his crewmates nor the rhythmic scrubbing of dishes could distract him from thinking about what was waiting for him back in his room.

The little bunk seemed warmer than it had before as Elijah shut the door and locked it behind him. He was hesitant to move toward the bed, but he couldn't deny the thrill of excitement tingling in his belly as he took a seat on the mattress. How was he supposed to do this? He didn't imagine that...inserting things was something you just did without any warm-up. But the captain was expecting a report.

Elijah double-checked that his door was locked, then undressed himself and slid under the blankets. He retrieved his borrowed paraphernalia and set both items aside, watching them out of the corner of his eye as he settled his head on the pillow. For a while, he just stared up at the ceiling and chewed his bottom lip uncertainly. He'd never really jerked off on command before—it felt strange to just be lying in bed having decided that he was going to masturbate instead of doing it as the urge took him. He settled into the mattress purposefully and closed his eyes, taking a deep breath in an attempt to ease some of the nervousness building inside of him.

He let his hand drift down his stomach and flatten against the warming skin just above the soft nest of his black pubic hair, sucking in a sharp breath as his fingertips brushed the base of his dick. He imagined it was the captain's hand there, slowly wrapping slender, calloused fingers around him and beginning to stroke him into hardness. He kept an unhurried pace, pausing to let a shiver run through him as he stretched his foreskin back fully and held it there, taut and tingling. The familiar feeling of his dick growing hard in his hand made him sigh, but it was the memory of the blond kneeling between his spread legs that sent fire through his blood.

Elijah's free hand found one of his nipples and pinched it firmly, drawing a hitching yelp from his throat. His hips bucked into his hand as he quickened his pace, lips parted and throat exposed as his shoulders arched away from the mattress. He could smell the older man over him, sweat and gunpowder and oil, feel his hand stroking him, and hear his low, murmuring voice praising him for the way he writhed under the touch. If it were the captain touching him, he'd be firm, but gentle. He'd run his hand down Elijah's thigh, over the tender skin behind his balls to press his fingertips against the ring of muscle slightly further. How could it have only taken one brief encounter to make Elijah long for the blond's hands so much? His own hand followed the path his imaginary captain took, the pad of his finger putting ginger pressure against his opening. It was an odd sensation that made his hips twitch upward and his breath catch. It felt so tight—how was anything supposed to fit in there?

He stopped the movement of his hands long enough to pat the mattress in search of the bottle of lubricant and clicked the lid open once he found it. The gel was startlingly cool on his fingers and even more so as he lowered them to slide between his legs, the slippery touch unfamiliar and strange. Rather than get his sheets sticky, he kicked them away, spreading his legs in the open air to allow himself better access. His slick fingers pressed against the tight muscle, each tiny movement sending a lick of electricity up his spine as he imagined the captain bent over him, whispering in his ear and teasing him until he relaxed. With a gentle push, the tip of Elijah's finger slipped inside, and he gasped, his soft gaze snapping open at the sudden intrusion. The tense burning sensation faded after a moment of stillness, and he dared to press deeper in time with a slow, unsteady exhale. He could only describe the feeling as intense—even this small stretch quickened his heart and tightened his stomach, threatening to overwhelm him.

His cock jumped against his stomach as he slid deeper into himself, and he took it in his free hand again, pumping slowly in time with the careful movement of his finger. When he retreated enough to push back in, he added another finger and winced slightly against the increased pressure. The captain would make sure he enjoyed it. He would take his time and work him up until he was ready, distracting him from the passing discomfort with tender bites to his nipples or neck. He would whisper to him and bring him to the brink of orgasm, then deny him so that he panted and gasped with need underneath him. His own hand wasn't enough.

Elijah let his fingers slip from himself, whimpering at the sudden sense of loss, and he squinted through the spots in his vision in search of the toy the blond had given him. With his dick aching from the removal of his hand, he squeezed more of the lubricant into his palm and smoothed it over the thick end of the plug, then placed it just at his entrance. The soft silicone felt foreign compared to the warmth of his fingers, but Elijah shut his eyes and let out a long breath as he pushed the toy into himself. As soon as the widest part slipped through his opening, the first wave of the plug's unusual shape put pressure against a spot deep inside that shook a startled moan from his lips and caused a tremor in the muscles of his thighs. The curl at the narrow end of the toy pressed into the skin behind his balls and made him hiss with pleasure, heels digging into the mattress as his back arched.

For a while, he couldn't even bring himself to move the plug—his own fight for breath and shuddering was enough to brush it against whatever it was inside of him that pulled the air from his lungs. His hand moved automatically back to his seeping cock, stroking faster than before and gasping out soft cries with every helpless jerk of his hips. In desperation, he slipped his fingers through the loop at the base of the plug and eased it in and out, each push against the spot inside him blurring his vision. It wasn't his hand running over the length of his dick, squeezing the tip with every pass. It wasn't his grip moving the toy inside of him and making him cry out. It wasn't a toy at all that was pushing into him, spreading him wide.

"Fuck," he whispered, lifting his hips from the mattress in an attempt to take more and groaning with frustration when the plug would go no deeper. Tension built in his belly, each wave of pressure washing fire over his skin, until he panted out a whining moan and spilled his orgasm onto his own stomach in pulses that flashed his vision white. He milked the last few drops of semen from his quivering cock and slowly settled back onto the bed, unable to calm his breathing. One more shaky cry fell from him as he eased the plug out of him and let it drop to the mattress, and then every muscle in his body gave out.

Elijah laid sprawled on the bed, the forgotten bottle of lubricant half empty and dripping onto the sheet near his pillow and his skin trembling in the cool air of the room. He couldn't pretend to care about the sticky mess he'd left all over himself or the drying gel on his hand. When his heart finally began to slow, he took a deep breath and let it out with a puff of his cheeks. At least that was one thing he'd be able to tell the captain with confidence that he really, really wanted.

6

Elijah didn't emerge from his bunk until the crew had been up and about their duties for hours. He'd used the last of the captain's lubricant when he'd woken up in the wee hours of the morning and spotted the wiped-clean toy still sitting on the shelf by his bed. His second orgasm of the night had taken longer to build to but had been even more satisfying. The trade-off was that he slept through the crew's breakfast and found a clean-up job waiting for him in the mess hall. The other unfortunate side-effect was having to bundle up his sheets and sneak them down the ladder to the lower deck for washing, all the while paranoid of being caught by his taunting shipmates.

When he'd convinced himself he'd escaped detection, Elijah made himself a cup of coffee and poured a second cup to carry with him to the bridge. They'd been en route to Tadmor for some time now, and while he was sure most of the flying was automatic on long trips like this, he imagined it must still be tiring to be the one in the pilot seat. So he offered the woman a smile as he stepped through the sliding doors and lifted the mug in front of him like a white flag before she could grump at him to leave.

"I thought you might want a pick-me-up," he said, peeking around the cup at her, and the woman softened—just slightly.

"That part of your cabin boy duties?" she asked as he took the steps down to her seat in front of the massive window.

"Well, there's nothing left to clean without me invading people's privacy, so I'm just sort of winging it from here."

She snorted and took the mug from him. "And bringing me coffee was the best use of your time you could think of?"

"I tried to see if Park needed any help, but that...didn't go so well."

"Park's an asshole. This ship is his baby, and god forbid anybody else tries to lay hands on it."

"Yeah, I kind of get that impression. Oh—" Elijah paused and dug some sugar packets and dried creamers out of his pocket. "I didn't know how you take it."

"Black. But thanks." She tilted her head at him with a sly grin. "We all know how you take it, though, don't we?"

A faint frown wrinkled the boy's brow as he pushed the small packets back into his pocket. "What?"

"You know. You and the captain. The way you came out of his room yesterday looking all rumpled? I know what he's like; no way did he let you be on top."

"On t—" Elijah snapped his mouth shut and stared pointedly down into his coffee cup with a snort. "I'm just trying to work and do my part, and all I got were jokes about being a prostitute or people back home fucking cows. Why is everybody so worried about me and him?"

"Well, it's a small ship. Not much in the way of gossip, usually. And I can't speak for everybody else," the pilot chuckled, "but you've seen the captain, right? And you've got a pretty face and a certain farmboy charm about you. Helps me sleep at night to imagine you two getting all sweaty together."

"Oh my god." Elijah couldn't decide whether to laugh or find a bag to put over his head. "You're making too much out of me being in there one time."

The woman leaned forward in her seat. "Ha! So you *were* getting sweaty together?"

"It's really none of your business."

"Maybe not, but I want the juicy details of your affair anyway."

"There's no affair. There's no nothing."

"Suit yourself, kid." She sat back and took a long slurp of her coffee as she returned her attention to the panels in front of her. "I don't need your confirmation. I have a rich fantasy life."

Elijah sighed, lingering near the steps to drink his coffee. Stars passed by them outside the window, and the pilot stretched in her seat, scratching at the coppery hair at the base of her ponytail. She was young, probably not much older than Elijah himself, but life aboard a ship had put a few premature wrinkles at the corners of her eyes. After a while, she glanced sidelong at him.

"Crew calls me Brooks, by the way," she said with a faint smirk on her thin lips. "You should too."

"Oh—Elijah," he offered in return, smiling. It was the first real sign of friendliness he'd seen since leaving home, and it lifted a little of the weight from his shoulders.

"Good to meet you, Elijah." She tilted her head toward the co-pilot's seat beside her. "Have a seat if you're gonna hang around. We came out the other side of the gate yesterday, and we'll be coming up on the Glowing Eye nebula soon. It's a good one."

The boy hesitated, but then a broader smile parted his lips, and he took a seat in the co-pilot's chair, careful not to touch any of the controls. The two of them sipped their coffee in silence for a few minutes while Elijah stared down at the console in front of him. The display showed a simplified map of their surrounding area with their intended path marked with a dotted line that arced across the screen. "Can I ask you a question?"

"You just did. Ba-dum tss. But you can ask me another," Brooks answered, grinning sidelong at him.

"Why are we passing through Schedar to get to the Tamanin system from Gamma Cephei?"

The pilot's brow lowered into a slightly less-friendly stare. "You a navigator as well as a pretty face?"

"It just seems out of the way."

"It's because the FTL gate at Deneb has been out of service. Found that out the hard way the last time we had to pass through this area."

"Even so, couldn't we have used Delta Cyg? We could have shaved off—I don't know," he shrugged, "maybe a whole day?"

"There's no gate at Delta Cyg."

Elijah tilted his head at her with a frown. "There is as of a couple months ago," he said. "I saw it on the updated chart the last time the

Federation ship came for a pickup."

Brooks opened her mouth for a rebuttal and then grimaced. "I haven't been able to update our charts since the last time we were by Merope about six months ago."

"Really? Six months? But so much can change in—"

"I know," she sighed. "I do what I can. I fly the ship, I keep up with our inventory and our registry, I maintain the weapons and shield systems on the front end—and use them when I need to. I plot all the routes and watch the scanners. I'm just one me. So sometimes we take a little longer getting somewhere, I guess. But I have to choose sleep on occasion."

Elijah turned in his seat to face her. "I didn't mean anything by it," he said in a softer voice. "I just thought—"

"It's fine, kid. It's a small ship. Just drink your coffee and enjoy the view." She nodded her head toward the front of the ship as the first hints of flowing carnelian lights appeared at the edge of the window.

Elijah slipped from his seat, abandoning his mug on the floor nearby, and took up a place in front of the pilot's chair. The nebula came into view slowly—Elijah couldn't even try to comprehend how far away from them it was—but he waited patiently for the pink and blue iris to fill the window, his forehead resting on the thick glass.

He'd listen to any amount of taunting for more views like this.

· · ◆ · ·

It was approaching the middle of the day before Elijah finally stood before the door to the captain's cabin with the once-again-cleaned toy safely in his pocket. He didn't feel so hesitant to knock this time.

The blond's stern face shifted into a playful expression at the sight of the boy in his open doorway. "Come to give your report?"

"Yes, Captain."

"About time."

"I was on the bridge, sir. Brooks let me see the nebula."

The captain snorted. "Ain't she a sweetheart? Come inside."

Elijah did as he was told, growing familiar now with the sound the cabin door made as the lock slid into place. He slid the plug from his pocket and offered it to the blond with just a touch of heat in his face. The captain waited a beat, then lifted his eyebrows questioningly at the younger man.

"And the other?"

Elijah managed a sheepish smile. "I, uh. I used it all."

"Did you now?" the captain chuckled. "Were you just mighty careful, or was that from multiple uses?"

"Multiple, um...multiple uses."

The captain tilted his head and took a step closer, carefully plucking the toy from Elijah's extended hand. "So that'll be a 'yes' for that on your list, huh?"

Elijah licked his lips before finally peeking up to meet the other man's pale eyes. "It's a 'yes, please,'" he clarified, and the blond's nostrils flared almost imperceptibly.

"Well, since you asked so nice." The captain reached out to let his fingers run through the boy's dark waves, gripping him firmly at the back of his head. "But it'll have to wait. I have prep to do before we get to Tadmor." He released Elijah and gave his cheek a quick brush with his thumb before removing himself completely. "You're going to behave yourself, right?"

"I'm not *actually* a kid, you know."

"Oh, I know. A kid wouldn't have spent the night doing the things you did."

Elijah chewed his lip to keep from showing too much of his smile, but he had no defense.

"Since Chimera got such a good scrub-down yesterday, why don't you take some time before we dock to look this over again?" The blond turned to his desk, setting aside the plug as though it were a completely normal thing to have on a table and taking up his tablet. He offered it to Elijah. "That list is right where you can find it. Might be more comfortable looking it over when I'm not staring at you."

Elijah held the tablet in both hands and nodded. "I'll...make some decisions."

"Good boy. Now get out. I need to make a call."

The boy nodded again and excused himself, pausing outside the captain's door once it closed and looking down at the tablet with a brisk sigh.

7

Elijah spent the next couple of hours sat on his freshly-laundered sheets, staring at the screen of the tablet in his lap. Some of the things on the list were easy to agree to now that he had...experimented with himself a little. Others he had to open a net search to even visualize. He worked his way through the list one by one, alternating among blushing heavily, cringing with distaste, and feeling the stirrings of erections. When he'd made a mark for everything on the captain's list, he put the tablet away and went to the showers to spend a while under the cold water.

With a full two more days of empty space between the Chimera and its destination, Elijah had a lot of time to kill. He'd been tired before—worn out, stressed, and sick of the routine that had been his life for the past twenty years—but he'd never really been *bored*. Bored was something new altogether. He sat in his little cabin, napped, organized his few belongings for the seventh or eighth time, and got shouted at and run off by Harper the one time he tried to wander the cargo hold.

Elijah spent some time memorizing the layout of the ship. It wasn't difficult, as the ship was large but was mostly cargo space—he confirmed the other crew members' living quarters along the same hall as his own when he spotted Davies moving back and forth from the med bay, and he found what looked like Park's quarters hidden in the engine room tucked at the back of the cargo hold. It would take him a while to really get a feel for the ship, he was sure, but he liked it already. Despite its age, it was sturdy and solid, and it felt lived-in. He just hoped the crew could come to accept him.

The showers became silent when he walked in, and they stayed that way until he left. He tried to make conversation in the mess hall, but Park and Harper always left as soon as he arrived, the First Officer ignored him, and Brooks only wanted to know if he'd seen the captain lately. Only Davies would chat with him, but Elijah could only take so many sympathetic looks before he excused himself and retreated back to his bunk again. Acceptance seemed like a long way off.

He half expected the captain to summon him at any moment—or was it hope? He certainly couldn't ignore the tugging he felt whenever he went for coffee and saw the blond's cabin door shut tight at the far end of the hall. But the captain seemed to keep to himself. Elijah rarely heard his voice in the corridor. Didn't he get lonely?

He was able to amiably pass the next afternoon playing cards with Davies in the med bay and listening to stories of the ship's past adventures. Most of the exciting ones involved dramatic things like double crosses or ambushes, but some were as simple as "the time Park passed out drunk and Shaw had to carry him back to the ship." Elijah liked hearing both kinds—especially since it meant he'd finally learned the name of the captain's surly First Officer.

The intercom startled him as Brooks' voice crackled over the speaker in the hall.

"Approaching Tadmor colony. Prep for dock."

Elijah dropped his cards without hesitation and clambered up onto the examination table to peer out the window there. Tadmor was a desert planet, sporting a massive dome just like the one on his home colony. As they passed through the atmospheric barrier and eased into the docking arms, Elijah's nose pressed closer to the window. This definitely didn't look like his home colony. Dhat-Badan was mostly farmland or pastures, with only a small town center and distant farmhouses, but this place was a mess. The docks were at the top of a few tall towers where ships were moored by massive metal arms, and elevators led down from the catwalks into the colony itself. The area below the docks was cluttered and crowded with bodies moving through what looked like some kind of market—awnings and unlit flood lights formed rows of cobbled-together shops that filled the sprawling space. Beyond the market, more towers grew, littered with tiny balconies. It looked more residential, but the structure was unsteady. Each tower seemed to be built of pre-fabricated apartment blocks stacked on top of each other like a puzzle game. Wires ran haphazardly between the towers, clearly strung up to bring electricity higher as the towers grew. Open stairs along the outside edges of the towers appeared to be the only method of moving from floor to floor aside from some narrow catwalks here and there between them.

The whole thing looked kind of crappy, if Elijah was honest.

He looked over his shoulder at Davies, who was calmly tidying the deck of cards. "This is Tadmor?"

The man lifted his eyes at the question, not seeming irritated by the boy's hasty ending of their game. "Sure is. One of the outposts, anyway. It's a trading port, which is a polite term in this sector for a slum. You'd be better off staying on the ship."

"Are you kidding? I didn't come all this way just to stay on the ship."

Davies shrugged, leaving the boy to his decision in favor of shuffling the cards and laying out a game of solitaire. Elijah practically ran from the med bay, rushing down the hall toward the gangway doors. He skidded to a stop in the airlock entry, where the captain, Harper, and the surly First Officer—whose name Elijah still hadn't heard—stood waiting for the doors to depressurize. The captain had put on a leather coat with a grey fur collar and secured his Jericho 9mm pistol in its holster on his belt. The First Officer wore a sawed-off shotgun strapped to his thigh, and Harper appeared unarmed, but the coat he wore was much too large for his skinny frame, which made Elijah almost certain that he was hiding more than a few firearms. All three of them turned to look at Elijah as he took another step forward.

"Where do you think you're going?" the captain asked, already looking back down to make sure his holster was secure.

"I'm coming with you! I want to see this place."

"This ain't a field trip, kid."

Elijah snorted in frustration. "Well then it's a good thing I'm not a student."

The captain ticked an eyebrow at him and stared at him for a few beats, silently questioning the wisdom of his backtalk. The boy settled under the look, though Elijah still frowned across at him. "We're here for business," the blond said. "You'll get in the way."

"I can keep my mouth shut," Elijah promised. "I won't cause trouble. Just don't leave me stuck in here."

The captain gave a low sigh, his eyes shutting briefly as his head fell toward one shoulder. After a moment, he huffed and straightened with his eyes on the young man beside him. "Harper. Arm him."

Harper scoffed, then paused as he realized the other man was still looking at him. "You're serious?" At the captain's nod, he grimaced and reached into his coat, retrieving a small pistol that he spun in his hand to offer grip-first to Elijah. He glared suspiciously up at the darker boy as he took the weapon from him.

The captain tilted his chin toward Elijah. "You know what to do with that, kid?"

Elijah tucked the pistol into the back of his belt. "My dad taught me how to shoot. Don't worry about me."

"Well all right." He looked up at the hulking man at his shoulder. "Shaw, keep an eye on him."

The gangway door hissed out a stream of air, and the captain turned to face the broad walkway as the airlock doors slid open to allow them out into the colony.

"By the book, gentlemen," the captain said without turning his head. He led the way down the towering catwalk and to the elevator, which was just big enough for all four of them.

Elijah craned his neck to see over the people around him as they entered the marketplace, once or twice taking a few steps backward to catch a second or two more of the piled contents of the stalls they passed—exotic fruits, plants, and hung meats, as well as spare parts and electronics he couldn't identify. He desperately wanted to wander, but he kept close by Shaw and Harper, never letting the captain out of his sight. It was crowded in the market, and it had a less than pleasant smell. The port was mostly full of humans, but Elijah did his best not to stare at the aliens they passed. Until getting dropped off on Omicron, he'd only seen them in vids—no one but human Federation soldiers ever came to Dhat-Badan.

When they turned a corner into an alley, the crowd thinned a bit, and the captain stopped them at a block near the end. He banged on the door with his fist, and a screen to the side of the doorway flickered on. The face staring back at them was a kineta—a tall alien race with downy fur all over their bodies. They had long muzzles with slits for noses and sharp, canine teeth, and elongated ears that turned like satellites to follow nearby sounds. They might have been considered cute by human standards, but this one stared out at them with round black eyes narrowed, and Elijah could see a hint of its teeth in its sneering smile.

"Captain," it said. "I've been expecting you."

The door gave a thunk as it unlocked, and a furry, four-fingered hand pulled it open. Elijah followed his new crewmates inside, but the second the door shut again, the muzzle of a gun was forced under his chin by the burly-looking kineta who had let them in. Elijah lifted his hands automatically and looked over at the captain, who was already reaching out to stop Shaw from pulling his shotgun.

"You brought me a new face, Captain," said the kineta behind the large, rounded desk at the center of the room. Its voice had a soft rumble underneath it in person, as if it might have had an extra set of vocal chords. "I don't like new faces."

The blond offered him a congenial smile. "That's not the way to make friends, Shrike."

"I don't like making new friends, either."

"I just managed to get a new hand on my ship; don't scare him off on his first run. Come on." He took a step closer to the desk, showing his lack of concern with the possibility that Elijah was about to get his head blown off.

The alien studied him for a moment, then nodded, and the gun was lowered from Elijah's chin. The boy let out a silent breath of relief and tried to steady his heart. The guard was still glaring at him, but Elijah noticed Shaw out of the corner of his eye, watching the alien with just as much suspicion. It put Elijah slightly more at ease to know the First Officer was on his side.

"I'm at dock 42-B," the captain said, moving the conversation along from less adversarial topics. "You ready to pay?"

The kineta at the desk tilted his head up at the man. "I may have another shipment for you, actually. Are you picking up?"

"Maybe. Where's it going?"

The alien hesitated, just for a beat. "Altera."

"Oh fuck off," the captain scoffed.

"Now, listen before you mouth off—"

"You want me to ship something from *your* warehouse straight to the Earth Federation's front door? Altera's security is tighter than a virgin's asshole."

Elijah swallowed, lips pressed together.

"I'll pay you double the normal rate," the kineta pressed.

The captain gave a soft, pensive snort. "And who am I delivering this to, exactly?"

"I'll tell you that if you agree."

He sucked his teeth and looked down at the floor with his hands on his hips. After a moment, he glanced up at Shaw and Harper in turn, seeming to ask their opinion without speaking. Elijah wished he knew them well enough to participate in the silent conversation, but all he saw was three men looking at each other, so he just stood back and listened. Finally, the captain spoke again.

"I want two and a half."

"Getting a little greedy, Captain," the alien sneered.

"Call it hazard pay. I don't even go near Proxima Centauri at all if I can help it, and you're asking me to drop a shipment right under the Federation's nose. Two and a half."

The kineta eyeballed him, drumming his fingers on the surface of the desk. Then he gave a snort, his ears flattening against his head. "Fine. Two and a half."

The captain glanced over his shoulders at his waiting crew. "Harper, take the kid and go unload. We'll be along."

"Yes, Captain." The young man turned Elijah by his sleeve and ushered him out the door, leading him back through the marketplace toward the docks. Elijah quickened his step to keep up with him, leaning to catch the other boy's attention.

"Are we really going to Altera?" he asked, and Harper grimaced up at him.

"That's not a good thing," he pointed out. "It's actually a terrible thing."

"But it's the biggest station in the Federation!" Elijah countered. "It must be amazing!"

"Amazingly easy to get thrown in prison."

"But you guys are—" Elijah checked himself and dropped his voice to a conspiratorial murmur. "You guys are smugglers, aren't you? Don't you have, you know, ways around security and customs and things like that?"

Harper frowned. "Captain seems to think we do." He urged Elijah into the elevator up to their dock and scowled at the inside of the doors with his hands tucked grumpily under his armpits.

Brooks let them back onto the ship, and Elijah followed Harper back down to the cargo bay, but when he moved to push the lever that would open the main doors, Harper smacked his hand.

"Not yet," he said. "First we unload."

"What? How can we unload without opening the doors?"

Harper ignored his question and moved over to a cluster of massive boilers at the far end of the room. He climbed a maintenance ladder to the top and twisted a rusty valve to open the top of the nearest boiler, then reached his arm inside. A moment later, something metal gave a ringing clunk, and the front of the boilers opened as one large door, revealing a secret compartment hiding six unlabeled metal crates. Elijah's mouth dropped open. They weren't boilers at all—they were just empty husks.

"Move those other pallets out of the way," Harper commanded. Elijah scurried up to the controls and used the track-run forklifts built into the cargo bay to shift the other crates aside. He moved the machine in the wrong direction a few times, causing Harper to shout angrily at him from across the room, but he soon got the hang of the controls and successfully made a path from the false boilers to the bay doors. The visible pallets were labeled, and Elijah noted that they were all common, standard things—textiles and dry goods that the crew didn't need to hide to ship.

Harper clambered down the maintenance ladder and shoved the first crate out of the hidden compartment on its rollers. Elijah moved down the metal steps and crossed the cargo bay to help him move the others.

"You put fake boilers in cargo to hide contraband in?"

"No," Harper grunted as they shouldered the crate forward. "The boilers are real. Or I guess they were. Captain replaced the water treatment system on this rig years ago. It's still back there. The new model takes up half the space, so we left the bones in.

"Huh." Elijah glanced back at the open boilers and smiled faintly. It was clever.

Once the crates were near the door, Harper climbed up to shut the compartment again, and then Elijah was permitted to open up the main bay doors. Another kineta was waiting on the catwalk with a hover truck, so the three of them loaded the heavy crates onto the back. The alien didn't speak, and neither did Harper, so Elijah kept his mouth shut, too. When the truck was loaded, the kineta drove it away from the ship with its illicit goods safely stowed. Harper tugged Elijah back up the ramp and onto the ship by the scruff of his shirt, then shifted the lever to draw the bay doors closed again. For a little guy, he sure did feel comfortable dragging Elijah around.

Elijah glanced between the young man and the closing doors. "That's it?"

"That's it. What did you expect?"

"I don't know," Elijah shrugged. "I guess I thought smuggling would be more...exciting."

"Exciting is bad," Harper said slowly, as though explaining to a child. "Exciting means problems. We don't want exciting. We want easy and simple and profitable."

"I guess so. So what do we do now?"

"Now we wait for Captain to get back and tell us what we do now."

"Oh. I can't go out?"

Harper's green eyes narrowed at him from the top of the stairs near the forklift controls. He watched him for a long moment before speaking. "What are you doing here?" he asked.

"What do you mean?"

"I mean *what are you doing here*? You expect me to believe you just showed up out of nowhere and convinced the captain to let you join up just...because?"

Elijah frowned up at him. "I wanted to get away from home. Is that so hard to believe?"

Harper grunted and leaned on the catwalk railing. "Park says you slept your way on board. Is that true? You sleeping with the captain for a spot on the ship?"

Elijah sighed through his nose. He wasn't ashamed of what he'd done, but he didn't want this to be an ongoing subject of conversation with the rest of the crew. "I offered him what I had in exchange for a chance," he said. "He accepted. Anything else is between him and me."

The young man considered him for a while, biting his lip and drumming his fingers anxiously on the metal railing, but then he nodded. "Captain will be pissed if he gets back and you're not here," he said as he straightened. "Wait until we get orders, and then maybe you can go and see the port."

He climbed the ladder back into the interior of the ship without giving Elijah the chance to reply, leaving him alone in the cargo bay. Elijah puffed out a soft breath. He guessed that counted as acceptance.

8

The captain's voice came over the intercom just as Elijah was about to risk escaping to the docks without permission, freezing him with guilt a few feet away from the decompression doors.

"Everybody to the bridge. We need to have a talk."

Elijah was the last to arrive. Brooks was in her pilot seat, and the captain was leaned against the heavy chair next to her with his arms folded. The rest of the crew were spread around the small bridge, waiting to hear what their leader had to say. Elijah kept to the back with his eyes on the frowning blond.

"So here's the deal," he began, scanning the faces of his waiting crew. "I took a difficult job. Risky. It's on Altera."

A burst of various disbelieving replies came from the crew who hadn't been present for this decision—Brooks scoffed and Park swore, and Davies pressed his hands into the console in front of him to lean forward as though he could check their captain for fever from across the room.

"Yeah, yeah, I know," the captain said over the top of their voices.

Elijah took a single small step forward. "But he said he's paying double, right? So isn't it fair?"

The captain's lips curled into a sardonic smile. "Kid, anytime someone offers to pay you double, that generally means it's only half what you'd charge them if you knew the whole story. But this is doable," he said as he returned his attention to the rest of the crew.

"We just need to make some adjustments."

Park bent down to lean his elbows on the back of the nearest chair. "How do you expect to get Chimera past all those fancy Federation scanners? Altera's a hell of a lot pickier than those FTL gate weigh stations."

"We were gonna have to move up in the world eventually, right? I don't know about you, but I'd like to retire someday instead of spending my golden years looking at your ugly mug, Park." The engineer raised his middle finger in reply, but he didn't interrupt. "I told Shrike we have some stops to make first, and he's willing to be patient if it means getting his cargo onto Altera without a fuss. So we're gonna make our next drop, and then we'll head for Jannat, and I'm gonna talk to Ungolo. If anybody knows how to get onto that station without getting shot, he does."

"And how much of our score are we gonna have to pass on to him to find out?"

"Don't you worry about your cut, Park."

Elijah raised his hand slightly to draw the captain's attention, earning himself some snickers from the crew around him. "Who's Ungolo?"

"He's a thengisi information broker."

The boy perked up, a smile on his face. "A thengisi? Really? They don't normally leave the Southern Ring, do they?"

Park smirked sidelong at him. "Look at you, knowing things."

Elijah huffed at him. "I know things."

"But you've never seen one, have you?"

He opened his mouth to retort and was forced to shut it again. He *hadn't* ever seen one.

"No," the captain cut in, "the thengisi don't normally leave the Southern Ring. We're going to Jannat. It's a satellite station orbiting their outer colony planet, and it's the closest aliens are allowed to come to Ekhaya—the thengisi homeworld. We're liable to have a time getting on there to begin with, so you be on your best behavior, kid, hear? Thengisi don't take kind to being gawked at."

Elijah nodded. "Yes, sir."

He thought the blond's eyes lingered on him for just a moment too long at being addressed as "sir," but then he turned his gaze on the first officer. "Shaw, you make sure we're stocked up on the basics, and we'll get out of here tomorrow and head for our next drop at Indira. Until then, y'all do as you like. Need a volunteer to stay on the ship." Davies lifted his hand in agreement, and the captain nodded at him. "Thanks, doc. I'll see the rest of you back on board and ready to go at 0700, you hear?"

"Yes, Captain," came the small chorus of replies.

"Now fuck off."

The crew headed for the exit door en masse, but as Elijah took his first step forward, the captain gave a quick, sharp whistle, and the boy looked over his shoulder to find the older man pointing at him.

"Not you."

Elijah waited awkwardly while the others filed out, not missing the teasing side-eye Brooks gave him as she passed. Once Harper had slid down the ladder just outside the bridge, and Elijah was left alone with the ship's captain, he stood at a safe distance while the other man watched him.

"So," the blond began. "You came out; you kept quiet; you followed orders. That's a promising start."

Elijah dropped his gaze to the floor for a moment to hide his brief smile. "I didn't want you to regret bringing me along."

"And what about your first time on a new planet? Got big plans?"

"I don't really know. I've never exactly had a lot of free time before. At home, if I wasn't working in the barn or the pasture, my mom always had something for me to be doing back at the house."

"Come on," the captain said with a smile, "even farm colony kids know how to have fun. You a drinker?"

"Sometimes."

"Ever had a Lasterian Snakebite?"

Elijah paused. "Is that something you drink?"

"I'll take that as a no." The captain pushed away from the co-pilot seat supporting him and moved toward the boy. "Come on then. You want to have a drink with me?"

The smile on the older man's face put a little flutter in Elijah's stomach, but he refused to let it show on his face. Was he seriously being asked out for a drink? Was this a Captain-crewman thing, trying to feel him out as an underling, or was he just trying to get

Elijah drunk so that he could take him back to his cabin? Or did he genuinely want to get to know him? Elijah bit his tongue in an attempt to force back that thought. He probably just wanted to keep an eye on the farm boy and make sure he didn't bring any trouble back to the ship on his first night out. He was being babysat—which was fair, he guessed, but it still made him feel like a kid. Being actually *called* "kid" all the time didn't help that, either. But with a babysitter or without one, he wasn't about to say no to going back onto his first new planet and seeing more of the port. So he nodded.

"Okay. Let's have a drink."

It was still daylight as they stepped into the elevator at the end of the catwalk leading away from the ship.

"I'm not used to drinking while the sun's up," Elijah said with a chuckle as the doors closed. "Back home, if us kids were doing any drinking, it was late at night, past curfew."

"Tadmor gets 19 hours of daylight," the captain answered. "Day and night are a little more loosely-adhered-to concepts here. 'Specially to visitors."

Elijah nodded, but after that, the pair was silent on their ride down the elevator. The quiet was too awkward for the boy to bear, so after a time, he spoke up again.

"I saw the cargo space hidden in the old water treatment system," he said. "That's smart."

The captain chuckled. "Ain't I just? Most places we go just scan cargo ships for weight and hope the right number means they're only carrying the stuff they say they are. Chimera is an old VSA-7 on the outside—and on paper—so she's expected to have certain specs. The more of her guts I replace, the more weight I free up for cargo without tripping any alarms when we pass through weigh stations. Her engine's new, too, so there's some more space in a compartment under there if I need it."

"What about places that have more than weight scanners?"

He shrugged. "That's case by case. Not everywhere has the interior scanners like Federation stations—like Altera. Sometimes the cargo's small or light enough that we can fudge it, since inspectors aren't likely to find our goodies even if they come on board to look. Who thinks to check inside the boilers when there's a cargo hold full of boring stuff like rice? But mostly I try not to take jobs that take us through heavy-duty security."

Elijah smiled up at him. "Not a big risk, big reward type of guy?"

"Big risk tends to end in death, not big reward. I'll stick with safe and profitable."

"Then why did you take the job to go to Altera? That sounds like the definition of big risk, big reward."

"Well," the captain said with a faint sidelong smirk, "I've been meaning to upgrade the ship anyway. This'll give me the money to do that."

The elevator clunked to the ground, interrupting their conversation, and the doors creaked open. The captain walked out first and didn't look back, clearly trusting Elijah to follow him. Elijah had to dodge humans and aliens alike who all seemed determined to walk right into him as they made their way through the marketplace, despite the way they all moved out of the captain's way as he walked. He'd clearly been here before, so maybe they knew him—or maybe there was something about the way the blond carried himself. He certainly looked at home in the dirty market, and he walked with a casual stride, as though none of the surrounding bustle interested him in the slightest.

They turned a corner and found themselves in front of a broad set of doors marked only by a neon sign in the shape of a bottle and a shot glass. Easier than trying to decide on a written language everyone would know, he guessed. The captain walked through the doors as they slid open in front of him, and Elijah followed him into the dimly-lit room. It was noisy inside—thumping music and clinking glasses and a couple dozen voices all talking over each other. A cluster of people were dancing in a cramped space in one corner, including—Elijah was pretty sure—a scantily-clad female kineta. He averted his eyes and followed his companion's lead toward an empty table near the wall, taking a seat across from the other man. A human waitress approached them, and the blond leaned an elbow on the table to smile up at her.

"Two Snakebites, please, honey."

The woman tapped her knuckles on the table with a nod. "You got it, sweetie." Then she was gone, disappeared back into the crowd.

Elijah leaned forward so that his captain could hear him better. "You know I don't actually have any money. My chip has maybe five credits on it."

"I'll take it out of your paycheck," he answered with a wink that made the boy's heart skip.

Elijah did his best to move along without acknowledging the feeling. "So, I still don't know your name."

"Yep."

Elijah waited, but the other man didn't speak again. "Are...you going to tell me?"

"Nope."

"Why not?"

"Because I'm 'Captain' to you."

The boy frowned, but he thought it was better not to argue. "Okay," he said instead, "so what is this drink, exactly?"

"Strong," the other man laughed.

"But what's it made of? What's in it?"

He shrugged one shoulder. "Who knows? Just drink and enjoy, Or, you know, vomit. You got any allergies?"

"Uh—"

The woman reappeared at their table and placed two lowball glasses in front of them, each one filled with something murky and yellow over a couple blocks of ice. She vanished as quickly as she arrived, leaving them to their drinks, and Elijah picked up his glass and inspected the contents. Something inside was swirling a darker golden yellow, further muddying the liquid inside. He grimaced faintly.

"This looks like piss."

"Maybe it is piss," the captain chuckled.

"You think it might be piss and you still drink it?"

"It's a big, beautiful galaxy, kid, full of all kinds of new and exciting experiences. This one happens to taste good. If it's piss, I don't want to know. Why ruin a good thing? Skål." He clinked his glass against Elijah's and downed the drink in a couple of long gulps.

The boy hesitated a second longer before following the other man's example. It was disgusting. Elijah coughed, but didn't quite gag at the burn of alien liquor pouring down his throat. He steeled himself for half a moment before swallowing the rest down just to get it over with, and by the time his glass made it back to the table, his head was already swimming.

"I think that actually is piss," he grunted, restraining another cough. "And if it is, I'd hate to meet the thing it came from."

The man opposite him laughed. "Enjoy the life you've chosen, kid."

"I chose piss?"

"You chose the unknown. That includes strange and unfamiliar alcohol."

Elijah chuckled softly, turning his empty glass in his hand. "Great."

"Just don't drink too much. I want you coherent when we get back to the ship."

"Why? Is there work to do before we leave tomorrow?"

"No. I have some questions for you in my cabin. Important questions."

"What—oh. Oh." Elijah felt heat rising in his cheeks that wasn't from the alcohol.

The blond was smiling slyly at him. "It's more fun if you're coherent before I make you completely *in*coherent."

Elijah kept his eyes on the table, knowing that looking up into the other man's pale eyes would only stoke the growing fire starting in his belly. He didn't want the blond to read the eagerness on his face. He only glanced upward when the captain waved at the waitress for another round, and she plunked two more glasses down on their table. The second one didn't go down any easier, but at least it gave him a few moments to settle himself enough to look the other man in the face.

"So I like to know who I have on my ship," the captain said as he leaned back in his chair. "Who do I have on my ship when you're on it?"

"I'm pretty sure I told you the other night whatever there is to know about me," Elijah chuckled. "I'm from Dhat-Badan. That right there ought to tell you just about everything."

"That just tells me where you came from—doesn't tell me *who you are*. And just because I like the sounds you make when you come, that doesn't mean you'll be any good to my crew." He paused just a moment to enjoy Elijah's faint blush. "I know you can do as you're told on a basic drop, at least. I know you're willing to offer your body to a stranger to get a ride on a ship. I know you say you want to see the galaxy. But if I'm going to trust you to be on the Chimera, I need to know what's under your hood."

"Is this an interview?"

"It's a little late for an interview," the captain answered. "And I've already decided to keep you around for now. No offense, but you don't seem like much of a threat. But that doesn't mean I've decided to trust you. And you've gotta have my trust, kid, if you're going to stay on my ship."

Elijah nodded. "I understand," he said. "But I'm pretty boring. There really isn't that much to tell."

The blond's lips curved into a slow smile, and he lifted his hand to wave the waitress back over without taking his eyes from the boy across from him. "There's always more to know."

· ● ◆ ● ·

"Don't even get me started on *privacy*," Elijah snorted as he tried to drain the last few drops from his newly-empty glass. The table wasn't quite full of them, but they—along with the tray that until recently had contained an impressive pile of fried bar food—were starting to encroach on the boy's elbow room. "Forget about it. I have four older brothers. My youngest-older brother *just* moved out of the house three months ago, and my older-older brother only a year before that. My oldest brother moved out when I was sixteen. Sixteen," he said again, leaning forward on the table to look closer at the captain. "I lived in a house with seven other people in it until then—because let's not forget about Aunt Sarah, who moved in after her husband died when I was nine. I shared a bedroom with *all* of my brothers ever since then. From nine years old to three months ago, I couldn't so much as roll over in my sleep without somebody else knowing about it. You ever have to jerk off behind a barn?"

The captain watched him with a barely-restrained laugh behind his smile. "Can't say that I have."

"It sucks," Elijah confirmed for him.

"That why you couldn't sleep on the ship? Not enough other bodies crowding you?"

The boy dropped his eyes and shrugged with a faint, embarrassed smile. "I guess so. I'm not used to being alone. It's a nice change, but some things you just get used to, you know? I didn't have to fight to make sure I got some breakfast this morning."

"Well I can't guarantee you won't have to fight Harper someday. Boy eats enough for three his size."

"That's still not a lot though, right?" Elijah asked, and he held his hand up near his chin to indicate Harper's short stature.

The captain barked out a laugh and slouched back in his chair. "You're not as shy as you seem, are you?"

"Do I seem shy?"

The blond shrugged. "Guess I figure all small colony farm boys are shy."

"Hard to grow up shy when you're sharing a bathroom with five other guys—and a couple of them just plain don't care if you're trying to jerk off. I had to get out of there." He leaned his arms on the table and looked down at the swiftly-melting ice in his glass. "All my life, the only escape I had was dreaming about being somewhere else. *Anywhere* else. I watched vids; I got on the net when I could. We didn't always have the best connection out there. I thought about what it would be like to get up there—out beyond the dome that kept us in. That dome felt like...like the walls of my cage. I couldn't even go everywhere on the planet I was stuck on because it was blocking out the poisonous freakin' atmosphere."

"You know," the captain said, "not everybody thinks it's all that great up here, either. We've gone a while without a job and had some pretty lean times. Imagine the Federation made sure y'all got all the food you needed."

"That's not all there is to this life, is there?" Elijah looked up at him with a soft furrow in his brow. "Just a full belly and a blanket? I want more than that. I want better than that. I don't want to be a story that didn't get told—I want to experience...everything," he said, splaying his hands as if he could express the vastness of the universe. "If that means some of those things are bad, then...I guess that's the trade I'll have to make for the great stuff."

The man across from Elijah watched him in silence for a few beats, but before he could open his mouth to reply, the boy was startled by a pair of slender hands on his bicep. The laughing young woman wordlessly tugged him out of his seat, tilting her head toward the dance floor. Elijah glanced between the girl and his captain as though asking permission to leave his seat, but the blond only smirked and slightly lifted his glass from the table in encouragement.

Elijah was not what anyone would ever call a *good* dancer, but he'd had enough to drink and the music was loud enough that he could pretend. The girl held his hands, touched his arms, and pulled him deeper into the press of bodies both human and not. He found himself laughing and moving to the thumping bass, letting the alcohol free his hesitation, but he couldn't keep his eyes from drifting back to the table he'd left. The captain sat leaned back in his seat with a fresh drink in his hand, and every time Elijah looked, he found the blond staring back at him through the crowd with an intensity in his pale eyes that made the boy shiver.

The young woman who had dragged him out seemed tireless—not to mention very drunk—and Elijah enjoyed trying to keep up with her. He didn't even notice the touch at the small of his back until he looked over his shoulder and saw the captain's now-empty chair. He froze as he realized it was the blond behind him, the heat of the other man's breath on his skin.

"Let's get back to the ship, Elijah," the captain said against his ear, softly and firmly, as if there was no room for disagreement.

Elijah's stomach tightened again, but he couldn't tell if it was anxiety or anticipation. "...Okay."

His captain paid for their drinks while Elijah pulled himself away from his dance partner with a smile, and they walked out together back toward the docks. Elijah wasn't entirely steady on his feet after his drinks, and he got distracted by the wares at some of the shops they passed, but his companion didn't seem to mind walking leisurely to give the boy time to look around and take in the atmosphere of the market. As they rounded a corner close to the docks, a pair of men stood facing them, purposely blocking their path. The captain stopped when he caught sight of them, and he let out a long sigh.

"Hey there, Captain," one of the men said, sneering the title like an insult. "I see you made it back."

"Isn't that crazy? It's almost like I had work here."

"Work that you snaked out from under us back on Talos."

"Is that what we're calling it when you try to charge eight thousand credits for a low-risk five-parsec jump, and Emesin takes a better offer?"

The man pointed an accusing finger at him and snarled, "You had no right to cut in on our negotiations!"

"Cry me a river, Paolo. Be reasonable next time and maybe you'll get more work. Now piss off; you're in my way."

The one called Paolo lurched forward and swung, barely missing the captain's chin as the blond backed out of the way. He moved to place himself between Elijah and the two approaching men, putting a hand out to keep the boy behind him.

"Stay back, kid."

Elijah frowned at the back of his head as the others drew near, one of them reaching out for the collar of the captain's coat and dragging him closer. When Paolo raised his arm to strike again, Elijah stepped forward, turning the man sharply by his sleeve and snapping out a punch that connected hard with his jaw. Paolo stumbled backward and scowled across at Elijah as soon as he found his footing.

"You should have listened to your boyfriend, kid."

"Fuck yourself," Elijah spat, and he got snatched by the front of his shirt for his trouble. He took a few hits to the stomach and face, but once he got Paolo's neck securely into the crook of his elbow, the other man began to drip significantly more blood onto the ground than Elijah had. When his attacker grew heavy in his grip, and Elijah's knuckles were raw, he shoved him away, leaving him to tumble back against the nearest wall. Beside him, the captain was bleeding from the mouth but had his opponent on the ground, his boot connecting with the man's ribs once more before he backed off.

The two men helped pick each other up and retreated around the corner with vengeful promises on their lips. Elijah stood beside the captain, both of them panting. At least Elijah felt sober now. The blond spit a mouthful of blood onto the ground.

"Assholes," he muttered. He turned to Elijah and took him gently by the chin, turning him to one side and then the other for inspection. He didn't look much better than the boy felt, but he had a soft frown on his lips as he studied the bruise making Elijah's eye ache. "That's gonna swell," he said. "Come on."

9

Back on the ship, Davies looked up from his little sofa in the med bay and sighed when he saw the state of the two men in his doorway.

"Already?"

"This wasn't my fault," the captain insisted. "Just a couple of bitter drifters looking for trouble."

Davies urged Elijah up onto the examination table and set about gathering a few bandages and packets of gel. He passed the boy a cold pack to hold against his eye and dabbed at a cut at the corner of his mouth with a fresh cloth. "You couldn't even keep the kid out of trouble on his first run?"

The captain smiled, wincing a little as it stung his broken lip, and he looked at the boy out of the corner of his eye. "I don't think I have to worry about him. You really know how to throw a punch, kid."

Elijah chuckled and glanced back at him with his uncovered eye while Davies smeared gel over the cut on his lip. "It's not always boring on the farm."

"I guess not."

Davies shook his head and softly sighed as he fastened one small adhesive bandage over the corner of Elijah's mouth and several on the broken skin of his knuckles, and then he turned his attention to the captain and similarly patched up his few injuries. He commanded him to rinse his mouth with a diluted gel and spit the bloody mixture out in the sink before he gave a grunt that Elijah assumed meant they were done.

"Luckily, it wasn't too serious this time," he said as he gathered up the empty gel packets. "Probably a good thing we're getting out of here in the morning."

The captain worked his jaw a little, seeming satisfied with the work the rinse had done. "Anybody else back yet?"

"I don't think so. You know Park will be at the scrapyard until ten minutes before we leave."

"Yeah, I know. I'm gonna be in my cabin; buzz me if anything life-threatening happens."

"Will do, Captain."

The blond headed toward the door and paused as it hissed open, glancing over his shoulder at Elijah and beckoning him to follow without saying a word. The boy slid off of the examination table and thanked Davies on his way out, then followed the captain out into the hallway with a growing tension in his chest. He knew that there were important questions waiting for him in the other man's cabin, and he couldn't stop replaying that sly smirk curling his lips as he promised to make Elijah completely incoherent once they got there.

· ● ◆ ● ·

Elijah stood in the captain's cabin again, trying to keep his eyes away from the bed as his host closed and locked the door behind them.

"You haven't brought me my tablet back," the captain said without looking at him. Elijah froze, but the look the blond gave him over his shoulder had a teasing edge to it.

"I...sorry," he answered. "I have it in my bunk, I can—"

"I do need it back," the captain cut him off, "and not just because I'm interested in your answers. But for now, I'll give you a pass."

"Thank you, Captain," Elijah said automatically, and the older man paused as he turned to face him at the head of the bed. Elijah stepped closer when the blond beckoned him forward with two fingers, stopping only at the light touch of the taller man's fingertips against his chest.

The captain lifted his hand to the boy's face, one knuckle touching under the dark-eyed boy's chin to draw his eyes upward. "How about for tonight, I just be very specific?"

"O...okay."

"What I want to do to you tonight—if you'll let me—is to strap you face down on this bed by your wrists. It won't be too tight; just enough to keep you where I want you. Then I'll put a blindfold on you, and I'll touch you. Wherever I want. However I want. You won't be able to see what I'm about to do. Then, when I'm ready, I'm going to hit you. Lightly, at first, on your ass or the backs of your thighs, until your skin is flushed and hot. Then I'll hit you a little harder. I'm going to want to hear you whine. When you're used to that, I'll hit you a little harder, and once your cock is dripping, if you beg me, I'll touch it. But you won't come until I'm finished with you."

His thumb brushed Elijah's cheek, touching the edge of his bandage and causing a pleasant sting. "Does that sound like something you want, Elijah?"

The boy's mouth was too dry for him to even consider answering with words. His stomach was tight, and he could already feel his dick beginning to press against the buttons of his pants just from the low, even promise in the other man's voice. He'd never known this was something that he wanted. He still wasn't positive. It was a little scary—but his heart was too high up in his throat and beating too fast for him to pretend it didn't sound exciting. Finally, he nodded.

"I do," he said, a shiver running up his spine as the pad of the captain's thumb ran over his bottom lip.

"One more rule," the blond murmured, and Elijah tried to swallow away the lump in his throat at the quiet, intense look in the other man's pale eyes. "This one's important. When we do this, you're going to be making a lot of noises. I need to be able to hear the difference between the usual kind and the kind that means you aren't having fun. We don't know each other too well yet, so it might be hard for me to tell. So, if you need me to ease up, back off, slow down—you say 'yellow.' You need me to just stop, you say 'red.' You got me?"

Elijah nodded again, and the captain gripped his chin a little tighter, avoiding the cut on his face. "And when I ask you a question, you answer me politely. Understand?"

"Yes," Elijah tried again, though his throat was dry.

"Yes, *Captain*," the blond corrected, the command firing a spark in Elijah's belly.

"Yes, Captain," he half whispered.

"Good boy." The other man released him and took a small step backward. "Now get undressed for me."

Elijah glanced down at his half-hard dick and hesitated just a moment at the thought that the captain would know he was aroused from the simple description of what was to come. But he found his hands moving automatically, unlacing his boots and toeing them off along with his socks. He stood and tugged his shirt off by the collar, leaving it aside near his boots, and then fumbled slightly with the buttons on his pants. He avoided the other man's eyes as he slid his pants and underwear down his hips, shivering as the cool air touched his erection. When he stood nude in front of the ship's captain, he dared to peek up at his face, but the blond was only watching him, blue eyes traveling the length of the younger man's lean body.

"Get on the bed, Elijah," he said after a moment. "Hands and knees."

Elijah crawled up onto the bed, already feeling a tremble of anticipation beginning in his skin, and as the captain approached him and took him by one wrist to fasten it into a cuff, he noticed for the first time that it was definitely a permanent fixture, as were the numerous D-rings hanging from the lower edge of the mattress. The cuffs could be attached anywhere around the bed. Elijah allowed himself to be strapped down by both wrists, the short strip of leash between his cuff and the bed leaving him very little room to move, and he lowered his chest to the mattress at the soft, urging pressure of the other man's hand between his shoulder blades.

He thought he'd feel embarrassed with his hips lifted and his ass in the air, but the shift of the mattress behind him as the blond moved to kneel between his legs and his gentle touch moving up Elijah's spine to the back of his neck settled a warm calm over him. He peeked up to watch as the captain retrieved a soft blindfold from the small cabinet above the headboard and stayed still as it was slipped over his eyes. The cloth was cool against his cheeks and just snug enough to completely black out the light of the room.

The blond's fingertips explored his back, his sides, his hips, pressing gently into his skin. Elijah flinched away at first on instinct, unaccustomed to being blind and in such a vulnerable position, but he relaxed slowly under the older man's steady touch. He was taking his time, calloused hands running over every inch of his torso and pausing every time Elijah's breath caught in his throat as though he was memorizing the boy's most sensitive spots. Elijah's skin began to tingle with prickling warmth under the caress, and he couldn't be sure if his lightheadedness was from the drinks he'd had or from the way his breath had become just a little bit shorter.

The sudden smack of pain on the meat of his ass snapped him back to reality, and he jerked forward away from the hit automatically, but the skip of his heart settled as a firm, warm hand ran over the tender spot, wiping away the sting. As soon as he relaxed, another strike came, burning the skin just enough to make him jump. Every hit sent electricity up his spine, and every one was followed by a reassuring caress that soothed his increasingly tender ass and thighs. When he stopped flinching from the gentle smacks and settled a little deeper into the mattress as he relaxed, the sheet a welcome coolness under his cheek, the audible crack of skin on skin drew a startled yelp from his throat.

"All right, Elijah?" the captain's low voice asked from behind him, fingernails scratching lightly over the burning skin.

"Y-Yeah," he murmured, and he received an even sharper smack for his answer, his fingers clenching tightly around the straps leashing him to the bed.

"That wasn't very polite."

"Y...Yes, Captain," Elijah panted, squeezing his eyes shut even underneath the blindfold in an attempt to steady his breath.

"Better."

Elijah gasped as another hit landed on his ass. Even the air moving across his skin made him tremble now. The muscles in his thighs quivered, threatening to give, but the man behind him wouldn't let him drop. Every time Elijah fell a little closer to the bed, the captain struck him harder, causing him to jerk upwards again with a gasping moan. Even in the darkness the blindfold allowed him, Elijah could see spots in front of his eyes as he hid his face in the rumpled sheets that muffled his whimpers. His body jerked forward with each strike and eased back with each firm stroke of the captain's palm over his raw skin.

When the blond squeezed him in both hands, urging his hips a little higher and spreading him open, Elijah heard his soft hum of approval and shivered. His cock twitched, the tip briefly kissing the bed and leaving a thread of precum between the sheet and his skin. The flicker of friction startled a sharp moan out of him, and his hips instinctively twisted forward in search of more, but the captain slapped him in the back of the thigh and shot him back up again.

"Not yet."

Elijah whined in response, the desperation in his own voice surprising him. The other man hadn't even really touched him yet, and his dick was quivering with want. He panted and moaned through the hits that followed, teeth clenched and shoulders hunched as he braced himself with a straining grip on the straps of his cuffs. When his knees finally began to slip, unable to support his weight, the captain hooked an arm around his waist to keep his hips raised and bent over his back, his teeth sinking into the heated skin of Elijah's shoulder.

"Do you want me to touch you, Elijah?" he whispered behind the boy's ear. "Do you want me to make you come?"

For a moment, Elijah couldn't manage more than a shaky moan. The man above him was patient, though the press of his warmth against Elijah's back did little to help him gather his thoughts.

"Yes, Captain," he said, breathless and gasping, but the blonde only nipped at the back of his neck.

"You can beg better than that."

"P...Please, Captain," Elijah whispered.

"Please what?" he breathed, his words hot against the brown skin between Elijah's shoulder blades.

"Please...please let me come. Please, Captain."

"Good boy," he growled, and the praise shot straight to Elijah's groin, sending a shudder through him. The blond's free hand snaked around him, fingers curling around his straining dick and drawing the breath from his lungs. Elijah bucked into the touch and almost finished immediately, but the other man squeezed him so tightly that he went still. He didn't give Elijah time to rest; as soon as he had a brief moment to settle, his hand began to work over the boy, stroking him firmly and steadily. The fabric of his pants felt impossibly rough against Elijah's raw skin, but he could still feel the press of the blond's erection grinding into him over the burning sting.

Elijah could barely think. His body was overwhelmed with sensation that overlapped the boundary between pain and pleasure, and he felt himself pressing back against the man above him, desperate for more of his touch. The captain's teeth left sharp bites along the back of his shoulders, and his arm kept Elijah supported as the boy's breath grew more and more unsteady. Elijah heard himself moan and beg for release in a voice that barely sounded like his own, letting out a shaky cry as the blond's thumb ran over the tip of his cock. Every muscle in his body tensed, and he half sobbed into the mattress as he finally gave, back arching and wrists jerking against his restraints. He spilled thick ropes of white over the captain's fingers and onto the bed, his hips twitching with every pulse his orgasm sent through his stomach.

He couldn't catch his breath, but he went slack in the other man's grip, feeling like he was melting into the sheets as the blond eased him gently back onto the mattress away from the mess he'd made. He barely noticed when his wrists were set free; all of his attention was focused on getting enough air to his foggy brain. Gentle hands ran over his back and down his arms, massaging the tension out of his fingers. The blindfold slid away from his eyes, but he didn't have the energy to open them. He felt the captain's fingers running through his hair and fell into sated stillness, exhaustion overtaking him and slowing his breath into the steady pattern of sleep.

Elijah woke under the captain's heavy blanket and opened his eyes to narrow, sleepy slits. His body felt like it weighed a thousand pounds, and his ass and thighs were still sore and burning. He managed to turn his head and found the blond sitting in his chair, beaded hair loose around his shoulders and chin leaned into one hand on the surface of the table. He was shirtless and bootless and had a tablet in front of him, and he frowned down at the computer screen he was hunched over. Elijah's eyes traced the colorful tattoos up his arms and over his shoulder blades. He couldn't make out all the details, but there were some flowers, a purple and green nebula silhouetting a constellation, and a woman's weeping face half hidden by a sheer veil. They probably all had stories. Elijah wondered if he would ever hear them. The captain looked up when the boy managed to stir and caused a soft creak on the mattress.

"Welcome back," he murmured, and his slow smile sent a different kind of warmth into Elijah's chest. "How are you feeling?"

"A little beat up, honestly," he said. "But fine." His voice sounded dry, and the other man must have noticed, because he gestured to a glass of water on the small table beside the bed. Elijah sat up slowly, grateful for the coolness of the liquid as it ran down his throat.

"I haven't scared you off?"

Elijah smiled down into his glass and shook his head. "I'm definitely discovering something new about myself," he chuckled. Then he paused. "But...is this really fine for you? I mean, that's twice now that we've...whatever we did, and both times it's kind of—seemed all about me. Not that I'm complaining," he added, his face flushing slightly under the other man's amused gaze. "But I guess I thought that you'd want to...you know. Get yours, I guess?"

"You don't have to worry about me, Elijah. I have plenty more planned for you—if you're willing."

"I...think I am. Is it always that intense?"

"It can be as intense as you want it to be."

"Seems like there's a bit of a learning curve. At least, my ass thinks so."

"I'm happy to teach you. And your ass."

Elijah set his glass aside and flinched as he shifted on his rear, but the sting wasn't an unpleasant reminder. He leaned back against the headboard and looked over at the reclined captain. He had clearly gotten comfortable, but the space on the bed next to Elijah was still cool. He hadn't slept.

"What time is it?"

"Midnight or so."

"Do you not sleep?"

"Well, there seemed to be an unconscious farm boy in my bed," the blond teased.

Elijah didn't know how to reply. He didn't want to push by suggesting they share the bed if the other man was trying to keep his distance, but he couldn't help the subtle weight of disappointment in his chest at the thought. He looked down at his hands in his lap and chewed the bandage at the corner of his mouth. When he looked back up, the blond had settled back in his chair and returned his attention to his work.

"If we're going to do this more, can I ask you something?" Elijah spoke up.

"Sure."

"What's your name?"

The captain paused. He dropped the tablet to his lap with a small sigh, but there was a faint smile on his lips. "Won't take no for an answer, huh?"

"I just figure if I'm going to let you tie me down and spank me, the least you can do is tell me that."

"All right, all right." He set his tablet aside on the table and leaned his elbow on the arm of his chair with his cheek on his fist. "It's Leslie. Almstedt."

"Why didn't you want to tell me before?"

"It's not a very intimidating name, right? You don't get far in this business with a name like 'Leslie.' So better to just be 'Captain,' you know?"

Elijah hesitated. "I like Leslie," he said in a quiet voice. "Can I use it?"

The blond seemed a bit taken aback by the question. He opened his mouth as though he meant to instantly reject the idea, but something made him pause. His pale eyes matched Elijah's brown for a few beats, and then a resigned smile quirked the corners of his mouth, and he nodded. At Elijah's grin, he lifted one warning finger. "Not in front of the crew. Only Park knows, and he knows better than to say it out loud."

Elijah mimed zipping and locking his lips, unable to keep the smile from his face. "You got it, Les."

The captain's eyebrows lifted slightly, and Elijah almost swore he saw a touch of color beneath the light beard on the other man's cheeks before he cleared his throat and turned back to face his computer screen. "Anyway, fuck off so I can get some sleep. Park won't let up on you if he thinks you spent the whole night in here. And bring my tablet back."

Elijah wasn't offended by the man's gruff tone. They weren't friends, after all, and they definitely weren't anything more than that. They just...had an arrangement. Elijah could live with that. He slid out of bed and tugged his clothes back on, tucking his socks into his boots and his boots under his arm. He only paused a moment at the door, glancing over his shoulder at the captain's—Leslie's—hunched back.

"Night, Captain," he offered as the cabin door slid open at his touch, and then the other man peered back at him.

"G'night, kid," he called back, waving him off without looking up.

10

It was difficult to get to sleep. Elijah's rear still felt warm, and his mind was full of memories of the captain's hands on him. Not just the captain—Leslie. He'd trusted Elijah enough to share a secret with him. It was trust the boy intended to deserve. On the Chimera, he'd be able to see all the places he'd ever dreamed of, and he could earn his place with—well, not entirely honest work, but work, anyway. That was enough for him.

Elijah sat up on his cot, the blanket pooling around his hips, and he squinted in the dark for his knapsack. He bent over the edge of the bed and dug inside the bag for his little notebook, clicking on the light by his bed on his way back upright. The book was well worn, the edges of the paper softened by repeated thumbing, and the ink on some of the early pages had begun to fade. He'd written all his hopes in this book—ideas for jobs he might get on far-flung worlds, planets he longed to see and the routes he might take to get there, carefully plotted and marked in pencil under dim lamps before his brothers griped at him to shut it off and go to sleep. But the back few pages were the most important. There, he'd started a list of things he wanted to do—someday. Some of them were simple, and some were bigger, but every one was impossible on the colony of Dhat-Badan.

He found his pen and ran his fingertips over the aging ink on the first page of his list. He'd started it so long ago, when the idea that he could ever leave his colony behind had first entered his mind. Today he was able to mark some off for the first time.

~~Ride in a starship.~~ Chimera.

~~Visit an alien planet.~~

~~Meet a kineta.~~ April 6, 2186. Tadmor.

Elijah suspected that some of the other things on the list would take a lot longer to complete—things like "fly a starship" or "visit 100 different planets"—but at least now he would have the chance. He chewed his bottom lip in thought as he turned the page. Some of them he might never accomplish. "Ride a giant sea worm on Ganthar 6" could probably safely be filed under "thirteen-year-old pipe dreams." His eyes landed on one entry that he remembered writing in the middle of a bout with late night melancholy a few years ago, and he flushed with embarrassment.

Fall in love.

He'd come home from a party in his uncle's back field attended by the same few people he saw all the time, listening to the same music, drinking the same beer stolen from their parents. They'd told the same stories, made the same jokes, and sat around the same bonfire the same way they'd done for years. Elijah had spent some time kissing one of the girls who favored him and sneaking side glances at the boy who helped at his family's farm, but it had all felt so…empty. He'd escaped the party and sat in his corner of the shared bedroom lamenting his lot in life, and he'd added one more impossible dream to his list. Kissing was fun, but none of that sort of thing had ever lit a fire inside him—and now that he knew what real want and desire could feel like, he felt even more like everything he'd done before had been hollow.

Elijah shut the book, laid it aside on his little shelf, and flicked off the light as he settled back onto his cot. Whatever he had going with the captain may have been exciting, but Elijah wouldn't be doing himself any favors by confusing it with being in love. He had too many other things on his list to worry about checking that one off just yet.

• • ◆ • •

In the morning, Elijah showered without even a single moment of eye contact from Park, shaved with a spare razor Davies had provided him, and threw away the bandage clinging to his cheek from the night before. The gel seemed to have done its job; only a tender red spot remained where the cut had been.

He felt more relaxed aboard the ship than he had the day before. He knew his way around the decks, and he was beginning to recognize the subtle hums and bangs that meant they were detaching from their docking bay. He heard the pilot announcing their departure over the intercom and smiled at the thought of continuing his duties as normal. This really could be his home.

The ship itself didn't need a lot of maintenance cleaning now that Elijah had given every deck a good scrubbing, but the mess hall seemed to be in a constant state of disaster. The rations in the kitchen were all prepackaged and simple to prepare, but they weren't very satisfying. These were the "basics" Shaw had taken all that time to gather? There had been countless market stalls on Tadmor with fresh vegetables, meat, and other goods, and instead, Shaw had subjected his crewmates to this freeze-dried, nutrition-less crap. The kitchen didn't have much in the way of cooking supplies, but it at least had a stove, and Elijah had seen a couple of pots and pans in one of the cabinets. Maybe he could make something decent after their next stop—if the captain was willing to give him some money. Or was he going to get a cut of the next shipment's payment? Elijah needed to ask him about more than their sex arrangement if he planned on staying on board the Chimera.

He made a pot of coffee, washed the leftover dishes, and scraped a few old condiment stains from under the counter before he allowed himself to peek into the little viewing room by the med bay and sit by the window for a while. He didn't see the captain until he was cleaning up after lunch. He barely heard the soft hiss of the cabin door down the short corridor from the mess, but the slow measure of Leslie's boots on the metal floor was unmistakable. Elijah smiled over his shoulder at the blond, wiping the suds from his hands with one of the few clean towels in the kitchen. His smile faded instantly at the stern frown the other man directed at him as he approached, and he retreated half a step before his hip hit the counter, trapping him between the captain's leaning arms.

"Captain," the boy said softly, overly aware of how close Leslie's face was to his. Was he angry? Elijah thought they had almost shared a moment back on the planet the night before, but the blond certainly wasn't looking at him like they'd gotten any friendlier.

"You're slacking, kid," Leslie murmured, his pale eyes locked firmly on the younger man's dark orbs.

"I am?"

"Mhm."

Elijah's brow knit in confusion. "I swept, and I did the laundry Brooks asked me to—"

The captain tutted at him, and the soft scolding settled a weight in Elijah's belly.

"You still have my tablet."

Elijah froze. He meant the checklist—Elijah had left it in his room again. "I'm sorry. I'll go get it right now," he said, but he made no move to attempt an escape from behind the barricade of Leslie's arms.

The captain lingered, those predatory eyes tracing Elijah's flushed face just long enough for the heat to spread to his stomach before Leslie pushed back and waved him away with a casual gesture.

"Hurry up, now. I'll wait for you in my cabin."

"Yes, Captain." Elijah hurried as fast as he could without slipping on the smooth floor, his palms burning as he slid down the metal ladder to the crew deck. He had let his "assignment" slip his mind, and now the captain was probably going to think up some extra punishment for him. The thought sent a pleasant twist of anticipation through his insides. When, exactly, had he come to want a punishment?

He took the tablet from his little bedside table and rushed it back up the ladder to the captain's door. Leslie took it from him with a stoic glance and urged him backward toward the bed to wait while he skimmed the boy's responses.

Elijah sat where he was directed, watching the subtle working of the captain's jaw while he slouched comfortably in the chair by his desk.

"You're a lot more adventurous than I thought you were," Leslie chuckled after an endless, tense silence. "But I guess I should know better by now, shouldn't I?" He set the tablet down on his desk and propped his boots up on the edge of the mattress, blocking the way between Elijah and the door. "You know, even after we leave, it's going to be another four or five days before we get to Indira. You're not going to get cabin fever with all these long trips, are you?"

"I hope not," Elijah answered honestly. "I just wish there was more I could do around here. Everybody seems to have a job but me."

"You just keep doing your part when we land, and don't worry about the rest until I tell you to. I'd have at least one less limb than I've got today if not for Harper, and you think his ass does anything on board except sit in his bunk and play those VR games? You're fine."

Elijah smiled and exhaled his relief. "Okay. I'll just stay out of engineering."

Leslie snorted softly. "Yeah, that's best." He tilted his head toward the tablet to draw their conversation back to its purpose. "Now, you looked this over carefully, right? Didn't check yes anywhere you meant no?"

"I don't think so. Some of it was way out there for me, but a lot of it was…just out there enough, I guess?" He licked his lips and lowered his eyes. It would be too difficult to tell the other man just how much he'd been dreaming about some of the things on that list.

"Is that right? Like being spanked?"

"Like being spanked," the boy confirmed with a laugh.

"You liked the pain, or you liked being tied up?"

"Both, I think. Hard to tell if it was one more than the other. I probably need to try more," he added softly, peeking up at the pale eyes watching him.

"Is that right," the captain said again, dropping his feet from the bed to sit up a little straighter. This time it sounded much less like a question. Leslie flicked his gaze down to the floor beside him and nodded toward it. "Come here, Elijah."

He hesitated, unsure what exactly the other man wanted from him, but when he saw the subtle flaring of the blond's nostrils as he met his eyes again, Elijah moved forward on instinct, settling on his knees on the metal floor by the arm of his captain's chair. Leslie reached out to cup his chin and draw his face upwards, his thumb tracing the boy's lush bottom lip. He watched Elijah for a while, the soft warmth of his hand and his even gaze quickening the boy's heartbeat in his chest.

"You like doing as you're told, don't you, Elijah?"

He swallowed thickly before he could answer. "Yes, Captain."

"You like it when *I* tell you what to do."

"Yes, Captain," Elijah said again, a little more hoarsely. His head turned toward the other man's palm before he could help himself, his lips parting over Leslie's calloused hand. His tongue pressed against the pad of the blond's thumb, and Leslie gripped his chin tighter with an audible hiss of breath. A moment later, the captain pulled his hand free, leaving Elijah slightly lightheaded and mourning the loss of the other man's touch.

"Then I'll give you some orders," Leslie said easily as he stood. "Get up and pull down your pants."

Elijah pushed himself up, fumbling with his belt while the captain opened the small cabinet at his headboard. He sat down on the mattress at Leslie's soft command, his pants bunched around his knees, and his breath hitched in his throat as the captain kneeled in front of him.

"I'm going to put this on you," the blond said evenly. He held out his hands and showed the younger man a small strap of leather strung with a few thick metal rings separated by smooth bolts. "I want you to wear it out of here, and I want you to keep wearing it until I bring you in here to take it off."

"You're going to put it...*on me* on me?" Elijah clarified, gesturing toward his exposed groin.

"That's right. You'll be able to keep it on without trouble—walking around, sleeping, going to the bathroom, all that—but these rings here will keep you from masturbating. And these little sensors," he added, touching the cool metal circles between the rings, "will sense if you're about to come, just in case you're determined, and they'll give you a real little shock to put a damper on the idea." The captain looked up into Elijah's frowning face and chuckled. "You see, that look you get and those sounds you make when you're pushed over the edge?" He reached up and slid his fingers through Elijah's hair, his grip tightening on the back of the boy's neck. "They belong to me. Every single one. And this is going to make sure I get what's mine."

Elijah trembled under the touch, squeezing the blanket under his hands so tightly that his knuckles ached. He stared down at the metal and leather in Leslie's hand with a boiling, nervous excitement in his belly. He had ticked "maybe" beside the item on the list called "chastity belts" simply because it hadn't seemed too scary a concept after a basic net search, but having it explained to him was entirely different from looking at stock photos.

"How—" he started, then stopped to clear the dryness from his throat. "How does it come off?"

"I'll show you, if you let me put it on. Will you do that for me, Elijah?" Leslie's palm was hot against his skin, his voice soft, and his gaze steady. He looked up at the boy in the warm, quiet room, loose yellow waves falling over his shoulder as they slipped free of his low ponytail. His orders were firm, and he took no argument outside the doors of his cabin, but he would have waited patiently all afternoon for the boy to make up his mind. There was only one answer Elijah could possibly give to this man.

"Yes, Captain."

"Good boy," Leslie purred, and Elijah shivered as he removed his hand from his neck.

Elijah jumped at the heat of Leslie's fingers on his cock, but he didn't have long to enjoy it—the captain seemed adept at securing the device. One cool ring slipped over Elijah's balls, settling snugly against him, and the rest slid easily over the length of his dick, the last resting around the soft crown of skin at the head. With one quiet snap, Leslie secured the whole thing in place. It was loose enough to be comfortable now, but Elijah suspected that if he got a forbidden erection, it would be uncomfortably tight.

"This," the captain said, pointing toward a slightly larger sensor disc at the end of the leather nestled in Elijah's pubic hair, "is how it comes off. Just touch it there."

Elijah did, but the metal only flashed red twice, and the straps didn't budge. He looked up at Leslie in confusion and found him smirking faintly.

"Sorry, I wasn't clear," the blond chuckled. "I meant that *I* have to touch it there. It's coded to my fingerprint." He put his hands on either side of Elijah to push himself to his feet and gestured for the boy to do the same. When Elijah had carefully adjusted himself and fastened his pants and belt again, Leslie brushed his knuckles under the younger man's chin and tilted his head at him with a sly smile. "Now get on with your duties, cabin boy."

· · ◆ · ·

Elijah struggled to walk normally for the rest of the day. Every movement reminded him of the leather and metal surrounding his cock and threatened to test the limits allowed to him. Every time he passed someone in a corridor, he felt they must have known his secret somehow. This wasn't just a hurried walk back to his room hiding a small dildo in his pocket—how long would he have to wear this thing for? He'd been too overwhelmed to think to ask. What if it was days? What if it was weeks?

He retreated to his room long before he was ready to sleep. He couldn't take his crewmates' eyes on him, but lying on his cot turned out to be no better. His every thought was obscured by the memory of Leslie's curling lips, the captain's hands clutching his hips and stinging his rear with every strike. There was no way for him to distract himself with the constant touch of the device around him. And he was right—an erection was definitely uncomfortable.

Elijah covered himself with his blanket and squeezed his eyes shut, panting into his pillow at every unintentional jerk of his hips. Even the brush of the sheet against the heated skin between the rings was enough to make him whimper, but he didn't dare try to overcome the barrier. He didn't want to risk tempting the electric shock, no matter how mild the captain said it was.

11

Elijah appeared in the mess the next morning with bags under his eyes, grateful that someone else had made a pot of coffee before he arrived. Any sleep he'd gotten had been fitful and short, interrupted by every touch of fabric anywhere near his hips. Park, Brooks, and Harper were already seated at the long table to eat their rehydrated breakfasts, and Elijah could feel their eyes on him as he passed them by in his search for caffeine. He took his place at the far end of the table with his mug in both hands and hunched over it, hoping the smell alone would help keep him awake.

"Jesus, kid," Park snorted. "You look like shit. You have a bad night with the captain or a really good one? Or maybe you were up missing your favorite cow?"

"Fuck you," Elijah muttered as he took his first blissful sip.

"What'd you say to me?" Park's chair squeaked on the floor as he got to his feet. He leaned his hands on the table to glare across at the younger man, but Elijah just stared back at him with a frown on his face.

"You don't have to give me shit all the time just because I'm the only one getting laid around here."

Brooks barked out a laugh that brought red to both Park and Harper's faces, but only the taller man snapped back.

"You're walking that wire, ain't you, new kid?"

Elijah set down his mug again without taking his eyes from the scowling engineer. "If you want to back that mouth up, you tell me when, Park. If not, I suggest you take any grievance with me to the captain instead of wasting all your time trying to piss me off, 'cause one of these days it's gonna work."

The older man hesitated, but Elijah wouldn't look away. He could sense the subtle shift as Park sized him up, trying to see if he was worth the potential scrap. Elijah had seen it more than once and had occasionally gotten his ass kicked by one of the older boys back on Dhat-Badan for his trouble, but he knew that his hard labor on the farm had left him notably more imposing than a limping engineer. Elijah held his gaze until Park clicked his tongue in annoyance, shoved his tray away from him, and stalked from the mess hall with a curse on his lips.

"You tell him, kid," Brooks laughed.

"He shows up here," Harper muttered with a shake of his head, leaning his chair back on its rear legs, "he shows up here, and now he's in good with the captain and sowing discord among the crew—"

"Don't use words you can't spell, Harper," the pilot cut him off. "Give it a rest with the conspiracies and let the kid have his coffee before he's got to deal with this bullshit."

Harper grimaced in annoyance and took up the remaining half of his muffin as he headed toward the ladder to the lower deck. "Make sure the kitchen's clean, cabin boy," he said over his shoulder.

Elijah sighed as the young man's steps faded down the ladder shaft, and he leaned his elbow on the table with his chin in one hand.

Brooks tilted her head back to drain the last coffee from her cup and thunked it back down on the table. She let Elijah takes a few sips of his coffee in silence, then leaned forward on both elbows to look at him a little closer.

"So," she finally started. Elijah flicked his eyes over to her, since moving his entire head felt like too much effort. "It was a good night, right? With the captain."

"Jesus fucking Christ," Elijah sighed. He scooted his chair from the table and carried his coffee with him back to the ladder, ignoring the pilot's laughter as she shouted after him that she was only trying to be sympathetic.

He finished his coffee back in his bunk, shifting awkwardly on the bed every few moments to adjust the position of his imprisoned prick. Just like Leslie had said, it wasn't uncomfortable, and he had managed to take his morning piss without any fuss, but it was certainly a constant reminder of the captain and what Elijah wished was touching him instead of the leather and steel.

It was easier to spend the day locked away in his cabin than to face the rest of the crew. He distracted himself with reading a book that Davies had let him borrow, but not even the killer-for-hire mystery could keep his mind off of their own ship's captain. He made it a few hours before he managed to get himself shocked by the device, at least.

When the crew deck was silent, and Elijah hadn't heard any sounds of movement for some time, he finally risked making his way to the bathroom for a shower. He didn't know if it was safe to get his device wet, but Leslie hadn't said anything about *not* getting it wet, nor had he called Elijah back to his cabin to have it removed for over a day and a half, so he figured the captain must have known he would shower at some point. At least, he hoped so. He laid his change of clothes on the bench and started up the water behind the half-wall, grateful for the echo of splashing in the empty room. The hot water was a relief, unknotting the tight muscles down his shoulders and back, and he shut his eyes to enjoy it for a while.

His respite was interrupted by the hissing of the far door, and he froze. He slapped off the water as quick as he could and tried to inch his way back to his towel behind the tiled half-wall, but found himself face to face with Brooks before he could make it around the corner.

She spotted his secret immediately and let out a laugh that reverberated around the room so loudly that Elijah instinctively shushed her.

"Is that what was wrong with you?" she asked, wiping tears of mirth from her eyes with the back of her hand. "Holy hell, kid. You've landed yourself in a whole new world, haven't you?"

"Please," Elijah sighed as he snatched up his towel to cover himself. "Please don't say anything."

"Oh, this secret is *so* safe with me," the pilot chuckled.

"Thank you."

"Thank *you*," Brooks echoed, giving him a mock salute as he hurried out of the locker room dressed but still damp.

· • ◆ • ·

By the middle of the next day, Elijah was suffering. He couldn't cool down, and he read the same paragraph of Davies' book four times before he gave up and tossed the worn paperback to the foot of his cot. There was very little he could will his body to do except cover his face with his pillow and keep his hands squeezing it tightly in a desperate attempt to keep them from reaching down for his dick. His erection strained helplessly against the metal rings, but he refused to undo his pants to free it. As sensitive as he was, even the movement of the air in the room might set off his next electric shock. It wasn't a painful jolt, exactly—but intense and pulsing, and definitely uncomfortable in a way that Elijah found hard to admit he liked.

He had been lying still with his eyes shut under his pillow for almost half an hour when he heard the click of the ship's intercom and the captain's stern voice over the speaker.

"Hey new kid; come see me. Now."

Elijah had never moved faster in his life. He flinched a little as he pushed off of his bed, but the tenderness of his neglected prick was easily forgotten in his rush to get down the hall and up the ladder to the captain's door. He banged on the entrance a little too hard and practically fell inside when Leslie opened the door.

"Look at you," the captain chuckled as he pressed the door lock. He paused a moment to look the boy up and down, a smirk curling the edge of his lips as he took in Elijah's flushed face and the faint sheen of sweat glistening on his collarbone. "You're in a state, ain't ya?"

"Please, captain," Elijah panted softly. "Please take it off."

"Now you're giving the orders?" Elijah whimpered in frustration as Leslie laid a hand on the boy's chest and walked his fingers slowly down his stomach. "You don't like wearing it after all?"

"It's—" Elijah swallowed before continuing. "It's more intense than I expected."

"How many times have you been shocked?" Leslie traced the

buckle of Elijah's belt under his shirt, causing the boy's breath to catch in his chest, and when the captain's hand ran smoothly down the tight fabric covering his erection, Elijah jerked and grit his teeth, the jolt swaying him on his feet.

"A few," he admitted with a dry voice.

The captain's eyes were locked on him like prey as he pushed gently on Elijah's hip, urging him back toward the bed. "Then I reckon it's about time you got those pants off."

Elijah backed up as quickly as he dared, already fighting his belt as he hit the mattress. He struggled to keep his attention on the work of his hands; the captain's steady gaze on him was already enough to make his heart race. He desperately wanted—*needed*—Leslie's hands on him, and he wasn't above begging for it. In fact, he felt his dick give a little jump as he realized he hoped the blond made him beg for it. The man had made a complete mess of him, and Elijah hadn't even seen him in two days.

Leslie took a step to close the distance between them, but he'd barely put the weight of his knee on the bed between Elijah's legs when the intercom speaker gave a brief squeal of feedback.

"Captain to the bridge," Brooks' voice announced with a touch of urgency. "Got a ship hailing us on the private frequency. I think it's Kaffir."

Leslie paused, watching Elijah's uneven breath pass through his parted lips, and then he let a tiny huff slip as he pulled away. "Sorry, kid," he said on his way to the door. "It'll have to wait."

"Are you kidding me?" Elijah called after him, but the cabin door was already open. The door gave a hydraulic hiss as it slid closed, and Leslie didn't hear the boy shout, "At least take it off!" Elijah slumped back onto the bed with one arm draped over his eyes and groaned in defeat. If he tried to remove it himself, he would only get shocked again. He gave himself a few moments to regain what composure he could muster before tugging his pants back up his hips and buckling his belt, then stalked sourly from the captain's cabin.

He crossed the mess hall and lurked by the door to the bridge, but when Shaw brushed by him and let himself through without hesitation, Elijah followed.

"Came out of fucking nowhere, Cap," an unfamiliar voice was

saying over the speaker by the copilot's seat, where Leslie leaned with his hands on the arm of the chair to listen. The man had an accent that Elijah couldn't place, and he spoke so quickly that a lot of his words seemed to blend together. "They blasted my engines to shit and made off with my cargo. I'm stranded."

"You're lucky you're alive," Leslie snorted.

"You're telling fucking me. So how about it? You going to prove I'm even luckier? Give me a tow?"

The captain hesitated, working his jaw in thought as he stared at the speaker. "And how do I know those corsairs aren't waiting behind a moon somewhere? You sound like bait to me."

"Bait!" the man repeated, clearly offended. "You think I'd help those pricks? You think I'd do that? To you?"

"Dunno. Would you?"

"Depends. What are you hauling?" The man gave a boisterous laugh, and Leslie exhaled softly through his nose, but Elijah couldn't tell if it was amusement or irritation.

"Can't help you, Kaffir," he said after a moment. "Maybe you'll float into a colony in a couple years."

"Captain, you're killing me! You leave me here like this, and I'll haunt you until the day you die, then I'll haunt you through eternity."

"You can't haunt a dead person."

"Watch me fucking try, arkadaş. Come on. I pulled your ass from the fire back on Delta Parada, and you treat me like this? Me."

Leslie's head slumped forward between his hunched shoulders, and he glanced behind him at Brooks and Shaw. His eyes paused for just a moment on Elijah, but it was Shaw that he tilted his head at in a silent question. The First Officer grunted his disapproval but shrugged one shoulder as if to say it was the captain's decision.

"Fine," Leslie sighed. "Give my pilot your coordinates, and we'll stop and pick you up. We're heading to Indira; we'll drop you off there."

"You are a blessing, and a gentleman. I still have a bottle of whiskey left—I'll thank you properly, my friend."

"Yeah, yeah," the captain grumbled, gesturing for Shaw to follow him as he walked away from the console toward the door. Elijah followed at a distance, but he could still hear Leslie's quiet command once they were back in the mess hall outside.

"Get Harper. I want you two keeping both eyes on him until we dock, you feel me? And keep him out of the hold."

"You got it, Captain." Shaw slid down the nearby ladder to the deck below, leaving the two of them standing in the kitchen.

Elijah looked over at him with confusion knitting his brow. "Isn't this guy your friend? Why are you so suspicious of him?"

"I don't have friends, kid," Leslie answered with a shake of his head. "No such thing in this business. You'll see."

· · ◆ · ·

Kaffir was a tall, well-built man of nearly forty, with dark skin, hair that was only slightly more pepper than salt, and a bright smile. He greeted the Chimera's captain with a handshake that pulled into a hug, which forced a tight-lipped smile onto the blond's face as they parted. The newcomer made himself at home right away, seemingly oblivious to the guarded stares of Shaw and Harper constantly at his shoulder. Kaffir apparently traveled alone on his small ship, making the same sorts of deliveries as the Chimera—only relying on the speed and stealth of his ship to keep him from the Federation, instead of hiding his wares in plain sight the way Leslie did. He ate a meal from their stores, shared the harrowing tale of the corsair ship gaining on him over the course of a day before finally opening fire and warning him to either let them board or salvage his wreckage, exchanged some catching-up stories, and then vanished with Leslie into the captain's cabin to share his remaining bottle of whiskey.

Elijah had sat quietly by while the men chatted and laughed, the device restraining him mostly forgotten during the extended conversation. It was strange to see the captain being so easy with someone—even when the two of them were alone, Leslie was guarded and aloof. But no matter what he'd said about having no friends, he certainly seemed friendly with this man Kaffir. A knot grew in Elijah's stomach as the two men left, and Kaffir's hand found the small of Leslie's back at the entrance of the captain's room. Then the door shut behind them, and the others dispersed back to their various duties, but Elijah sat staring at the doors at the end of the corridor with a weight in his chest.

12

Elijah had no reason to linger on the thought of what Leslie and Kaffir spent their time doing. It was none of his business. He knew that in the rational part of his brain—unfortunately, that part was fast diminishing, since Elijah had now spent three full days confined in the device, and the captain had yet to remove the restraining metal rings from Elijah's privates. Every time the boy saw him, he was either on the bridge checking on Brooks or making a brief appearance in the mess hall before retreating back to his cabin with Kaffir. Elijah did his best not to listen at the door every time he entered the kitchen. He cleaned up after an unsatisfying breakfast following another night of fitful sleep, and he was about to escape to his bunk with a second cup of coffee when the captain's doors slid open across the corridor.

Kaffir stepped over to the counter without voicing a greeting and leaned across Elijah to pour his own cup, yawning loudly as he stirred in his packet of sugar. He apparently hadn't felt the need to put on a shirt before coming out, and his lack of belt left his pants slung low on his hips. Elijah made a point of not looking at him despite the other man's close proximity. He reminded himself that none of it was his business, but when Leslie appeared in the mess a moment later looking more than a little drained, he couldn't help the unpleasant thump in his chest. He locked eyes with the captain for just a moment before staring down at his coffee with a determined frown. He edged away from their guest and did his best not to let his irritation show.

"Shaw," Leslie said, drawing the attention of his silent First Officer. "Why don't you take Kaffir below deck and show him your collection? He's a big admirer of custom work."

For the first time, Elijah saw the barest hint of a smile on the large man's face, but Kaffir was frowning.

"What sort of custom work?"

"Go on and have a look. Shaw never gets to talk shop. Go on now," he said again, waving them both away with no further room for argument. Kaffir followed the First Officer down the ladder with a skeptical look on his face, and as soon as they were out of sight, Leslie focused pale eyes on Elijah.

"And you," he said, "get in here."

Elijah hesitated a moment, wavering between bringing his precious coffee with him or leaving it behind, but when the captain's door opened again, he quickly pushed the cup to the back of the counter and hurried to follow him. Even the sight of Leslie's hand on the door lock was enough to make Elijah's breath catch, despite all his worries.

"What's that look on your face, Elijah?" Leslie asked. He tilted his head at the boy, and Elijah could tell he hadn't slept. He looked drawn, and his small, teasing smile was missing its spark.

"No look, Captain," he answered. "I just...it's been three days."

"And how are you holding up?"

"Please take it off," Elijah said, more aware than ever of the heavy rings encircling him now that he was alone in Leslie's room again. But it smelled wrong. It didn't smell like the scent of Leslie—faint shampoo and gunpowder. It smelled like Kaffir. "Please take it off," Elijah said again, a little weaker. "I know you've been busy," he went on, unable to keep the mild spite from his voice.

"Listen to you," Leslie chuckled. "Is that jealousy?"

"I'm not," the boy protested, but the flush of heat in his face gave him away. Even if he did have no reason to worry himself with what the captain did when he wasn't around, and even if he couldn't say it out loud, he had to admit it to himself. He was jealous. He didn't like the thought of Leslie forgetting about him.

"Well, let's get that thing off you, anyway. Get your clothes off."

Elijah started to unbuckle his belt, but he paused. "All my clothes?"

"Shaw will keep Kaffir busy for a long time, and I have plans for you. Now are you going to ask more questions, or are you going to do as you're told?"

Heat blossomed in Elijah's chest, and he tried not to look like he was rushing to get undressed. He left his clothes in a pile by the desk and stood trembling in front of his waiting captain, the rings of his restraint suddenly much tighter around his growing erection. He sat down at Leslie's soft command and allowed the other man to slip the black blindfold over his eyes again.

"You tell me if this hurts too much," the captain murmured somewhere close to his ear. Elijah jumped as firm rubber fastened tight over one of his nipples and then the other, the cool, thin chain between them settling against his chest. It was painful, but it was pain in the same way Leslie spanking him was pain—hot and piercing and dizzying. He sucked in a breath of anticipation as he felt the mattress shift behind him, and Leslie's fingers ran smoothly down his forearm to place a familiar-shaped object in his hand.

"I want you to put that in your ass for me," Leslie said. He turned Elijah's free hand palm-up and poured some of the slick gel over his fingers. He seemed to sense the boy's hesitation, but he only gave a low chuckle that sent a shudder down Elijah's spine. "Don't you worry. I'll take it off soon."

Elijah shifted awkwardly on the bed in an attempt to get into a position to comply. His breath caught in his throat as he felt the captain's hands on his shoulders.

"Lean on back, Elijah."

The boy did as he was told, unable to keep the soft whimper from escaping his lips as he laid back not against the headboard, but against the captain's bare chest. Leslie's arms encircled him loosely, and Elijah could feel his clothed thighs against his own bare hips. It took him a couple of breaths to settle against the older man's skin, but his erection was growing too painful to ignore. He allowed his legs to fall open and pressed slick fingers against his entrance, already more confident as he prepared himself for the width of the toy. It wasn't exactly the same one, but it gave him the same delicious burn as he slid it deep inside himself. As soon as he touched the bundle of nerves inside of him, he let out a cry that became a whine as his restraint shocked him back to reality.

"You are tender, aren't you?" Leslie's voice rumbled in his ear. He gave a light pull to the chain resting on Elijah's chest, tugging the snug clamps on his nipples. "You like these?"

"Yes," Elijah panted, not quite managing to take a full breath. "Yes, Captain."

The captain's scruffy cheek brushed the side of Elijah's neck. "You want me to take that off for you so that you can come?"

"Yes, please, Captain," he begged, unashamed. Every movement of the toy inside of him was sweet torture, and he writhed against the older man behind him, twitching his hips upward desperately and hissing as the leaking tip of his dick touched his stomach.

"And you're gonna stroke that pretty cock for me?"

"Yes, Captain."

"Good boy," Leslie growled, and a single touch of his thumb to the sensor released the metal ring at Elijah's groin, allowing the blond to guide the device off of him with a gentle hand. Elijah replaced it immediately with his own, gripping himself as firmly as he dared and beginning to pump his fist in time with the movement of the toy. His hips moved on their own, grinding into his hand as his head fell back against Leslie's shoulder.

Somewhere in his hazy mind, Elijah heard a soft click, and a ragged moan ripped from his throat at the sudden vibration deep within him.

He swore, hand releasing the end of the toy to grasp madly at the man behind him. Leslie's teeth bit into his shoulder as his back arched, the sharp pain keeping him from pulling too far away, and Elijah's breath fell from him in desperate whines. This wasn't enough. Leslie was all around him, but his hands were placidly at his sides, not doing the work that Elijah so desperately wanted from him—the work he was being made to do on his own. He needed more. He turned his head to hide his face in the few free tresses of blond curled against Leslie's neck and let the smell of the other man's sweat fill his nostrils and draw him closer to a brink that seemed impossible to cross. His own hand just wasn't enough.

"Les, please," he breathed in a weak voice, and he heard the man behind him give a low, deep sigh. The blond's calloused hand finally laid just at his knee, burning a trail across his skin as he drew slowly down the inside of Elijah's thigh. The heat of his palm on trembling flesh flung Elijah over the edge that seemed so impossible to breach before and scraped a shaky moan from him that seemed to fill the warm air of the cabin. Leslie's hand was a lifeline, keeping him from losing himself completely as he spilled his climax on his belly and chest with each blinding pulse.

Every muscle in the boy went slack as he collapsed against his captain's chest. He whimpered and shuddered once more as Leslie carefully slid the toy from him with a practiced hand, but the warmth of the other man left Elijah in too deep a daze for him to hope to move.

· • ◆ • ·

Elijah woke some time later underneath Leslie's blanket. He squinted into the overhead light and wiped the sleep from his eyes with the balls of his hands. His blindfold sat on the nightstand next to what he assumed were the small clamps that had been on his nipples before. The bed was warm, and it smelled like Leslie again. He didn't want to get up. So he didn't—he tugged the blanket up closer to his chin and shut his eyes again, but he didn't get to stay that way for long before the cabin door opened, and he was forced to stir.

"There you are," the blond called. He'd dressed himself again and re-tied his hair. He dropped down to sit on the mattress nearby while Elijah sat up, slowly and reluctantly. "Have a nice little nap?"

"Sorry," Elijah chuckled. "I feel like I take up your bed a lot."

"I'll let you know when you've worn out your welcome. Feeling all right?"

Elijah nodded. He glanced toward the door and felt a guilty weight settle in his chest. "I guess I should—go, right? Kaffir's probably seen enough of Shaw's guns to last him a lifetime."

"You really are jealous, huh?" The captain let out a laugh. "Didn't take you for the type."

"I'm not jealous," he insisted. "It's none of my business."

"No, it's not," Leslie confirmed. He pushed to his feet and stretched his arms over his head with a soft grunt. "But I'll tell you for nothing that it hasn't been any fun keeping that asshole busy in here."

Elijah frowned up at him. "But you guys seemed so friendly before. Why are you...staying in the bedroom with him if you don't even like him?"

"You think I'm gonna let that thievin' shit loose on my ship? Better to let him think he's in good with me and not let him out of my sight. I owed him a debt, that's all, and I like my books to be square. Fuck, but it's exhausting sleeping in that chair. Neck's sore as shit."

Elijah stared down at the blanket bunched at his hips and tried to keep his smile from showing. Leslie was reassuring him, in his way, he was sure. It might not have been any of his business, but Elijah couldn't deny that he felt better knowing his imagination had run away from him.

"But you're right," the captain sighed. "I guess I'd better let Shaw off the hook and keep actin' like a good host. You go on now, and I'm gonna see if I can't catch a few winks before I go get him."

Elijah dressed himself quickly, shivering a little at how exposed he felt in just his underwear and pants without the restraining device around him.

"Make sure the others don't need anything," Leslie called as Elijah approached the door. "I don't want anything holding us up once we're coming in to dock."

"Yes, Captain." Elijah smiled over his shoulder. He didn't miss the little smirk the blond threw him as he waved him away.

13

When Brooks announced over the intercom the next morning that they were approaching Indira, Elijah raced for the bridge to look out the window. The pilot barely acknowledged him bursting in now—he'd been coming to put his face against the window at least once almost every day. Indira shone blue even at this distance; pale clouds rolled over the water, broken only by the imposing metal structures towering over every landmass of the sprawling archipelago that would support one. As they drew nearer, Elijah could spot waterfalls pouring from cliffs of red stone, circled by long-bodied, winged creatures that looked like they should be too heavy to fly. Beyond the dots of land their ship approached, there was only water—sparkling blue-green as far as he could see, dotted with the white caps of waves. With his forehead and hands pressed close, he let out a soft laugh, his fingers curling against the cool glass.

"It's an ocean world," he said, breath briefly fogging the view in front of him.

"Yeah," Brooks agreed. Elijah could hear the unspoken "so what" in her voice.

"I've never seen an ocean before," the boy answered without taking his eyes off of the endless waves.

"Man, but you are backwater," the pilot laughed, but Elijah didn't mind.

The intercom clicked on above them, and only the captain's voice could draw his attention from the steadily approaching water as Brooks lowered the ship toward the docking bay.

"Shaw, Harper, new kid—get down to the airlock ready to go," the captain commanded through the crackling speaker. "We've got a drop to make."

Elijah lingered by the window a few moments more, until Brooks clicked her tongue at him in a warning.

"Don't make the captain wait, kid. You'll regret it."

"I'm going," he assured her, giving her a bright smile on his way to the door.

He was practically bouncing on his toes at the airlock door while the other men gathered behind him. They had to wait for Brooks to unhitch Kaffir's ship from the tow line and make sure it was capable of remotely docking, which seemed to take at least two lifetimes.

"Aren't you going to miss me, Captain?" Kaffir asked from somewhere over Elijah's shoulder.

"Dearly," Leslie drawled, paying more attention to checking his Jericho than to what their guest was saying to him.

"You have to come with me to Abassi someday. The courtesans of the Valstiba will make you forget all of your worries, I promise you."

"What makes you think I've got worries?" the captain answered. A sly smile pulled at his lips as he glanced sidelong at the other man.

"I didn't say they were warranted. A man so far up his own ass he thinks he's any safer by not telling even his closest friends his real name obviously has many worries on his mind. I will get it out of you someday, arkadaş. You'll see."

Leslie only snorted at him, but Elijah paused. He smiled, using all of his willpower not to look back at the blond and give himself away. Kaffir didn't know the captain's name. He didn't know that the captain hated him. But Elijah knew. The boy bit his lip and allowed himself a single quick sigh through his nose. The feeling more than made up for the torture of the last few days.

When the captain finally hit the release on the wall and allowed them outside, Elijah was the first out of the depressurized corridor. He barely heard the warning words that followed him—he needed to get outside.

The landing dock was enclosed, but he raced down the echoing corridor, dodging between men checking manifests and crew unloading crates of cargo, until he reached the outer doors and almost crashed into a passing kineta in his rush to get out. As soon as the salty, whipping air of the planet hit his face, he only managed a few more steps before he slowed to a stop with his eyes on the cerulean sky.

The sky. Not a ceiling, not a ship's hull—not a distant, oppressive dome, locking him in and keeping the world out with its constant, churning engines. Just the sky. Nothing but air between him and the endless galaxy. He was small, insignificant, in the face of all the nothing that pressed down on him. Elijah stepped forward to lean his elbows on the railing of the catwalk, unable to move his gaze from the passing clouds. Small and insignificant—but free.

"Hey kid!" the captain called from behind, startling him, but even as Elijah turned, he couldn't wipe the smile from his face. "The hell's wrong with you?" the blond scolded.

"There's no dome here," Elijah answered, lifting his hands as a laugh fell from his lips. "There's nothing."

"Big fuckin' deal," Harper sighed, but the captain only watched his newest crewman with one hand on his hip and a subtle smile touching one corner of his mouth.

"Job first," the blond said, just a little gentler than before. "Then sightseeing."

Elijah nodded and stood up straight, biting his lip to keep his smile somewhat contained. "Yes, Captain."

Leslie shook Kaffir's hand and sent him on his way with a friendly smile, but he made sure that the other man was out of sight before he led his crew to their next contact. The others seemed to be purely for intimidation purposes on this drop—Shaw bristled even burlier than normal, and Harper made no attempt to hide his fidgeting with a switchblade knife from his belt. The man who paid them was sweaty and hunched, licking his lips anxiously as his eyes darted from the screen of his computer to the captain's stoic face. Elijah didn't know why the man needed to be intimidated, but he guessed he probably wasn't contributing much to the effect, since he still hadn't been able to pull the grin from his lips. The captain just kept him at the back.

Once they'd finished their business, Elijah returned to the Chimera to help Harper unload the cargo. It took a bit more work this time, as the crane controls sparked and gave out—causing a lot of swearing from Park—but Elijah was able to shoulder the last crate off its tracks and up the small ramp to the waiting transport vessel. He ached a bit from the exertion, but when the captain dismissed him with orders only to be back on the ship before nightfall, Elijah bolted.

The broad tower they'd landed on took up almost the entirety of the island, but if he leaned over the railing, he could see the water hitting the rocks far below. He walked the length of the tower, stopping at market stalls, talking with people who passed by, and trying to take in the sights, but his eyes kept drifting back to the ocean below. The distant water stretched on forever, only disappearing from view when it curved over the horizon.

Elijah used a few of the scant credits left on his chip to buy a couple of strange purple fruits and a bottle of a fizzing drink, the name of which he hadn't been able to pronounce no matter how many times the laughing insalar had repeated it for him. The laughter seemed strange in the insalar's voice, as they all sounded almost like they had two sets of vocal chords moving at once. It was an unusual, echoing effect that Elijah enjoyed listening to. This alien had been friendlier than the other insalar he'd met briefly so far—they all looked preternatural and distant, with their all-black eyes and long, ink-colored hair, but this one had a single bright red streak that framed his face. He'd happily chatted with Elijah and told him the best place to get a good quiet view of the water from the colony's catwalks.

Now Elijah sat with his treats at the end of a long balcony along the outside of the market level, his legs dangling over the edge and his elbows resting on the metal rail as he chewed. The wind was sharp but warm against his cheeks, and he shut his eyes between bites to enjoy the touch of the unimpeded sun on his skin. It felt different, even if he was imagining it.

When he'd finished his fruit and licked the last of the sweet juice from his fingers, he leaned back from the railing and patted his pocket. He tugged the little notebook from its place and opened it carefully. At home, it had seemed like a list of daydreams. But as Elijah looked out over the water, his feet hung a mile above an island on a world light-years away and a conversation with a silver-skinned alien only an hour behind him, his list didn't seem so out of reach. He pulled his pen from his pocket and opened his book to the back pages, and he smiled as he bent over his knee to mark out his next completed tasks.

~~Stand on a planet without a dome.~~

~~See an ocean.~~ *April 11, 2186. Indira.*

"Keeping up with your diary?" a voice said nearby him, and Elijah jumped as he fumbled to keep his notebook close to his chest. He looked up and found the captain standing at the end of the balcony, one hip leaned against the railing and his arms crossed over his chest. He smiled back at the playful smirk on the blond's lips.

"Sort of," he answered as the other man stepped closer to him.

"Spotted you out here all by your lonesome and thought I'd make sure you weren't lost," the blond drawled, looking out over the water rather than meeting Elijah's smiling face.

"Just enjoying the view." He lifted the notebook slightly to indicate the page he was on. "It's my first time seeing an ocean, so I had to cross it off my list." Leslie tilted his head, glancing down at the ratty paper while Elijah ran his thumb over the line he'd made. "This list is important things I want to happen before I die. I heard my uncle call it a bucket list. You know, before you kick the bucket?" The boy chuckled and lowered his head so he didn't have to look his captain in the eye. "I know it's stupid."

"Not the worst I've heard." Leslie grabbed onto the rail and slid down beside Elijah, letting his own legs hang over the side as he helped himself to a sip of his cabin boy's unpronounceable drink. "How many have you crossed off so far?"

"As of today?" Elijah pretended to count on his fingers, then laughed. "Four."

"Well that's sad," the captain snorted, and he set the bottle back down between them.

"Hey, I'm new, okay?" He smiled at the blond's teasing sidelong glance. "I just wish I could get down there. I've never been swimming, either."

"Really? No swimming holes back on the farm?"

"No natural ones. I knew a kid who snuck into the reservoir once, but he couldn't get out again and died in there. Everybody was drinking corpse-water for a week and didn't know it. So it put a damper on that idea right quick."

"I bet." Leslie leaned his elbows on the rail and looked out over the water. "But you can't swim in this water anyway. I heard tell it's too salty; humans just float on top."

"Even getting in at all would be amazing." Elijah gave a soft sigh and let his chin rest on his arms on the railing.

"And swimming's on your list, I take it?"

Elijah nodded without looking up at him.

Leslie watched him a moment, a pensive furrow in his brow. Then he pushed himself up and nudged the boy's thigh with the toe of his boot. "Come on."

Elijah frowned up at him as he stood, tucking his notebook back into his pocket. He followed his captain around corners and down hallways and elevators, even squeezing through a couple of narrow passages that he was almost sure they shouldn't be using. Leslie paused at a heavy doorway, then leaned his shoulder against it, the rusted metal groaning in protest as he put his weight into opening the door. Pale sunlight pierced the dark hallway, and Elijah flinched, squinting ahead of him as Leslie looked back with a sly grin on his lips.

The metal under their feet gave way to smooth red stone, and less than fifty meters away, green waves washed up in a gentle rhythm against the sloping clay. Elijah could feel the smile on his face, but he couldn't make any words come out as he took slow steps toward the edge of the water. It smelled like salt and summertime—at least, what he imagined summer would be like, since Dhat-Badan's climate was carefully regulated and temperate. He inched closer to the waves as the metal door thunked shut behind him.

"It's so big," he said, mostly to himself, but he looked over at the sound of Leslie's soft snort of laughter.

"That's what I like to hear."

Elijah frowned at him in feigned disapproval and took one more step closer. He paused, chewing his bottom lip a moment, then made his decision. He tugged off his boots one at a time, stuffed his socks inside, and pulled his shirt over his head by the collar.

"You're really getting in?" the captain asked from behind him, and

Elijah beamed a grin over his shoulder.

"I'm not going to waste this." He unbuttoned his pants and slid out of them without hesitation, then moved into the warm water and let it wash over his ankles, his toes sinking into the silken clay. A second later, he was up to his waist, laughing as he had to brace himself against a stronger wave. He waded until the surf splashed up onto his chest, his arms spread wide as he tested the sensation of his hands running through the deep water. He could already feel it trying to eject him toward the surface. Laughter fell freely from him as he struggled to keep his toes in contact with the bottom, and when he finally let go, he bounced to the surface with a splash that popped him upward and almost tumbled him upside down. He had to spit out a mouthful of briny water as he surfaced, kicking wildly in an attempt to right himself, but when he shifted to look behind him, Leslie stood silently on the shore, his arms folded across his chest and only a subtle smirk touching his lips.

"Well?" Elijah called. "Are you coming?"

"And shrivel up in that salt? This is your new experience, kid, not mine."

Elijah fought the abundantly-buoyant water until he could almost touch the bottom again, though he'd drifted slightly farther away from the rocky beach in his struggle. "But I can't swim! What if I drown?"

"Then I guess I'm out a cabin boy," Leslie answered.

Elijah scoffed as though he was offended, but he hesitated, allowing himself to sink into the water up to his chin as he watched the other man. He should have been happy enough to see the ocean and be able to get in it himself—but he couldn't deny that he wanted the captain beside him, laughing, water dripping down his bare torso in the afternoon sun. Elijah sank down a little deeper as he felt a familiar stirring in his belly. The thoughts that had filled his head and fueled his fantasies through the nights of their voyage were still fresh in his mind, as was the sensation of the blond's chest pressed so firmly against his back. The captain definitely enjoyed teasing him—was it possible that Elijah could tease him a little, too?

The boy inched forward until his feet could touch the ground again, and he stepped toward the shore, the warm air feeling a little cooler on his wet chest the more he exposed it. He saw Leslie's eyes drift downward to the waistband of Elijah's soaked underwear, clinging almost transparent against the dark skin of his hips.

"I'd feel safer if you were out here, Les," he said, aware of the blond's gaze on his hand as he ran it idly over his flat stomach. "Just in case I need something to grab onto."

Leslie let out a soft huff, but Elijah caught the subtle movement as he licked his lips. "I ain't a lifeguard," the blond muttered, already shifting his coat down his shoulders. "But I guess it would look bad if one of my crew died on my watch."

Elijah smiled to himself as he sat back into the water, trying to find his balance with his feet slightly lifted from the bottom. He watched Leslie without shame while the captain removed his shirt and reached for the buttons on his pants, but a faint flush heated the boy's cheeks as the blond stepped free of his clothes completely. He apparently wasn't planning on swimming in his underwear—because he wasn't wearing any. Elijah tried not to stare as the other man approached, grateful when the captain's hips disappeared below the water line. Maybe he wasn't as cut out for teasing as he'd hoped. This was definitely an entirely different feeling from when he'd seen Shaw in the shower—and it was different from Elijah's first glimpse of the captain's naked body being in the dark of his cabin.

They floated together for a while, Elijah actively trying not to look over at Leslie's blatant nakedness and Leslie not bothering to pretend he believed that the boy was afraid of drowning. Elijah shut his eyes and let the sun warm his face. He was drifting in an ocean under an open sky on an alien world, light years away from the colony prison he'd left behind. He was doing it—he'd be able to cross a fifth item off his list now, and he had a lot more galaxy to see before he was done.

A sudden firm touch to his arm startled him out of his dozing, and he flailed, splashing salt water as he kicked his feet toward the ground—mostly unsuccessfully.

"Settle down," the captain laughed, pulling the helplessly floating boy closer to him. "Just don't want you to drift out to sea. There's more than one beast out there with a mouth bigger than your whole self."

"What?" Elijah jerked himself up against the other man's side, hand fastening firmly on the captain's bicep for stability. "Really?"

Leslie laughed, and Elijah looked up into his eyes. A few wet, blond tresses stuck to the sides of his face, fallen free from his messy bun, the silver beads in his hair glinting in the last low beams of the setting sun. A drop of water ran from his temple down his cheek, and Elijah's gaze followed its path to the blond captain's chin. He had to resist the urge to lick it away. He matched Leslie's pale eyes as he realized the older man was watching him, too. The smile hadn't faded from his lips, but it looked a little bit more warm now, and less teasing.

"Best get on our way," Leslie said, his hand slow to release Elijah's arm as he pulled away toward the shore. "Won't do to tell the others to be back by sundown and then miss my own curfew."

Even in the warm seawater, Elijah missed the heat of the captain's skin. He swallowed the feeling down, nodded, and edged back to standing on the clay beneath the waves. "Right."

14

With their delivery completed, the Chimera only had one more stop to make—the thengisi station Jannat. It was a long trip, even with the use of gates, but Elijah kept busy. The rest of the crew seemed to have adjusted quickly to not having to clean up after themselves. He did his part, and in between he sat in the little viewing room or visited with Brooks on the bridge—she didn't mind him so much anymore, as long as he didn't chat constantly. He was content to examine the ship's star charts and occasionally discuss routes with her.

The trip to Jannat was supposed to take nine days, so Elijah expected that a few would go by without him seeing the captain again, but he called the boy into his cabin after Indira was only a day or so behind them. Elijah wished he could say he was getting used to Leslie's hands on him, beginning to be able to control himself, but even the smallest smile or the soft clicking of silver beads in blond hair were enough to make the boy's heart skip. He was pliant and obedient under the captain's blue eyes, and all it took was a subtle tilt of the head to force Elijah to his place on the bed without question.

"I wanted to ask you something," Leslie began casually, approaching where the boy sat and folding his arms loosely in front of him.

"Okay," Elijah answered, remarkably calm even through the growing tightness of expectation in his throat.

"Do you like it when I tie you up? You liked it when I spanked you?" he asked softly, and the boy nodded.

"Yes, Captain." His voice wasn't quite so steady now. He couldn't help the little flip in his belly—Elijah liked the pain, admittedly, but the captain's constant care that he was enjoying himself was almost as good, in some ways.

"You liked not being able to move? Helpless while I took what I wanted from you?"

"...Yes, Captain." Elijah swallowed hard. This wasn't just a check-in. He knew that look on the blond's face.

Leslie leaned down close to Elijah's cheek, his teeth fastening onto the boy's earlobe just long enough to draw a sharp gasp from him. "Do you want me to do it again?"

"Yes, please," Elijah sighed. His fingers tightened on the edge of the mattress, desperate to reach up for the man above him but not daring to do so without permission.

"And you want me to touch you?" Leslie's free hand trailed down Elijah's chest and stomach, gripping his hardening dick firmly through his pants and drawing a shaky whine from him. "Like you touched yourself?"

"Yes," he panted.

"When you had that toy up your ass, were you imagining it was me fucking you?"

Elijah bit his lip in an attempt to hold in his gasp, his hips twitching up against the blond's hand automatically. "Y...yes," he breathed, and the other man's low, growling chuckle sent a wave of heat through his belly.

"Maybe if you're good."

"I'm—I'm good," Elijah promised, barely embarrassed anymore at the things coming out of his mouth.

Leslie laughed and gave the boy a hard squeeze that made him buck with need. "We'll see," he murmured, and Elijah whined as he pulled away. "Take your clothes off."

Elijah didn't even try not to rush this time—he had his boots and shirt off within moments. He should have been better at getting undressed by now, but the thought of what he really wanted being so close made him too eager. His shaking hands fumbled with the button on his pants one too many times, and he looked up as Leslie's hands covered his. The captain sat down on the bed and drew the boy around to stand between his knees, gently pressing Elijah's arms to his sides. His hands slid slowly up the boy's legs to his hips to keep him in place, and he leaned close to place a slow kiss on the younger man's flat stomach. The light brush of his beard made Elijah tremble, and he fought to keep from reaching for the soft blond hair in front of him. This was too intimate to bear—his throat tightened at the heat of the other man's lips on him. When Leslie moved his hands to unbutton Elijah's pants for him, the boy's breath caught in his throat and stayed there while the captain inched them down his hips and thighs. His legs almost gave out as Leslie's pale eyes gazed up at him from so close to his exposed erection.

"Is there something you want, Elijah?"

He didn't have the voice to answer. He knew what he wanted, of course—and the captain's hands resting casually at the backs of his thighs made his meaning clear—but he didn't know if he was really permitted to say it out loud. When he didn't answer, Leslie bent forward and nipped at the skin of his stomach, his hands moving to cup the soft flesh of Elijah's ass.

"Ask me," he murmured against the boy's dark skin. Elijah swayed slightly on his feet at the heat of the other man's breath on him. "Beg me. Tell me you want me to suck your cock."

"Fuck," Elijah breathed instead, the sound of his own rushing blood almost deafening him. "I—I do," he tried. "I want you to."

"Do better than that." Leslie bit him more sharply right over his hipbone, making him yelp.

"I—please, Captain," the boy panted, lost in the predator's eyes staring up at him. "Please suck my cock. Please," he hiccuped.

"Hold onto that pipe, Elijah," he commanded softly. The boy glanced upward to the low ceiling and reached up to grab onto the exposed pipe just over his head. "You don't let go until I tell you to."

"Y-Yes sir."

The blond gave a low growl of satisfaction and squeezed Elijah's rear to draw his hips closer, taking him into his mouth in a single long push and swallowing once the boy hit the back of his throat. A quivering cry fell from Elijah's lips at the sudden heat surrounding him, his hands tightening painfully around the pipe above him.

Leslie's tongue ran firmly along the thick vein on the underside of Elijah's cock as he withdrew, teeth pulling gently at his foreskin as he reached the tip. He ran his tongue through the slit to taste the pearling liquid there and caught the younger man's dark, lidded eyes.

"Do you like that, Elijah?"

"Y-Yes. God, yes," he whimpered. The captain slapped him sharply on the ass so hard that the boy cried out, but he didn't need to say anything. "Yes, Captain!" Elijah corrected himself, his head falling back as the blond swallowed him again. His arms trembled with the effort of holding himself upright, but the blond kept him still with a firm hand. Every soft sound that rumbled in the other man's throat sent a shudder up Elijah's back and quickened his breath. He wasn't going to last long like this.

Elijah moaned with frustration the next time Leslie pulled away from him, but a curl of anticipation twisted its way through his stomach as he watched the captain take his own middle finger into his mouth, wetting it with saliva before returning to his work. The captain's hand slid through the gap of Elijah's legs, and the boy jumped as the slick digit pressed between his ass cheeks and against his entrance. He couldn't control the sounds that fell out of him even at the first gentle pressure, and when the tip of his cock touched the muscle at the back of the other man's throat and he felt his finger slide into him, he almost lost his balance completely. It was completely unlike the sensation of the toy spreading him. That was Leslie's heat sinking deep inside him, his saliva easing him through the tight ring of muscle. It was Leslie's tongue on his dick, drawing him closer and closer to the brink of climax. Elijah shuddered as he felt Leslie push into him up to the knuckle, his remaining fingers splayed and pressing into the flesh of the boy's buttocks in an effort to get his finger deeper. A single minute crook of his finger almost made Elijah go blind as he brushed the spot inside him that the toy had introduced him to before.

The tension built inside of him until his whole body shook, but when he gave a desperate jerk of his hips, Leslie retreated, looking up at him as he licked excess saliva from his swollen lips. Elijah almost sobbed with want.

"Please, Captain," he said, trying to anticipate what the other man would want from him. "Please let me come."

Something dark passed over the captain's pale eyes. "No," he answered simply, and he let his finger slide free from Elijah, leaving the boy struggling to stay standing. Leslie left him there, clutching the pipe overhead with aching hands, and turned to the cabinet above his headboard. Elijah watched him through hazy eyes as he gathered a few long straps of leather, measuring and folding them along the length of his arm. The captain looked over his shoulder at the helpless boy beside the bed and smirked faintly at him.

"You can let go now, Elijah."

He did, gladly, shivering at the tingling in his arms and hands as he lowered them.

"Come over here and lie down. Face the wall."

Elijah wasn't confident at all in his ability to walk, but he managed to make it onto the mattress and onto his side without falling. Leslie's firm hand on his thigh sent a ripple of pleasure over his skin that caused a long sigh to escape him. He allowed the other man to spread his legs wide and bend his knees, wrapping the leather straps around his thighs and shins and securing them to keep his heels pressed snugly against his buttocks. Leslie trailed his hands up Elijah's sides and down his arms, then drew them together to bind his wrists in front of him with the last strip of leather.

"Is that comfortable, Elijah?" he asked. The straps were tight, and Elijah could barely move his legs, but the shivering the exposure caused in him was worth it. He nodded. "Good. Remember to tell me if you need me to stop."

"Yes, Captain," the boy whispered.

Leslie urged him to keep one knee bent toward the ceiling and reached up to one of the low pipes running along the ceiling. For the first time, Elijah noticed that a couple of them weren't pipes at all— they were solid bars, and this one bore a small pulley and hook that extended easily on its cord as the blond drew it downward. Leslie clipped the hook around the buckle securing Elijah's lifted leg and snugged it upward, the cord clicking softly as it locked into place. Elijah was left with most of his weight on the mattress but his bent knee keeping him just elevated enough to feel a tremble in his skin. He looked over his shoulder at the man who'd bound him and let out an admiring puff of air as the captain stripped off his shirt and tossed it aside. Elijah's eyes traveled over the colorful ink on his arms and chest and the few scars that marked his torso, telling stories of adventures and mishaps. He could feel Leslie's warmth this close to him, and he wanted more.

The captain let his hand travel slowly down the boy's side as he settled on the bed behind him, fingers tracing the space between his thighs created by his lifted leg. Elijah heard the faint click of a bottle cap and hissed as the cool gel touched him, quickly warming under the blond's fingers. Leslie slid a finger back inside him easily, soon adding another and beginning to move slowly into him and out again. The subtle burn made Elijah's heart pound, his dick quivering and aching to be touched. He could still see the faint sheen of Leslie's saliva on it when he glanced down, but when he moved his hips to try to find some friction against the sheet, the captain left a punishing bite on the flesh of his shoulder.

"No touching," he murmured, and he laved his tongue apologetically over the red mark he'd left, causing a shudder in the younger man.

Elijah twisted and jerked against Leslie's hand, desperate for more of him. He cried out when his fingertips touched the tight bundle of nerves inside of him, and his back arched so that his shoulder blades came to press against the other man's chest. Leslie's warmth spread through him like a wildfire, and the blond's soft whispers of praise against his ear hastened his breath until the addition of a third finger inside of him pulled the air from his lungs completely. Elijah struggled to buck into the touch, but the straps around his legs and the cord suspending him from the bar kept him from moving half as much as he wanted.

"That's it," the captain whispered, every brush of his lips against Elijah's skin igniting a new fire in him. "Show me how much you love having me inside of you."

Elijah hoped that the desperate pants and moans the man was drawing from him were proof enough, because he certainly didn't have any coherent thoughts to verbalize. His head swam from his racing heart and his quickened breath, and he closed his eyes against the spots that appeared in his vision each time Leslie pressed the pads of his fingers against the place inside that made his body flush with heat. He whined at the constellations of kisses the ship's captain was leaving across his shoulders and back, soft touches interspersed with a few nipping bites to make him jump. A breathless sigh escaped him as Leslie's arm fastened around his waist, tugging Elijah tightly back against his chest and pushing his fingers deeper into him. The blond's hand flattened on the boy's stomach just above his twitching cock, fingers dipping into the black curls at his base before wrapping around him with a firm grip.

"Fuck," Elijah sobbed, his head falling back against Leslie's shoulder and causing a soft tinkle from the silver beads in his hair. The blond moved both of his hands in perfect time with each other, thrusting and stroking the younger man until he trembled with unreleased tension. Elijah could feel Leslie's breath husky and hot against his ear and felt the hard press of the other man's erection against the small of his back. He wanted more than his hands.

"Please," he managed to whisper, though it was cut off by a sharp gasp as Leslie squeezed him, rolling his thumb over the precum leaking from the tip of his cock.

"Please what, Elijah?" the captain answered in a thick voice, cheek to cheek with the boy who panted and squirmed against him.

"Please, I want you—" He stopped to give a sudden moan at the firm thrust of the other man's fingers deep within him.

"You want me to what?"

Elijah squeezed his eyes shut tighter and wet his lips, taking a moment to try to find the capacity for a single sentence in his ecstasy-addled brain. "I want you to fuck me," he panted, hurriedly adding, "please, Captain," in anticipation of being spanked again.

Leslie's grip tightened on him, and Elijah was sure he felt the other man's cock twitch against his back. He shifted closer to the boy, the scruff of his beard tickling Elijah's smooth jaw and his lips just barely brushing the edge of the younger man's mouth as he whispered the two most torturous words Elijah had ever heard.

"Not today."

He groaned in frustration that quickly melted into incoherence as the other man resumed his attentions. Leslie had allowed him just enough movement to buck forward into his hand and back against his fingers, so Elijah jerked as much as he was able against the blond's more insistent pace.

"Come for me," Leslie growled against his ear, and it was a command Elijah couldn't help but obey. He swung his arms up over his head, wrapping his bound wrists around the back of the captain's neck to clutch him tightly against him as he exploded into his lover's hand. His fingers wove tightly into Leslie's pale yellow waves, and he turned his head to hide his face under the other man's chin as his hips twitched against his will, spilling his orgasm over Leslie's fingers and onto the mattress. His body jerked with every spasm until he slowly relaxed against the man behind him, unable to will any of his muscles into any further movement.

He gave a shuddering moan as Leslie's fingers slipped out of him, and at the blond's gentle nudging, Elijah released his clinging grip around his neck and let his limp arms fall back to the bed in front of him. He felt the loss of Leslie's warmth behind him as the other man slid away, but he sighed with relief as the captain unsnapped him from the pulley on the ceiling and dropped his weight back to the mattress. Leslie's hands were gentle on his thighs as he unraveled the straps keeping his knees bent and gently straightened them, massaging out the stiffness in his legs. Elijah's eyes could barely open, but he felt a faint smile curling his lips as he watched the blond unbind his wrists.

"Are you all right, Elijah?" Leslie asked, already much softer than he had been moments before.

"I'm fine," he promised as he rolled his newly free wrists. He glanced down at the obvious bulge remaining in the other man's pants and managed to turn enough to face him. He reached his hands tentatively forward and laid them lightly on Leslie's thighs for just a moment before they were gently but firmly removed. Elijah glanced up into the captain's blue eyes with confusion furrowing his brow.

"Why don't you let me touch you?" he asked, and the blond's small smile was so disarmingly sly that even Elijah's exhausted dick felt a faint twitch.

"Are you asking questions now?" Leslie said instead of answering. He bent forward with Elijah's wrists in his hands and nipped softly at the boy's knuckles. "You just keep doing exactly as you're told."

Elijah settled back against the pillow at Leslie's urging, accepting the soft cloth the blond gave him to clean himself up. He looked up at the man sitting on the mattress beside him—the man who not only hadn't shot him in the head for sneaking on board his ship, but who had taken him in when he'd asked for a job and taken great pains not to take advantage of him even when Elijah had thrown himself at him. He'd let Elijah set the rules all along. This man was stern with his crew, uncompromising when it came to business, and he was definitely commanding in his private life, but there was care behind his barked orders and a quiet gentleness in his eyes. Elijah felt a different sort of fluttering in his stomach as his eyes caught the captain's gaze. This feeling wasn't lust—was it longing? That was a little scarier.

"Les," he tried quietly when the blond took the soiled cloth back from him. The captain paused in the doorway to the small adjoining bathroom and waited, but he didn't turn around. "Can I stay here for a while?"

Now one blue eye peeked back at him. "Stay?"

"I mean, you always kick me out. Which is fine, it's your room, but...I'd just like to be able to talk to you. Out on the ship, it seems like business, you know?"

The blond chuckled. "It *is* business."

"I get it," Elijah insisted. "But in here...in here I can call you Les," he said, as if that explained the breadth of the complex emotions rolling around his own brain right now.

The captain let a few beats of silence pass while he moved into the bathroom and washed his hands, then he tossed the dirty cloth into the sink and turned back to face the nude young man on his bed. "Think you'll get better rations if you get in good with the captain?" he asked with a teasing smile on his lips.

"*Are* there better rations on this ship?"

The blond's snorting laughter made Elijah smile. "Not really; no. Well," Leslie added, "except for the insalari candies I keep under the bed. But those are only for special occasions." He tilted his head at the boy and let his eyes roam the length of his lean body. "And you don't want to know what you have to do for it to be a special occasion."

"I dunno," Elijah chuckled, "I've never had insalari candy, and you know how I like a new experience."

"I'll have to plan something for you, then." Leslie glanced over his shoulder into the bathroom. "Why don't you have a shower? More privacy here than the shared one belowdecks."

"I knew there would be perks," Elijah teased as he scooted to the edge of the bed. Leslie let him by, so he shut the door and turned on the water in the glass-walled shower. The shower head didn't even sputter; it was already an improvement over the shared locker room on the crew deck.

Elijah stood with his hand under the running water, waiting for it to warm up enough to step into. He stood under the stream and let a sigh fall out of him, his hands running over the lingering red marks on his thighs where the leather straps had held him. What Leslie did to him was intense and overwhelming. Elijah had never thought of himself as having a particularly submissive personality, but something about the way the blond looked at him, calmly commanding him and guiding him to sensations he'd never even imagined, made him want to do just that—submit. Leslie had proven over and over again that he had Elijah's comfort and pleasure in mind. Elijah knew that he'd do anything the other man asked of him, and do it gladly. He trusted him. It was definitely trust he was mistaking for deeper affection with that little flutter. It was a good feeling.

Elijah let out a small, quiet sigh and scratched his fingers over his scalp to rinse the sweat from his hair. He barely knew Leslie, really. Before he got carried away thinking thoughts that could get him in trouble, he ought to make an effort to hold a few more conversations with the captain that weren't about the ship or about the different kinds of bondage.

He scrubbed himself clean, flinching just slightly as he twisted to wash the remaining lubricant from himself. Maybe someday he would even come back from the captain's cabin without his ass being sore for one reason or another. When he turned the knob to stop the water, he paused just outside the glass partition. There was only one towel hung from a hook on the wall. It felt strangely intimate to dry himself with it, but it would have been even more awkward and domestic to call out and ask for a new one.

By the time he stepped back into the bedroom, Leslie had already stripped the stained sheets from the bed and replaced them, and was now relaxed with his back against the headboard, his eyes closed, and his fingers laced across his stomach. Elijah wasn't sure what to do with himself. He crept around the bed to gather up his clothes and dressed as quietly as he could, feeling a bit like an intruder. He froze with one arm in his sleeve when Leslie's eyes cracked open to watch him.

"Uh. Hey, Les," Elijah said, hoping his smile hid his uncertainty. "Sorry; were you sleeping?"

"Just picturing you in the shower," the blond chuckled.

Elijah smiled despite himself. He slid his other arm into its sleeve, then took a risk, moving to sit on the mattress at Leslie's side. He waited to be scolded or shooed away, but the captain only lifted a curious eyebrow at him. Elijah didn't speak, and Leslie didn't dismiss him. The captain rose after a few moments to stretch back in his desk chair and examine something on his tablet, and Elijah couldn't keep the smile from his face. The two of them sat together quietly for a while, the silence easier and more companionable for every minute that passed.

15

The captain called Elijah into his cabin every night for the next three days. Leslie let him stay longer before kicking him out now—he'd even told him a couple of stories about his earlier years, when he and Park were just starting out and had to stop for days to make repairs on the ship between every jump. He still didn't talk about himself much, but Elijah was beginning to see the man behind the "Captain" he showed to the world. He'd pulled himself up from working as labor crew on the same merchant ship as his parents, been through hard times, and was now the captain of his own seemingly successful ship. Even if he'd used less than legal means to get there, Elijah had a hard time judging him for it. He knew how restrictive the Federation could be—who was to say they were always right about what cargo should be illegal and what shouldn't?

Elijah was allowed another private shower in the captain's quarters after a particularly sweaty second round, and he emerged still wiping droplets of water from his hair to find Leslie hunched over his tablet as usual. He turned it off when he heard Elijah enter and spun in his chair to look at him.

"Thanks for letting me use the shower," Elijah said as he scrubbed the last dampness from his dark curls.

"Least I can do," the captain answered with a sly smirk. Elijah didn't miss the quick sweep of blue eyes over his bare torso as he circled the bed to gather his clothes. "So how many things you gonna mark off that list of yours on Jannat?"

"A lot, I hope," Elijah said with a grin, bouncing slightly as he drew his pants up over his hips. "I've always wanted to meet a thengisi, so that's one. I don't really know what to expect once we're there, though."

"What other sort of things are you missing?"

He paused. "A lot of it would probably seem...really boring to you."

"Well it ain't my list."

Elijah chuckled lightly and bent to scoop his shirt up from the floor. "I guess not." He put off answering long enough to hang his towel back up, but when he stood in the bathroom doorway and found the captain still watching him and waiting, he had to smile. As little as Leslie talked about himself, he always seemed curious about Elijah's exceptionally boring home life. The idea of staying in one place your whole life must have been just as foreign to him as growing up in space seemed to Elijah.

He leaned against the desk where Leslie sat, his hands resting on the edge near his hips. "It's mostly a lot of basic stuff. Like seeing an ocean. I've never even seen...rain, or snow. The atmosphere on Dhat-Badan was constant and sunny, since all the crops were watered by machine. Even the only animals I've seen are the cows we kept. I want to...pet a dog, you know? I just—I haven't done anything. I just want to see what's out there." He gave a small shrug and looked down at the floor instead of at the other man's face, feeling a touch of heat rising in his own cheeks. He decided not to mention the most embarrassing thing on his list—he didn't want the captain getting the wrong idea by Elijah even mentioning the word "love."

Leslie watched him without answering for a few beats, the muscles in his jaw subtly working as he considered. "Well I'm sure we can scare up a dog or two," he said with a faint smile.

· ● ◆ ● ·

While Elijah was clearing up after supper the next evening, his heart gave a little jump of anticipation when he saw the captain's cabin door open across the hallway, but he suppressed it when he heard the sharpness of the blond's voice calling out to the rest of the crew before they could file out of the mess. This wasn't Leslie come to fetch him for another night. This was the ship's captain with new orders. His entire demeanor was different. The slight glare in his eyes, the set of his jaw, the way he stood with one hand on his hip and kept the gaze of every subordinate in turn—the captain seemed to be a much harder person than the one Elijah was coming to know as just "Les."

"Y'all sit for a minute," the captain said, and the crew obeyed, chairs scraping on the metal floor as they resumed their places at the long table near the wall. "I want to make a stop before we get to Jannat."

"A stop?" Park spoke up immediately. "Where the hell is there to stop between here and those bugs?"

"Olmos, on Amerath 9."

The others seemed to understand, but Elijah didn't. "What's there worth stopping for?"

"It's an advance colony set up by the Federation," the captain answered. "They produce all the Praevad for the surrounding system. I thought it might be worth our while to pick up what we can before we go into thengisi territory."

Elijah frowned across the room at him in mild confusion. He recognized the name Praevad—it was a serious painkiller. One of his brothers had taken it for a while when he'd broken his leg, and it had left him more than a little loopy, but pain-free. He'd slept a lot. It seemed effective, but Elijah didn't see why they'd need it on board the Chimera.

"Is it that dangerous there?" he asked, and Harper snickered beside him, but Leslie limited his amusement to a small smirk.

"That ain't why," the captain said. "Praevad's safe for humans, but the thengisi cut it with something or other, and then it turns into what they call 'iwayini yokulala.' The wine of sleep. Pretty rough—and addictive—drug on them for whatever reason. It's illegal in their territory, and so's Praevad. So of course it sells for a pretty penny."

The boy's brow furrowed softly. "You want to sell them drugs?"

"I want to make money," Leslie clarified. "Don't make much never mind to me what they do with the stuff once it's out of my hands."

"I thought you said you were on board with this crew, kid? Scared of getting your hands dirty now?" Park smirked sidelong at him, and Elijah bristled.

"I'm not scared," he answered in a voice more sure than he felt. The idea made him a little uncomfortable. It was easy to ignore that he was on an actual smuggling ship, for the most part, since one of their captain's big selling points was that he never checked the boxes he shipped. Discretion on Leslie's part also meant that Elijah could pretend there was nothing truly harmful in the crates he unloaded. But selling dangerous, addictive drugs on purpose was different. *This* cargo, at least, was probably pretty universally considered bad.

His eyes fell to the floor as a lump of guilt settled in his chest. Did he really have any room to judge what the captain did?

"It's an easy side gig," the captain cut in.

"And that's the *only* reason we're stopping?" Park asked, leaning his elbows on the table and staring up at the blond with a suspicious frown. "Just makin' a buck, no interest in the planet Olmos is built on?"

Leslie snapped his gaze over to the engineer. "I didn't think I fuckin' stuttered. I'm stopping whether y'all are in or not. But if you let me use some of the credits from your next cut to make the buy, we can pick up even more Praevad and get an even better return. So show me them hands."

Park's skeptical expression remained, but he and the rest of the crew raised their hands in agreement without hesitation. Elijah locked eyes with Leslie for just a moment before he raised his own hand as well, albeit a little slower.

"All right then. Brooks, you plot the detour and get me an ETA. Let's make it a short stopover."

"Yes, Captain," the pilot answered. The others filed out of the room, so Elijah followed. He had agreed to be a part of the crew, after all.

· ● ◆ ● ·

Elijah stayed in his bunk the rest of the night, searching the net on the tablet he'd borrowed from Davies. He'd heard of the Amerath system, but nothing he could find about it seemed to justify Park's suspicions. Leslie's reasons for wanting to go were unsavory enough, weren't they? The planet seemed pretty normal—though Elijah was excited to see that it was a particularly icy climate. That would be one to check off his list.

He lingered somewhere between excitement and worry for the next few hours while they made their detour. When the ship settled on the planet's surface and the captain called him over the intercom to tell him to report to the airlock exit, he quickly settled on the side of worry upon finding Shaw and Harper missing from their usual places.

Leslie stood by the decompression door alone, wearing a heavy coat that brushed the backs of his calves. He turned when he heard Elijah's footsteps and gave the boy a quick look up and down with a small smirk on his lips.

"You heard this is an ice planet, right kid?"

Elijah looked down at his well worn clothing, which was definitely more suited to a climate-controlled farm colony than any kind of extreme temperature. He gave a sheepish smile and shrugged his shoulders.

"This is all I've got."

The captain watched him for a few beats, then snorted out a sigh bordering on irritation. He climbed back up the ladder to the upper deck and returned a minute or two later with another coat slung over one arm. He tossed it at Elijah, who scrambled to grab it before it could hit the floor.

"That'll do 'til you can get yourself a decent one," Leslie said, already returning his attention to the exit.

Elijah smiled as he slid the borrowed coat over his shoulders. It fit pretty well—as well as any of his standard hand-me-downs, anyway. Leslie waved away his thanks, and when the ship doors opened, they waited just inside the hull for decompression. Elijah chewed his lip and did his best not to bounce despite the excited pounding of his heart. An ice planet would be cold, of course—which was new for him to begin with—but would also have snow. Snow, with a little approved down time, meant snowballs, snowmen, maybe even sledding. At the very least, he'd get to see it and touch it. That wouldn't be enough, but it would be a start.

Leslie hit the release once the screen above the door let them know it was safe, and Elijah barely kept himself from pushing ahead of his captain. He rushed forward as soon as Leslie had stepped outside, eager to see the icy planet they'd landed on—and immediately regretted it. The wind cut across his face like a hundred knives, each stinging his skin and making his eyes water, and it blew so hard that he was almost bowled over on the slick pathway. On instinct, he scrambled back toward the ship mid-swear and hid in the safety of the airlock, clinging to the railing along the inside of the door and staring out at Leslie with eyes that showed his feeling of betrayal.

The captain laughed at him, though the sound was partly carried away by the wind. "Little cold, kid?"

Elijah's teeth chattered, and the air burned his lungs as he took a breath to reply. "What the fuck is this?" he half shouted. He released the metal railing as it grew too cold to touch and stuffed his hands into his coat pockets instead. "People live here?"

"Lots of 'em," Leslie answered.

Elijah watched his disbelieving scoff appear in front of him in a puff of steam. "How? And why is there no real dock?"

"It hasn't been here that long." The captain tilted his head away from the ship, urging the boy forward. "Come on. We've got work to do."

The boy hoped his whimper wasn't audible over the sound of the wind. This wasn't what he'd expected—this was miserable. He never thought he'd be grateful for the climate-control systems of Dhat-Badan, but this biting chill sank down to his bones and made him question if he could even walk to the captain's side, let alone all the way through the colony to the safety of the base ahead. He wasn't sure human muscles were meant to work in these temperatures.

"Yes, Captain," he said reluctantly, holding his pocketed fists close to his body as he tried again to make progress on the path. He ducked his shoulders against the wind and stayed close to Leslie's back as the captain led the way toward the main compound.

The buildings here looked more like permanent tents than proper buildings, made of steel frames and thick material drawn taut into the snow, but they kept the cold out well enough once the two were inside. The complex was massive and sprawling, with metal beams supporting the ceiling and leading off into infinite sterile-looking plastic corridors. Leslie seemed to know where he was going, so Elijah followed, grateful for the break from the howling wind that he was positive had left icicles on his eyelashes. No one seemed to pay them much attention—there were only humans around, some in Federation uniforms, some in work jumpsuits, and others in everyday clothes. Elijah couldn't quite put his finger on the sort of place this was; it seemed official and backwater all at once. Even the uniformed Federation officers just leaned against doorways and chatted, not minding the milling crowd around them. If this was a production colony, they probably didn't have much to do most of the time. It made it a good place to do the kind of business the captain was interested in.

Still blowing on his hands to bring life back into his fingers, Elijah stopped just outside a wide set of sliding metal doors and waited for Leslie to enter before following him. This place looked more like the markets Elijah had grown used to seeing on their stops at Tadmor and Indira—metal shelving filled with canisters and plastic-wrapped boxes, bins of smaller items filling the center of the room, and a long counter at the back, where a man meandered back and forth with more stock in both arms.

"Hey there," the captain called, and the young man behind the counter paused to drop his restock before looking their way.

"Hey," he answered with a professional smile. "What can I do for you?"

"Where's old Boles? Off drinking his profits?"

The man shook his head. "Retired off-world. I'm his nephew."

"Is that right," Leslie murmured. "Well, good for him. You're takin' up the family business then, huh?"

He chuckled and lifted his hands to gesture around the room. "Such as it is."

"What's your name, mister?"

"Frederick."

"Well see, here's where I'm at, Freddy." Leslie moved closer, stopping just short of the counter to lean his elbows on it. "I need some Praevad."

"You're in the right place," the man shrugged, not seeming to take offense at the captain's nickname. "We've got single doses in one of the bins up front, and I've got some packs back here if you need more."

"Nah, that ain't what I mean. I'm lookin' for a whole *lot* of Praevad. See, Freddy, I'm in the shipping business, and I got a big ol' order to fill."

Frederick paused and folded his arms across his chest. "You know there are purchase limits for indviduals. I can give you that much."

"Now, listen," Leslie went on, putting on his most charming smile as he looked up at the younger man. "Me and your old uncle had a unique agreement. I know there's all them restrictions, but I ain't an individual, you feel me? I represent an interest at large, and that interest needs a fair load more Praevad than the Federation thinks they oughta have." He tilted his head slightly, the beads in his hair clicking softly at the movement. "It ain't good business to keep product from who wants it, now is it?"

The young man stared at him in silence for a few beats. "You're talking about taking it to Jannat, right?"

"What you don't know won't hurt you, mister."

"But what I *do* can get me thrown in prison."

"Only if you tell."

Frederick sucked his teeth in thought, and for a moment, he only held Leslie's gaze in silence. Elijah shifted uncertainly behind his captain. This man could get them in a lot of trouble just for asking, but the blond didn't seem concerned about that possibility. After a long, tense silence, the man spoke again.

"How much are you paying?"

"Thatta boy," the captain chuckled, and he straightened to look the younger man in the face. "I can give you one and a half what each pack's worth—that's wholesale, now, but not cost."

"That's not very much, considering the risk I'd be taking."

"It's a hell of a lot more than you'll get selling it to the Federation."

"I think you can do better."

Leslie snorted softly, hands on his hips and jaw subtly working as he considered. "You think I can, huh?" He glanced down at the floor and scuffed one boot on the concrete before looking up at the other man again. "Tell you what. You an' me don't know each other. You don't know you can trust me. I aim to start all business relationships out right, so how's about I give you one and three-quarters this time? That's more than the standard rate, now, you feel me? Next time you'd best not be so greedy," he added with a quick, smirking wink.

The man stared at him in silence with uncertainty written on his face, and he briefly narrowed his eyes in thought before he took a step closer to the counter and nodded. "Just tell me how much you need."

"Good answer."

Elijah lingered nearby while the captain hammered out the details with the young man, half listening and half inspecting the bland containers on the shelves. He had gathered up a decent amount of dread at the thought of having to brave the cold again by the time Leslie called to him.

"That's it?" he asked, and the blond smiled at him.

"Business first; business done. But there's something else I want to show you."

16

Elijah struggled in the cold, especially as he followed the Chimera's captain away from the settled compound and into the snowy hills. The snow was definitely beautiful, and he risked frostbite by being unable to resist sticking his hands in a deep bank along the road, but this temperature was one task he would be happy to mark off his list and never experience again.

They walked for so long that Elijah began to question whether Leslie planned to murder him without witnesses, both of them fighting the wind that threatened to knock them back down the hill at any moment. Then the captain stopped in front of him and took him by the shoulder so he could lean in close to his ear.

"This is worth the walk."

Elijah frowned curiously at him but followed the last remaining steps to the crest of the steep hill. At the top, the wind stopped almost entirely, howling around the protective ridge of the surrounding cliffs. The sky was clear as glass above them, dotted with glimmering stars in a blanket of swirling purple and blue. The air around them seemed to sparkle, and it took Elijah a moment to realize that each glint was a tiny speck of ice caught in the whirling eddies of the wind, filling the night with fine, iridescent glitter. Beyond the curtain of swirling shards, vast ribbons of vibrant green waved softly across the horizon. Shimmering pillars seemed to ride the river of light as it drifted by them, flickering in and out of existence as if to an unsteady tune Elijah couldn't hear. Washes of brighter color ran swiftly along the underside of the band, disappearing into the dark surrounding the aurora as quickly as they appeared. Even the wind seemed to grow silent around them, leaving them standing shoulder to shoulder in the forgotten cold.

"Les," Elijah breathed in a cloud of steam, but he couldn't take his eyes from the waves of light and glinting ice streaming by above them.

"They call it diamond dust," the captain said, tilting his head toward the boy at his side. "It's a mighty rare sight along with an aurora like this." He gave a small shrug and kept his attention on the sky. "Thought if it wasn't on your list already, it might be somethin' you'd like to see anyhow. Since we're here."

"It's beautiful," Elijah whispered. He tore his gaze away long enough to smile broadly at the blond beside him. "Thank you."

Leslie shrugged away the boy's gratitude, but Elijah caught him glancing sidelong at him and saw the faint smirk on his scarred lip. Was this part of the reason they'd made the detour to come here? This is the reason Park had suspected? Elijah's cheeks heated at the thought even in the freezing cold. Leslie had thought to bring him here—even if his main concern had been the drugs, he'd still made the time to walk up this hill to show Elijah something amazing. He'd been listening when Elijah talked about the silly, simple things on his list. Elijah's stomach twisted under his borrowed coat, and he tucked his arms slightly closer to himself. This felt less like trust. This felt like...he liked Leslie. He liked him a lot. And maybe...maybe Leslie liked him a little bit, too.

They stood together in silence under the rolling colors of the sky. It was beautiful, and Elijah did his best to capture every moment in his memory, but he was distracted by the slightest movement of the man beside him. If things were different—if Leslie were different— this might have been a romantic moment. Leslie might have held his hand inside his pocket so they could both keep warm, or gazed into his eyes, or even tried to kiss him. Elijah would have let him. *Wanted* him to, even.

But Leslie wasn't different. Leslie was Leslie, and Leslie was aloof and distant and had made it very clear that he wasn't interested in more relationship than they already had. At least, Elijah thought he had. But things like this threw him off—Leslie was being kind to him, definitely, but that wasn't the same as romantic. Best to put those types of thoughts out of his mind completely. Elijah would only complicate things and make himself miserable trying to figure the other man out. He could just enjoy the sky and be satisfied standing next to someone whose company he enjoyed just as much.

Eventually, Elijah's shivering became too much to bear, and Leslie touched him on the arm to turn him back down the hill once he noticed.

"Had your fill?" he asked, and Elijah nodded, unable to contain his smile even though it hurt his icy cheeks.

"Not really," the boy replied, "but I think you'll have to carry my frozen body back if we stay here any longer."

"Then let's go warm you up."

Leslie's smirk shot straight to Elijah's groin. He nodded and let his captain lead the way back down toward the compound and the waiting ship.

• • ◆ • •

"Harper!" the captain's voice boomed from the cargo bay, drawing the scrambling sound of the young man's feet on the deck above without the need for the intercom.

The metal of the ladder squeaked under Harper's palms as he slid down to their level. He looked between Leslie and Elijah in confusion and subtly shrank from the blond's stern gaze.

"Why the hell is my cargo hold so empty, Harper?" he asked, and Harper paused and glanced around the room.

"Something missing, Captain? Nobody's been down here."

"Nobody came by to drop off that shipment we came here for?"

Harper shook his head. "I didn't know you'd done the deal already. Hasn't been nothing on the comms, even."

Leslie scowled at the floor, his hands on his hips and fingers drumming against his pockets. "All right then." He ticked his head to the side just enough to catch Elijah's eye. "Looks like we've got another visit to make."

Elijah followed his captain's brisk pace back through the blasting wind toward the compound. Leslie made no attempt to wait for him this time; he stalked along the narrow path through the snow and didn't even stop to brush the ice from his shoulders once they were inside. He made a bee-line for Frederick's store and stopped just inside the door, glancing at the few customers inside.

"Y'all are gonna want to get out," he called. A pair of women paused to eye him suspiciously, but the man nearby tapped one of them on the arm and urged them along with him, quickly and silently excusing themselves as Elijah scooted aside to let them by.

"Hey!" Frederick called from behind the counter. "You can't run off my customers like that!"

Leslie took a few steps toward the other man. "You got a shipping delay, mister?" he asked in a low voice, and Elijah could hear the threat in it. "Thought you'd have time to get my cargo to me three times by now."

"Your cargo?" the young man echoed with a tilt of his head. "What cargo's that?"

The captain visibly tensed. Elijah looked between Leslie and the shop owner and edged to stand more beside his captain.

"You don't want to make this mistake, friend," Leslie promised. "I dealt square with you—you done been paid, and I expect you'll get me my cargo and send me on my way with a goddamn smile."

"I don't remember making any deal with you." Frederick pushed up the hinged door on his counter so he could step through, and he moved just in front of the blond to make sure the captain knew he was the smaller of the two. "And even if I did, who are you going to tell about it? We didn't sign any contracts. You going to tell on me to the Feds? *You?*" He sneered down at Leslie and let out a soft, smirking snort. "Some drug-dealing smuggler is going to go to the soldiers and claim I ripped him off?"

Leslie took a slow, deep breath, and he let it out in an empty chuckle. He looked up into the other man's eyes without flinching. "You're new, mister, so I'll say it again in case you really are this fuckin' slow. I paid you—and I'll get what I'm owed."

"You'll get to leave this planet a free piece of shit instead of a jailed one," Frederick countered. "Now get the fuck out of my shop."

The captain shook his head. "All right. Remember, now, that you done this to yourself."

Almost faster than Elijah could see, Leslie had slammed his hand into the young man's sternum and knocked him to the ground. He had his silenced Jericho from its holster and leveled on the shop owner before the other man could recover, and when Frederick saw the barrel of the gun aimed at him, he froze on the floor with his elbows supporting him.

"Captain," Elijah murmured with worry in his voice, but the blond didn't look at him.

"Don't kill me," Frederick begged, all bravado gone from him now. "Please. I'll get you your Praevad. Just don't kill me."

"I ain't gonna kill you," Leslie said evenly. "That'd be a waste of a contact. But I can't have folks thinkin' they can fuck me over, you feel me?"

"I get it," the young man answered in a panic.

"I don't think you do."

The muffled thump of Leslie's Jericho sounded in the empty shop, making Elijah flinch, but Frederick's screams weren't so silenced. He clutched at his destroyed knee while blood fell in bursts from the broken skin, staining the concrete floor and spattering his shirt. The captain waited patiently for the young man's cries to ebb, never lowering his pistol. Frederick looked up at him with his jaw set in a grimace of agony, slightly rocking as he tried to hold his leg together.

"You're gonna get me my cargo," Leslie said, his voice low and dangerous. "Right fuckin' quick, you hear?"

"Yes," Frederick ground out. Sweat poured from him, and he was clearly struggling to keep from collapsing entirely.

"Yes, *Captain*," the blond corrected, and an uneasy chill touched the back of Elijah's neck at hearing the same command that had been given to him so differently in the other man's quarters.

The young shop owner had to take a moment to catch his ragged breath. "Yes, Captain," he finally said through gritted teeth.

"And next time I show up, you're gonna deal straight with me and thank me for my business, ain't you?"

"Yes, Captain."

"All right. I expect I'll see somebody from you by the time I get back to my ship."

He finally lowered his gun and glanced over to meet Elijah's stunned gaze, tilting his head to beckon the boy out with him. Elijah stepped forward to follow him, but caught movement out of the corner of his eye. From the floor, Frederick had managed to get one hand behind him and find the pistol in the back of his pants, which he now raised toward Leslie's back.

"Captain!" Elijah called in warning, his own gun already snatched from his belt and aimed directly at the shop owner's chest before the blond could turn around.

Leslie stopped to look over his shoulder and sighed through his nose as Frederick struggled to keep the gun lifted at all, let alone decide which man to aim it at.

"That ain't the way, mister," he said. He glanced sidelong at Elijah to make sure his own hand was steady, then took a step closer to the man on the floor. "I thought you was smarter than this. You go on and put that down, now, less'n you want my boy here to put a few more holes in you."

Frederick looked up into Elijah's face, trying to judge whether the boy had the mettle to pull the trigger, but Elijah kept his gun leveled at the other man's heart. He stared him down, unshakeable, until Frederick grunted in resignation and let his pistol clatter to the floor at his side. Leslie stepped forward to kick it aside and sighed as he stood over the bleeding man.

"See what you done, now?" he said. He took his time retrieving his Jericho from its holster and turned it in his hand to click the magazine free. He checked the remaining bullets in the clip and slid it back into place with a small sigh. "Now you gone and made me think you're deaf, friend. That means I'm gonna have to tell you twice."

"No no no—"

The shop owner's plea was cut off by the sound of another round firing. With his other knee shattered, Frederick's scream was a little weaker than before. He doubled over his own bloody legs, seeming to want to hold them but hesitant to put his hands on his injuries. Leslie crouched down beside him and rested his elbows on his knees, letting his pistol hang loosely in one hand between them. Some of the other man's blood had splattered onto him, but he didn't seem to mind the red droplets staining his coatsleeves and hands.

"Now, Freddy," the captain said, waiting patiently until the younger man managed to look up at him, "we understand each other, don't we?"

"Yes," he rasped in answer.

"You think long and hard on this next time you figure it's smart to try to put one over on one of us drug-dealing smugglers."

He rose, then paused for a moment and glanced over at the counter. He took a few steps to retrieve a small tablet from the surface and dropped it to the floor beside Frederick. He nudged it closer with the toe of his boot, the corner leaving a smear of blood as it trailed through one of the growing puddles.

"I'll have my cargo on my ship within the hour, Freddy," he said. He didn't wait for an answer before stepping over another puddle on his way to the door.

Elijah followed behind him, only turning and lowering his gun once the door was open. He tucked the pistol back into his belt and saw Leslie holster his own weapon, then tuck his bloodied hands into his pockets to keep them hidden on their way through the compound.

Elijah's heartbeat was surprisingly steady. When that man had pulled a gun on Leslie, he hadn't hesitated. Shooting someone to prove a point was farther than Elijah thought the captain would go—but then, he'd only seen deals that went well so far. He should have expected that things wouldn't always go smoothly, and that Leslie would have to respond with appropriate force. And after all, it's not like it was the first time Elijah had held a gun on someone.

By the time they reached the ship, the cargo doors were open, and Harper was directing a pair of workers while they unloaded a few crates from a transport car. The captain entered the ship through the open bay doors and gave Harper a sharp nod on his way by to the deck ladder. Leslie didn't say anything, but Elijah followed him to the upper deck and to his cabin anyway, feeling as though he hadn't yet been dismissed. At the door to his quarters, Leslie glanced over his shoulder at the boy behind him, then pressed the release on the door and stepped inside.

Elijah waited quietly while the captain shrugged off his coat and tossed it onto the floor of his adjoining bathroom. Leslie hesitated a moment, then held his hand out and gestured toward Elijah, who took the hint and pulled off the borrowed jacket to hand it back. With both of them discarded on the floor, Leslie paused in the bathroom doorway and leaned one elbow against it without turning around.

"You had my back, Elijah," he said softly. "Thank you for that."

"Of course. I wouldn't be much good to the crew if I didn't."

Leslie nodded, and Elijah lingered near the bed while the water ran in the sink. He watched through the open door as the blond put his hands under the faucet, splashing water up over the blood that had dried there in the cold.

"What you did to him," Elijah started. He hesitated until Leslie glanced at him out of the corner of his eye. "You needed to do it, right? To protect your reputation."

"That's right," the captain agreed. "If I let it slide, word gets out I showed my belly to some wet-behind-the-ears shopkeep, and other folks think they can do me the same way. I kill him, and I get no cargo and lose my money anyway. This way, I get what I want, and he's still got a working mouth to tell the story with." He looked over at the boy. "You think I did wrong?"

Elijah shook his head. "I get it. I don't...like violence. But I get it. You don't always have a choice, right?"

"That's the way I see it." He turned off the faucet, shook the water from his hands, and dried them on a small towel from the counter. When he'd finished, he set it aside and turned to face Elijah fully. "You didn't look much like a farmboy back there, the way you held that gun."

"I told you I knew how to shoot."

"That ain't the same thing, and you know it."

Elijah scuffed his foot as he looked down at the floor. "Well, you didn't spend much time on my farm."

"Oh?" Leslie chuckled and crossed the room to sit at his desk chair, wordlessly inviting the boy to join him. "More to that back-ass-of-nowhere colony than there seems, huh?"

"Well, it's not a huge population. A lot of big families. And the Federation gives better kickbacks to the more productive farms, but there's only so much to go around. Like a pool, and each family gets a percentage, right? So if you do better than your neighbor, your family gets better stuff." He gave a small shrug as he dropped down onto the mattress. "Lean times make people mean."

"Got into some cornfield rumbles in your day, did you? How do you even have lean times in a colony under a dome?"

"Cows still get sick. They die giving birth. Crops wither if the soil's not right. Things happen. And sometimes somebody who lost a few too many cows this season thinks he deserves to have a few of yours, so he sends his sons to come steal them. Then your dad sends you to go get them back, and to make sure they don't think they can do it again." Elijah kept his eyes on his feet. "So...I get it."

Leslie watched him without speaking for a few beats. "You ever shot a man, Elijah?"

He shook his head. "I've...shot *at* people. But nobody was really trying to kill anyone back home. Just warn them, or rough them up a little, you know? The worst I've done is nick Paul Green's arm and make him need stitches. We didn't usually bring guns, even, unless it was really serious. We just got into scraps." Elijah peeked up at the man across from him. "But you've killed people, right?"

"That's right."

"Do you feel bad about it? I know once, I...I beat Marcus Cane so bad he was in the infirmary for days. Fractured his eye socket. I didn't mean to, really, I just...sort of lost it. Went too far. And the way I felt after that, trying to get the blood off my hands under the hose behind the barn? I almost wished it was me they'd carried away instead, and I didn't even kill him. And you came in here and washed up like you didn't just cripple a man for life."

Leslie took a slow breath before answering. "The problem ain't washing the blood off your hands, Elijah," he said in a more subdued voice. "Blood comes off easy. Little hot water, little soap. The problem is you still see it there long after you done washed it off. I got a lot of stains only I can see."

Elijah opened his mouth to speak again, but the captain was standing now.

"You liked the light show, right?" the blond asked.

Elijah nodded.

"Then it wasn't a wasted trip." He tilted his head toward the door, and Elijah knew that *now* he was being dismissed.

17

It was only going to take them another day or so to reach Jannat. Leslie kept his distance the next day—Elijah guessed they had gotten a little too close to a real conversation for the captain's liking—so Elijah minded his own business and settled down in his own bunk to try to get some sleep. It didn't bother him. Leslie was a secretive person, and Elijah suspected a bit of a broken one. If he wanted to keep Elijah at arm's length, then Elijah could be patient until he was ready to get closer. And Elijah did want to get closer, he thought. He wanted the heat of the blond's hand gently at the side of his neck again. He felt a tug he didn't quite recognize somewhere in his belly. Up there on that hill, under the glowing sky, he really had wanted Leslie to kiss him. He'd wanted it to be romantic. But Leslie didn't even want Elijah to touch him—why would he want to kiss him? For that matter, why did Elijah want to be kissed? Kissing was intimate and romantic, and it was very different from what he and Leslie had been doing together so far. Kissing was something you did with someone you had *feelings* for.

Elijah gave a soft sigh in the darkness. Was he having some feelings?

He shifted on the creaky mattress of his bunk at the thought of the blond captain. In the stillness of his room, he could feel the tight straps around his legs and the press of Leslie's body against his back. He'd wanted the other man so close to him—inside of him, overwhelming him. It was kind of a frightening emotion. He'd had the odd daydream about boys his age back at home, but they'd been remarkably tame compared to the sorts of things Leslie had shown him over his short time aboard the Chimera, and Elijah had certainly never felt the uncontrollable urge to be dominated that he had earlier in the captain's cabin.

He felt a twinge in his groin and squeezed his eyes shut. It had only been a couple of hours since he left Leslie's room, and his brain knew that he needed sleep, but his dick didn't seem to care. The time didn't matter. His whole body ached for more of those wickedly smiling blue eyes. His mind kept drifting back to the blond's lean, naked body wading into the ocean surf. He imagined being allowed to put his hands on the blond's muscular torso, tracing his scars with his fingertips and kissing every inch of ink-stained skin. He pictured the way Leslie would bite his lip and gasp as Elijah touched him, finally permitted to wrap his fingers around his cock and stroke him the way the older man had done to him.

Elijah's fingers had started to work the button of his pants before he realized what he was doing, but a sudden banging thump on his door startled him into attention. He swung himself out of bed, shifting the front of his pants to better hide the beginnings of his erection, and hit the button to open the door.

Leslie smiled at him from the doorway, and heat rushed up Elijah's neck and into his cheeks. Of course he'd show up now. Had he somehow heard Elijah thinking about him? Had he been summoned by the boy's erection like some sort of dick spirit?

"Can I come in?" the blond asked, and Elijah stepped guiltily backward to allow him inside. "I've been thinking about what you asked me," Leslie said as he switched the door closed behind him. He set a small zippered bag on the floor beside Elijah's bed and straightened to look him in the face. "About asking to touch me."

Elijah's heart clenched. He hadn't done anything wrong, but he somehow felt like he'd been caught.

"Is that something that you want to happen?"

"Yes," he admitted, his throat feeling suddenly dry.

Leslie stepped close to him, his gaze keeping the boy from moving back. He tilted his head and dropped his eyes to the younger man's full lips. "And you think you'll be able to please me?"

Elijah swallowed the growing tightness in his throat. "I...think you'll tell me what to do so I can."

"Good answer," the blond chuckled. He lifted his hand and ran the pad of his thumb slowly over Elijah's bottom lip. "Do you want to try?"

"I do," Elijah answered, not bothering to hide the eagerness in his voice. His skin had already begun to prickle with excitement, and his breath caught in his chest at the next soft command he watched fall from the captain's lips.

"Then get on your knees."

The boy dropped immediately, settling back on his heels and lifting his eyes to the other man's face. He clenched his hands into fists on his thighs to keep them from shaking. This wasn't the same as touching. What if he was no good at it? What if he choked? He exhaled slowly as Leslie's hand caressed the dark curls at the side of his head, and he leaned into the touch automatically.

"My belt," the blond said. Elijah shifted forward an inch or two and forced his hands to grip the leather of the captain's belt, sliding the end free of its buckle and brushing it aside so that he could reach the button on the pants underneath. He wet his lips, trying to slow his racing heart as he unfastened the top button. Leslie apparently made a habit of not wearing any underwear, because Elijah could see the first curls of blond hair against light skin and the tip of the other man's hardening dick as soon as he began to ease his zipper downward. The deep, straining red was different from the dark brown Elijah was used to seeing on himself, and Leslie was noticeably larger than he was despite his slighter build, but the soft skin stretched in just the same way as Elijah's own as the blond gave a faint, eager twitch. Elijah slid Leslie's pants down his hips just far enough to free him completely, then hesitated and glanced upward, hoping for guidance.

"Go on," Leslie urged, his fingers tightening just slightly in the boy's hair. "Show me how much you want to please me."

Elijah leaned closer, uncertain, but he licked his lips once more before parting them to take the velvety skin into his mouth. He had to open his jaw wider than he expected to get beyond the tip, his tongue flattening against Leslie to make more room. He moved slowly, struggling to keep his mind on his task instead of becoming overwhelmed by the reality of what he was doing. Leslie—the man who had brought him to breathless, desperate orgasm over and over, who had left him raw and stiff from affectionate abuse, and who had watched him with such hungry eyes—was in his mouth, smooth and hard and pressing softly toward the back of his throat. He jumped slightly as he felt Leslie's fingertips brush his face, hand moving to lightly cup his chin and hold him steady.

"You look good with a cock in your mouth, Elijah," the blond teased, easing back from the kneeling boy's lips and pushing forward again into the soft moan he caused.

Elijah was allowed to rest his hands on the back of Leslie's thighs, but when he tried to reach up and slide his fingers over the length of his cock, he was brushed away with a gentle hand. He let his grip tighten on the fabric of Leslie's pants and followed the slow, easy pace the blond set. When he swirled his tongue over a certain spot near the head of the captain's erection and heard a low grunt in response, he grew bolder, shifting a little higher on his knees to try and let Leslie sink deep into the back of his throat. He was forced to retreat quickly, coughing softly as the other man slipped free of his lips with threads of thick saliva still connecting them.

"Good boy," Leslie hummed, taking him more firmly by the hair to pull the heat of the boy's mouth back over him. "You know, I saw that you left 'humiliation' on your list," he added in a low, dangerous voice. Elijah heard his own longing groan as he glanced up and caught Leslie's pale eyes on him, but he didn't break away to answer. "Is that something you want, Elijah? You want me to humiliate you and make you mine?" He forced himself a little deeper into the boy's mouth and exhaled sharply at the shuddering groan Elijah gave. "You like that idea, don't you? Being mine? Letting me use you however I want?"

The word "mine" sent a jolt through Elijah's stomach and groin, forcing his aching cock to strain against the front of his pants. He pressed forward to take the captain as deeply as he could, hoping his sigh was enough to convince the older man of his "yes."

Leslie tugged him backward, a whimper escaping the boy as he leaned back on his heels and had his gaze forced upward. "Is that what you want, Elijah? To be mine?"

"Yes, Captain," Elijah practically begged, moaning with satisfaction as the blond forced himself deeply into the younger man's mouth. He held onto Leslie's thighs as tightly as he could, the captain's hand in his hair setting a harder, faster pace. Elijah's eyes watered from the pressure at the back of his throat, and he had to break away periodically to take quick, gasping breaths, but each time he returned, moaning at every soft pant the man above him let slip.

"That's it," Leslie hissed. "Just like that."

The boy whined with need, fingers digging into the blond's legs, and then Leslie pulled him back again, holding him firmly by the hair and wrapping his other hand around his own cock to take his place.

"Open your mouth," he commanded, and Elijah did as he was told, his whole body trembling. His lidded eyes watched the blond stroke himself, and he could see the muscles in his stomach clenching below the hem of his shirt. Leslie's hips jerked once, and with a low growl sounding in his throat, he shot his climax burning hot onto Elijah's face, spilling over his waiting tongue and leaving heavy droplets on his lips and rolling down his chin. Elijah licked his lips to taste the bitter fluid, the muscles in his legs shivering just trying to keep him upright, and he struggled to catch his breath.

Leslie held his fingers in the boy's black hair for a few long, slow exhales, and then he eased him upward, touching under his chin to force Elijah to meet his eyes. "Now," he purred, "I'll show you what it's really like to be mine."

· · ◆ · ·

Park's quiet whistle echoed in the metal corridor as he walked with uneven steps toward the back of the ship. His knee had been acting up for a few days, but it was nothing he couldn't limp through. The bigger pain right now was the fuel injector that had been spitting sparks ever since they left Dhat-Badan. He'd tried his damnedest to fix it, but now it was threatening to shut the whole engine down, so it would have to be replaced. Luckily, he'd gotten a deal on a spare one a few months ago and tucked it away in storage. Now it was just a matter of finding the fucking thing. He'd tried everywhere he could think of and had zero luck, so it was down to the back room. Park was pretty sure the only thing they kept in there was old bolts that didn't seem to fit anything, some spare chairs from the mess hall, and a few strings of Christmas lights, but he had to check anyway.

The engineer stopped at the door and shifted onto his good leg with a soft grunt, banging hard on the switch beside the doorway in anticipation of it getting stuck like always. The lights were on inside, which was odd, but Park got his biggest surprise once he stepped into the room.

The new kid was kneeling on the floor by the far wall, naked except for a pair of grey briefs that did very little to hide his erection. He was sitting back on his heels with his legs spread wide by a metal rod tied to the backs of his knees, his wrists behind his back and strapped together up to the elbows. He wore a thick collar that leashed him closely to the heavy shelving behind him, and a pool of saliva had formed on one of his bare thighs, dripping from the ball gag that was tied tight around his face, forcing his mouth to stay open. The boy looked up at the sound of Park's footsteps, a sheen of sweat on his forehead and chest, and his dark eyes widened with horror as he recognized the man who had walked in on him.

"Jesus fucking Christ," Park swore, venom in his voice, and he retreated from the room far faster than he'd come in, flicking off the light on his way out and leaving Elijah in the dark once the door thudded shut behind him.

Elijah panicked. With the door to the storage room closed, he couldn't see an inch in front of his face. He pulled against the straps binding his arms but couldn't budge them, and even rising up onto his knees was tricky with the spreader bar keeping them open. Even if he could have, he wouldn't have been able to stand, since his leash kept him bound to the lowest shelf. Elijah had expected that "humiliation" would mean more of the same "yes Captain," "no Captain," and begging that they'd already been doing, but he had been sorely mistaken.

Leslie had tied him securely with the tools in his bag, making sure he was as comfortable as he could be, and he'd caressed his face, bit his earlobe, and promised to be back to finish him soon. He didn't know how long had passed since then. The waiting was sweet torture, and Elijah's imagination ran wild with thoughts of the captain's return. His prick had leapt to attention at the sound of the opening door and withered just as quickly as he caught sight of Park's appalled face. Now he was still tied up, locked in the dark, and he had been seen in the most compromising situation of his life by a man who he'd been trying to get to accept him as a crew mate and an equal.

The sudden light pouring in from the door a few minutes later made him flinch. He peeked toward the corridor through one squinting eye and heaved a sigh of relief when Leslie's silhouette came into focus. The blond rushed to his side and knelt in front of him, first unbuckling the gag from his face and allowing him to work his jaw back into place.

"Elijah, I'm so sorry," Leslie said immediately. He was already working on loosing the straps around the boy's arms. "No one ever comes in here; I didn't mean for anybody to see you like this. God damn Park picking the one god damn day," he huffed, but he sounded more angry with himself than with the engineer. Once Elijah's arms were loose, Leslie unsnapped the fastenings holding the spreader bar to his knees and let him settle more comfortably on the floor. He cupped the boy's face in both hands and lifted him to look him in the eyes, and Elijah's heart constricted at the gentle worry furrowing the other man's brow. "I'm sorry," he said again, the soft words seeming to pour warmth over Elijah's chilled skin.

"You mean it *wasn't* part of your humiliation plan for Park to see me naked? 'Cause that was pretty humiliating."

Leslie sighed. "Of course not. I should have locked the damn door," he scolded himself.

Elijah found himself smiling at the captain's fretting. He snorted softly and lowered his eyes for a moment before peeking back up into Leslie's anxious blue eyes. "The look on Park's face was pretty good, though," he murmured.

Leslie paused, the uneasiness melting from his face, and he cracked a smile. "Oh, my ears are still burning from the dressing down he gave me."

Elijah laughed, and the sound caused a soft, then a louder, relieved chuckle from the other man. Leslie leaned forward and touched his forehead against Elijah's, the breath of their laughter mixing for a brief moment before he pulled back to unbuckle the collar from around the boy's neck.

Elijah managed to get himself back to his bunk and cleaned up without running into any other members of the crew, which was a blessing. His muscles felt stiff from being held in one position for so long, but it was the kind of pain that made him smile as he stretched. Every little ache was a reminder of Leslie's hands on him. But they would be arriving at Jannat soon, so he would need to force himself to focus more on his work and less on what was asked of him inside the captain's locked cabin.

18

The thengisi station was massive, but it didn't look like any space station Elijah had ever seen before. The entirety of it was a cluster of intertwining tubes, twisting around each other, splitting and joining up again and jutting out at strange angles. Every rounded passageway was covered in vents, and a few were lined with rails that carried small shuttles at high speeds along the curving exterior of the station. Elijah barely heard Brooks talking on the comm behind him, both hands splayed on the glass and all of his attention on the approaching station. He watched with awe as they eased closer to the lit runway, and his mouth dropped open at the sight of the bay they pulled into. Everything inside was made of sleek blue metal that shone almost black in the lights from the ship, and the ceiling doors that closed above them were covered in rows of ridges as though the room itself had a ribcage.

He only tore his eyes away when he felt a heavy hand on his shoulder and turned to see the captain looking down at him.

"Go get geared up, kid. Tell Harper I said to arm you from the stock. We'll want to get straight to business. Aliens only get a twelve-hour clearance on the station unless you're government."

Elijah couldn't help the bright smile that parted his lips. "Yes, Captain," he answered almost before the other man had finished speaking, and then he was out the door and hurrying down the corridor to the armory.

The gangway doors couldn't open fast enough. Elijah had his chosen pistol in his belt, and he stood with the captain, Harper, and Shaw while they waited for the passage to depressurize.

"Thengisi are particular," Leslie said, watching Elijah closely to make sure he was listening. "They want things done the way thengisi do them, which doesn't always make a whole lot of sense to other people. The station's gonna mostly be dark because they're nocturnal. If anyone offers you something, even a drink or a chair, say no. If they ask again, you can say yes—if they don't, they weren't really offering it to you anyway. They don't care what your name is, so don't bother introducing yourself. You'll probably never be friendly enough with one to learn its name. Call them 'obhuti' if it's a male and 'osisi' if it's a female. The males are the ones with the horns. Oh, and if you get a little lightheaded, that's normal. They keep the station at a higher oxygen level than humans tend to want. Most importantly, don't make eye contact. It's rude."

"Where am I supposed to look?"

"Oh, you'll find other things to stare at, I'm sure."

The gangway door hissed before Elijah could question further. He'd seen pictures of thengisi before, but they were mostly sketches from his school books or quick sightings in vids he'd seen of large, multi-species stations like Altera. Thengisi were very rare outside of their home system—they were reclusive and mistrusting as a rule and only established an embassy on Altera in the last twenty years or so. No one on Elijah's home colony had ever seen one in person. He would be the first.

With that thought emboldening him, he followed his shipmates down the gangway and into the station. As expected, the docking bay was only dimly lit, with runner lights along the catwalk leading into the outer ring they'd been allowed to enter. A guard blocked their way at the next massive set of blue-black doors, and Elijah struggled not to stare open-mouthed. Then alien stood on two legs, just a little shorter than Elijah himself, its body a sleek black carapace. It was dressed in what looked like miles of cloth wrapped a hundred times around the torso and shoulders and falling almost to the floor like a tattered robe. The number of wrappings was apparently to leave space for two long arms that hung in the usual human way from its shoulders, as well as two matching pairs of thin, spindly arms with only three pointed fingers each, all four extending from the center of its chest. The alien held them protectively close against its torso and used its longer arms to grip a tablet and the strap of a narrow rifle slung across one shoulder. Large, golden eyes sat at the sides of its slick black head, framing the single massive, two-pronged horn that grew from the end of its elongated face. Elijah guessed this must have been a male.

The long mandibles at either side of the alien's jaw gave a minute clicking twitch as it opened its mouth to speak, revealing a thin row of needle-like teeth. "ICV-P Chimera," it said in a soft voice that rasped like an egg dropped into a hot pan. "Registration number D801-dash-5."

"Safely docked," Leslie answered. Elijah tried to spot what part of the Thengisi the captain was looking at and decided he must be looking slightly over the alien's shoulder to avoid impolite eye contact. "We have a delivery to drop off in sector seven, and we're requesting the remaining time as leave to refuel and resupply."

"Cleared," the alien confirmed, and it held the tablet out toward Leslie with one clawed hand. The blond pressed his palm against the screen, waiting until the tablet gave a quiet ping before removing his hand. The Thengisi turned it back to tap a few things on the screen, then gave a quiet clicking sound and moved aside to allow them to approach the doors.

"Thank you, obhuti," Leslie said.

"Walk wisely, ohambi," the alien replied as it tapped a code into a panel by the exit. The double doors snapped open suddenly, then eased slowly apart, making more than enough space for the crew to pass through. Elijah followed Leslie and the others into a tall corridor lined with the same riblike ridges as the docking bay, their footsteps echoing in the heavy silence following the thud of the bay doors closing.

"What's an ohambi?" Elijah asked, speeding up just a little to match pace with the captain. "That's not one of the words you said before."

"I think it means 'traveler' technically, but really it's a word for anyone foreign. Not exactly an insult, not exactly polite." Leslie shrugged one shoulder as they walked. "They are how they are."

Elijah let out a soft, pensive hum, prepared to speak again—but then they reached the end of the corridor. The passage ahead of them opened up into a cavernous hall, rounded and ridged all around except for the floor. A deep spine ran along the apex of the room, leading the way across to disappear into the tunnel at the opposite end. The open space still felt warm and close despite the vastness of the room, like a chitinous womb that seemed to throb inward with minute breaths. This entry area was clearly meant for the station's alien visitors—there were walk-up bar restaurants, arms repair shops, and a small clinic. Most of the people Elijah saw milling around the room were either human, kineta, or insalar, but the ones running the shops and restaurants were exclusively thengisi. They probably didn't trust anyone else enough to employ them. Aliens on Jannat were visitors, and visitors only.

"I want to check the incendiary place," Harper said, already drifting toward the row of shops along the far wall, but Shaw snatched him by his sleeve and pulled him back to his place a step behind the captain.

"After business," Leslie said without even needing to look back. He led them to a thengisi who stood at an arched door beside the single window in the entire hall—this one looked similar to the guard who had let them into the passageway, except that its head was narrower and sleeker, its mandibles small and almost delicate-looking, and its face lacked the heavy keratin horn. So this one was a female, Elijah guessed. He was glad they had the horns, at least; he would never have been able to tell them apart otherwise.

"May we ride, osisi?" Leslie asked when the thengisi turned its broad golden eyes to him, not quite rising high enough to meet his face. "We need to go to sector four."

"Sector four is restricted," she answered in that same crackling hiss, mandibles vibrating softly against her cheeks as though the very request was impolite.

"I'm expected by the isithethi Ungolo."

The alien held her tablet in the spare hand of an arm from her torso and turned to the large panel at her side, her more dexterous hands tapping and clicking on the screen in front of her. The thengisi didn't have eyebrows, really, or any part of their face that seemed to move except their mandibles and mouths, so it was difficult to tell if she was annoyed or not. Elijah wondered how they ever knew what the others were thinking if they weren't allowed to look each other in the eye and they had no discernible facial expressions, but he guessed that no species that couldn't communicate effectively with its own kind would ever make it to the stage where they were building space stations.

After a few more touches with her spindly fingers, the screen in front of the alien beeped softly. She tilted her head and turned to almost face the captain again. "You are expected, ohambi," she said, and she pressed a large release at the edge of her console that opened the door behind her. "I will direct your shuttle to sector four. Walk wisely."

"Thank you, osisi."

The captain urged his crew ahead of him and entered the small shuttle car last, barely missing having his ankle caught in the door. He took a seat beside Harper, leaving Elijah to take one of the two seats opposite next to Shaw. He peeked sidelong up at the First Ifficer, but Shaw just sat staring straight forward at the wall ahead of him, arms crossed over his chest and a grim frown on his face.

"Wipe that look off your mug, Shaw," Leslie said, his shoulders already more loose and his voice more casual than he had been while addressing the aliens. "Your concerns have been noted, and if you offend Ungolo and he kicks us out before he tells us anything, I'm gonna shove your fat ass out the nearest airlock, you hear?"

"Just don't trust bugs," the First Officer grumped, his massive shoulders rolling as he shifted his weight in his seat.

"See? That's what I'm talking about. Now you stow that shit." Leslie pointed an authoritative finger at the man twice his size without a care for the discrepancy. "You just keep your mouth shut 'til we get back to the ship, and we'll consider it a successful little mission. You feel me?"

Shaw's jaw tightened, and Elijah could see the man's fingers gripping his biceps.

"I can't hear you," the captain pressed.

The larger man heaved a resigned sigh. "Yes, Captain."

"That's better. Now you behave. Don't let the kid show you up."

Shaw's head turned almost imperceptibly toward Elijah, and the boy leaned away from him instinctively, but Leslie only laughed. The shuttle eased to a stop almost as quickly as it had started, and when the doors opened, the captain hurried them all out and dodged the door again as it shut behind him. The thengisi at this stop eyed them suspiciously as they passed, but Leslie didn't look at him, so Elijah didn't, either.

19

This part of the station was decidedly less alien-friendly. There were hardly any lights along the sides of the corridor, and the floor wasn't quite as even and sleek. Elijah felt the urge to reach out for the back of Leslie's shirt so that he could follow along in the faint light like a baby duckling but decided against it before he actually moved his hand. The captain walked without hesitation around the bending tunnel, up and down as the floor raised and dipped under their feet, and the others followed in tense silence. There were no friendly shops or restaurants full of chatting patrons here. Every door they passed seemed half melted together where it met the wall, almost like the dark cobalt metal had been poured into place. None of them had any signs or labels of any kind, but Leslie walked forward with purpose until they reached a narrow entry without even the tiny round lights that had dotted the walls so far.

The captain spared one final look over his shoulder at Shaw. His First Officer gave him a small nod, so he placed his hand against the wall beside the door. A panel that was indiscernible from the rest of the corridor to Elijah illuminated soft blue under his palm, and the doors made a small crack before they split in the center to allow them inside. Elijah gladly went last. The room they entered was darker even than the hallway outside, and once the door closed, Elijah could barely see Leslie's back in front of him. He heard a soft, rolling hiss from across the room and suspected that whatever else was in here could see them just fine.

"It's been a long time, Captain," a thengisi's rasping voice called, and a heavy step followed, making a scratching sound on the metal floor that sent a shudder up Elijah's spine.

"Glad you agreed to see me, Ungolo. I need a favor."

"Of course you do. Everyone needs favors, don't they?"

"I hope I'm not intruding on your hospitality," Leslie answered, and Elijah could hear the faint smirk in his voice.

"I'm not complaining," the alien said. "If people didn't need favors, I'd be out of business." It gave a hissing, rattling chuckle—at least, Elijah thought it was a laugh. A creepy one, but a laugh nonetheless. "What problem do you have that I can solve?"

"I need to get a shipment onto Altera. The kind they're not gonna like."

"Ah-haa," the thengisi breathed. "You don't have small problems, do you, Captain?"

"I try to have *no* problems, usually."

"If you didn't have any problems, you wouldn't have any money," the alien chortled. The amused clicking of its mandibles sounded like a snake's rattle. "And what have you brought me in exchange for solving this problem?"

"I have some information you aren't likely to have heard yet."

"That's a good start—assuming I haven't actually heard it."

"What else do you want? I'm scant on credits until I make this drop."

The thengisi gave a hissing sigh as though it was considering. "I do have a few errands to be run," it said, and Leslie laughed.

"I've been on your errands before, Ungolo," he said.

"I've still got the scar," Harper piped up.

"Memories make life more full," the alien answered a little firmly. Another heavy skittering sounded from across the room, and Elijah got the feeling that it was moving closer to them. "I want you to get something back for me," he said, definitely closer now. "Something that was stolen."

"Someone stole from you?" Leslie asked. "And they ain't so dead you got it back already?"

"This is a...delicate relationship, and one I intend to maintain. This individual believes I don't know it was him that did this disrespectful thing, and I want to keep it that way. So, I would ask that you perform a...I believe the human phrase is 'a bait and switch?'"

"Not quite, but I catch your meaning. So where is it?"

"Here on Jannat. You see; I don't even make you travel."

"Yeah, thanks."

"Your target has an office where I believe the stolen data drive is being kept. It's in sector one."

The captain gave a small, suspicious snort. "The only thing in sector one is the alien embassy. Your thief's an ambassador?"

"I worry about who he is; you worry about what he stole," Ungolo replied. "The drive will be in a private residence adjoining the embassy. It will be marked 615. It will be locked." His steps echoed in the room as he moved away, and Elijah heard the heavy click of a metal door opening and closing before the alien scratched its way back to them. "Replace it with this and bring the original back to me. You still have most of your twelve hours' leave; I expect you to return to me within six."

"Don't make it easy on me or anything, obhuti."

The alien's chittering laugh made Elijah cringe. "Easy is not what you get in return for asking me to get you clearance for Altera. Be grateful."

"I am grateful. And I'll get this done. I'll forward you the information I have as soon as I get back to my ship."

"Yes, you will. On all counts."

Elijah sensed the captain moving ahead of him in the dark, and when the door slipped open behind them, he finally caught a glimpse of the information broker in the dim light pouring in from the hallway. He wore a thicker, heavier version of the same wrapped robes Elijah had seen on the other thengisi, but he was missing one of his smaller arms, and five massive horns grew from the front of his head where the others had only had one. Two matching pairs curled toward his face and one larger horn curved upward into a viciously sharp point above his head, his slick carapace glistening even in the faint light. His heavy body almost creaked as he moved, and his mandibles shook with one last hissing chortle as the captain urged them out of the dark room. Elijah was glad to have the door between them again when it closed, but Shaw visibly shuddered.

"Creepy-ass thing," the large man muttered, and Leslie pointed a warning at him before heading off back down the hallway toward the shuttle. Once they were inside and moving back toward the ship, Harper pointed to the small drive the captain held in his lap, given to him by the thengisi broker.

"So this is my job, right? With the sneaking and the stealing."

"Probably," the captain answered, turning the drive in his hand. "Go check out the embassy and see what security's like in the area. Find this guy's place if you can, but don't do anything until you check back with me."

"Got it."

"I'll take Shaw to go meet with our drop-off in sector seven and catch you back at the ship when we're done."

"What do I do?" Elijah cut in, and the captain's blue eyes flicked up to him with a touch of amusement in them.

"You're itching to check out the station, aren't you? Just be back on the ship and ready to go within two hours. I want all hands available for this."

"Yes, Captain," the boy replied, unable to keep the smile from his face for the remainder of the shuttle ride.

· • ◆ • ·

Elijah practically burst from the shuttle car as soon as it came to a stop back at the dock station. Leslie dismissed him with a wave as they went their separate ways, and then the boy was wading through the crowd without a single look back. He didn't have enough credits to his name to be tempted by the wares of the shops lining the chamber—he'd yet again forgotten to ask Leslie about his pay in all the talk about new ways to orgasm—so he only browsed. He used a chunk of the few credits that he did have on his chip to treat himself to a strange-looking bowl of black noodles and unidentifiable meat in a clear broth. He had only been able to point to the half-empty bowl of his neighbor at the bar when he ordered, as he had no faith in his ability to pronounce the name printed on the board on the wall, but the meal was surprisingly delicious. It definitely tasted better than the drink the captain had pushed on him back on Tadmor, at least.

While he wandered, entranced by the curving, bone-like structures that made up the window formation by the shuttle and the seats and shop entrances around the massive chamber, he spotted a small cluster of booths with curtained-off entrances underneath a sign that read "Comm Terminal." He poked his head into one open booth and found a small stool and a terminal with a large screen and a slot to insert a credit chip. In the booths around him, people were chatting and laughing, some very casual and others speaking in low voices as though they didn't want to be overheard.

Elijah brightened immediately. These were public comms. He slid onto the stool in the empty booth and pulled the curtain shut behind him, which caused the screen on the terminal to flicker to life. The words "Insert Credit Chip" appeared in a few different languages, and Elijah slipped his card into the slot, hoping he had enough left to at least initiate a call. He bit his lip and grimaced in anticipation as the terminal displayed a spinning circle for a few moments, but then let out a breath of relief when it read, "Input Receiving Coordinates." He put in the coordinates for his home colony and waited with his palms pressing anxiously into his knees as the comm connected. He realized he had no idea what time it might be back on Dhat-Badan and cringed as he imagined waking up his father with a call from halfway across the galaxy.

The screen flashed black for just a moment, and a second later, his mother's face appeared, her thick black hair tied up in a french braid and her dark eyes drooping and exhausted. He saw the circles under her eyes and winced with guilt that only intensified when her face lit up into a smile of deep relief.

"Oh, Elijah," she said, half sobbing, her hands reaching out for her screen as though she could touch his face across the stars. "Where are you, baby? Are you safe? Have you been eating?"

"I'm fine, mom," he assured her. He swallowed down the growing lump in his own throat. He knew he'd been selfish by leaving, but he hadn't expected how her tears of happiness would hurt his heart. "Plenty to eat."

"How could you just go off on some stranger's ship without even a word to your father or I?" she snapped, her hoarse voice suddenly taking on the admonishing tone that had made him cower since he was small. "What were you thinking? Do you know how worried we've been? What if you'd been murdered or sold off on some alien slave market somewhere?"

Elijah smiled. The quick turnaround was actually comforting—it was the same method of softness and scolding she'd used his whole life, and it gave him his first little stab of homesickness to be reproached again. "I know it was stupid," he admitted. "But I'm all right. The captain of the ship gave me a job. It's a shipping vessel, and he goes all over the galaxy, mom. I'm on Jannat right now. *Jannat*," he said again, as if the first time couldn't have impressed her enough. "I met a thengisi! There are tons here. They're so different, and did you know you aren't supposed to look them in the eyes? It's rude. Oh— and I saw a kineta back on Tadmor, and I got to try a drink that I'm pretty sure should have poisoned me, and I just had these noodles that were black and slimy and weird but they were *so* good. And we went through some FTL gates, and I got to see the Glowing Eye nebula, and mom, it was so beautiful, it was crazy, and you wouldn't believe how *big* everything is out here, just the ships and the satellite stations, and—"

He stopped as his gaze finally fell back to his mother's face and he saw her watching him in patient silence, hugging one elbow to her as her fingertips rested lightly over her smile.

"I'm...really sorry I left so suddenly," he said, more quietly. "I just—"

"I know, honey," she interrupted him, sounding a little strained. "But you had to go, didn't you?"

"I did, I think. I know I did."

"You look happy."

"I...I am."

"Then everything turned out fine, didn't it?"

Elijah didn't try to fight his smile. "Is everything okay there?"

"Your father was furious when we found your note," his mother said. "But he was just worried. Your brother was—"

The terminal in front of Elijah gave a harsh beep, and an insufficient funds warning flashed in the corner of his screen beside a

15-second counter.

"Crap," he groaned. "Mom, I'm out of time for the call. You can send me messages and I'll try to answer when I can, okay?" He hurried to give her the Chimera's registration number before the call cut out, and he heard his mother's "I love you, honey; be safe" before the screen went black and the terminal spit his chip back out as if it was disgusted by his poverty.

Elijah sat for a few moments with his chip in his hands, clearing his throat once or twice and wiping at his eyes with the back of his wrist to make sure there was no trace of tears there. Then he took a deep breath, pulled open the curtain, and headed back toward the Chimera.

20

Harper had already returned by the time Elijah got to the bridge. He entered to find the entire crew gathered there just as before, with the captain standing near the window, but this time all eyes were on Harper.

"So the main problem," he began, running a weary hand through his mess of brown curls, "is that this guy's house seems to be behind a couple different card keys. Getting into the embassy sector is easy if you look human and pathetic enough, but the apartments are down an offshoot passage that needs a pass. There weren't any guards at the door, really, but there are enough wandering around that we'd have to get inside quick. I got a look down the hall when somebody went in, and there seem to be hallway doors every few apartments, each one of them locked, and then I assume a different lock for the apartment itself. The one closest to the door, that I got a look at, was 202, so I'm guessing 615 is gonna be pretty near to the back. If the lock system makes any sense, the card keys will only unlock enough of the hallway doors to get at the apartment you're assigned, meaning we can't just nab anybody's key, because if they only live in the 300-block, we're not getting all the way back to six with their key. So we pretty much have to have the key of the guy we're stealing from if we want to guarantee we can get in and out."

"Great," Park quipped, and Harper held up a hand as though he wasn't finished.

"The good news," he went on, "is that our guy in 615 is the human ambassador himself."

"How exactly is that good news?" the engineer asked.

"It's good news because it means he has a bodyguard," Harper said. "And that bodyguard will definitely also have a key to the apartment." The young man turned his arm to check the watch on his wrist. "*And* he also happens to be getting off his shift in an hour, *and* the secretary at the embassy said she sees him at the bar near the hangar bays all the time because this thengisi apparently has a thing for humans. Don't even ask me how that would work, because I don't wanna think about it. But there we go."

"Well then," the captain said after a few beats of silence. All attention turned to him as he settled back against the co-pilot's seat. "Sounds like we know what we're doing." He looked over at Harper. "You happen to know if this bodyguard has a thing for female humans, or male ones?"

"The secretary was pretty detailed in her disgust, so she made sure I knew that he was into guys. But does that even matter when you're talking about a thengisi and a human person? That's not making any babies no matter what you do. Eugh. Can you imagine what that would look like?"

"Stay on target, Harper. This ambassador—you know where he's going to be for the next while?"

"I told the secretary some sob story and said that I needed to see him, but she said he's all booked up in meetings for the next six hours and I'd have to come back. So, that's our window, I guess. Assuming he doesn't have to run back home for anything."

"We won't need more than that," the captain said. He pushed away from the chair and moved to stand closer to his waiting crew. "All right. This sounds like we have a plan. Harper, you come with me back to the bar, and we'll see if we can find this bodyguard. You too, kid," he added with a glance in Elijah's direction. "Between the three of us, hopefully one of us will take his fancy."

"Bets," Brooks cut in with a raise of her hand. "Twenty credits the xenophile bug goes for Elijah."

The boy frowned across at her, but Park was laughing.

"No way," the engineer said. "Cap's the prettiest, hands down. I'll take that bet."

"You kidding? With that boyish charm? The kid's practically got a sign around his neck that says 'take advantage of me.'"

"I do not!"

Harper seemed mildly offended. "Who's betting on me?"

Brooks stared at him for a beat. "I'm sure your mom loves you, Harper."

"Fuck you, Brooks!"

"All right," Leslie interrupted, quieting the room immediately. "Let's get out there and see if we can find our friend. Y'all hold down the ship 'til we get back."

"Yes, Captain," came the expected chorus of answers.

• • ◆ • •

Elijah only recognized a couple of the drinks on offer at the bar near the docking bays, but at least the glass the thengisi bartender put in front of him was the right color for alcohol instead of murky and piss-like. He settled at a table with his crewmates and sipped his drink—which would also have to come out of his pay, since Leslie had paid for it—until he saw Harper nudge the captain with his elbow. A new thengisi had appeared nearby, his dark robes wrapped snug around his bulky torso.

"He's got that broken horn," Harper mumbled. "Just like she said."

Elijah tried to look without looking like he was looking. Harper was right—the alien who approached the bar had the same pronged horn extending from his face as the others, but one split was off-center and asymmetrical, leaving a whitened stain where part of it was missing.

"Well," Leslie said with a light sigh, "wish me luck. Harper, I'll signal you if he's not taking the bait."

"You got it, Captain."

The blond drained his drink, pushed himself from his seat, and approached the bar with his empty glass in his hand. He leaned against the bar top right beside the thengisi with the broken horn, and Elijah could see his lips move as he greeted the alien but couldn't hear what he said from this distance. The captain had a charming smile on his face and seemed to be edging closer to the thengisi bodyguard as he spoke, but Elijah could tell that he was using the lack of eye contact to scan the alien's body for where he might be keeping his card keys. Elijah spotted it before Leslie did, he thought—a small metal folio tucked into one of the folds of the guard's robes on the opposite hip from the flirtatious captain at his side.

He leaned over to try to subtly point it out to Harper, but he was distracted by Leslie's hand reaching up toward the alien, his fingertips lightly brushing one broad mandible. The sight made the hairs at the back of his neck bristle and his hand tense around his half-empty glass. He didn't like it, he realized with a faint throb in his gut. He didn't like seeing the captain's hands on anyone else—not even a random alien he didn't know, and not even for the sake of a job. Not when he had that slow smile on his lips that should have been only for Elijah. He felt a shameful heat in his cheeks and took another drink to hide his embarrassed frown. He couldn't let this get to him. The captain was just flirting so that he could get what he needed from the thengisi. He'd probably flirted his way to many, many things before. And it wasn't like Elijah had any claim to him at all. But those rational thoughts didn't make his chest feel any less tight.

The captain was tilting his head at the alien, chatting with him easily. Then Elijah noticed the quick cut of the blond's eyes back toward their table and the soft double tap he gave the bar top with two fingers. Harper got out of his chair without hesitation, but Elijah touched his sleeve before he left the table.

"On his right hip," he murmured, and the lanky young man nodded his understanding before making his way to the bar.

Elijah watched, feeling fairly useless, while Harper stood at the thengisi's right side and did his best to distract him from the captain's flirtations. For a while, they seemed to be vying for the alien's attention, but then the guard clearly made his choice—he turned his back on the captain almost completely and leaned close to Harper, one slender arm from his torso reaching out to caress the young man's sleeve. Leslie accepted defeat but lingered nearby, sipping from his refilled glass and watching Harper's hands repeatedly reach for the thengisi's hip with obvious clumsiness. Elijah tried to hide his cringe in his glass.

Harper almost got close once, and then the alien drew close enough to him that Elijah saw his mandible almost touch Harper's cheek, his hand moving somewhere Elijah couldn't see, and he lost it. Harper visibly flailed his arms as he recoiled, and he must have said something rude, because the thengisi pushed away from the bar with every inch of him looking angry. Leslie's smile was more tense now, but when he tried to calm the guard, the alien turned to glare directly at him with one large yellow eye. The thengisi pointed one clawed finger at the captain and Harper in turn, and then shouldered his way forcibly by the smaller man on his way out of the bar.

Elijah followed him automatically, leaving his drink behind at the table and walking a short distance behind him. He had no idea what he was doing, but he knew that he'd only get one chance to do it. The alien was stalking through the crowd toward the shuttle car gate—if he got there, he'd be gone, and so would their opportunity to get his key. Elijah quickened his pace as much as he could without drawing attention to himself as he circled the room, weaving through travelers and hurrying to cut the alien off at the gate. When he was finally ahead of him, he turned, half jogging back across the room and slamming directly into the approaching thengisi. He caught himself around the alien's middle and tried to catch the metal folio as he fell, but the clip it was attached by was stronger than he expected. The guard heaved him up with both hands on his shoulders and forced him away, and Elijah gave a quiet cry and collapsed against him again with all his weight on one foot.

"I'm so sorry, obhuti," he said, keeping his eyes demurely lowered as his hands pressed into the hard carapace of the guard's torso. "I've hurt my ankle somehow."

The thengisi gave a soft grunt of annoyance but paused as if he was unsure how to proceed.

"Please, just—can you help me to that bench? Forgive me, obhuti. I won't trouble you more."

"Ought to mind where you're going," the alien clicked in a rough voice. He kept three of his hands on Elijah as he half dragged him aside toward the nearest bench, leading him between a group of kineta lingering around the entrance to a shop, and sat him down.

"Walk *more* wisely, ohambi," he grumbled over his shoulder, already turning to start back toward the shuttle gate.

Elijah watched him go, waiting until he'd disappeared into the shuttle car before giving a long sigh. He patted his shirt and untucked it from his belt to let the folio slip free from where he'd hastily tucked it while they walked. How the thengisi hadn't noticed his fumbling with the clip, he didn't know—maybe frustrating him had been more effective than flirting. He slipped the folio into his pants pocket and rushed back to the bar, where Harper was flinching under the captain's scolding as the blond pushed him aside to move toward the exit.

Leslie almost bumped into Elijah on his way out and seemed about to snap at him, too, but the boy put a stalling hand on his arm and plucked the folio from his pocket to press into the other man's palm. The captain paused, looking between the stolen item in his hand and the smiling face of the young thief.

"I sure hope the key we need is in there, because he's probably gonna get real pissed if he gets bothered by any more humans today," Elijah said.

The captain's anger melted into quiet laughter, and he nodded with a gentler look in his eyes as he met Elijah's gaze. "Good job, kid," he said softly. Then he turned to snatch Harper by the back of his collar and pulled him along as he led the two of them out of the bar. When they were a safe distance away, Leslie handed the folio back to Elijah.

"I need to be visible when this happens," he said. "I'm supposed to have business here, so I can't just vanish. I'll be finishing up with our contact and loading the next shipment."

He meant selling the Praevad to an alien who was going to turn it into drugs, Elijah knew. The thought still made him uncomfortable, but along with everything else they had planned for the day, it seemed a minor sin.

Leslie looked between the two younger men. "You two can handle this, right?"

"Wait," Elijah interrupted. "Just us?"

"Don't worry," the captain chuckled. "Harper's better at break-ins than he is at picking people up." He reached into the back pocket of his pants and handed Harper the small disc drive given to him by the information broker. When Harper reached for it, Leslie pulled it back to force the other man to look up into his face. "You are, aren't you, Harper?"

The curly-haired boy glared up at his captain with as much venom as he dared. "I am," he insisted, and he took the drive when Leslie offered it again and tucked it into one of his many coat pockets. "At least the bug was going for it with me," he grumbled.

"Less bitching and more doing your job, huh? If you're caught breaking into an ambassador's apartment, I ain't gonna be able to get you out of the jail they throw you in. And you do *not* want to go to a thengisi jail."

Elijah almost asked why, but then decided he didn't really want to know—at least not until he was safely back on board the Chimera. The captain shooed them away, and Elijah let Harper lead him to the shuttle car back to sector one and the embassy.

There were even more aliens crowding the lobby of the embassy than there were in the welcome area. People clustered in front of desks and waited in lines, frustrated and impatient sighs easily heard from every corner of the room. Elijah could only imagine what so many people could have to talk to the embassy about—he didn't suppose the thengisi took in many refugees.

He followed Harper through the mass of people filling the embassy floor, squeezing between lines and excusing himself as he brushed shoulders with a few waiting travelers. The deeper they went, the fewer people there were, but the more Elijah worried that they'd be questioned. Harper stopped him just before they rounded a corner in a back corridor, and they waited at the end of a short hallway for the sole thengisi to disappear out of sight.

"Hurry," Harper said, and together they rushed for the door in the center of the hall. Elijah scanned a card from the bodyguard's folio that made the terminal beep harshly and turn red, cursing as he tried the next. Harper tapping him impatiently on the back didn't help his nerves, but the third card caused a gentle ping, and then the doors cracked open. They got out of sight and deeper into the corridor before the doors even finished opening, and by the time they closed again, Elijah was already scanning the card through the terminal at the next security block.

The hallway felt even more suffocating than the rest of the station—the same dark, ridged metal made up the corridor around them, but the walls were tighter and the ceiling was lower than the rooms in the rest of the embassy. Elijah had to squint in the darkness to see the terminals the deeper they went and the father from the lights of the main hall, and his racing heart made his breath even shorter. Finally, they reached the last door, and as soon as they were through, Harper began to run his hands along the walls in search of the signs marking the numbers on the apartments. Elijah peered at one, but didn't recognize the script.

"You know how to read thengisi numbers?" he asked, his whisper sounding booming in the empty hall.

"Mostly," Harper admitted in a hiss, eyes narrowed at the signs as his hands brushed over them. "I think it's this one. Try the card."

Elijah did as he was told, swiping the card through the slot in the terminal and sighing with relief when it made a soft beep. Harper shoved him inside and pressed the button on the wall to shut the door behind them. They both stood for a few moments in the darkened apartment, neither able to see very far in front of them. Elijah only knew Harper was still right next to him because he could hear the other man's quiet, wary breathing. Then he heard a soft click, and a beam of light shone forward from the little flashlight Harper held.

"You couldn't have done that in the hallway?"

Harper frowned up at him. "In the hallway, somebody might have seen it. Now shut up and look for someplace a bug alien ambassador might hide a stolen disc drive."

Elijah went as far as he could in the opposite direction from Harper while still having the benefit of the fringes of the other man's flashlight beam. The apartment wasn't as sparse and creepy as Elijah had expected; the walls still had the same rib-like lines and slick feel as the rest of the station, but there were rugs on the floor, and the seating arranged in a circle in the side room looked plush and comfortable. There was even a tea set laid out on one of the tables near the largest sofa. It was good to know that not every thengisi was as menacing and strange as Leslie's friend the information broker.

The pair of intruders checked tables, drawers, and even a hidden compartment behind a painting, but found nothing. Finally, Harper sat on the floor behind a large desk with a personal terminal, his own small tablet in his hands while Elijah held the light over him. Harper tapped at his screen, glancing between the numbers and lines there and the sleek metal lock on the bottom desk drawer. Without touching the keypad on the lock itself, Harper clicked it open after a couple minutes' work and stuffed his tablet back into his coat.

"Hold the light steady," he said, and Elijah leaned over him to shine the beam at a better angle. Harper tugged the drawer open and peered inside, reaching in to feel through the scattered contents. He let out a quiet, triumphant noise, and when he pulled his hand back, he held a small drive identical to the one he'd carried in.

"Got you," he murmured. He passed the drive off to Elijah and replaced it in the drawer with the empty one, carefully rearranging the drawer's contents to hide the fact that they'd been tampered with. He slid it closed slowly, and the lock clicked back into place. "Now let's get the hell out of here."

Elijah gave him a hand up and slid the drive into his pocket, then followed his crewmate back toward the front door of the apartment. Just a few steps away, Harper stopped short in front of him, and Elijah plowed into his back in his rush, almost knocking them both over. Elijah didn't have to ask what had stopped him. There was a voice outside the door. Harper grabbed hold of Elijah's sleeve and reached out for the flashlight, both of them fumbling to turn it off. Harper nearly dropped it in his haste, but it clicked off as the terminal outside gave its quiet beep. Elijah found himself pushed sideways toward a nearby closet, and then his back was against a set of shelves stacked with boxes that gave puffs of dust as he bumped them, and Harper was pressed close against his front in the narrow space as the door clicked quietly closed.

"Don't get any ideas," Harper hissed under his breath, noticeably uncomfortable at being so tight against the boy.

Elijah couldn't help his soft scoff. "No problem there," he muttered, the other man's offended snort the only answer he could get out before they heard the sound of the apartment door slipping open.

Both of them went dead quiet, struggling for absolute silence in the dark closet. Elijah tried to think of anything but what the inside of a thengisi prison was like, but his imagination ran rampant as he listened to the footsteps passing by just outside the door of their hiding place.

An eternity passed in that tiny space, Elijah standing so still that his muscles ached with the effort. What if the ambassador was just home for the night? What if he'd cancelled all of his appointments and meetings to come home and have a nice luxurious supper at home? Maybe invite a few guests over? Elijah fought to keep his breath steady and silent and could sense Harper doing the same beside him. Just when he thought the muscles in his calves would snap from standing so motionless for so long, Elijah heard the footsteps go by them again, followed by the quiet sliding of the front door.

They waited, their ears straining for any hint of sound. When none came, Harper moved, easing away from Elijah by increments as if he expected the door to whoosh open again at any moment. He put his hand on the closet door and turned the handle slowly before poking his head out. He waited again, watching the front door suspiciously, and then he stepped out, pulling Elijah along with him. He didn't have to say a word to get the boy to follow him to the door. Once they were back in the hallway, it took everything Elijah had not to sprint for the end of the corridor. The pair had to stop at one of the connecting doors to wait out a female thengisi who seemed unable to end her conversation with the male lurking by the door to her apartment. When he gave up at last and allowed her to escape inside, Elijah and Harper slipped by.

When they finally arrived back in the main lobby of the embassy, Elijah felt like he hadn't breathed since they entered the apartment. He wanted to laugh, but Harper still looked surly as he walked beside him.

"Why are you making that face?" Elijah asked him. "We got it, didn't we?"

Harper didn't answer right away. They walked a few more steps before the shorter man looked up at him from under his soft mop of curls. "Will you be real with me for a second?"

"Uh, sure?"

"Am I ugly?"

Elijah almost stopped walking. His brow furrowed as he looked down at his crewmate. Harper was skinny, and a little short, and Elijah suspected he looked younger than he was. His reddish hazel eyes were slightly wide, his cheeks dusted with an uneven pattern of freckles. He was twitchy and suspicious and always seemed to be studying you, but—Elijah gave a small shake of his head and answered honestly.

"No."

"You hesitated," Harper said with a scowl.

"I didn't!"

"Just because I'm not tall and blue-eyed and perfect like I came out of an underwear ad doesn't mean that not even a creepy perv bug would want me," he grumbled, hands in the pockets of his coat as they approached the shuttle car gate.

"I think you proved earlier that a creepy perv bug *would* want you, actually," Elijah chuckled, and Harper's hand snapped out to thump him in the arm almost faster than he could see.

"She didn't think so," Harper said more quietly.

Elijah's expression softened. Harper spoke to the thengisi manning the shuttle gate and stepped into the car first once the doors opened. Elijah took a seat across from him and let a few moments pass before he spoke again.

"You mean Brooks?"

Harper straightened a little in his chair, and the mild look of panic that tightened his lips told Elijah that he'd been caught. "She didn't have to be such an asshole about it, that's all," he said, giving a purposeful scoff before turning his head to look out the window at the passing twists of the station outside. "Anyway, forget I said anything."

"I'm sorry I insulted you," Elijah offered. "I'm sure under different circumstances, I'd love to be shut in a closet with you. We can try again when we get back to the ship if you want."

"Fuck you," Harper spat, and he hunched in his seat and crossed his arms, but Elijah smiled faintly at the light kick the smaller man gave his knee.

21

The captain had praised them both upon their return, then commanded that everyone else stay behind while he delivered the drive to Ungolo. While Harper and Park prepped the ship for departure, Elijah lingered on the bridge with Brooks.

"We're going to Altera next, right?" he asked.

"Seems that way," the pilot answered without looking up from her terminal.

Elijah hesitated, not sure if she would be offended by his question. "How are we getting there?"

Brooks paused and glanced over her shoulder. She watched him standing awkwardly by the stairs down to the pilot seats and ticked an eyebrow at him. "How would you get there?"

The boy's eyes lit up. "We'll have to go by the Southern Cross," he said. "But if we take the usual route we'll have to pass through the Coalsack. If we reroute to swing by Beta Crucis, I think we can shave off a few hours."

The woman stared at him a few moments, then cracked a small smile and tilted her chin toward the navigation console behind her. "So make it happen, kid. I'm busy with the paperwork."

Elijah waited for a moment as though he expected her to rescind the offer or maybe call him an idiot, but then he stepped up to the large terminal and took a seat. The screen was different from the ones he'd been allowed to look at on the Federation ships, but the basics seemed similar enough. He scanned through the star charts loaded into the terminal and logged the route he'd chosen to take them from Jannat to Altera, and he smiled to see that the computer's calculations confirmed his suspicions that his way would save them time. Brooks even grinned at him when he sent the information to her console for confirmation.

The bridge doors hissed behind them, and Elijah turned his head to see Leslie enter with a casual stride.

"All set, Captain?" Brooks asked. The blond nodded.

"As set as I can get us. Everyone on board?"

"All accounted for."

"Then let's get starside. We have an important delivery to make."

"Yes, Captain."

Leslie's eyes cut sideways toward Elijah, his head tilting slightly. "You got a new job, kid?"

"I asked him to help me with navigation, Captain. Kid's got an interest, so I thought I'd put him to work."

"Fine by me," the blond chuckled. "Got our course to Altera plotted?"

"Yes, Captain," Elijah answered promptly.

"Good. Then come with me." Leslie beckoned him to follow with two fingers and turned to leave the bridge without looking back. Elijah hurried after him, walking a step behind him down the now-familiar corridor toward his cabin. He tried to ignore the butterflies coming to life in his stomach, but after the surprising rush he'd gotten from the successful break-in, he couldn't help the way his skin subtly tingled at the thought of the older man praising him with more than words.

Leslie opened the door to his cabin and locked it once Elijah was inside with him. Elijah waited for the usual offer to sit, but it didn't come. The captain stepped close to him and reached out to run his fingers through the boy's hair, settling his hand at the side of Elijah's neck with his thumb lightly resting on his jaw. His touch felt warm in the cool air of the ship, but it still sent a shiver up Elijah's spine. There was no escaping the soft gaze of those grey-blue eyes, especially this close to his own face.

"You're more useful than you let on at the start, aren't you?" the captain asked, a sly smirk curling his lips.

"I told you I wanted to earn my place." Elijah was grateful that his voice wasn't betraying the pace of his heart yet.

"You saved my ass, getting that card key the way you did. And Harper said you kept your cool during the retrieval. This isn't too much adventure for you compared to your farm?"

"If I didn't want excitement, I wouldn't have come."

The corners of Leslie's eyes crinkled faintly with his smile. "Good. And you know how to read star charts? You're turning out to be a pretty smart investment, Elijah." He brushed his thumb over the soft line of the boy's jaw.

The boy's stomach gave a little flip. He ought to ask some practical questions while he had the captain alone—about his pay, or about his future on the crew, or even about what the other man had planned for him beyond today. He needed to do it now, before he got lost in the slow movement of Leslie's tongue as he wet his lips.

"I—can I talk to you about something?" he forced himself to say despite the protests of his dick.

"Sure." The captain didn't seem fussed by the change of tone. He removed his hand and dropped back into his desk chair, folding his hands in his lap to listen.

Elijah fidgeted a moment before sitting on the mattress across from the other man. "So," he started, not quite meeting the other man's eyes, "I definitely don't want to have the 'what are we' conversation, so...don't think that's what this is."

"Saying it makes me think that's exactly what this is."

"It's really not," Elijah promised. "I just—I'm trying to be practical. I really like what we do together. I want to keep doing it. But is it really going to be the only reason I'm here? If I do say stop someday, then...what? Do you just leave me at the next drop and tell me 'good luck?' How long do I have to be here before that's not what happens?"

Leslie gave a faint grunt as he pushed himself into a straighter seat, and he cleared his throat before answering. "Well, let's see, now. In the time you've been here, you've helped unload cargo for delivery; you've cleaned the ship from stem to stern; you pick-pocketed a thengisi ambassador's bodyguard, broke into that ambassador's apartment, and stole a disc drive; and you've apparently started doing

Brooks' navigation for her." He let a smirk cross his lips as he looked at the boy. "Sounds to me like you've already got more than one job on board this rig. You're liable to overexert yourself."

"So that means...I can just stay?"

"Here's the deal, Elijah." Leslie reached out to give the younger man's knee a firm, decisive pat. "I like you. You've got a good head on your shoulders, you work hard, and you follow orders. That's more than a lot of ship's captains get from their crew. You keep doing what you're doing, and I'll treat you the same as everybody else—you're here until you wanna leave or you fuck up so bad I can't keep you. Sound good?"

"Yeah," he answered, a relieved, laughing sigh slipping out of him. "That sounds great."

"As far as you and me personally, well—same deal. As long as we're both having fun, we can carry on. If and when that stops, so do we." He shrugged. "Maybe that means you don't want to be on my ship anymore if you're only taking one kind of orders. I'm not gonna worry about that 'til it happens. I recommend you don't, either."

Elijah nodded, looking down at his hands in his lap, then peeked up at the blond with his lips twitching into a smile. "So does that mean you're actually gonna pay me one of these days, Captain?"

"Little shit," the blond laughed, and he put a hand on Elijah's shoulder to push himself up to standing. It was a familiar gesture that sent a pulse of warmth through the boy's chest. "I'll make sure you get your cut."

"Yes, sir," Elijah answered. He stood and headed for the door feeling much more at ease. He definitely shouldn't overcomplicate things. He'd just keep going as things were, and maybe the captain would want to get closer to him too—maybe not. Leslie was making it as easy on him as possible; Elijah didn't have to tortue himself. He had enough work to do, after all.

His mind was full of images of what Altera would be like, how many aliens would be there, and what sorts of things he'd be able to find to spend his hard-earned credits on. Definitely food. Updated star charts. Maybe even some things to make his little closet seem more like a home. He could call his mom again, since they were cut short before—he might even get to talk to his dad or his brothers. Most excitingly, he'd get to see the most advanced station in the Earth Federation. He had no idea what the information broker had given the captain that was going to allow them to get there in one piece, but Leslie hadn't seemed worried, so Elijah tried not to worry, either.

• ● ◆ ● •

Elijah was able to settle into a routine during the long trip back into Federation space. He kept the ship clean, he gave Brooks some relief watching the ship's monitors when she needed to sleep, and he made sure there was always a fresh pot of coffee in the mess, since the crew didn't all keep quite the same hours. He also spent almost every night locked in the captain's cabin with him, which was torturous—both in the way that made his body tremble and for his faintly aching heart. He wouldn't say he was pining, but having the captain so close to him but still somehow at arm's length was wearing on him. One night, Leslie caught him in the little viewing room off the med bay, and they sat together on the patched-up couch and just watched the stars and blackness beyond the glass. Leslie had admitted he was glad to find another person who thought the emptiness of space was just as beautiful as the stars, but when Elijah had smiled at him and the comfortable silence went on a little too long, the blond had locked the door and had the boy's pants off within seconds.

Leslie frequently cut off the conversation when it got too intimate—instead of telling Elijah more about how he came to be on such good terms with a thengisi information broker, he got permission to try hot candle wax on the boy's stomach. That was pretty nice. Instead of talking about where his parents were now, he had fastened a collar and leash around Elijah's neck and bitten his ear, erasing any other thoughts from the younger man's brain. Over the course of the last ten days, Elijah had been tied to the captain's desk chair, blindfolded, and edged for hours before being allowed to orgasm; he'd been made to kneel on the floor with his arms bound while the captain used his mouth; he'd been spanked, suspended, and strapped down in half a dozen different ways. He'd even tried "sounding" at the captain's offer, which apparently involved the insertion of smooth metal rods into the urethra—but that was the first time Elijah had used their agreed-upon safeword and put it a stop to an activity. He still cringed a little to think about it.

Elijah did still find time to sleep, since the captain always dismissed him from his quarters rather than share the room overnight. It was a boundary that the blond was apparently unwilling to cross. Elijah wasn't hurt by the drawn bedroom line specifically, but he couldn't lie to himself and pretend he didn't sometimes wish he could fall asleep with the subtle movement of Leslie's chest under his cheek.

· · ◆ · ·

On their final day approaching Altera, Elijah at last got the nap he'd been hoping for, and when he woke up, he made his way toward the kitchen to scrounge up a snack before they arrived. He heard an angry voice from inside and stopped with his hand on the ladder leading to the upper deck.

"I don't care about your god damn reasons, Cap," Park snapped. "The hell are you thinking leaving your damn toys lyin' around where anybody might walk in on 'em?"

"Don't call him that," Leslie's voice answered firmly, and Elijah's heart jumped a little at the captain coming so immediately to his defense. "I said I was sorry. What the hell do you want?"

"I want you to get your head out of your ass. Or out of his. Or whoever's up whose ass with whatever the fuck you two get up to."

"Fuck you, Park."

"No, man, you listen to me," the engineer pressed. "You know I don't give a shit about what you do with whatever pretty fuckin' boys you pick up on these shithole stations. But you pick 'em up and you leave 'em there; you don't bring these people onto the Chimera and act like they're crew. What the hell are you doing with this kid?"

"He wanted a spot," the captain said. "We ain't so hard up we can't split the cut another way for an extra set of good hands."

"What good hands?" Park asked, his voice a little louder. "The kid's not a soldier; he's not a doctor; he's not a pilot—he sure as hell's not a mechanic. How good his hands are wrapped around your dick don't count, Cap!"

"Now you shut your damn mouth. He's made himself useful on two drops now. He's helping Brooks with navigating. He can learn the rest."

Park gave a disbelieving scoff, and a few beats of silence passed before he spoke again. "You're soft on this kid."

"I ain't soft on him," Leslie insisted.

"Yeah, man, you are. He spends half his time in your room gettin' who knows what done to him, and he's gonna get paid for moving some damn boxes around? Give me a fuckin' break, Cap."

"He moves more boxes around than your crippled ass has in years."

The engineer's voice dropped a little lower. "I'm trying to keep your head on straight here, Cap. You're my friend. I don't want you losing your damn mind over some pretty kid and being the fuckin' wreck you were last time."

Elijah's heart tightened on the deck below. Last time?

"You don't talk to me about 'last time,'" the captain said in an even, dangerous voice.

"I'm the only one who can talk to you about last time!" Park almost shouted. "You need to think about what the hell you're doing before you get—"

Elijah heard a chair scooting sharply on the floor. "I said I ain't soft on him, so I ain't soft on him! The kid came right up and offered himself to me, so I'm taking what I want until I'm done with him. When I'm bored, I'll drop him at the closest station, give him his last paycheck, and say fare-fuckin'-well; is that all right by you?"

"...Yeah, Cap. That's fine by me."

Angry footsteps startled Elijah into movement, and he rushed in hurried silence to the end of the corridor, slipping around the corner by the med bay and pressing his back to the wall in case Leslie came down the ladder. He heard the captain's boots echoing in the opposite direction and let out a slow, full breath, but it did nothing to calm the twisting ache in his stomach.

What had he expected? He had thrown himself at the other man and begged for a place on the ship. So all that talk about being a real part of the crew, getting his own pay, and making his own choices— had that all been just to make Elijah feel better? Had he been imagining the warmth in the blond's words? Park made it sound like the captain did this all the time—picked up young men he liked, slept with them, and forgot them. Had he really promised Elijah anything more?

He could ignore the throbbing in his chest. He should ignore it. He'd known the captain for only a couple of weeks, and he had spent most of that time in his bed. He'd just been feeling attached because of the sex. Not even sex—not really. Maybe he wasn't as cut out for a "mutually beneficial" relationship as he'd thought he was. But the thought of telling the smirking blond that he wasn't going to do it anymore? That he didn't want him? The lie felt bitter in his mouth before he even gave it words. He would just have to be more aware, and not daydream about kissing and gentle touches just because someone had wanted to sleep with him. If he felt uncomfortable the next time the captain called him, he could just say no. It could be that simple, couldn't it?

Elijah went back to his bunk to give Park time to leave the mess hall. The last thing he wanted was to have to look him in the face so soon after their accidental encounter, let alone after the conversation he'd overheard. But by the time he got to the kitchen, it was all he could do to pour himself a cup of coffee and sit and stare at it for a while.

He poured it down the drain when Brooks announced their approach over the intercom.

22

The Space Station Altera was the pride of the Earth Federation. Looking at it from the window at the front of the bridge, it was impossible to really appreciate its scope. It was so big that it actually started to seem small, like it might be a really close up toy instead of a massive station that was home to millions of humans and other aliens. It was a giant ring with two perpendicular passages crossing at the center like spokes on an unimaginably large wheel, and every inch of it was gleaming white in the surrounding darkness. A hundred thousand lights pulsed brightly around the rim of the wheel, slowly changing to red as they led the way downward to the center of the spokes and the extended docking bays.

Elijah kept as close to the glass as he could until the mass of the station disappeared around them as they drew near enough to dock, and then, once he got the okay from Brooks that he wasn't needed, he made his way toward the armory and the landing near the gangway doors. The captain was waiting there, as always, with his long hair tied back into a low, messy bun and his dark jacket brushing his hips as he folded his arms. No matter how much time they'd spent together over the last few days, it was still difficult to see him outside his quarters. This wasn't Les, the man who touched him gently and whose eyes made promises of affection that he didn't intend to keep. This was the captain of the Chimera, who planned to drop him at the nearest station the second he stopped being sexually interested—or interesting. It hurt his heart more than he wanted to let it, no matter how he'd tried to convince himself that Leslie's assurances were honest. He simply had no way of knowing.

Leslie turned to look over his shoulder at him as he approached and seemed to pause for just a moment, his eyes flicking up and down the boy's body before focusing on his face.

"All right, kid? Look like you saw a ghost."

"Yeah," he assured him, glad for the steadiness of his own voice despite the uncertainty of his thoughts. "I'm fine, Captain."

"Then look sharp. And stay unarmed. They'll send someone in to inspect the ship and check the cargo."

"And that's...okay?" He glanced back as Harper appeared in the hallway behind him. "I mean, the information broker—he gave you what you need, right?"

"Ungolo promised me we'd be all set."

"And you stake all our lives on his word?" Harper spoke up, and the captain turned stern, pale eyes on him.

"An information broker ain't much good if his information ain't true. And Ungolo is a real good information broker."

The curly-haired young man's face pulled into a skeptical grimace. "If you say so, Captain."

The intercom beeped, interrupting before Leslie could scold the boy. The captain held the button to answer, and a minute later, Elijah was standing in front of a tall, stoic man in a crisp federation uniform. The navy blue shirt and pants were smooth and stiff, and the officer's insignia and rank gleamed importantly from his chest. The high collar of the uniform shirt even made the man's clean-shaven jaw and stern face look more official, somehow. Maybe they were regulation, too. Elijah looked down at his dark grey work pants that were slowly wearing away at the knees and his stretched out brown henley shirt that had already lost a couple of buttons, and he suddenly felt like a slob. Maybe he could spare some of his first real paycheck for a new change of clothes.

The man stepped into the landing without looking up from the tablet in his hand, leaving them waiting in tense silence while he finished scrolling through whatever he was reading. When he finally looked up, his eyes scanned the three men briefly before landing squarely on Leslie. "You're the captain?" he asked, and the blond moved a step forward.

"Yes sir, that's me."

"You're due for inspection before any of your crew can disembark. I'll need to see your cargo."

"Right this way." The captain led the stoic inspector down the corridor toward the rusty ladder into the cargo bay. Harper and Elijah shared a quick, uncertain look before following at a distance.

In the cargo bay, the two young men lingered by the doors, watching anxiously while the captain walked the inspector through the rows of crates filling the hold. Elijah knew that the containers' legality was kind of a crapshoot—some were boring and totally legal, some were legal goods but unregistered cargo, and the ones hidden away inside the cover of the empty water treatment system were both unregistered and likely to be very, very illegal. If the Federation found those, Elijah wasn't sure what would happen. Harper seemed to think they'd all be lined up and given two shots in the back of the head. They would probably all be thrown in jail, wouldn't they? At the very least, Leslie would. Elijah chewed his lip, his eyes locked on the man in uniform.

The inspector scanned each crate with a small spherical device that shone its blue fan of light across every box in turn, and he checked the data it sent to the tablet in his other hand. When he reached the back of the room and the boiler structure, he paused, and Elijah could sense Harper's whole body tensing beside him. The inspector cupped the little scanner in the palm of his hand and ran his fingers along the barely-visible line marking the break where the secret door opened. Elijah tried to ask the captain what they should do with nothing but his eyes and a nervous frown, but the blond only spared him a brief flick of his eyes before returning his attention to the inspector.

The uniformed man turned his head to look over his shoulder at Leslie. "Open this up, please," he said evenly.

"Harper," the captain called without hesitation, and after a second's pause to peek at Elijah, Harper hurried down the stairs and clambered up the boiler's maintenance ladder. The door gave a heavy thud as Harper twisted the valve to open the lock. The inspector waited patiently while Harper shoved the door open, unfazed by the noisy creaking of the metal hinges.

Once there was space, he stepped inside and lifted his handheld scanner toward the crates of definitely-very-illegal cargo they'd been given by the kineta on Tadmor. Elijah couldn't unclench his hands from the railing, but he felt himself leaning so far forward that he might go straight over if the inspector took very much longer. The man in uniform made a small, pensive sound, and then he stepped out of the hidden compartment and stood facing the captain. He slipped the scanner back into his pocket and tapped his screen a few times before turning the tablet to offer it to Leslie.

"You're all clear," he said. "Hand here, please."

Elijah had to stop himself from shouting, "Really?" That would definitely have been suspicious, so he settled for exchanging a silent, disbelieving look with Harper from across the room. Even the captain hesitated uncertainly, not yet raising his hand to touch the tablet screen.

"You just came from Jannat, right?" the inspector pressed. He lifted his eyebrows at the blond with a subtle tilt of his head. "You're *all. Clear.*"

Leslie paused just a moment more, then placed his hand on the offered tablet and waited for the soft beep that allowed him to move. The inspector spun the tablet and tapped at the screen with the same stern look on his face as before, all trace of conspiratorial hinting vanished in an instant.

"You're set," he said. "How long will you be staying?"

"Four days," Leslie answered, and the inspector gave his screen another few quick touches.

"Cleared." He finally looked up and gave the captain a brief nod. "Welcome to Altera."

· • ◆ • ·

Elijah waited until the gangway doors were closed behind the inspector before he started laughing. Harper even let out a laughing sigh of relief, but the captain turned back to them and settled them with a quieting gesture.

"All right," he said, stifling their laughter but not their excitement.

"That was really it?" Elijah asked. "Ungolo can just make federation inspectors *ignore* our cargo?"

"An information broker trades in secrets and favors, kid. It'll be no mistake that particular officer was our inspector. He must have owed Ungolo something, or wanted something from him. He'll get his debt settled by somebody else who needs to know something. Not sure I'm capable of wrapping my brain around the web that sneaky bug must keep track of. Now settle down and try not to act like we just got away with something."

Leslie turned to press the button on the intercom, and Elijah and Harper waited while the captain's voice echoed over the ship's comm system. "I'm gonna go track down Shrike's contact while the boys unload. Shaw, you get down here and come with me. Everybody else—shore leave. Four days. Park, you take the first rotation on board. Behave yourselves."

The intercom clicked as he released the button on the wall. Elijah kept his jaw tight when the captain turned back to face them, fighting not to read too much into Leslie casually referring to him as one of "the boys." Did he think of Elijah as part of the crew or not? He tried to force the worry to the back of his mind. He had work to do.

"Y'all get back down there and get Shrike's crates off the ship," the captain said, pulling him back to reality. "As soon as I make contact, I'll have them send a transport. Harper, you make sure everything gets on there. Not a trace left behind, you hear?"

"Yes, Captain."

"Once it's gone, y'all clean up the hold and get it sorted for the next drop. Then you can go."

"Yes, Captain," Harper and Elijah said together.

The pair worked quickly, moving crates and taking lists to give to Brooks for the registry. They finished easily and looked out through the doors over the cargo ramp, but there was no one waiting for them, so they passed the time by taking turns playing rounds of a shooter game on Harper's tablet. A pair of men in a hover transport appeared after an hour or so, and the young men hopped down from their seats on top of the crates. The men at least greeted them and helped them load the cargo, but they weren't any chattier than Shrike's men on

Tadmor had been.

When they were finished, Elijah stood beside Harper on the empty catwalk and peeked sidelong at him. He almost asked if the other man wanted to go out onto the station together, but before he could even form the question, Harper had given him a quick mock salute, told him to close up the cargo bay, and scampered back across the hold to the exit. That answered that, he guessed.

He was eager to explore Altera and see everything the Federation's flagship station had to offer, but instead he lingered near the gangway landing. It would be stupid to ask Leslie to come out with him, wouldn't it? They'd had so little time and too much to do on Jannat, but it would be nice to have someone to show him around, or just to walk with for a while. It had seemed too easy and normal to just have a drink with the handsome blond back on Tadmor—but that time, Leslie had invited him. And back then, Elijah hadn't yet spent any time with a warm, affectionate feeling in his belly.

Elijah paced the corridors around the landing, rubbing his palms on his pants to keep them from feeling too clammy. It was rational for Leslie not to be attached to him, but that didn't mean that Elijah had to pretend he wasn't interested in *him*. Nothing had changed, really. The captain didn't owe him anything. Elijah just had to keep his head on straight.

When the captain's boots sounded on the deck ladder, Elijah jumped. He tried to turn the corner casually, as if he was heading for the gangway at that moment by complete coincidence, and he gave his best smile as the captain met his gaze.

"Hey, kid," he said easily. "Heading out for your big Federation adventure?"

"I—yeah, I think so." He hesitated and forced himself not to wipe his palms again and draw attention to them. "I was actually going to ask if you wanted to...come with me, I guess. You know, just—it'd be nice to have someone to show me around."

"Thought you were glad to be off on your own, farm boy," Leslie teased, and the sly smile on his lips made the boy's stomach ache. His soft tone was too sharp a contrast to the harsh shouting he'd directed at the ship's engineer that day. "Lonely already?"

"The difference between here and home is that now I pick my

company," Elijah answered, refusing to take his eyes from the other man's face.

The captain hesitated, frowning faintly as though he didn't want to answer. Before he could try, a side door thunked open nearby, and the Chimera's pilot appeared, pulling her shaggy ginger hair into a ponytail as she walked.

"Sure," Leslie said quickly, and he nodded toward the woman as she approached. "Hey Brooks. The kid here wants some company for his first Altera excursion. You want to come with?"

"If there's drinks involved, sure," Brooks answered, and Elijah smiled at her to hide his disappointment. A group of three wasn't exactly what he'd had in mind—but he definitely didn't want to say that out loud, let alone in front of the taunting lady pilot. "I can play tour guide for a little while."

"Great," Elijah said, hoping his smile didn't seem too forced.

23

Inside, Altera was sleek and shining, with high walls, vast windows, and busy transports that shot to and from a hundred airlocks set at intervals along the massive open space. It was the size of five or six cities and just as crowded. Every level was like its own town—there were restaurants, shops, housing, and even green spaces with real, living trees and beautiful water fountains. Statues of Federation heroes lined the broad walkway from the docks, and banners bearing the colors of the various branches of the Federation hung from every spare space on the walls. After staying so long on the cramped Chimera, being in the citadel of the Federation and looking up at the distant ceiling almost felt like being back at home.

Elijah walked close beside the captain, though Brooks was more chatty with him. Leslie wouldn't hold his gaze and tended to give brief answers to his questions. Elijah split the cost of new star charts with Brooks and sat for a while looking over them with her at one of the many bars on their level, drinking their beers and checking over the updates to the charts loaded into the Chimera's navigation system. The captain sipped his drink and listened with far less interest in star charts than either of his subordinates had, but Elijah caught the blond watching him silently more than once. Each time, he tried to offer the man a smile or draw him into the conversation, but Leslie seemed too distracted to participate. Elijah told himself he was imagining it, but the other man even seemed to be sitting unnecessarily far away from him. This was more than the regular distance Leslie always kept between them—it was almost cold.

When they'd finished their drinks and were preparing to move on to the next level for further exploration, the captain stopped at the door of the bar instead of following them.

"I've got some things to take care of here," he said, speaking to Brooks more than to Elijah. "So I'll catch y'all back on the ship. Make sure you're back in time for your rotation," he added with a pointed look at the pilot, and then he turned with his hands in his jacket pockets and walked away from them into the crowd.

Elijah watched his back until it disappeared, unable to keep the slight slump out of his shoulders. This hadn't been the outing he'd hoped for at all. Leslie would barely even talk to him. There must be something else on his mind—Elijah hadn't given the other man any reason to start avoiding him. At least, he didn't think so.

He swayed a little as Brooks elbowed him in the arm and looked down at her smirking face.

"Trouble in paradise, kid?" she asked. Elijah must have shown more of his disappointment on his face than he intended, because her expression softened as she looked up at him. "Something happen for real?"

"No," Elijah answered honestly. Nothing *had* happened. Nothing real, anyway. All the confusion was just in his head—his growing feelings for the captain, his frustration, his likely overreaction to the captain's conversation with Park—none of it had happened to anyone else.

"I get the feeling I was intruding on what might have been a date," Brooks pressed, and Elijah sighed through his nose.

"Not much chance of that when one of the people making up the date invited you in the first place." He gave a dismissive wave and tried his best to smile. "It's fine. I think me and Cap have just...misunderstood each other."

The woman hesitated, eyes narrowed suspiciously at him, and she chewed the corner of her lip for a moment. "I get it," she said, nodding her head as though she'd made a decision. "So where to next, kid?"

"Well," Elijah started, then paused, looking down at himself and pulling at a loose thread near the collar of his shirt. "I guess I thought I should get some clothes that aren't falling apart."

"You're god damn right you should." Brooks slapped him on the back and tilted her head toward the nearest transport station. "Come on. Let's make you look a little less bumpkin and a little more renegade starship crew."

· · ◆ · ·

Elijah let Brooks help him choose a couple of new pairs of pants and shirts from the store she recommended. She tried to talk him into buying a long shirt that had the front of the torso cut out of it to show his stomach, but he adamantly refused despite her assurances that the captain would love it. He instead put on a hardier pair of black work pants with a bit of decorative piping along the hips and thighs, a grey long-sleeved shirt, and a warm jacket that zipped up at an angle and wrapped a high collar around his chin. He hadn't realized how worn and old his clothes felt until he slid on a new pair of boots that actually fit him snugly and hadn't had the insoles worn down by two years of hard work.

"Not bad, kid," Brooks assured him as she handed him his bag. He'd thrown his old clothes away but spent the credits on a couple of similar outfits—mostly to avoid having to hide out in his underwear while he washed his single set of clothes in the middle of the night. "You want to go get some ice cream, finish drowning out your sorrows?"

"I don't have sorrows," Elijah laughed.

"I know the look when a cute boy's got sorrows. I don't aim to get into your business, but if there's something I can help with, you can ask."

"It's not just my business I'd be telling," he admitted in a softer voice. "But I'm fine—promise. You don't have to keep babysitting me. I'm sure you have stuff you'd rather be doing."

"Well all right," the woman said, giving him a teasing smirk. "But I'm gonna check your bunk for empty pints later on."

"Feel free," he chuckled, but he hesitated when they exited the store. "Brooks," he started, only briefly glancing up at her face from the floor, "this might be a weird question—and you might not even know the answer—but...do you know if the captain has ever done this sort of thing before? Like with me, I mean. If he's...brought people on the ship for the same reason he brought me."

"Feeling jealous, kid?"

"It's not that. Just something he said made me wonder about it." It was only half a lie—but he wasn't about to tell Brooks that he'd been eavesdropping on an argument between the ship's captain and its engineer.

The pilot shrugged. "I've seen people pass through before when we stop somewhere. He's not the only one who brings people back sometimes—we've all got needs, don't we? But the captain's always kept it strictly eyes-front straight to his cabin and back again, you know? We've definitely never added someone on to the crew because the captain liked the look of their ass."

"I'm flattered, I guess."

"Don't worry; I'm sure you've got more going for you than that cute little bubble butt."

"What—I don't have a bubble butt!" Elijah resisted the urge to twist around and try to look, but Brooks laughed anyway.

"Whatever helps you sleep at night."

"Anyway, I also I wanted to ask something else weird."

"Hit me."

"Do you know if there's...some sort of—I don't know," he stalled, letting out a quiet laugh to hide his embarrassment. "Some sort of...store where I could find some...things that you'd use—you know, privately—"

Brooks stared at him, deadpan through his stammering. "You're trying to ask me about a sex shop?"

"I...guess so? It's weird; sorry. Never mind."

She sighed and turned him by the shoulder to point him toward the nearest transport. "Level six, sector B. The place is called 'Midnight Confessions.' I assume it's still there—I haven't been here in a while. If it's not, try level two. It's pretty grody there; you'll probably find something."

"I don't think I want someplace 'grody.'"

"Then you'd better hope Midnight Confessions is still open." She gave him a little shove between the shoulder blades to move him along.

Elijah laughed, and he waved at her as they parted ways on the broad concourse. He walked with his bag in hand, hesitant to even take the transport to level six. A thought had been rolling around in his head ever since Leslie had abandoned them at the bar—maybe Elijah was coming at this all wrong. He'd been so worried about his feelings, and about that desperate, thumping beat of his heart as he looked up at the blond and longed for those lips to close over his—he stopped mid-stride and snorted a quick breath in and out to center himself. Those exact thoughts. Those were the ones he needed less of. He was going too fast. He refused to be the person who fell in love after a month of knowing someone. Even thinking the word "love" gave him a bubbly, uncomfortable feeling in his stomach. That wasn't what this was. This was—a crush, maybe. He could allow himself a crush. And he could prove to a crush that he wasn't going to be like whatever happened "last time." He could expand the number of things on Leslie's list that he had first-hand knowledge of.

He rode on the transport squeezed between a woman in a sleek suit whose eyes never left her tablet and an insalar in an almost-sheer toga whose eyes never left *him*. This one had a streak in his dark hair, too, but it was green. Elijah wondered if they all had them and he just hadn't noticed, and if they were natural, or what they meant. He drummed his fingers on his knees with his bag tucked between his ankles and looked straight across at the opposite wall instead of letting his attention drift to the lean alien beside him. He was certain he could feel the insalar looking at him as he left the transport, so he took the long way to sector B to avoid his admirer realizing his embarrassing destination.

The shop's windows were blackened, but the sign above the sliding doors read "Midnight Confessions" in neon purple calligraphy, so Elijah swallowed once and walked through the entrance. The store itself was dimly lit and smelled of heady perfume, and every wall was lined with boxes and displays—some of which Elijah could identify and some he couldn't. An entire section was dedicated to lacy lingerie, which was somehow even more embarrassing to look at than the strangely-shaped silicone toys. He didn't even know what he was looking for. What could he possibly do that would impress someone as obviously experienced as Leslie was?

A woman appeared at his side so silently that he jumped.

"Can I help you find anything?" she asked with a smile, and Elijah was sure the one he returned looked more like a grimace.

"I'm...not sure?"

"Just exploring? I can help you with some ideas, if there's anything you're interested in." She watched him evenly, a practiced lack of judgment in her voice.

Elijah hesitated. There was no point in coming here at all if he was going to be shy. He didn't feel shy around Leslie—and if being tied up and spanked didn't make him shy, it would be ridiculous to be self-conscious about just looking around a sex shop. This woman did this for a living. If anyone could help him figure out what he needed, she probably could.

"I guess I'm looking for something I can...surprise someone with."

"What kind of someone?"

"Um. Well, I'm not sure. We're sort of not really in a—but it's—"

The woman let a bit of amusement touch her professional smile. "I mean is it a woman or a man? Or someone not human?"

"Oh—oh!" He laughed. "Sorry. It's a man. A human man."

"Got it. So are you looking for something for you, or for him?"

Elijah's brow furrowed slightly. "For...me, I think. He's more, uh...aggressive than me, I guess you'd say."

She ticked an eyebrow at him and tilted her head. "How aggressive are we talking? Are you looking for something in the 'aggressive' department?"

"Pretty aggressive," Elijah chuckled. "But I...feel like he's probably already got everything like that that he needs."

"Well, if it's a surprise..." The woman trailed off and beckoned him to follow her with one crooked finger. She led him to a display full of small foil packets and stood to one side to let him see the rows of discreet packages. "Have you ever worn a cock ring before?"

"A wh—" Elijah felt heat in his face despite his intentions. "Uh, no. No I haven't. Is that...is that exactly what it sounds like?"

"Pretty much," she answered with a smile. "It's meant to restrict blood flow, so it helps make your erection firmer and delay your orgasm. Does that sound like something you and your human man would like?"

"I...I think so. It's something that I can do...to myself?"

"It wouldn't be much of a surprise otherwise, would it?" the woman teased. "Yes. For a beginner, I'd recommend these." She picked up a blue packet and offered it to him. "It's made of silicone, and they're disposable, but you can use them a half dozen times before you need to throw them out. They're perfect for trying out."

Elijah took the packet from her and fidgeted with the firm ring inside the foil. He had no idea what he was doing. What was his plan? To just sneak into the captain's quarters, wait there with his pants off, and hope for the best? He didn't know anything about seducing anyone—when it came to the girls he'd been with, there had usually been a couple drinks at a party involved, or else Corinne had left him a note to meet her somewhere after dark. It was a far cry from trying to come on to someone like Leslie, who Elijah expected had seen just about everything under a dozen suns. But he'd left Dhat-Badan to have new experiences, hadn't he?

"How do I put it on?"

The woman smiled at him. "It's easy. Once you're hard, you just put a little bit of lubricant around the inside of the ring and stretch it on so that it's snug right at the base of your penis."

"That's it?"

"That's it. Do you need some lubricant?"

Elijah was positive that Leslie would have an abundance in his cabin, but he'd rather not go digging through the other man's things. So he said, "Yes, please."

With his purchases tucked safely away in the bottom of his clothing bag, he made his way back to the transport that would take him to the docking bay. He looked straight ahead of him the entire way and tried to quell the butterflies already moving in his stomach.

24

Elijah had mildly panicked outside the captain's door, but it had been unlocked, and no one had answered his knock, so he stepped inside and hurried to slide the door closed behind him. The room felt strange without Leslie in it—quiet and still, like being in a classroom after school or in your parents' bedroom. It smelled like the captain. Elijah could smell his sweat and the leather of his jacket, and the faint, warm scent of his skin. The boy lingered by the entrance a while, not sure how to proceed. The sheets were rumpled—had Leslie slept again, or were they still a mess from the last time Elijah had been there? He chewed his lip, his stomach clenching slightly at the thought.

He took a determined breath and let it out with a puff of his cheeks. If he was going to do this, he'd better hurry up and do it before the captain came back and found him just standing around creepily in his room. Elijah stripped down but hesitated with his clothes in his hands, taking a few false starts in either direction before settling on tucking them out of the way on the bottom shelf of the captain's nightstand. He dug the foil packet and the small bottle of lubricant from the bottom of his bag and then shoved it to the side of the nightstand before he took a seat at the edge of Leslie's mattress.

"Intense Pleasure for Longer," the packet promised. Elijah stared down at it for a moment's worth of hesitation, then tore it open. The fat little ring inside the foil was thick and stiffly malleable. Elijah spent a few moments squishing it experimentally between his fingers and glancing uncertainly between the small circle and his own soft dick. He stretched the ring between his thumbs to test its elasticity, trying to eyeball it against his anticipated girth. It was surprisingly stretchy. The woman hadn't said anything about sizes, and Elijah wasn't so blessed that he was breaking records, so it would probably be fine, right?

The little folded instructions inside the packet told him essentially what the woman in the shop had said—get hard, put it on, and enjoy. Getting hard would be the easy part, especially lying in Leslie's bed with the smell of his hair in Elijah's nostrils. Elijah propped up a pillow, leaned against the headboard, and took his small bottle of lubricant from the nightstand to run a drop around the inside of the ring as he was told. He set the ring carefully on top of its open packet at his side and settled back. If this was the easy part, why did he feel so nervous about touching himself in the captain's bed? He'd answered his own question—because it was Leslie's bed. Elijah hadn't done anything in this bed that hadn't been at the express command of the handsome blond. He shut his eyes and imagined Leslie's voice in his ear, whispering to him to spread his legs and touch himself. Elijah's hand slid down his torso and wrapped around his awakening prick, slowly beginning to stroke it into readiness.

When he felt his stomach jump for the first time, he stopped himself and took a calming breath before he looked down at the ring again. His hands shook just a little as he picked it up, and he bit his lip in concentration as he stretched the ring wide, shifting his hips to get a better angle as he slid the slicked silicone down to the base of his cock. He touched it a few times to make sure it was going to stay in place, and then he paused, waiting for something amazing to happen. He gave his dick a few experimental strokes, but there wasn't any of the "intense pleasure" the package had suggested. He felt a little numb, actually. And slightly cold to the touch. He lifted his erection and let it bounce back against his stomach once or twice. Was he missing something? He checked the instructions again, shifted the ring around his base, but everything seemed to be in order. Maybe the intensity came later?

The sound of footsteps outside the door startled him, and he shoved the empty packet off of the mattress in a rush and scrambled back to the center of the bed. Should he pose? Don't be stupid. But he had to lay somehow. Maybe he should have found the captain's straps.

A click and a sharp hiss sounded the impending opening of the door, and Elijah managed to get into a somewhat-reasonable position against the headboard, but he was halfway through pulling the blanket up around him, deciding that defeated the purpose of being naked, and kicking it away again when he looked up to see Leslie standing in the doorway.

The blond stared down at him with blatant bewilderment on his face, his grip tight on the strap of the bag over his shoulder as the door closed behind him.

"Hey there," he said after what felt like a millennium of tense quiet.

"Hey," Elijah answered, a thousand times more awkwardly.

"You letting yourself in now?"

"I wanted—I thought you might...want to try something else," the boy said, hoping he sounded more enticing and sexually-awakened than he felt as he forced his legs to spread slowly. "I got you a surprise."

"So I see," Leslie murmured, and he dropped his bag to the floor as he approached the bed. He ran one warm hand up Elijah's bare thigh but paused before he reached his hip. "You're getting more adventurous," he said, his eyes on the boy's suddenly much hotter erection.

Elijah shivered under his touch. "Is that bad?"

"Absolutely not," the captain chuckled. His pale eyes traveled up Elijah's torso until he met the boy's gaze. "Now, what is it exactly you thought I might want to try?"

Elijah struggled to keep his eyes from the other man's thumb casually brushing the inside of his thigh. "I was wondering...how much weight those bars on the ceiling can hold."

Leslie's nostrils flared almost imperceptibly, and a slow smile crept across his face. He leaned forward slowly, his gaze dropping to the boy's full lips. "Enough," he purred, his grip tightening on Elijah's tensed leg muscle.

• ● ◆ ● •

The smooth leather straps had warmed quickly against Elijah's skin, and Leslie had tightened them carefully snug around him, but it had still been a slightly disorienting experience to be lifted from the mattress and left to sway a foot or so above the bed. His arms were bound behind his back, his forearms tied together and strapped firmly to his sides, and he was supported by the chest, waist, and hips, his thighs spread and legs kept bent by ropes tying his ankles close to his rear. Elijah shifted as Leslie pulled on the pulley strap, raising him up just one more click before securing him. This was definitely the most exposed Elijah had ever felt, but his body wasn't responding with fear—every inch of his skin burned with anticipation, and his dick ached from lack of stimulation.

"All right, Elijah?" Leslie asked as he circled around to the boy's front. "Comfortable?"

"Yeah," he croaked in response. He tried to swallow but had no luck wetting his throat. The captain had removed his shirt and jacket, and Elijah found it difficult to lift his eyes from the taper at the other man's waist. The scattering of scars on his torso did little to mar the view. His pants hung low enough to show just a touch of curls, and the way he stood with one hip slightly cocked felt like a promise of good things to come—especially with Elijah's head positioned almost precisely at hip height.

Leslie reached out to cup Elijah's chin and draw his gaze upward. "Yeah?" he echoed, and Elijah quickly corrected himself.

"Yes, Captain."

"Good." He gave the boy's cheek an affectionate stroke with his thumb. "You wanted to try something a little rougher? Something that hurts a little more?"

"Yes, Captain," Elijah breathed, his skin prickling expectantly. He wanted the same wash of heat that he had felt the first time the captain had struck him—the surprising rush of pleasure following the sting and the tingling, tense anticipation of the next hit. If it impressed Leslie, then all the better.

"Something harder than my hand," the captain murmured to

himself, and he crouched to tug a shallow trunk from underneath his bed.

Elijah couldn't see beyond the open lid, but his pulse quickened as the sight of the thin rod Leslie produced, one end wrapped to form a handle and the other bearing a small, flat flap of leather. He'd been around enough animals to know a crop when he saw one—but they'd never made his dick twitch with excitement before. Leslie ran his fingers down the length of the rod slowly, allowing Elijah to watch his measured movement before slapping the crop experimentally against the palm of his hand. The soft crack caused a tight heat in the pit of Elijah's belly, and he peeked up into the captain's smirking face.

Leslie moved closer to him, and a single swift flick of his wrist brought the flat end of the crop sharply up against the boy's stomach, causing his back to arch away instinctively from the sting.

"No slouching, Elijah," the blond said firmly.

Elijah's muscles clenched, his bonds digging into his skin as he hung slightly straighter in them.

"It's handy that you're wearing that cock ring," Leslie mused as he tilted his head at the boy. "I don't want you leaking all over my bed until I'm ready for you to come." He gave the front of Elijah's thighs a quick swat with the crop, making him jump, and then he reached for the cabinet by the headboard to retrieve the soft blindfold Elijah recognized. He slid it onto the boy's face with gentle hands, and Elijah's world went dark.

The cover served its intended purpose—all of Elijah's attention was on the sensation of the cords keeping him aloft, the sound of his own expectant breathing, and most importantly, the anticipation in his chest as he waited for any sign of movement from the other man. He didn't hear the captain take a step, but he felt the first strike of the crop against his ass and hissed, his thighs tensing in their ropes. That. That was what he wanted. That burning in his skin, the slowly receding wave of pain that surged forward again with the next hit before it could fully wash away. It was more painful than Leslie's hand—a sharper, more focused pain—but it sent that much more of a thrill up the boy's spine, curling pleasure at the nape of his neck.

Whenever Elijah began to relax and sink into the sensation, Leslie snapped the crop on his stomach or the fronts of his thighs, startling him back into attention. His entire body trembled with effort, and as the blows came faster and harder, Elijah started to wince at them. He tried to breathe slowly to keep his focus, but the pain was becoming overwhelming, and his soft, eager moans were beginning to change into flinching whimpers. He remembered what the captain had told him when they started—that if it was too much, he should use the words Leslie had told him and say so. But he would be disappointed, wouldn't he? That maybe Elijah wasn't as much fun as he'd thought. He'd said they'd keep doing this until one or the other of them wasn't having fun anymore. If Elijah was too soft, would Leslie stop having fun? Somewhere in the rational part of Elijah's brain, he knew that he should speak up. Every new hit washed an unpleasant burn over him, and he was almost certain the captain had broken the skin. But he couldn't make his mouth form the word to make it stop. Stupid crush, stubborn determination, or unexplained affection he couldn't quite admit—whatever the reason, the thought of Leslie never wanting to touch him again was enough to make him grit his teeth and try to wait out the other man's abuse of his backside.

He hoped that the captain would notice—that he would sense his partner's discomfort and stop on his own—but that relief didn't come. Finally, when Elijah felt the prickling heat of what he was sure was a drop of blood rolling down the back of his thigh, he choked out one more breath and managed the word, "Red!"

Elijah held his breath, half expecting the next blow to land regardless, but the captain had paused.

"What?" Leslie asked, sounding a little short of breath himself.

"Red," Elijah repeated, a bit weaker this time. The blindfold was lifted from his eyes a moment later, and Leslie grabbed hold of the loose strap to release the pulley lock and lower the boy down to the mattress. His hands worked quickly on Elijah's bonds, freeing his limbs and allowing him to relax onto the bed with wincing slowness. Elijah didn't realize until he flexed his hands that he'd been clenching them so tightly that his fingernails had left marks in his palms. For a few breaths, Elijah couldn't do more than lie still, the sheen of sweat on his skin chilling him in the ship's processed air.

"Turn on your side," the captain said, urging the boy over by his shoulder. "We need to get that off you."

Elijah's brow furrowed in confusion as he was moved, but realization made him jump as the blond's careful hands slid the silicone ring from him, and he laid back down on his stomach with guilty heat in his cheeks. "I'm sorry," he said softly, and he heard the slow exhale from the other man's nostrils.

"Why did you wait until it was too much?" Leslie asked him. Elijah recognized the slight accusation in his voice, though the other man was clearly trying to hide it.

"I'm sorry," he said again, but the captain was already walking into the bathroom. Elijah pushed unsteadily up onto his elbows and looked over his shoulder as Leslie returned with a small first aid kit.

"I ought to make you walk to the med bay yourself and let Davies see this," the blond answered sharply. He flattened a hand on the small of Elijah's back. "Keep still."

Elijah hissed at the sting of the antibacterial gel the other man smoothed across his skin. This had backfired. He hadn't been able to hold on til the end. Now Leslie was irritated at him, and for good reason—all he'd proven was that he couldn't be trusted to know his own limits. He laid still while the captain cleaned up his broken skin, his chin in the blanket and his eyes on the floor. When the blond's hands left him, he peeked up and saw a stern frown looking back at him.

"You have to tell me if you're not ready for something," Leslie insisted. "If something hurts too much. I can't read your god damn mind."

"I know," Elijah answered. He slowly sat up, feeling for the first time like he ought to cover himself in front of the other man. This wasn't how he'd wanted this to go at all. "I just wanted to—"

"I don't care what you wanted to do," the captain snapped. "You've stopped me before when it was too much. I know you know how. What the hell's the problem now?" He stood in front of Elijah with his hands on his hips, but none of the playfulness remained in his stature. The man gave a huffing sigh and scratched roughly at the back of his head, softly tinkling the metal beads in his hair as he looked away from Elijah's face. "You're just a kid," he muttered with a frown. "I ought to've known better."

"I'm not a kid!" Elijah protested—though he felt very much like one right now. "I just—I'm new to all this stuff, okay?" He didn't say what was really lurking in his chest, waiting to be shouted. He didn't say that he just wanted Leslie to be kind to him, like he had been before. That he wanted to make him happy even if it meant being uncomfortable himself. That somehow, over the span of just a few weeks, Elijah had gone from desperate and curious to wanting the blond captain's hands on him any way he could get them there—to wanting to taste his lips and hear the measure of his breathing as he slept. Elijah wanted to talk with him, drink with him, see new worlds with him. He wanted to know everything about him and tell him everything there was to know about himself. Most of all, he wanted Leslie to want these things, too. He wanted the Chimera's captain to be soft on him.

"Les," he tried again, not missing the subtle crease in the other man's brow at the use of his name, "I'm sorry, I didn't—"

"I think you ought to go," Leslie interrupted. "You're gonna want to rest if you still want time to explore the station before we leave."

Elijah's mouth snapped shut, and his fingers curled into the rumpled blanket at his sides. He swallowed once before he moved to the edge of the bed.

"Yes, Captain," he murmured softly. The blond was already brushing past him, and the bathroom door slid shut a moment later, leaving Elijah alone in the cabin to dress himself. He flinched as he pulled his pants and underwear up over his tender ass but hurried to slip on his shirt despite the sting. He gathered up his shopping bag and hesitated as he spotted the cock ring still sitting where Leslie had left it on the nightstand. Should he take it with him? Or leave it?

Elijah reached out to pick it up, then bent to take the foil packet and instructions he'd left discarded on the floor. It had been a stupid idea. With a heavy weight in his chest, he tucked the embarrassing reminder into his bag and left the silent captain's quarters. Maybe this had all been a stupid idea.

25

Rest simply wasn't happening. Elijah had returned to his room long enough to put away his things—including hiding the cock ring in the very back of his single drawer—but the thought of lying there on his bunk and running over the last hour in his head a hundred times nauseated him. He needed something to occupy himself. Something to take his mind off of the way Leslie had looked at him with such annoyance and disappointment.

He made his way to the bridge and settled gingerly into the seat behind the navigation console so that he could update the ship's star charts. He focused on the data transfer, double checking the coordinates they'd entered for their next destination and pretending he couldn't feel the ache in his chest or the invisible weights tied to his limbs. No amount of calculations was going to be able to keep him from the overwhelming sense that he'd ruined everything. He could have just kept doing what they'd been doing—it was fun, and new, and hot as hell. Even being strung up and hit with the crop had been great at first. If he'd just been honest and told Leslie to slow down...

Elijah leaned his elbows on the console and put his head in his hands. Why did his stupid heart have to make everything so complicated? He was being ridiculous, and he knew it. He couldn't help how he felt. If he had feelings for Leslie, then he had them—but he *could* help what stupid things he did in response to them. He wanted to be honest. But how could he admit to the captain how warm he made Elijah feel when he'd heard him threaten to leave the boy behind at the nearest station when he got bored with him? And now he'd made him angry by not keeping up his end of their deal—by breaking their trust. It was still so early, and they'd only known each other for a brief while, really. Just a few weeks. The best thing to do would be to apologize again once they'd both calmed down, and try to set his feelings aside for now. Like he should have done before he got the bright idea to wait naked in the captain's bunk.

The boy let out a faint, suffering groan, but he was startled upright by the sound of the bridge doors hissing open. Brooks tilted her head at him from the entrance.

"What are you doing here, kid? Midnight Confessions didn't work out?"

"Not exactly. Anyway," he continued immediately, hoping to cut off any further questions, "I wanted to get these new star charts in. They're even better than the ones I had back home. I guess that's what you get on a station like Altera."

Brooks peered at him in silence for a moment, then pressed her lips into a thin line as she walked by on her way to the pilot's seat. "I just came to check on the monitors before I headed out again," she began in a casual tone, leaning over her console without sitting. "The bunch of us are going out to have a few drinks at this club called Vertex on level two. You coming?"

"Everyone?"

Brooks's console gave a quiet ping at her touch before she leaned away and turned back to face him. "Well, not Davies. Teetotaler, you know. But everybody else. Captain said he might come later."

Elijah hesitated. Maybe that was what he needed. Forget about his apparently somewhat-unwelcome feelings for Leslie, his screw-up, and his embarrassment, and just be part of the crew for a little while. That was why he'd come out here in the first place, after all. It hadn't been to get into a relationship—of whatever kind he and Leslie had. He'd come to have new experiences and meet new people and see new things. And Brooks thought enough of Elijah to invite him, which to him spoke volumes about his position in her esteem.

"Sure," he said. "Sounds fun."

"Then move your ass, cabin boy," the woman answered, already moving toward the doors again.

Elijah stood and hurried after her. "I thought I was navigator now?"

"Probationary," she teased.

· • ◆ • ·

Club Vertex was a little grody, just like Brooks had warned him level two was. The bar looked like it used to be a warehouse—bare metal beams and vents criss-crossed the high ceiling, and the floors were all smooth metal. Second- and third-floor lofts with harsh steel railings encircled the main floor, which was split between high-top tables, extended couches, and an open dance floor, all surrounding the expansive circular bar. The whole place was dimly lit with red lights, and the air thumped with music so loud that Elijah felt it in his chest. Brooks, Park, Harper, and Shaw had claimed one of the long sofas against the wall, and Elijah sat with them, his elbows on his knees and a beer in his hand. He'd seen Shaw actually crack a faint smile a couple of times during one of Park's rants, and though Harper kept glancing around toward the exits, he had relaxed, too.

It was nice to forget about his personal drama for a while. He drank, shared a few stories, and even ventured out onto the dance floor once he had a few pints of beer in him. Others came and went from the crew's table, chatting and visiting the way fellow drunks do, and once when Elijah returned to the table to take a rest and finish his beer, an insalar in a nearly-sheer blue robe lounged on the sofa next to his shipmates. It was hard for Elijah to keep his eyes off of the alien—his silver skin shimmered in the moving lights of the club, dancing shadows across the sharp dips in his collarbones. Fully black eyes followed Elijah intently as the boy sat nearby. His face was calm and familiar and ethereally beautiful, and the slow smile he gave Elijah, half hidden by a glimmering curtain of long, loose black hair that spilled over his shoulders like flowing ink, made the skin on his arms prickle into goosebumps. When the alien ran long fingers through his hair to push it from his face, a hidden teal blue streak appeared at his temple.

"There he is," Park was slurring from across the table. "That there's our ship whipping boy, ain't you, kid?"

"Yeah, yeah," Elijah grumbled as he reached for his half-empty glass.

"We were just talkin' about you. 'Bout how you like to get all tied up and knocked around."

"Give me a fuckin' break, Park," the boy sighed. He drained his glass and thunked it back down onto the table with the others. "Ever since I showed up, all you've talked about is who I'm fucking and how I like it. I'm gonna think you're in love with me," he taunted, drawing a bubbling snort of laughter from the Chimera's pilot.

"Fuck you," the engineer snapped back. "I walked in on you all naked and trussed up like a dog; I get to talk all the shit I want."

"You were trussed up?" Brooks asked. She sat forward on the sofa, suddenly interested. "Trussed up like how?"

"Gagged and all," Park went on. "We all know how Cap likes 'em. It's a wonder you can ever even sit down, boy."

Elijah put his face in his hands and rubbed his palms vigorously over his cheeks to settle himself before he looked up again. "So anyway, if you're done telling the whole world my goddamn business," he said with a glare in Park's direction, "can we just pretend to get along or at least leave each other alone? Just today?"

The engineer scoffed into his glass but let the matter drop. Brooks told a story about the time she got drunk and spent twenty minutes banging on the airlock of a ship that definitely wasn't the Chimera and demanding to be let in. She had to be hauled away to sleep off the booze in a jail on Sigma Barton 6—which, she assured them, was one of the nicer jails she'd ever been in.

The entire time she was talking, Elijah could sense the insalar's eyes on him. He ordered another drink to distract himself from the black orbs staring unabashedly at him and the folds of delicate cloth tied at the insalar's waist, barely hiding the shape of the lean body beneath. Elijah felt heat creeping up the back of his neck, but he couldn't tell if it was from the alcohol or from the tiny little curl of a smile on the alien's lips.

"I always wanted to ask," Elijah said, hoping conversation would break the insalar's steady gaze. "The color you guys have in your hair." He gestured to his own head as though the alien wouldn't understand the concept of hair without the corresponding gesture. "Is it natural or not? I've seen lots of different colors."

The insalar exhaled lightly in amusement. "No," he answered, and Elijah almost wished he hadn't spoken—his voice was rich and low, and the sound vibrated softly in the way of his kind. That didn't help the warm feeling in Elijah's skin.

"So what do they mean?" he went on in an attempt to keep the conversation light. "I thought they might be family-related, bloodlines or whatever, or maybe social some way? Do the insalar have a class system sort of thing?"

The alien laughed then, but it didn't sound like the friendly vendor Elijah had met on Indira—it was a dark, sardonic sound, and the smile that followed put a pit in the boy's stomach. "We have a system called fashion, sweet boy."

Elijah paused. "Oh." He laughed, not minding when Harper snorted beside him and called him a fucking idiot.

The mood at the table did grow more relaxed, especially once everyone had had enough to drink that they became a bit drowsy. Elijah could feel the evening coming to a close, but he kept glancing over his shoulder toward the entrance to the club. Brooks had said that Leslie might join them. That didn't seem to be happening. Was he still on the ship? Was he alone—or not? The thought gripped Elijah's heart like a vice.

"Fuck y'all, I'm goin' to bed," Park finally slurred, and when he stood to leave, his bad knee buckled under him.

Shaw rose and hooked the engineer's arm over his shoulder to escort him out of the bar. Brooks and Harper weren't too far behind, but when Elijah emptied his last glass of beer and turned to say good night to the lingering insalar, the alien reached out one pale hand and wrapped slender fingers around the human's wrist.

"Not yet," the insalar murmured with a sly smile on his lips, and Elijah didn't try to pull away. He let himself be led from the table by the wrist, weaving through the crowd until the alien paused to exchange a few words with a man beside a black door and then following his insalar guide through to what appeared to be a small, private room. The sound of the music outside was muffled in here, but the bass still pulsed in Elijah's ears. The insalar kept a light hold on Elijah as he turned back to face him.

"I had something I wanted to discuss with you."

"Not sure how good a conversation I am right now," Elijah chuckled. He squeezed his eyes shut for a moment, but it did nothing to clear the alcohol from his brain. "Conversationalist."

The alien moved in close to him, his free hand reaching up to find the zipper pull of Elijah's jacket and give it a little tug. "Then you should just do as you're told."

"What?"

Elijah stumbled as the insalar jerked him down by the arm, and his knees hit the floor. He swayed for a moment until the other man's fingers fastened firmly onto his shoulder. The alien bent down and gripped the boy firmly by the hair at the back of his head, urging him to look upward and offering a faint smirk as he leaned in to run his tongue over the corner of Elijah's mouth.

"This is the way you like to be treated, isn't it?"

Elijah couldn't make himself form any coherent words. He tried, but his eyes were locked onto the alien's hand as he pulled at the intricate knots keeping his robe in place. Hints of a flat, silver-skinned stomach held Elijah's attention as the sheer cloth came loose, and he flinched slightly at the press of the alien's fingernails at the back of his neck.

"If you're good, I won't leave any marks," that low voice promised. "Your captain never has to know."

Elijah stared blearily up at the insalar for a few beats. Leslie didn't care about him. Whatever they might have been building toward, Elijah had ruined it. He was probably on the verge of being kicked off of the ship anyway, or at least not being invited back to the captain's quarters. The man in front of him was lean and beautiful and wanted him—only for the night, probably, but he wanted him. Why shouldn't he? He didn't owe Leslie this kind of loyalty. Elijah chewed his lip uncertainly, but when cool fingers brushed down his cheek and began to unzip his jacket, he shook his head.

"No," he said, pushing the alien's hand away from him. "I don't—I mean, thank you, but I'm gonna go."

"That's not the way a good little slave behaves," the insalar scolded with a soft click of his tongue. He took a firm hold at the side of Elijah's neck and forced him to meet his dark gaze as he slid a hand inside the boy's somehow now-open jacket, his fingernails scraping sharply across Elijah's skin on the way down his chest. "Let me see how well you serve your master."

"I said—no, man," Elijah pressed, turning his face away from the alien and shutting his eyes to curb a spell of dizziness. He didn't want this. He didn't want a stranger in a back room of some club. His stomach twisted inside of him, but he managed to push to his feet and take a step back. He didn't want this. He wanted Leslie. Whether the Chimera's captain wanted him or not—no matter how much it hurt his heart—Elijah couldn't lie to himself. He wanted Leslie. Only Leslie.

The insalar shoved him back against the door with one hand at the center of his chest, his smirk transformed into a faint scowl.

"You want me to be rougher with you?"

"You're gonna take your hands off me," Elijah answered. He stared into the alien's narrowed black eyes and waited for him to move.

"You are badly behaved," the insalar murmured, and Elijah sighed through his nose, his patience worn thin by the alcohol.

"One more time," he said, hoping that was enough warning, but the alien took hold of his belt rather than retreating. Elijah pushed him backward—not gently. The insalar spat at him and said something in a language Elijah couldn't understand, and the boy flinched as the drops of saliva hit his cheek.

Elijah honestly didn't intend to take a swing at the alien. But the next thing he knew, the insalar had stumbled backward with green blood pouring from his split lip. He shouted something that sounded angry, and the door opened so hard behind Elijah that he was knocked forward a step. The large man who had let them in now took Elijah by his open jacket collar and dragged him out of the room.

"Come on, kid," the man grumbled as he hauled Elijah away from the doorway where the insalar still snapped vulgarities at him. "You oughta know better than to start shit in here."

"I didn't start it!" Elijah protested, but his plea fell on deaf ears.

He was going to go to jail. His first night really left to his own devices on Altera, and he was going to be arrested. There was no way he had enough credits left for bail. Maybe he could call Brooks, or Davies—asking the captain was definitely out of the question, even if he'd find out eventually. There was no way Elijah could face him. He'd be lucky if Leslie let him back on board at all after this.

Just as Elijah was half-carried to the back door of the club, presumably to wait for the authorities, there was a loud and fast clicking sound, and the man carrying him suddenly jerked and went still, then collapsed to the floor in a heap. A moment later, Elijah was being pulled by the hand out the door and down the back alley. He followed at a run without question, and he'd already been led around the corner before his mind cleared enough to recognize the messy blond bun and pale eyes that glanced back at him.

26

Elijah ran, gripping Leslie's hand tightly and panting for breath with shouting and heavy boots close behind them. He ran until the captain rounded another dark corner and shoved him forward into a narrow nook between two tall stacks of cargo crates. Leslie urged him into a little crevice made by a gap in the long containers and pressed him against the metal with a silencing hand over his mouth, and they waited in tense silence until the sound of pursuing footsteps passed them by and faded into the distant noise of the station.

When their breath had a moment to slow, Leslie gingerly released him, taking the half step backward that their tight quarters allowed. The blond ran a weary hand over his mouth and rubbed at the back of his neck with a sigh.

"The hell were you thinking, kid?"

Elijah didn't answer. He just stared across at the ship's captain with a heavy pain in his chest. Leslie wasn't supposed to come for him. Leslie was going to drop him at some colony and bid him fare-fuckin'-well. He wasn't soft on him. Elijah had broken their agreement and ruined everything—Leslie wasn't supposed to come to his rescue.

"Something go wrong with your little rendezvous?"

"I didn't—"

"If you're gonna fuck aliens on shore leave, you should at least do it where you're not liable to get thrown out."

"But I wasn't—"

"Don't you know how to stop before you've had too much to drink? Stayin' out all by yourself—"

"Why did you help me?" Elijah cut him off, more loudly than he meant to. His breath caught in his throat in a hiccup that he had to force his voice through. "Why do you keep pretending that you care?"

Leslie stopped, and he stared at Elijah as though the younger man had slapped him. "The hell's that supposed to mean?"

Elijah's next breath came out in what he hoped didn't sound too much like a sob. He didn't have the strength to keep it all inside anymore, and if it meant he got left behind right here, then that's what it meant. "You're—you're kind to me, and then you're not. You act gentle with me and then kick me out of your room. You took me to see the ocean, and you climbed half a fucking mountain with me to show me lights in the sky that you didn't even think were on my list yet. You *remembered* my list. And then you tell Park you're gonna get rid of me as soon as you're bored, and you act like you don't want to be alone with me, and I fucking ruined it trying to do what you wanted, and—" He heaved out another weak breath and slumped back against the crate. "And I'm in love with you and I don't even know if you like me."

Leslie didn't speak for a long time. Elijah couldn't even look at him. It was all he could do to keep his breath steady with his eyes on the ground. He knew the heat in his face wasn't from the alcohol anymore. He'd said it out loud. He'd given voice to the thought he'd avoided for so long. Now the only thing to do was steel himself for the answer he feared was coming.

"Of course I *like* you," Leslie finally said. His voice was soft, and a long, slow sigh fell out of him as if he'd been holding it in for some time. "Elijah, I...I didn't mean to make you think I was playin' games. I'm sorry."

Elijah was almost more afraid to look at him now. He slowly peeked up to meet his eyes and found a face that looked almost as miserable as his own. "I wasn't—trying to fuck any aliens," he murmured, not sure what else to say. "He just—he heard Park talking all this crap about the kind of stuff me and you do, and he pulled me into that room, and I tried to tell him no, but he wouldn't listen. He said he...knew what I liked."

"So you socked him one? I saw him come out bleeding."

"I—yeah," he admitted.

They both stood in silence for a while, Elijah's heart beating so hard he could feel it pounding in his ears. Leslie hadn't addressed his actual confession—maybe that was the kindest thing he could have done, given the situation. But the quiet still made Elijah sick to his stomach.

"Elijah," Leslie started, and then he stopped. He sighed and folded his arms across his chest as he leaned back against his crate. "I owe you an explanation, I think."

Elijah watched him, waiting patiently while the blond gathered his thoughts.

"You heard Park giving me shit about you. So you heard him mention the last time."

Elijah nodded.

"The 'last time' he meant was...hell, it was years ago. I was...in a real relationship, you know? At least, I thought I was. I got my head up my ass about this insalar that—" He snorted and shook his head. "I loved him. I thought he loved me. I saw him off and on for a long while, when I was in the area, and whenever I finally got up the courage to ask him to come along with me...he laughed at me. Said we'd been having fun, but that was it. Said I shouldn't be so serious. I didn't take it so good."

"I'm sorry, Les," Elijah whispered. His distance, his blustering at Park, his unwillingness to get close—it made sense now.

The captain waved off his apology. "I didn't want to do that again. So since then, it's been strictly one-offs. I thought I could keep it together with you if I didn't let you too close. But...you turned out to be so..." Leslie broke into a resigned smile and shook his head without lifting his eyes from the floor. "You're too much for me, Elijah. Park saw straight through me, but I guess I did all right if you couldn't tell, at least."

Elijah's throat was so dry he could barely swallow, but he tried. "Couldn't tell what?"

"That I'm soft on you," the blond said, at last looking up into the younger man's dark eyes. "I'd been across the bar a while, trying to figure what I should say to you after what happened earlier, and when

I saw you go off into a private room with someone like that, it...tore me up. I know I spent all this time saying we should mind our own business, but...I think I let you turn into my business."

"I thought I was crazy," Elijah choked out.

Leslie closed the gap between them and cupped the boy's face in his hands, his thumbs brushing Elijah's heated cheeks. "That's my fault," he said gently. "I was trying to keep from hurting myself again, and I hurt you doin' it. I'm sorry, Elijah."

He looked up at the captain with his lips pressed firmly together, refusing to accept the prickling of tears touching the backs of his eyes. "I should have told you to stop sooner, before."

The blond nodded. "You should've. But I should have noticed you needed me to. And I shouldn't have lost my temper about it. I'll do better. If you still want me to," he added in a softer voice.

"I want you to," Elijah confirmed in a whisper, and Leslie smiled.

"I'm 'bout to cross a line, now," he murmured, edging ever so slightly closer.

"Yours or mine?"

"Just mine, I hope," Leslie chuckled. "I didn't think to put kissing on the checklist."

Elijah's heart was in his throat, but he managed to speak. "I...it's a yes," he whispered.

Leslie's slow smile threatened to burn Elijah to his core, and when the blond leaned in and brushed his lips over Elijah's, the boy's hands fastened onto his captain's sides on instinct. He let Leslie draw him close with gentle hands at the sides of his neck and eagerly parted his lips to meet the blond's deepening kiss. Leslie's body pressed him into the cargo crate so tightly that he could barely breathe, and he gave a soft, helpless whimper as the other man's tongue ran over his own.

Elijah struggled not to gasp for breath when Leslie finally broke free of him, fingers tangling in the blond's shirt as he placed one, then two soft parting kisses on the boy's lips before leaning back to look at him with a faint smile.

"Ready to come back to the ship with me?"

Elijah nodded, not sure where he was ever going to find the breath to speak again.

• • ◆ • •

Back aboard the Chimera, Leslie led the way down the short corridor of the crew deck with Elijah's fingers loosely woven with his own. The sight kept a constant burning in the boy's cheeks, and he lamented having to release his captain to follow him up the ladder. The ship was mostly quiet, no doubt full of a crew sleeping off their booze, as Leslie unlocked the door to his cabin and allowed Elijah inside.

It wasn't like the other times Elijah had stayed the night. They fell to the bed together, already fighting for air between kisses, and pulled at each other's clothes with desperate hands. Elijah's stomach tensed pleasantly at every soft, panting breath the blond let out against his ear as they pushed aside just enough clothing to be able to touch skin to skin. Leslie let Elijah touch him, and the boy savored every inch of pale stomach under his palm on his way to what he really wanted. Leslie's hand on him was maddeningly hot, and Elijah whined at the soft bites the other man left on his bottom lip and jaw as the two of them found a rhythm together, each stroking and squeezing and struggling to choose between air and the lips of the other.

When they were both spent, and Leslie had gently cleaned Elijah's stomach of sticky fluid with a soft towel, he laid back down beside the boy and ran his fingers through his dark, sweat-dampened hair.

"Stay," he murmured. He leaned in and pressed a single long kiss to Elijah's lips. "Stay this time."

Elijah didn't think he'd ever slept so well.

• • ◆ • •

In the morning, Elijah finally got the view he'd dreamed of— Leslie's calm, sleeping face on the pillow beside him, blond hair tousled and breath slow and even. Elijah almost didn't dare move for fear of waking him, but in a moment of bravery, he leaned down and touched a kiss to Leslie's barely parted lips. The blond gave a soft grunt and rolled over onto his stomach, hiding his face in the pillow, so Elijah just smiled and eased out of the bed. The captain probably wouldn't mind if he helped himself to a shower—he was soft on Elijah, after all. The thought made him bite his lip to keep from smiling like too much of an idiot.

Leslie was still asleep by the time Elijah finished dressing himself, so he let himself out of the room to make some coffee. Last night's alcohol had left him with a pounding headache. The mess hall was actually quiet for once, so Elijah got to at least briefly enjoy his coffee in silence before the others arrived. They all looked about like Elijah felt—minus, he supposed, the lingering butterflies in his stomach.

Park had barely poured his cup of coffee when the captain's cabin doors hissed open. The engineer opened his mouth with a sarcastic remark already on his lips, but before he could voice it, Leslie had stridden up to him and connected his fist with his friend's jaw. The coffee cup hit the floor and shattered, and Park fell back and half bounced against the counter top on his way down. The rest of the crew, including Elijah, stared in shock as the captain pointed an accusing finger at the floored engineer.

"That's for not using your head," the captain growled. "Because you had to run your damn mouth about your own crewmate, the kid almost got into serious trouble last night. If I hadn't been there, it would have been even worse than it was."

Park didn't move to get up. He glanced over at Elijah, who didn't quite know what kind of face to make.

"I'm fine," he said after an awkward pause. "It was just, after you guys left, that insalar, he—"

"He tried to lay hands on him," Leslie finished for him. "Thought he got to do what he wanted with him because of the things you said. After all y'all left his drunk ass alone." He reached down to help the engineer to his feet and crossed his arms once Park was standing on his own. "I know the kid's new. I know y'all don't always all get along. But we're all crew. And I expect you to act like it, you feel me?"

"Yes, Captain," came the chorus of answers.

"Good," he spat. "Now clean up that damn mess."

Leslie stalked back to his cabin and let the door lock thump shut behind him, leaving the rest of the crew in stunned silence after the scolding. Elijah moved to wipe up the spilled coffee out of habit while Park looked on guiltily. The others inched their way out once they had their coffee cups in hand, Brooks toward the bridge and the rest down the ladder to the deck below. Elijah scooped the broken ceramic into the garbage and rose to wring out his rag into the sink, not quite sure whether he should be the one to break the silence.

As he laid the washrag over the edge of the sink, he heard Park sigh behind him.

"Kid," the engineer began, rubbing awkwardly at his neck, "I...did wrong. I didn't mean to actually give you any trouble."

"I know that," Elijah assured him. He smiled faintly over his shoulder before turning to face the other man. "And I know you're just trying to look out for your friend when it comes to me. It's fine." He lowered his voice to a murmur and leaned in slightly closer. "We both know Les is softer than he acts, right?"

Park gaped at him for a moment, which was satisfying, but then he snorted out a soft chuckle and nodded. "All right, kid. I hear you. Then you and me are square." He offered Elijah his hand, and the boy took it with a nod in return.

"We're square. But it's Bennett."

"What's that?"

"My name. It's not 'kid.' It's Bennett."

Park scoffed and cuffed the younger man on the shoulder. "Just stay away from my engines, Bennett, and we'll get along fine."

27

With three full days of leave left on Altera, Elijah felt like he was on vacation. Leslie did do a little exploring with him, though Elijah noticed that he was still much more Captain-like than Leslie-like when they were in public. He didn't mind. It was better only having that side of him in private.

On their third day, Elijah used one of the public comm stations to call home, but got no answer. That was strange. His mother was very rarely far from the house. He left a voice note making sure they had the Chimera's registration number so that his family could send messages if they wanted, but he didn't think too much of it. He had enough on his mind—the expansiveness of the station, the course he needed to plan to their next destination, and his new footing with Leslie. Elijah had admitted to being in love, which the captain had yet to reciprocate exactly, but Elijah wasn't bothered. It was enough to know that Leslie was prepared to let him in, even just a little bit. He could be patient.

That evening, Elijah was lingering in the captain's quarters while Leslie showered, and the intercom buzzed on the desk as the blond emerged from the bathroom.

"Cap," Brooks' voice came through the speaker. "Is Elijah in there with you? He's not answering at his bunk."

"He's here. What do you need?"

"I have a message for him on the bridge. You'd...probably better come hear it, too."

Elijah and Leslie exchanged a brief glance, and the captain tossed his towel aside to reach for his clothes.

"Coming now."

Brooks already had the message up on the main view screen when they entered the bridge. Elijah recognized his oldest brother's face in the still shot, but something was wrong. He looked dirty and harried, and a cut above one of his eyes was seeping blood. Elijah moved close to the screen as Brooks started the video.

"Elijah," his brother began in a hoarse voice. "God, I hope you get this. I don't have much time. A ship came here—got us to let them in with an SOS and just started mowing people down before it even landed. A bunch of people came out and started yelling and rounding everyone up. Administrator Howe's been...making some kind of illegal drug. I don't know. They said they wanted it. They've locked everybody up, and they're making them work in the warehouses Howe had set up. The animals aren't getting fed, they burned some of the fields—they're shooting anyone who tries to fight back." He glanced over his shoulder and waited a beat as though listening before turning back to the screen. "We need help, but they've blocked our communication with the station. The Federation cargo ship isn't due for another six months. Nobody's coming. I'm hoping this gets through—you've got to tell somebody. You've got to get us help—"

A loud crash came from behind his brother's back, and the screen gave a spark of static and then went black as a single gunshot sounded.

"Daniel!" Elijah called in a panic, knowing his brother couldn't hear him. He stood in front of the blank screen, unable to breathe. He looked back at Leslie as if the captain might tell him what to do, but the blond was staring at the floor with his hands on his hips and a grim frown on his face.

"We have to go," Elijah said. He looked between Brooks and the captain in desperation. "We have to help them. We have to—to tell the Federation, tell them to send soldiers, something!"

"They ain't gonna listen," Leslie said quietly. He lifted his head to look Elijah in the face. "You said your colony's, what, four hundred people? The hell does the Federation care about some farmland? They'll just send more colonists out there later on if need be."

"But it's a *Federation* colony!" Elijah protested. "They have to protect it!"

"They don't and they won't," the captain answered. "And what d'you reckon they're gonna do when you tell them the colony got attacked because of all those drugs it's been making?"

Elijah's heart sank. It didn't exactly make his colony look good. Had that been what the Administrator was having shipped off-world? Was it why he'd met Leslie at all?

He sighed. "But...I can't just do nothing. I can just—I can leave that part out. I have to tell someone. They'll help—they have to help."

"Feel free to try, kid."

Elijah left the bridge without waiting to be dismissed, and he rushed from the ship as soon as the gangway airlock was open. This was Altera—the heartbeat of the Federation. He would be able to get help here. Leslie didn't trust the government, but they weren't going to just abandon one of their own supply colonies. Elijah asked for directions from every person in uniform that he saw and finally found his way to the Office of Colonial Affairs. He tried to push his way to the front desk and was immediately rebuked and told to take a number. When he tried to tell the woman behind the glass that it was an emergency, she only calmly explained that everyone in the room had an emergency and that he would have to wait his turn.

He paced for a while, then sat when he began to get some irritated stares, but he couldn't help the rapid tapping of his heel. Every moment that he spent here was another that his family was suffering.

He waited for over an hour before he was called back to the front desk, and then he was made to fill out half a dozen pages of paperwork about himself, his colony, and the reason for his visit. It was excruciating. Even when he tried to turn the completed tablet back in, the woman shooed him away again and said that he would be called. Another twenty minutes later, he was called to the desk of a haggard-looking woman who didn't even look at him as he sat down.

"ID number?" she asked mechanically, only pausing to glance up after Elijah had rattled it off to her. "And what can we do for you today, Mr. Bennett?"

Elijah huffed. What the hell had been the point of filling out the paperwork if she was just going to ask him anyway? He did his best to explain without incriminating his entire colony, and the woman nodded and hummed appropriately while he spoke.

"I'm sorry; are you actually listening?" he asked after the sixth "mhmm," unable to keep the irritation from his voice. "I'm telling you that my whole colony is being held captive or shot right now! You need to send people out there to help them!"

"Sir, once we have all the information, I assure you that your request will be forwarded to the appropriate authorities."

"Forwarded—what the hell does that mean? There's no time to *forward* things! People are dying!"

"People are dying all over the galaxy, Mr. Bennett," the woman said flatly, staring at him with an unsympathetic frown. "The Federation gives all the help it can to its citizens." She glanced toward the door to dismiss him. "Thank you for your time. We will investigate the issue and do what we can."

"Are you fucking kidding me?"

"Sir, if you raise your voice again, I will have you escorted out."

Elijah bit his tongue, snorted in frustration, and wished he could slam the sliding door on his way out of the office. Leslie was right. They weren't going to do anything. That meant someone else had to do something.

· • ◆ • ·

"Absolutely not," Leslie said immediately, as if he'd just been waiting for Elijah to get back and ask. He folded his arms and leaned his hip against the co-pilot's console. "We've got deliveries to make, and even if we didn't, ain't no way in hell I'm taking the Chimera into some kind of battleground."

"Deliveries?" Elijah echoed in disbelief. "How can you care about your deliveries more than this?"

"They're how I keep this crew fed," the captain countered firmly. "We miss a deadline, skip a drop, take off with some cargo—my reputation's ruined, and I've got no more work. Chimera's got no more work. We're done. I can't risk that."

"Daniel said they're shooting people! I can't just go make

deliveries! I have to help my family!"

"I feel for you, kid; I really do. But you're asking me to put my ship and the souls aboard her in danger for the sake of a colony we don't even know can be saved. I just can't do it. It's gotta be a no."

"But L—Captain," he corrected himself with a brief glance at Brooks, who seemed to be making a point not to listen. Elijah stepped closer to the blond and looked up into his face. "I have to help them. *Please.*"

Leslie sighed softly through his nose, watching the boy's suffering face. His brow furrowed uncertainly, and Elijah saw the hesitation in his eyes, but then the captain shook his head. "I'm sorry, Elijah."

Elijah let out a short, empty scoff, and he stepped back from the other man, running both hands through his hair and shaking his head as he made his way to the door. This couldn't be happening. He moved automatically down the deck ladder and to his bunk, but he couldn't stop the pacing movement of his feet in the tiny room. Leslie had told him no. Leslie had looked him in the eye, known his family was dying, and still said no. Still expected him to follow orders and make their drops on time like everyone he'd ever known wasn't being held captive. The same person who'd stood beside him on a mountaintop, and who'd kissed him so softly, and who'd slept peacefully with Elijah's head on his shoulder.

He finally stopped pacing, sank onto his cot with his head in his hands, and broke. He took ragged, heavy breaths and let his tears finally fall to the floor. He couldn't do it. He just couldn't do this. He couldn't be so cold.

A soft knock on his door startled him. He almost didn't answer, not sure he could look Leslie in the face, but when Brooks called quietly to him, he wiped his eyes with the collar of his shirt and leaned over to press the release on the door. The pilot stepped inside and stayed at the edge of the room, holding her elbows in her hands as the door slid shut behind her.

"I won't ask if you're okay," she said, and Elijah chuckled without humor.

"Good."

"Just give Cap some time. He always chews on things like this for a while—he has a lot on his shoulders, you know? But he'll come around. He's a good man."

"Is he?" Elijah heard the bitterness in his voice and shut his eyes to try to swallow it down before he looked up at her again. "My family doesn't have time, Brooks. Even if we left right now, it'll still take days to get to Dhat-Badan—and that's days of who-knows-what being done to them. If they're even still alive. Maybe I saw my brother get shot in that vid. I don't know." He shook his head and stood, then took a step toward his shelf and began to scoop his meager belongings into his worn knapsack. "I can't wait around for the captain to decide if he's a good man or not."

"Whoa, hold on now," the pilot started, but Elijah turned on her.

"I can't hold on!" He stopped and took a breath, clutching the strap of his knapsack tight. "I'm sorry. But I can't stay. I have to help my family. If the Chimera won't take me there, then I'll find another way."

Elijah approached the door and waited for Brooks to move. She looked up at him with the corner of her mouth caught uncertainly in her teeth.

"I know why you think you have to go," she said. "Just make sure you think about what you're leaving behind."

He shook his head, though his stomach ached and breathing was difficult. "He chose this ship over me. I have to choose my family over him." He put a hand on the pilot's arm to gently move her to the side. "Thanks for being a friend, Brooks."

"Elijah—" she started, but he was already out the door. He hit the release on the airlock and slung his knapsack over his shoulder on his way through the open gangway.

It wasn't easy, even on a station the size of Altera, to find someone willing to give him a lift all the way out to Dhat-Badan—especially with the limited credits he had to his name. He eventually negotiated passage on a tiny, rickety ship piloted by a single old man who was sufficiently moved by his plight, but was told in no uncertain terms that it would be the quickest of all drop-offs, as he wasn't interested in getting into trouble with whoever was attacking the colony. The man spent the entire trip back to his ship alternating between telling Elijah what a damn fool idea it was and praising him for being so loyal to his family. Elijah mostly tuned him out, and once they were aboard, he found a space to sit on the cramped deck and held his knapsack so tightly in his lap that his fingers hurt.

This was the choice he had to make.

28

Park took his time getting up the ladder to the mess hall, as he always did. His knee complained every time he climbed to the upper decks, but it wouldn't be worth the expense trying to add elevators to this piece of shit ship. He'd been trying to steer clear of the mess hall as much as possible for the past couple of days for fear of meeting a still-pissed-off captain, but he needed to eat. He'd made it halfway through his coffee and rehydrated potatoes when Brooks came clomping up the ladder, blowing by him to bang on the captain's door.

"Where's the fire, Brooks?" he asked, and the pilot huffed at him over her shoulder as the cabin door hissed open.

"Elijah left," she said to both of them, but her eyes were on the captain's face.

"He's a grown-up," the blond answered with what sounded like forced indifference. "We're not leaving 'til tomorrow anyhow."

"Cap, I mean he *left*," Brooks clarified, her eyebrows lifting to help make her point. "He said he's going home."

The captain hid it well, but Park could see the flash of panic in his eyes. The engineer leaned his elbows on the table and frowned over at his friend while the blond cleared his throat.

"Well, that's his choice, ain't it? Could have said something on his way out."

"You're okay with this?"

"He's a grown-up," Leslie repeated. Park heard the strain in his voice, even if Brooks didn't. "He wants to go throw his life away for the same folks he couldn't wait to get away from, that's on him."

"Cap," Brooks sighed, but he cut her off with a sharp, dismissive wave.

"Forget about it. Sorry you lost your navigator, Brooks." He turned without waiting for an answer and left them in the silence following the heavy thunk of his cabin door lock.

Brooks puffed out her cheeks in a huff and dropped down in a chair across from Park. She gave a helpless shrug. "Well is that supposed to just be fuckin' that?"

Park looked past her at the captain's closed door, but he didn't speak.

"That poor kid," the pilot murmured. "He shouldn't have been here at all, should he? He let Cap chew him up and spit him out."

"Maybe," Park said under his breath. He didn't say what he was thinking—that what had really happened was the total opposite. He looked back at her after a pause. "What's he talking about, throwing his life away?"

"Some message came in that his colony's being attacked. Everybody's getting shot up or locked up. He asked Cap to take the Chimera back there to help, and Cap said no, of course. I tried to stop him leaving, but he wouldn't listen."

"Well, they wouldn't like each other so much if they both weren't stubborn assholes," the engineer grumbled. He gave a gruff, long-suffering sigh and ran a hand over his short black hair. He didn't want to have this conversation. He didn't want to be the one coming to the kid's defense—but if he didn't, it would be him that would be forced to pick up the pieces.

"All right," he grumped, decision made, and he flattened his hands on the table to push himself up. "Keep the mess clear a while, will you? There might be some yellin' here in a bit."

"Don't get kicked off the ship yourself," Brooks warned as she stood.

"His ass knows he can't do without me. Go on," he urged her, and once she was down the ladder, he took a couple of limping steps to the captain's door. When Leslie didn't answer his knock, he tried again.

The intercom speaker on the door clicked on, and the captain's voice came through.

"Fuck off, Park."

"You'd best let me in there lest I start tellin' your business through the door."

"I ain't got nothin' to say to you."

"Well I got somethin' to say to you. I'm filin' a grievance with my ship's captain, and he'd better damn well listen to it."

A few beats of silence passed, and Park heard Leslie's sigh through the intercom before the lock clicked and the door slid open. Park let himself in and stepped farther inside without hesitation to slide the expected whiskey bottle farther away on the desk. Leslie allowed it to be scooted from his hand, but he glared up at the engineer with a scowl on his face.

"Thought you weren't soft on this kid," Park said.

"Can't ever mind your own fuckin' business," Leslie mumbled, half muffled by the glass of liquor he raised to his lips.

"And you're damn lucky for it."

"Will you just say whatever you've got to say and get gone? I'm busy."

"Yeah, I see that." The engineer leaned across Leslie when he tried to take back his bottle, and he set it on the floor beside the desk, out of reach. "I warned you not to lose your mind over a pretty face."

"This kid come after *me*," Leslie insisted, tapping one finger on the surface of the desk to accentuate his point. There was a faint redness in his face that Park recognized—he must have already been drinking before Brooks even knocked. "All watery-eyed and practically beggin' me. Says he's in love with me, and then soon as I don't turn my whole damn livelihood upside down for him, where's he at? Fft." Leslie settled back in his chair and made a zooming gesture with one hand. "Gone."

"D'you even hear yourself?" Park leaned against the desk to give his leg a rest and stared down at his glowering captain. "I don't know who you think you're foolin', but it sure as hell ain't me. I'm supposed to believe you're *surprised* a kid like that run off to go rescue his colony? Ain't you met him?"

"And what the hell am I supposed to do about it? He wants us to fly in there like big damn heroes, but this is a smuggling ship, and it sure as shit ain't full of soldiers."

The engineer sighed through his nose. "So you're gonna let him go off and try to be a hero all by himself."

"He made that call, not me. He's the one decided to leave."

"But you love him, right?"

Leslie scowled up at his friend as though the question was an accusation.

"You don't have to say it out loud to me, man. But you've never come after me like that because of someone else before. You laid me out 'cause of him. And Lord knows he's been stuck to your heels since he got here. I'm the last one who should be encouraging this foolishness, but this kid don't strike me as the type to cause you the same troubles as you had the last time. Maybe you oughta put more stock in him."

"Different troubles, same result," Leslie grumbled. "Still got my ass left behind."

"Oh, quit your bitchin' and get your head on straight, will ya?"

"I didn't ask you to come in here and give me a lecture, asshole, so—"

"He's gonna die, Leslie. You know that." Park leaned down to keep the blond's gaze when he tried to turn his face away. "You let him go back to that colony on his own, he's gonna get himself killed tryin' to do the right thing, and he's gonna hate you for it with his dyin' breath. That what you want?"

Leslie didn't answer. His eyes were on the empty glass he slowly turned in his hand.

"Now you know I'm not generally in favor of takin' big risks, but if you love this kid, you'd better think real long and hard about whether you wanna let him die out of spite and stubbornness, or whether you wanna do the right thing even when it don't make no sense."

The captain was silent for a while longer, and then he leaned forward to set his glass back on the desk. "Get the fuck out, Park," he said in a low, tired voice.

The engineer hesitated, eyeing the heavy slump in his friend's shoulders. "All right, Cap," he finally said. "You're the boss."

• • ◆ • •

Park lingered around the mess hall and the bridge for a while, listening for the sound of Leslie's cabin door to tell him his friend had made a decision. None came for so long that he almost gave up and went to bed, but then the ship's intercom crackled.

"Everybody to the bridge. Need a meeting."

Park exchanged an uncertain glance with Brooks and took a seat nearby to wait for the others. The captain appeared last, taking his usual place by the co-pilot's seat to address his crew. His cheeks were still a touch ruddy, but he had lost the hopeless scowl on his face and replaced it with the determined pale gaze that Park knew.

"Y'all might notice we're one less," he began, allowing a beat for the others to look around the room at each other. "That's what I wanted to talk about. Our cabin boy took off because of a message from home asking for help. Dhat-Badan is apparently being held down by some folks up to no good, and people are dying. I tried to tell the kid we couldn't just up and go on some rescue, so he went alone."

Leslie sighed and looked down at the floor with his hands on his hips. "Y'all know I never intend to do anything that's gonna risk what we got. But," he added with a pointed glance at Park, "my engineer gave me a hell of a guilt trip, so I put it to y'all. If you think we should go help, we help. If you want to stick to our route, we'll do that."

"He went alone?" Davies echoed from the back of the room. "Who is it that's attacking, exactly?"

"Don't know. Nobody good. Somebody with enough firepower and big enough balls to try to take over a four-hundred-person colony. Y'all can watch the vid if you want, but suffice it to say the one who sent it may not be with us anymore."

"Corsairs?" Harper spoke up, and Leslie shrugged one shoulder as he leaned back against the console chair.

"Could well be."

"I fuckin' told you guys he wasn't on the up and up! Fuckin' corsairs, man, he—"

"Cool down, Harper," Brooks sighed. "As if it's the kid's damn fault he's got people shooting up his colony."

"Don't like dealin' with no corsairs," Shaw said, his low, rumbling voice quieting the others in the room. "They got their hands on that colony, it's good as gone anyhow."

"But can we let him go by himself?" Davies asked. "He's one of us."

The crew exchanged uncertain glances, but Park's eyes were on the ship's captain. Leslie kept his gaze on the ground as if his attention might influence the decision, his knuckles turned white from their grip on the back of the chair behind him. He'd tell himself it wouldn't be his fault if something happened to Elijah because the crew chose not to take the risk, not him. He'd tell himself, but he wouldn't believe it.

"The kid stuck his neck out for us more than once," the engineer said. "I might not like him, but he pulled his weight on board. That makes him one of us in my book."

"Until we try to land on that shithole and find out he's just bait," Harper countered, but his frown was a little different from before.

"Get a grip," Brooks scolded. "He's a good kid and you know it. And he is one of us," she added as she looked out over the rest of her shipmates.

"Don't mean all of us gotta die," Shaw said. He took a deep breath and sighed it out. "New people are always trouble."

Leslie finally looked up at them as he pushed away from the chair. "So let's put it to a vote."

29

Elijah felt more than a little cramped on the old man's rickety ship, especially after the first two nights spent curled up on a footlocker in the corner. He'd been spoiled by getting to take so many naps in Leslie's bed. At least, three days out, Elijah's clothing was starting to smell more like his unshowered musk than the blond's sheets. He'd take his blessings where he could get them.

He did his best to put the captain of the Chimera out of his mind. He had no idea what was really waiting for him back on Dhat-Badan, and the last thing he needed was to be distracted by heartsickness. His family was counting on him. So whenever he caught himself remembering any soft smiles he'd once seen on the blond's scarred lips, he pushed the memory away—though he wasn't always as successful as he would have liked. In the quiet of the ship, he sat hunkered down against the hull with his worn little notebook on his knees, and he pressed his lips into a slightly bitter frown as he crossed out the line on his list that he'd avoided looking at for days.

~~Fall in love.~~

He couldn't bear to write the captain's name beside it. He would remember.

By the fifth day, Elijah was sick to death of the dry rations the old man had on board, but he was still grateful that his host was willing to share them at all. The pilot didn't ask him many questions about their destination, and Elijah was glad—the less he knew, the less likely he was to get into trouble for helping.

When they finally exited the nearest gate and began their final approach toward Dhat-Badan, Elijah took his place at the old man's shoulder, leaning over the back of the pilot seat as the colony came into view.

"Don't get too close yet," Elijah said. "The scanners will pick you up and alert the Administrator's office." He reached across to point at a spot on the map illuminated on the console's viewscreen. "There. If you can swing around and land near the terraforming generators, there's a back way into the dome for maintenance. I can get in if you let me out there."

"Ain't the whole point of having a dome that you can't breathe outside it, son?"

"I've made the run from the door to the generator and back before. It's just over two minutes. I can do it."

The old man seemed skeptical, but he flew his little ship around in a broad arc to avoid the area Elijah said would be noticed by scanners, and within minutes, he was touching down on the golden sand, the grit blown up by the ship's engines barely noticeable in the howling winds of the constant storm outside. Elijah tied one of his old shirts around his nose and mouth to protect against the sand, fixed his knapsack on his shoulders, and stood ready to press the release on the airlock as soon as the old man gave him the signal.

"You're crazy, kid," the pilot said with a shake of his head. "Go give 'em hell."

"Thanks for the ride," Elijah answered, and when he got the okay, he took a deep breath and hit the switch on the door, immediately letting in a torrent of sand. He took a moment to brace himself against the wind, then stepped out. He didn't hear the door close behind him, but when he glanced back over his shoulder a few feet away, he felt the push of heat from the engines as the ship took to the sky again.

He struggled to fight the urge to breathe as he made his way toward the massive generator complex as quickly as he could manage in the punishing wind. Every kid who grew up on Dhat-Badan had the dangers of inert gas asphyxiation drilled into them since birth. Just three breaths, they were told. Just three breaths outside the dome, and you'd pass out—and then you'd take the next two breaths, which would kill you. But it was only two minutes from the generator to the door. Maybe a little more from where he'd been dropped off.

Elijah counted seconds in his head as he forced his way through the wind tearing at his clothes, squinting through the curtains of sand buffeting him. The dome wall hummed as he approached, pale blue and translucent, reaching up farther into the sky than Elijah could see and much farther around than he could hope to walk in a day, let alone on one held breath. The faint light it gave off barely shone through the sandstorm, but the small glow was familiarly oppressive as the wall took over Elijah's field of view, and his heartbeat fell back into time with the deafening, rhythmic thump-thump-thump of the generators as if he'd never left his colony at all.

By the time he reached the airlock decompression door built into the one ground-level exit from the dome, his head was pounding. His vision dimmed as he opened the casing on the keypad lock, and he prayed they hadn't changed the maintenance passcode. It took him two tries to get it right with the world blackening at the edges of his eyes, but then the door hissed and creaked open. He rushed inside, slapped the metal pad to close the door again, and collapsed against the wall while the door ground shut against the wind. Elijah slid to the floor, pulling his shirt away from his mouth and gasping deeply as the decompression chamber filled with breathable air again.

He let his head rest against the metal wall while his senses returned to him. That was step one done. Step two would be figuring out what the hell was going on inside without getting himself caught or killed. That was going to be a lot harder.

Elijah got to his feet once he'd caught his breath, and he moved to the far end of the decompression chamber to lean against the door. There wasn't much chance of him being able to hear anything from the other side, but he tried anyway. There were no loud noises, at least. He would have to just risk it. He pressed up the release lever for the door and stood back as it pulled open, waiting for a couple of breaths in case he was about to be shot.

The corridor was deserted. Elijah had never spent much time in the compound, but there were usually at least a few maintenance workers around; the terraforming generators required a lot of upkeep. Today, Elijah assumed the workers were preoccupied.

Snugging his knapsack up tight around his shoulders, he made his way down the hallway toward the exit. Along the way, he ducked into a supply closet and supplied himself with a length of cord, a flashlight, and a heavy wrench. It wasn't the best weapon option, but he wouldn't have felt right taking any guns with him from the Chimera—and if everything went well, he wouldn't need to rely on it for long.

Outside, the colony he knew was in bad shape. Daniel was right—a few of the fields still smoldered, filling the air with lingering trails of black smoke. Some of the fences were broken or riddled with bullet holes, and as Elijah entered into the pasture, many animals lay dead and bloated in the mud. There should have been people out working these fields. He shouldn't have been able to go this far without seeing a single soul. He should have been here to help. He'd been selfish to leave. If he'd been here—he stopped himself before that train of thought could go any farther, leaning against the thick door of a still-standing barn while he paused to get his bearings. If he'd been here, he'd be dead or captured, just like everyone else. He wasn't a hero.

Elijah looked out over the pasture toward the massive, unfamiliar ship looming above the dock. If he wasn't a hero, why the hell had he come back here all by himself?

Suppressing his sigh, Elijah crept closer toward the center of the colony and the growing sound of movement ahead of him. When he finally spotted someone, he ducked behind a corner to avoid being seen and peeked around the edge of the wall. The town center was nearby, and people he didn't recognize sat on piles of cargo crates stacked haphazardly throughout the courtyard, each one with a rifle slung over his shoulder. They chatted among themselves, some carrying open bottles of liquor, others hunched over boxes to play cards. Elijah scanned the open space and tried to quickly count them before retreating back around his corner, but there were too many to get an accurate number. Maybe thirty. There must be more somewhere else, guarding the colonists, making them work. He would need to find where they were keeping everyone. He needed to make contact with someone—anyone—before he could hope to put together a plan.

He waited, silently watching the dirty-looking men and women who lingered nearby until he overheard one of them shouting complaints about having to give food to the captives. He followed the protest away from the town center and back toward one of the larger barns, but he stopped in his tracks as he reached the far end of the square. The flagpole at the edge of the courtyard had been strung with corpses—three men hung by thick ropes around their neck, their arms and legs left to dangle beneath blue, bulging faces. Administrator Howe was at the center, flanked by his two aides. The gruesome warning made Elijah sick to his stomach. He pulled his gaze away and forced himself to focus on the barn ahead of him.

The tall doors were chained up tight behind two armed guards, who seemed just as put out as the man hauling the cart of moldy-looking bread. Elijah crept around to the side of the barn to listen while the doors were unchained. A few people inside shouted at the man bringing their meal—women's voices, he noted—but mostly the complaints were subdued. They had been in there for days—a lot of the fight must have gone out of them.

He waited for the sound of the chain sliding through the doors again and made his way toward the back of the building. The small opening near the roof was unguarded. They must have taken the ladder away inside. Here, he was a fair distance away from the noise of the men and women in the square. It was only twenty-five feet, maybe. It wouldn't be the first time he'd scaled the back of a barn—though, admittedly, this was a bit riskier than clambering up some scaffolding to crouch in the hayloft during hide and seek. But right now, this was his best option.

Elijah hesitated for a breath or two, staring up at the distant window, then he set his jaw and reached up to let his fingers find the familiar nooks and crannies in the wall. It was a much slower, more difficult climb than it had been when he was a child, made more so by the weight of his knapsack on his back, but it was quiet enough—for now—that he could take his time. He was grateful for the surface of the hayloft once he reached the little window, and he spent a minute flattened on the wood, catching his breath. When his heart had settled a little, he eased himself forward on the loft until he could lean his head over the edge.

The barn was full of people—but only women and children. They must have been keeping the men separately. To keep them in line by threatening their families, he guessed. Pathetic. Elijah scooted out a little farther and made a soft "psst" noise until he attracted the attention of a small group just underneath him. As soon as their eyes found him, their faces lit up, and he had to quickly put a finger to his lips to urge them not to shout.

"Elijah!" one of the women called in as loud a whisper as she dared. It was Abigail—one of the girls his age who *wasn't* his cousin. "Oh my god, Elijah!" she breathed as she edged closer to the loft, drawing the attention of the women around her. "Someone go get Hannah! Elijah's back!"

Elijah's heart gave a solid thump as he spotted his mother's haggard face approaching through the crowd. She didn't appear to be injured, but she looked exhausted and weary. Even so, her eyes lit up when she drew near to her son, and the smile that parted her lips was undampened by the last few days.

"Elijah," she said. "How in the world?"

"I got a message from Daniel. I hitched a lift and came in through the generator gate—they don't know I'm here. Don't worry," he assured her. "I'm going to...do something."

"When is the Federation coming?" his mother asked. All the eyes in the barn seemed to be on him now.

"They're...they're not."

"What do you mean, they're not? They have to!"

"Well they're not. I tried. It's just me, mom. But I'm going to help." She let out a sigh of motherly worry, so he quickly went on, "Where are they keeping everyone else?"

"In Marlowe's barn, I think," one of the other women spoke up.

"Okay. Just—I'll work something out. Just sit tight and be safe, okay? I'll be back soon. I'm gonna get you out of here."

"Oh, be careful, baby," his mother pleaded, and he gave her the most encouraging smile he could manage as he slunk back toward the window.

He waited for a group of men to pass nearby before hooking his cord to the nearest beam and easing his way down the wall again. On solid ground, he pressed the release on the clasp and stuffed the cord back into his knapsack, then made his way toward the home he'd left behind. There would be things there he needed.

It took him longer than it should have to get back to his childhood home—the corsairs had apparently been ransacking the colonists' houses, so there were a few people lingering in the residential areas. Front doors had been left open, clothing strewn across the floors and the ground outside, and the Miller house, at the end of Elijah's block, was no more than a pile of burned debris now. Even assuming they were able to fight these intruders off, it was going to take a long time for the colony to recover.

Elijah approached the propped-open door of his house without being spotted, but he stopped dead when he turned the corner into the living room and found himself face to face with a leather-clad, bearded man with a bandolier looped across his chest.

"Where the fuck did you come from?" the man snapped, his hand already reaching for the gun strapped to his hip.

Elijah rushed him without thinking. He couldn't afford to let that gun go off, even if it did miss him. Others would hear. He slammed his shoulder into the corsair's chest and sent both of them crashing to the floor. The other man was bigger than him, and Elijah struggled to turn the barrel of the gun away from his own face as they wrestled on the floor. Before the corsair could fire, Elijah managed to knock the pistol from his hand, but he got himself stuck in a neck hold in the process. His heels scraped on the floor as he fought the man's iron grip, fingers prying uselessly at a thick forearm. He couldn't breathe— but he could still reach the heavy wrench tucked into the back of his belt. He swung it desperately over his own head into the face of the man holding him, his growl of pain enough reprieve to allow Elijah to slip free. Gasping for air, he forced the dazed corsair to the ground and straddled him, pinning his arms under his knees and leaning his weight into pressing the cold metal of the wrench handle against the other man's neck.

The corsair fought, frantic gurgles escaping him as he slapped and pushed at any part of Elijah he could reach. Elijah stayed put, his own breath ragged and unsteady as he forced himself to hold the weapon against the man's throat. He almost shut his eyes to keep out the sight of the corsair's reddening face, but he couldn't bring himself to look away. The man hissed a few last breaths through gritted teeth, spotting Elijah's shirt with saliva, and his flesh gave a sickening, squelching crunch as his windpipe collapsed. Elijah's hands slipped at the sudden movement, and he fumbled to keep a grip on his weapon, but the corsair's limbs had gone slack and his bulging eyes had lost their light.

Elijah took shuddering breaths, the wrench clattering to the floor as the weight of what he'd done settled on his shoulders. He pushed himself off of the lifeless man with quivering hands and sat for a while with his back pressed into the wall, trying to calm the feverish pace of his heart. He'd killed him. He'd killed him.

A soft, sobbing sigh escaped him, but he stifled it quickly with the back of his hand. He wished Leslie was there.

30

Elijah pressed the balls of his hands firmly into his eyes to stop the faint burning that had begun there. He couldn't afford to wait—and he definitely couldn't waste time wishing the blond ship captain was with him. After one more steeling breath, he rose to his feet and dragged the corsair by his ankles down the hallway and into the bathroom, then shut the door to close him inside after taking the bandolier for himself. He tucked the stray pistol into his belt and carried his wrench in one hand as he made his way through the rest of the house.

The trap door to the basement was still shut tight under the rug in his parents' bedroom. Allowing himself a brief sigh of relief, Elijah tugged open the door and slunk down the wooden steps beneath, easing the door shut behind him. He clicked the bare lightbulb on at the bottom of the stairs and started past the shelves of dry goods and emergency rations toward his true goal. The crate looked untouched, but Elijah didn't allow himself to feel hope until he pried open the lid and saw the stash of rifles inside. His father had always had an untrusting nature, and he'd justified the cache of secret supplies by saying he wanted to be able to "protect his family." Elijah had never known against whom, exactly, but now he was grateful for his father's paranoia.

He counted the guns in the crate and the boxes of ammunition as he laid them out on the floor. It wasn't a lot, compared to what they were facing—just a couple dozen long rifles and a few reloads for each—but it was going to have to be enough. It was definitely better than nothing.

Elijah helped himself to some of the rations stored away in the basement and filled his knapsack with as much as he could carry. He loaded all of the rifles, strapped three of them together, and kept one close to his hands. Then he waited. It would be night soon, and he'd have a much easier time moving around. He sat at the bottom of the steps and tried not to let his heels tap too anxiously on the floor. When his watch told him the sun should have set, he made a cup of lukewarm coffee with the supplies on the shelves and downed it all at once, then slung the strung-together rifles over his shoulder and made for Marlowe's barn.

With the rifles hidden in a nearby bush, Elijah made the climb up to the hayloft, his fingers and arms aching from the effort by the time he made it through the narrow window. He leaned down over the edge of the loft and hissed at the people beneath him, who had already huddled into their places for a night of unrestful sleep.

"Look there," one of the older men said when they noticed him, elbowing the man beside him. "It's Bennett's boy!"

"Where's Daniel?" Elijah asked. "Is he okay?"

"He got shot," the man answered in a whisper, the ripple of conversation moving through the crowded barn. "He's been in and out, but the doc thinks he's going to make it. He's over in the corner there," he said with a gesture toward a wall too dark for Elijah to see.

"Elijah!" his father's voice called, and the boy spotted him and his older brothers stepping over legs to reach the foot of the hayloft.

"I got Daniel's message," he said. "Here—food." He dangled his knapsack over the edge and let it drop into his brother's hands to be distributed among the others. "I have some of the guns from the basement—we can get the others."

"Good boy," his father said with a nod. The man had a hard face, even darker than Elijah's from his years spent working in the sun, but there was still a touch of warmth there as he looked up at his son.

"Here's what I figure." Elijah settled down on his belly to get a little closer to the others. "I'll take James, Andrew, and Ethan with me back to the house to get the rest of the guns. We'll bring them back in here, and then find a good position outside, and when they open those doors in the morning, we'll be ready. We'll need to get to Wilton's barn—that's where they're keeping the women and children. We don't want them to be able to use them as hostages."

"And Booker's wife is the best damn shot in the colony," one of the other man spoke up, chuckling.

"We need all of those we can get," Elijah agreed. He turned his eyes back to his father, whose firm gaze hadn't left him since he appeared. "At dawn, we're going to take back our home."

His father hesitated a moment, like he wanted to say something, but then he just nodded and jerked his head toward his older sons. "Go on; get up there."

With a bit of teamwork, the men were able to lift Elijah's brothers, one at a time, high enough for Elijah to grab onto their arms and haul them up the rest of the way. A few of the other men said that they had guns hidden away in their houses, as well, so Elijah made mental notes of the route they should take back. He and his brothers spent the rest of the night moving guns back and forth from the barn, taking turns making the climb up the side of the wall to lower them to the people inside. The last trip, they delivered a few guns to the women, but asked them not to make a move until the others were able to get to them. Finally, as dawn was approaching, his brother Andrew took a spot above the courtyard, where his sharpshooting skills could be put to effective use, and Elijah and the others settled in a flanking position.

"Glad to see you didn't run off completely," James muttered beside him while he checked his ammunition.

"Just because I want more out of life doesn't mean I don't care about my home," Elijah retorted.

"Sure seems that way when you take off without a word to anybody and leave us to hear mom cry about it for a week."

Elijah frowned down at the gun in his lap, but before he could let the guilt sink in, Ethan spoke up beside him.

"Will you shut up? Half the people here want to get off this goddamn rock; Elijah's just the only one with enough balls to actually go. Also, the place is full of pirates right now, so if we could maybe focus on that instead of on being a bitter shitheel, that would be great."

"Fuck you," James snapped, but he let the subject drop. Ethan nodded sharply at Elijah's grateful smile, and they waited out the rest of the night in silence.

· • ◆ • ·

When the chain was slipped from Marlowe's barn door, and the first shots rang out, the tense quiet of the night was forgotten, lost in the chaos the morning sun brought with it. Corsairs fell in waves as the men forced their way out, but once the invaders had recovered from the shock, both sides ended up huddled behind crates or buildings, reloading and taking shots when they dared. The colonists may have been defending their home, but they were no soldiers—and the corsairs were showing no mercy. The few men who risked the trip managed to open the doors of the women's barn, but that only added to the chaos. The majority of the women fled to the fields with their children, and the ones who stayed held their guns just as firmly as the men, but the colonists were simply outclassed.

Elijah fired when he had an opening, and a few times he saw his bullets sink into the chest of men across the courtyard. It was a lot easier to pull the trigger than it should have been. The shouting and gunfire around him was deafening, and he tried not to flinch as men he'd grown up with fell to the dirt around him. One of the corsairs threw a grenade, and James yelled at the others to take cover, but even from where he scrambled behind the corner of a building, the explosion rang in Elijah's ears. A piece of something clipped him in the side of the head, sending a hot flow of blood from his forehead to his cheek. He spared half a moment to wipe it away from his eyes and rushed back out with his brothers beside him, the high-pitched hum in his ears muffling the sounds of the gunfire.

Elijah hunkered behind a supply crate and split the last carton of ammunition with Ethan. The corsairs' numbers had been thinned a little—he thought, at least—but they were far more organized than the colonists had any hope of being. Elijah, his brothers, and the rest of the people he'd come to help were pinned down and out of bullets, and more than a few of them were bleeding out behind the barricades. Elijah paused with his back against the crate and wiped the blood from his eyes again. Had he really come all this way just to die on Dhat-Badan after all?

An explosion high above them brought an abrupt stop to the gunfire. The dome gateway burst open in a shower of sparks and metal, and the air around them became a whirlwind as the colony's protective barrier was broken. The gale lifted clouds of dust and anything light enough to be thrown, forcing colonists and corsairs both to crouch together and hide their faces from the whipping wind. Elijah squinted through the dust toward the source of the explosion and saw something massive swirling the smoke pouring from the gate, and he couldn't stop the laugh that fell from his lips as he recognized the shape that appeared as it sank below the obscuring cloud.

It was the Chimera.

As soon as the ship was clear of the broken gate, the colony's emergency backup systems came to life, sealing the gap in the dome and allowing the air to settle. The Chimera's engines still blew dirt and grit around the courtyard as it approached, but more importantly, the ship's guns began to fire on the corsairs, scattering them from the courtyard. The cargo bay door's hydraulics hummed as it opened, and Elijah saw Leslie, one hand on a strap to steady himself and the other holding his Jericho at his hip.

Brooks' voice crackled over the ship's speakers at the first pause in gunfire. "That's right, assholes! You'd better run!"

The Chimera drew close to the ground, and Leslie, Shaw, and Harper dropped from the bay doors. Harper immediately began tossing grenades toward center mass of the corsair forces, and Shaw walked toward them as if he was bulletproof, firing his shotgun at anyone who dared to show their face. The ship's captain spotted Elijah in the chaos as the corsairs were scattering and took a place behind the barricades of crates, dropping his duffel bag to the ground before the surrounding colonists.

"Y'all get the hell up and at 'em," he shouted to the men who stared in disbelief. "This here is an assist, not a rescue!"

They all hunkered down to reload, the ship's arrival giving them just a few moments to breathe in the panic.

"I thought you didn't want to be a fuckin' hero," Elijah called as Leslie dumped cartons of ammunition from his bag and tossed them to the men around him.

"Count your blessings, kid!"

"My blessings?!" Elijah snatched up a box of bullets and reloaded his weapon without taking his eyes from the blond. "Are you supposed to be a damn blessing?"

Leslie ducked as a shot rang out, pressing his back against the crate beside Elijah. "We might wanna put a pin in this conversation, huh? Just 'til we ain't gettin' shot at?"

Both of them rose to rest their guns on the crate and fire toward the line of recovering corsairs, then crouched back behind the barrier when the lull ended.

"You're good, you're terrible," Elijah shouted over the sound of the firefight. "You're gentle, you're rude—you say you care about me but you can't help my colony, and then you show up anyway?! If you're just jerking me around, do me a favor and don't give me any more blessings!"

"I came back, didn't I?"

Elijah flinched away from a bullet that hit the crate and paused to fire back before continuing. "Why?! Just so you can have it over me for next time? Just so you can try to get some cheap labor back on your ship?"

"Because I love you, goddamn it!" the captain snapped.

Elijah paused. The other colonists were still shooting around them, but Leslie's pale eyes held his gaze, a stern furrow in his brow.

"I love you, okay? I acted like an idiot and I can't fix it, but I'm here now because I love you. So can we please kick these corsairs off your colony and *then* have a nice long talk about it?"

Elijah's mouth didn't work. His brain barely worked. He hesitated a moment, but then he smiled, just a little, and the pair of them rose again to fire.

With the help of the Chimera's guns and its crew, the colonists began to make progress. Leslie shouted out orders to organize them, and they were able to slowly begin to make their way across the courtyard.

"Who the fuck are you, anyway?" James asked when the captain addressed him.

"I'm the one who's here savin' your hide, son, so you'd best get your ass up on that baler like I told you and keep on shooting."

Ethan shouted at him to just listen for once, and James did as he was told. The Chimera landed a short distance away from the fighting, and the colonists moved forward, ducking behind cover as they found it and pushing the corsair line steadily back. Elijah stuck close by Leslie's side, glad for his presence despite his protests. A shot rang out nearby them, and Leslie grabbed the shoulder of a man to jerk him backwards out of the line of fire.

"Dad!" Elijah called as he recognized his father being pulled behind the wall. "Are you okay?"

"That's your dad?" Leslie chuckled. "Good to meet you, man." He paused to reload and glanced sidelong at the older man. "Say, let me ask you somethin'. I'm lookin' to start a family of my own someday— what's your stance on spanking? You do a lot of that with your boys?"

"Are you fucking kidding me right now?" Elijah snapped as he threw a glance back at his father's puzzled face, but the captain only laughed and moved forward without him, hopping a fence to take a place behind a shipping crate.

When the corsairs finally began to retreat and barricade themselves inside the nearby general store, Brooks fired another heavy round from the Chimera, demolishing the walls of the building and dropping the roof on top of them.

Elijah's father snapped out a rare curse in Leslie's direction. "We'd like to have a colony left to live in by the time you're done helping!"

"I see where Elijah got his mouth from," the captain muttered, but he was promptly distracted by the sound of the corsair ship's engines roaring to life. He touched the tiny earpiece on his left side and spoke loud enough for his pilot to hear him over the sound of the fight around them. "Brooks, light that shit up! If they get that rig off the ground they'll crash right through that gate!"

"Yeah, that would be super irresponsible," Elijah sighed, and Leslie took the time to turn his head slowly toward him.

"Can we not?"

They both ducked down, Elijah pulling his father with him, while Brooks followed her orders. The corsair ship gave almost pained-sounding dings and thumps as the rounds hit it, and when one of the engines finally blew, it sent a few corsairs flying back toward the courtyard as they attempted to escape. It only took a few more shots from the Chimera and the emboldened colonists before the empty hands of the remaining corsairs began to appear above the battered crates and fences. The captain called to Brooks to cease fire and moved forward from his crate with his Jericho in both hands, stepping into the courtyard under the cover of a dozen more colonist rifles.

"Where's your captain?" the blond barked, and he focused his pistol on the first man who rose to speak.

"He was...on the ship," the corsair said with a sidelong glance toward the smoking wreckage.

Leslie snorted out a soft chuckle. "Well, seein' as y'all ain't got a ship no more, I guess you don't need a captain anyhow, do ya? Get your asses out here and get on the ground, and if I see a single gun in hand or a single stray dog tryin' to hide, I swear I'll scrounge up just enough bullets for every head we ain't put extra holes in yet." He turned to scan the crowd for his crew before snapping at them. "Shaw! Harper! Y'all get over here and keep these assholes in line."

While the pair set about tying the hands of the surrendering corsairs, the captain of the Chimera holstered his pistol at his hip and returned to meet the exhausted, empty stares of the colonists of Dhat-Badan. There wasn't a clean face among them, and every breath Elijah took had a little sting of smoke from the burning buildings around them. Men and women who had fought lay bleeding and groaning around them, tended to by old Doc Burke as well as Davies, who had appeared behind the line at some point. The colony was a mess, and they couldn't yet know how many had died defending it—but they had defended it. They'd won.

"So," Leslie said in a slightly subdued voice, his hands on his hips. "Who's in charge here, then?"

Elijah's father took a step forward. "They killed Administrator Howe. The Federation will have to appoint someone."

"Then you'd better call them and let them know you've got some corsair hostages and a busted gate. Maybe that'll convince 'em to send somebody."

The older man sighed through his nose and shook his head, but there was a small smile on his lips. "You've saved Dhat-Badan, mister. More than that, you kept my family from being killed. I didn't know that I liked Elijah running off the way he did, but if he's making friends like you out there, then I guess he's done all right."

"Don't thank me too much. You ain't seen my bill yet," Leslie added with a quick wink in Elijah's direction.

Elijah found himself smiling, though he tried to hide it from the suspicious glance his father threw him.

31

Elijah helped his brothers chain the corsairs inside one of the barns that still stood and did what he could to aid the wounded while Leslie and the rest of the Chimera's crew raided the corsair ship. The way Harper came out laughing and half dragging a large crate, Elijah suspected the trip wasn't going to turn out to be a complete waste of time for them. It seemed deeply quiet now, despite the sounds of people moving and working all around him. Anything would have seemed quieter than gunfire.

He saw Leslie talking with some of the older men in the colony, including his father, but when the captain headed back toward his ship, Elijah followed him. He stopped him with a firm grip on his bicep and stared down the automatic, threatening look the other man threw over his shoulder.

"I need to talk to you," Elijah said, and Leslie's expression softened into what might have been resignation.

"Yeah," he said after a beat of silence had passed. "I guessed you would. Come on."

He led Elijah up the familiar path to his quarters, the corridors echoing strangely with the bay doors open below, and shut them inside his cabin like he had so many times before. He seemed hesitant to move into the room, but Elijah didn't give him the chance. He stepped forward and hugged him tight, his chin resting on Leslie's shoulder and fingers twisting into the back of his shirt. The blond tensed in his grip, hands awkwardly out at his sides as though he wasn't sure he was allowed to put them on the boy who held him.

"You really came," Elijah said softly, half muffled by the fabric of Leslie's shirt.

The captain relaxed in Elijah's hug, and he allowed himself to slowly wrap his arms around the boy. "I guess I did," he murmured with his cheek against Elijah's hair.

"Eventually."

Leslie let a sigh slip from him. "I got no excuse, Elijah. I just—"

Elijah pulled back from him, shaking his head, and he put a quieting hand on his chest. "Did you mean what you said?"

The blond hesitated. "I said a lot of things—"

"That you love me."

Leslie's face burned slightly red, and he lowered his eyes a moment as though bracing himself before looking back up into the younger man's face. "I reckon I do."

"Can you say it when we're not in the middle of a firefight?"

The captain gave a soft, scoffing chuckle, and he reached up a hand to lightly touch the boy's face. "I love you, Elijah."

Elijah kissed him almost before the words had fully left his lips. He pulled his captain close to him, and the heat behind his kiss was slow, like relief. He held onto it for as long as he could, and when he finally had to break it to breathe, he was smiling. But when he opened his mouth to answer, Leslie stopped him.

"Before you say anything, there's somethin' else I've gotta tell you, too."

Elijah frowned up at him in confusion.

"I'm the reason those corsairs came here. At least, I probly am."

"What?" Elijah retreated from him, and Leslie didn't attempt to stop him. "What the hell do you mean, you're the reason?"

"To get us onto Altera, Ungolo wanted information," the captain explained, his brow knit in guilt. "I had information nobody else had—the Chimera was the first ship to carry that drug off of Dhat-Badan. So I told him about it. I told him there was a little farm colony that was hoping to be a new source. So I guess he told somebody else. That's how information brokers work," he added, as though to further justify himself.

Elijah scoffed and put a hand to his forehead as he tried to understand the other man's words. Leslie had sold out his colony for money. He'd put them all at risk so that he could smuggle who-knows-what onto Altera Station for profit.

"Elijah, I had no way of knowing who Ungolo would give that info to," Leslie went on. "It could have been a shipping company like us, or a dealer who would have come and made your Administrator rich. It's just bad luck that corsairs ended up with the information."

"Bad luck?" Elijah echoed, letting his hand drop. "Bad luck?! My brother got shot! People died! The colony is all but destroyed—they burned the fields, Les! They killed the cattle! Do you know how long it's going to take to come back from this? If ever! We'll be lucky if my whole family isn't relocated! We lost everything; do you get that?! And it's because of you!"

"I know it is," the blond answered solemnly. He looked like he didn't really want to meet Elijah's eyes, but he didn't turn away. "And I thought you oughta know it all before you—made any decisions about me."

Elijah shook his head, a humorless laugh falling from him. "Yeah."

Without another word, he hit the release on Leslie's door and walked out of the cabin, and he didn't stop until his feet were back on his colony's ruined soil.

· · ◆ · ·

Elijah had a lot to keep him busy. He worked with the other young men to move bodies and dig graves; he helped put out the last lingering fires; he nailed doors back into place and hauled furniture back upright. He worked until his hands were raw, turning away everything offered to him but water. By the time evening was approaching, he was moving by mechanical inches, working on autopilot until his brother Ethan finally snapped at him to go home, and he obeyed.

By the time he made it back to the house, his mother had somehow returned it to some semblance of order—so much so that he was almost able to ignore the spot on the living room floor where he'd broken a man's windpipe. His mother cleaned the neglected wound on his forehead while he sat on the bed he'd abandoned weeks before, trying to count how many hours it had been since he'd last slept. When she urged him down onto the mattress with a firm hand on his shoulder, his head barely had time to hit the pillow before unconsciousness overtook him.

The sun had been up for a while by the time he finally roused. His mother refused to let him out of the house to work with the others until he'd eaten something, so he sat at the same kitchen table he'd been eating at his entire life and sipped his coffee while he waited for her to finish his pancakes. He'd missed the smell.

She sat beside him once he had his plate, and she let him eat in peace for a while before she spoke. "You really saved all of us, Elijah."

"Mom, come on, don't—"

"But you did. You were millions of miles away, living the life you wanted, and you came back for us. Alone. You risked your life for us, and we have this colony back because of you. It's important that you recognize that."

"I just did what I had to. Nobody else was going to help," he added bitterly, and he lowered his eyes to scoot some pancake remnants through a pool of syrup.

His mother waited a few moments, and then she reached out to lay her hand on his, stilling its movement. "That's why you came home yesterday, instead of going back to the ship that took you from here?"

Elijah tried to take a breath to steady himself, but it didn't help. "I don't—I don't even know if I should have gone," he said in a weak voice. His mother's comforting hand on his back broke down the last of his defenses, and she moved his plate away just in time for him to put his head in his arms on the table. "I thought I could trust him," he said without looking up. "He said he needed me to trust him. But *he* told that information broker about the drugs Administrator Howe was making! He practically led those corsairs here!"

Hannah gave a small sigh, and she inched her chair closer to him to gently stroke his hair while he hiccuped. "You mean that captain?"

He lifted his head after a few more breaths and wiped his face on his sleeve before answering. "Mom, I—I should tell you, I—part of the reason I stayed on that ship, I..." He swallowed the lump in his throat, but it reappeared immediately. He wet his lips, trying to find the will to say the words he needed to say—the words that he had never spoken aloud to his family because he knew they would have been a disappointment to his father.

"The captain and I," he started carefully, "are..." He sighed. "I like...I like men."

"Oh, baby," his mother said with a soft laugh. "I know."

"You know?"

"Of course I do. We all know. That's one of the reasons why I wasn't so upset about you leaving—I know all the boys your age here at home, and I don't like your odds." She smiled at him and brushed the hair from his reddened eyes. "Now tell me about this captain."

Elijah let everything out under his mother's patient gaze. He told her about offering to sleep with Leslie for a ride on the Chimera, about how it had become more than that, about every wonderful and frustrating thing the blond had done since Elijah had first stowed away on his ship.

"And now he tells me that he loves me, and he's sorry, but that he sold us out so he could make money? And I just—fuck; is this what love is supposed to be like?"

"Love is patient," she said. "Love is kind. You know how it goes. But love is hard, and it doesn't always solve problems. This man sounds like he's got a lot of walls, and it's not your job to climb them. Maybe they could be taken down, in time—but that would take both of you, and first you'd have to decide how much you're willing to forgive. He is the reason those awful people came here, but it wasn't his intent; he seems like he hasn't always been honest about his feelings with you, but he's tried."

She leaned down and tilted her head to offer him a faint smile. "I think that a man who can admit when he's wrong, who can do the right thing even when it hurts him, is a good one, even if there are layers of bad on top. But only you can decide if you think he's worth the heartache he's given you and probably will give you. You always have a home here—and there are a million other ships you could sneak away on. We're right here until you make up your mind."

Elijah nodded, though the weight on his shoulders didn't feel any lighter. "I should...I should get back to helping," he said after a moment. He pushed away from the table and gave his mother's hand a gentle squeeze. "Thanks, mom."

He was scolded more than once throughout the day for not listening when people spoke to him. He had too much on his mind to focus very well. It did cheer him slightly to see the crew of the Chimera helping out around the colony. The sentiment turned sour when he reminded himself that they were trapped here until the Federation arrived to repair the gate anyway, but he still smiled when Brooks tracked him down to hug him and say she was happy he wasn't dead.

Leslie was nowhere to be seen, and Elijah was glad. He didn't know how he could look at him right now. Everything logical in him was telling him to wave goodbye as the Chimera left Dhat-Badan behind and to try to hitch a ride on another ship. He wasn't too old to join the Federation, either. That would get him out in the galaxy, at least. He wasn't useless—he had options. He had options that probably wouldn't involve crying into his breakfast over a man who'd strung him along like a lovesick puppy. A man who'd set him on fire more than once, who'd confided in him and laughed with him, spent late nights with him, swum in the ocean and stood at the top of a mountain with him, put his business at risk for him, and admitted his part in Elijah's troubles when silence would have served him better.

Elijah sighed heavily as he leaned against a nearby wall to take a break from hauling burnt lumber. It was hopeless—he loved the stupid bastard anyway.

But there was too much to do for him to be selfish. His colony needed every able hand available, and there was no decision to make until the gate was fixed. The last thing he needed was to rush into something he'd turn out to regret. So he'd work, and put his feelings out of his mind the best he could.

The house was quiet in the evening since Elijah was the only son left at home. Dinner with his parents was awkward, but he didn't get the dressing-down he'd half expected from his father for running away. Helping break the whole colony out from a hostage situation had gotten him out of a talking-to and an I-told-you-so, at least. The only words his father had for him at all were to tell him that he'd managed to get in touch with the nearby station, and that he'd gotten their assurance that the Federation would have a repair crew out within the week.

A week gave him some time to make up his mind. And the day's hard labor left him exhausted enough that sleep came easily, so he was spared the suffering of staring at his ceiling and torturing himself with thoughts of the Chimera's captain.

By the fourth day, Elijah had settled into the constant fatigue he remembered from before he'd left the colony, but he still hadn't seen Leslie. He'd chatted with Brooks and Harper sporadically, and he'd even seen Park helping to repair some of the colony's machinery, but the captain either hadn't been leaving his ship or was actively avoiding him. Either option was fine, he supposed. Elijah wasn't going to chase after him—at least, he didn't plan on it—so if Leslie wanted to cut off contact, then maybe Elijah wouldn't have to make a decision at all. Maybe there was no space left for him aboard the Chimera. The thought hurt, but maybe it was an easier hurt to deal with than the alternative.

He ate the meal his mother cooked that evening and cleaned up all the dishes just like he always had, not even looking up when he heard the sound of a knock on the door. People had been coming and going so frequently over the past few days that even knocking was beginning to seem like a cursory measure. But Elijah's sudsy hands stopped moving when he heard a familiar, low voice from the doorway.

"Evening, ma'am. I'm here for Elijah, if he'll see me."

"I'll ask," was all his mother would promise, and she left the front door ajar to poke her head into the kitchen. She watched her son's face for a moment before speaking, but they both knew she didn't have to say who it was. "Do you want to talk to him, honey?"

"Yeah," Elijah answered after a moment's hesitation. He reached for a towel to dry his hands. "I'll talk to him."

His mother let Leslie inside, and Elijah led him into his formerly-shared bedroom and shut the door. It felt like a strange reversal, having the captain in his room. Leslie didn't move too far from the door—he just stood with his hands in his pants pockets, glancing subtly around at the slowly-grown collection of knick-knacks on the shelves.

"This is the childhood home, huh?" he asked, his voice soft. "You really fit five boys in here?"

Elijah stayed a bit more than arm's reach away from him. He couldn't quite relax, despite the other man's obvious attempt to lighten the mood. "We managed," he said simply.

Leslie lowered his eyes to the floor, and Elijah felt a little guilty for shutting him down. It couldn't have been easy for him to come.

"I...guess I wanted to ask where you reckon I stood. I didn't come to beg. But I hear the Federation will be here soon, and...as much as I've got wrong these weeks with you, my conscience won't let me up and leave without tryin' one more time to ask you to forgive me."

"Les," Elijah sighed, and the captain glanced back up at him with a faint frown on his lips.

"I know you can—should—do better than me. I ain't even asking if you want to be with me. But whether I deserve to or not, I love you, and the thought of leavin' you here, where you tried to hard to get away from, and you hatin' me all the while, just...it tears me up." He paused to take a short, steadying breath. "So, if you want it, there's a spot for you on the Chimera when we leave. Even if all you want's a lift to the next station. And if you want to stay shut up in your bunk the whole way and give me the finger on your way out, then...at least I figure I've helped you a little bit in the end."

Weight settled in Elijah's stomach as though he'd swallowed a ball of lead. "You...damn idiot," he murmured. He stepped closer and gave the other man a light shove by his chest, which Leslie accepted without resistance. "Even now, when I think you're going to let me go, you just...can't you just let me keep thinking you're terrible?"

"Elijah—"

"I'd given up on you. I came back here on my own because I thought money mattered more to you than I did. Then you tell me about the information broker, and you vanish? In a colony with four hundred people on it, a good number of them dead now, you still manage to fucking disappear."

"I didn't figure you wanted to see me."

"I didn't! It would have been easier! It would have been easier to forget you if you'd just...left. But here you are. You're so..." He stopped, pressing the balls of his hands into his eyes to push back the burning feeling. "So...goddamn selfish."

The words hung heavily in the air for a few beats before Leslie spoke again, his voice sounding a little strained. "That what you want?" he asked. "You want me to just take off, so you can forget me?"

"Stop asking me what I want!" Elijah huffed as he dropped his hands.

"Well goddamn, Elijah; am I selfish or not?"

"I don't know! That's the problem!"

Leslie ran a frustrated hand through his hair and audibly sighed. "Just tell me what you want from me, Elijah. Please."

"I want *you!*" Elijah slumped forward in resignation, letting his forehead rest on the blond's shoulder. "I want you," he said again, almost whispering. "I just want to know it's not a mistake." He reached one hand up to curl his fingers into Leslie's shirt. "I love you," he admitted. "But I've still got half a mind to kick you out of here and never look at you again. I'm setting myself up to be hurt, being with you."

"That's funny," Leslie said in a soft voice, "here I was this whole time thinkin' I was set up to get hurt."

Elijah smiled, though his heart was aching. "So...what?" he asked through a tight throat. "Do we just keep running, afraid of risking anything in case we get hurt?"

Leslie cupped the boy's cheeks in his hands to draw his gaze up, and Elijah fought the urge to lean into the touch, trying to keep his pulse steady under the heat of the other man's hands.

"I can't promise I'll never hurt you," Leslie murmured. "Anybody that'd say they could is a damn liar. I can promise I'll try. I can promise to listen when you tell me I'm bein' an asshole or a fuckin' idiot or both. That's the best I can do. If that's not good enough for you—" He paused to give a soft, sad chuckle. "Hell, Elijah. You've run this show from the start whether you know it or not. If you want to call it quits on me, there ain't nobody in the galaxy who would blame you. Least of all me. But I'm willin' to risk it if you are. I'm just sorry it took me so long to get there."

Elijah hesitated, watching Leslie's pale, pained eyes. He loved this man. Despite everything, and against all good judgment, Elijah loved him. Leslie had made mistakes, and been withholding, and they'd frequently misunderstood each other—but, when pushed, he'd always shown Elijah that he could trust him. They could work on how quickly he came around to doing the right thing. Elijah hadn't behaved perfectly, either. And after all, had Elijah really come this far to start being afraid now?

"I'm willing to risk it," he said, and Leslie's lips closed over his with enough force to drive the air from his lungs.

32

There was still a lot of work to do on Dhat-Badan, but a Federation ship arrived two days later to rebuild the dome gate and allow travel again. Once it was able to open, a ship took away the corsair prisoners, which at least removed the threat of a counterattack from hanging over the colonists' heads. A small number of Federation soldiers and engineers remained to help with the repairs, and Elijah's father said that shipments of new cattle and seed would be arriving before long. The colony wasn't going to be abandoned.

Leslie and the crew of the Chimera were thanked officially for their aid in protecting a Federation colony, and unofficially dressed down by a uniformed man with a clipboard for the "entirely unnecessary" destruction of a very expensive gate. Even so, Elijah saw the captain of the Federation ship shake Leslie's hand and privately exchange words with him that the boy suspected were far kinder than the bureaucrat's.

With the Chimera loaded with spoils from the corsair ship—as well as more homemade baked goods than they would ever be able to eat—and the gate repaired, Elijah had to say a real goodbye to his family. His mother still sniffled, and his father asked him again if he was sure, but no one tried to stop him. Even James shook Elijah's hand and wished him well, though he didn't seem very pleased about it. Daniel had been on his feet for the last couple of days, so he came to see Elijah off at the Chimera's open cargo doors and gave him the tightest hug he'd ever had.

"You didn't have to come back," he said quietly, and he pulled back and put a brotherly hand on the smaller man's shoulder. "You did good, Elijah."

"I'm just glad I got your message."

Daniel smiled at him and mussed his hair, pausing as he glanced over his brother's shoulder and tilted his chin at the blond captain standing deeper in the cargo bay. "So that's the real reason you're leaving again, huh?"

Elijah grimaced. "Mom told you?"

"Mom told me," he chuckled. "But it's a good thing. I think the only gay guy on the colony is Jacob Gray, and he's way too old for you. And also he picks his nose. I've seen it. You don't need that in your life."

Elijah dropped his head to laugh and looked back up at his brother. "Thanks, Daniel."

"Take care of yourself out there. I'd tell that captain of yours what I'd do if he hurts you, but I'm pretty sure he could take me, so you're gonna have to handle him on your own."

"Don't worry about me," Elijah said with a smile. "I've got him right where I want him."

· ● ◆ ● ·

Elijah was able to watch his home colony disappear behind them without hiding behind crates this time. It felt good to have a real place, even if he still didn't know where he was going. The crew treated him like he'd never left, though Brooks did make a comment or two about the availability of Elijah's youngest brother. He cleaned up the mess hall, which had clearly suffered some neglect in his absence, and spent some time on the bridge helping plot their next route. It was easy to fall back into rhythm with the hum of the ship's engines under his feet. He even had a few more personal belongings to put away in his bunk now that he wasn't sneaking away at a moment's notice.

He only started to feel tense after the crew had eaten their supper and he'd cleaned up the kitchen afterward. He hadn't spoken to Leslie much since they'd left, and now his heart seemed loud as he tried not to look at the closed doors of the captain's cabin. The dynamic between them had changed. How were you supposed to treat someone once you'd both admitted you loved each other? Could it really just be the same as always? Every glance, every casual conversation, felt heavy now. Elijah wasn't even sure he would be keeping his own bunk now, but he hadn't wanted to presume anything. Leslie clearly liked his privacy—that wasn't going to change overnight. The ship was cramped quarters to begin with; Elijah would understand if he still got kicked out of the captain's room regularly. He just hoped that having that kind of practical conversation would come as easily to Leslie as asking about butt plugs had.

The cabin doors hissed open across the room, almost making him drop the last cup he was washing, and he looked up as Leslie moved close to the counter.

"Getting right back to cabin boy duties?"

"I didn't think you accepted crew who earned their keep in 'I love you's," Elijah chuckled, but he paused as he saw the red that flushed across the other man's cheeks.

Leslie cleared his throat and reached up to scratch the back of his head as an excuse to lower his gaze. "You're not gonna be shy about that, huh?"

Elijah bit his lip to keep his smile in check, and he set the clean cup back with the others. Leslie was embarrassed. He may have been older than Elijah, and more worldly in general, but when it came to real relationships, Leslie was just as new to all of this as he was.

"Don't worry, Captain," he said softly. "I won't speak out of turn in front of your crew."

"I know you won't," the blond answered sternly, but Elijah could hear the bluster in his threat. Leslie gave another little cough and leaned his hip against the counter to look Elijah in the face, clearly trying to reverse the direction the conversation was taking.

"I want you to come to my cabin when you're finished here," he said.

"Yes, sir," Elijah nodded, unable to keep tense excitement from bubbling in his belly. "I'm done. If you're ready for me."

Leslie tilted his head back toward the door and led the boy into his quarters. The familiar thunk of the lock matched the pounding of Elijah's heart, but he didn't have much time to let his nerves get to him—the blond had Elijah pressed between his body and the cool metal almost as soon as the door closed, muffling his soft, startled sound with a kiss. Leslie's tongue parted his lips, caressing him with a heat that shot straight to his groin. He sighed at the gentle touch of the other man's hands on his face, and when they parted to breathe, Leslie stayed close, his forehead pressed lightly against Elijah's.

"Didn't know I could miss someone this bad," the captain murmured with a smile on his lips. "Not sure I like it."

Elijah let his fingers twist into Leslie's shirt at his waist. "Well, I live here, so you'll probably be sick of me more than you'll miss me from here on."

"I doubt that." Leslie pressed another lingering kiss to his lips and brushed his fingertips through the soft hair at the back of Elijah's head. "I do need to ask you if you expect, or...want anything to change. Between us. "

Elijah smiled. Even if he couldn't always count on Leslie to make good decisions, at least he was reliably open and willing to initiate the difficult conversations.

"Do you want anything to change?" Elijah asked, and the blond lowered his eyes.

"I've never done this before. And I've been the one screwin' up so far. So you're the boss. You wanna start from scratch, just get a drink sometime, do it properly—we'll do that, and I'll quit draggin' you in here. Even if all I want is to strap you down and show you how much I missed you," he added in a lower voice. The pad of his thumb brushed Elijah's bottom lip, bringing up goosebumps on the boy's arms. "But you just gotta tell me how you wanna go from here, and that's what we'll do, understand?"

Elijah saw the uncertainty in the other man's pale eyes, and his heart gave a pleasant thump. Leslie was trying. He did have a lot of walls built up—but maybe he'd made a little crack in the first one for Elijah to come through. That wasn't nothing. Elijah dropped his gaze to the floor a moment to hide his smile, and he crept his fingers toward the blond's metal belt buckle.

"Yes, Captain," he murmured.

Leslie's sharp intake of breath was audible as he took the boy by the wrists and walked him swiftly backward toward the mattress. A soft laugh fell from Elijah's lips as he was pushed back onto the blanket, but it quickly died at the predatory look in the pale eyes that stared down at him.

"You've been asking me for something for a while," the captain said, his gaze dropping to Elijah's full lips. Electricity coursed through the boy's skin at Leslie's light touch to his jaw. "Do you think it's about time I give you what you want?"

Elijah tried to swallow but couldn't quite get past the lump in his throat. Even with all the time he'd spent in this room, on this bed, and despite his repeated gasping pleas, Leslie had never actually had sex with him. Not really—not without using a toy in place of himself. Elijah had only even seen the other man orgasm a small handful of times. Usually he just worked Elijah into a babbling, sweaty mess, then excused himself sometime after the boy had passed out. Elijah sometimes pretended that the blond was just the other side of the bathroom door, panting and stroking himself to completion with the taste of Elijah's sweat still on his lips, but he had no idea if it was true.

"Please, Captain," Elijah managed to get out. He wanted to reach up to Leslie's belt but didn't dare touch him without permission. Not when he had that slow, taunting smirk on his lips.

"Then you'd better get ready for me," the blond answered. "Take your clothes off."

Elijah did as he was told, tugging his collar up over his head and easily sliding out of his boots, pants, and underwear. No matter how many times he'd been in the captain's quarters—in however many compromising positions—it still made his heart race to see Leslie's eyes trailing down his body, those slender fingers toying idly with his belt buckle while he waited for the boy to undress.

Leslie reached into the cabinet above the headboard and dropped a small bottle of lubricant into Elijah's waiting hand. He watched patiently as Elijah settled against the pillow and splayed his legs wide. Elijah couldn't hold the other man's intent gaze; just knowing the blond was watching him and hearing his soft intake of breath as Elijah slid gel-slicked fingers between his legs was enough to make the boy's skin burn with embarrassment and excitement. Elijah's eyelids fluttered shut as he pressed a slow finger inside of himself, the muscles in his thighs tightening at the pleasant burn. He knew better than to try to touch his own erection without permission, though it pulsed torturously against his stomach, demanding his attention. His breath came in shallow pants as he stretched himself with his fingers, desperate and impatient for the heat of the other man.

The subtle dip of the mattress and the touch of Leslie's fingers at the back of his head startled him, but a soft moan fell from him as he parted his lips to follow the blond's guiding hand and take him into his mouth. The press of Leslie's cock at the back of his throat was almost too much for him, but when his hand slowed between his legs, the captain gave his nipple a sharp pinch as a reminder. He whined around the other man, satisfied by the tightening clutch of Leslie's fingers in his hair. He was learning the right ways to move his tongue to make the stoic captain hiss, and he was able to take him much deeper than the first time. Every little gasp Leslie made sent a jolt through Elijah, twitching his own suffering prick.

"Good boy," Leslie rumbled above him, and he tugged Elijah away from him to allow him to breathe. "Hands and knees."

Elijah reluctantly removed his fingers from himself to twist into his commanded position, but before he could settle, Leslie was over him, fastening his wrists into the leather cuffs Elijah knew well by now. He strapped him to the bars at the headboard and spread his knees beneath him with a light touch, then slowly ran his fingertips over the curve of Elijah's ass, sending a shudder up the boy's spine. The first strike was almost gentle, but Elijah still jumped and bit his lip. He waited for the next slap of Leslie's palm on his skin, gripping his restraints against a blow that didn't come.

"You know," the blond purred as he leaned over the younger man to give his ear a soft bite, "I was thinking about what I should do to keep you from runnin' off again." He let long fingers run lightly over the boy's throat and settled his hand on Elijah's collarbone. "And I think I've come up with something good. You want me to keep you here, don't you, Elijah?"

"Yes, Captain," the boy breathed, unable to keep his hips from grinding back into the man above him.

"And you're not going to run away from me again, are you?"

Elijah shut his eyes and let a soft, smiling sigh escape through his nose. He heard the uncertain plea hidden under Leslie's command, no matter how the captain tried to hide it. He twisted just enough to catch the other man's eyes and tilted his chin to risk pressing a warm kiss to the corner of Leslie's mouth.

"No, Captain," he murmured. He did his best to keep his smile in check at the stunned look on the older man's face, but coherent thought was wiped from his mind as Leslie crushed his lips with a kiss. Elijah whimpered at the intrusion of the captain's tongue and tried to follow him when the kiss was broken, gasping at the smooth heat of Leslie's cock against him as the other man leaned forward to reach into the cabinet again.

Elijah stayed still while Leslie fastened the leather collar around his neck, and he sucked in a sharp breath as he was jerked gently backward by the strap hooked to him like a leash. He groaned in frustration at the loss of Leslie's warmth against his back, but his skin tingled from the light press of leather kept taut against his throat. The captain's free hand struck his backside again, making him pant, and then Leslie spread him open, and the burning caress of his tongue against Elijah's opening brought a sudden, shivering moan from the younger man. His hands clenched around the straps holding him to the bed as if they might save him from drowning, but they couldn't keep the constant, panting cries from escaping him. Leslie squeezed the flesh of his thighs and let his palm brush agonizingly lightly down the underside of Elijah's dripping cock as the boy's entrance softened under the careful attention of his tongue.

Elijah's legs quivered underneath him at every touch, steadily losing the ability to support his weight the longer Leslie's mouth was on him. If he started to slack, the captain would tug on his leash and force him to straighten his back and press harder into the blond's tongue. When Leslie finally broke away from him, Elijah could barely breathe, his knuckles white and fingers aching from holding onto his restraints. He let out a helpless moan as the mattress shifted behind him and he felt the hot pressure of Leslie's dick against his entrance.

"All right, Elijah?" the captain asked softly, his voice muffled by the pumping blood in Elijah's ears. His hand splayed gently across the dip of the boy's lower back, a little cool on Elijah's overheated skin. "Are you ready?"

"Yes," he half sobbed in reply. "Please, Captain. Please."

Leslie eased forward, guiding Elijah's hips back with a sure hand, and wanton cries fell from the boy's lips as the blond entered him, stretching him with a sweet, overwhelming sting. Elijah choked even without the small pull on his leash, his whole body shuddering at the sudden fullness that was completely unlike any of the toys Leslie had used on him before. It was almost too hot for him to bear—and the first slow roll of the captain's hips against his backside made him whine and hide his face in the pillow. Leslie took his time with him, making certain the noises the boy made were from pleasure and not discomfort. Elijah could sense the tension in the man behind him, who, judging by the dig of his fingers in Elijah's hips, was clearly struggling to keep his composure. Leslie ground against him with slow, experimental rocks of his hips, listening for every cry and hitch of breath until he found the spot inside of Elijah that the boy had grown to know well. Elijah jerked against his bonds, desperate to escape or push back—he couldn't decide. Leslie kept him from moving too far with a firm hand on his leash, and he picked up his pace, his careful movements turned relentless.

Elijah was lost. He couldn't breathe, couldn't think, couldn't move except as his lover pulled him. Leslie's knees pressed his thighs farther apart, and the blond's hips smacked hard into his backside at a rhythm that even his racing heart struggled to match. Hours might have passed that way, or maybe only moments—Elijah's mind was fogged with the pleasure that spread over every inch of his skin, burning him alive from the inside out. In his haze, he knew the captain's name fell from his lips in a plea, but no punishment came. Instead, the blond paused just long enough to reach forward and unfasten him from the headboard, leaving his wrists bound together as he hauled Elijah up to kneel in his lap. The boy's head fell back at the gentle tug on his leash, his strapped wrists thrown over his head behind him to hold onto Leslie's neck for dear life. He moved on instinct, lifting and dropping his hips onto his lover's cock deeper than he thought possible, and a cry almost like a sob ripped from him as Leslie's hand finally slid around his own dripping erection.

"I want you to come for me, Elijah," Leslie growled, his breath hot and close by his ear where Elijah held him with fingers knotted in blond waves.

The boy couldn't even muster a "Yes, Captain." He just moaned, caught helplessly between his lover's expert hand and the pounding burn that filled him every time he pressed back into Leslie's lifted hips. Even if he'd wanted to, he wouldn't have been able to hold back with the captain's rough command against the skin of his neck. He only made it a few more thrusts and twists of Leslie's grip around him before he cried out, spilling his climax onto his own stomach and his lover's hand. He only slowed the movement of his hips, unwilling to give up the press of Leslie's cock deep inside him, but his whole body tensed again as the blond lifted his hand to slide his semen-slicked fingers past Elijah's parted lips. His own fluid was salty on his tongue, but he dutifully licked every drop from Leslie's probing fingers, gasping as the man beneath him thudded upwards again.

"Where do you want me to come, Elijah?"

The question itself sent lightning through the boy's exhausted body, and his fingers tangled tighter in his lover's hair. "P...Please, Captain," he managed, every breath a struggle as the air was pushed from his lungs with each thrust of Leslie's hips.

"Please what?"

"Please—inside me, please—"

Leslie held him tightly by the leash and the hips, keeping him firmly in place as he thrust up into him at a frenetic pace. It was all Elijah could do to stay upright in his lover's arms, panting out pitiful moans, until he felt the tension in the man beneath him slowly rise and finally snap. Leslie's heat shot into him, causing his back to arch against the blond as he rolled his hips in a few more slow movements, allowing them both to settle in the deafening, silent moments following their stillness.

Elijah only unclenched his aching fingers when Leslie gently touched his hands, easing them back to his front and undoing his straps. He helped the boy slide off of his lap and lie back onto the mattress, where he fell and stayed, feeling as though his body was made of liquid. Leslie let him collapse there in a daze, but for once, he didn't immediately get up to fetch a cloth to clean him with. He just carefully unbuckled the collar from his lover's neck and slid it free, abandoning it on the floor beside the bed, then laid down with his arm over Elijah's waist, his hand settling near the beat of his still-throbbing heart. Elijah smiled despite his exhaustion, settling back against Leslie's chest and lacing his fingers with the other man's.

"Can you say it now?" he asked softly, and he felt the soft puff of warm air against him as Leslie chuckled.

The blond pressed a long, lingering kiss to the sweat-glistening skin at the base of the boy's neck.

"I love you, Elijah," he whispered, squeezing his lover's fingers in his own.

Elijah bit his lip and had to find his voice through the tightness in his throat. "I love you too, Les."

33

The gate of the dome protecting the colony of Dhat-Badan opened to receive the Chimera, and Elijah waited from his regular place at the navigation console while the decompression and sterilization systems did their work on the ship. It had been eight months since he'd last seen his home colony, and he could tell even through the windows in the bridge that things had mostly been able to return to normal following the corsair attack. The fields bloomed with crops, cattle grazed in their pastures, and people moved to and fro in the distant town below.

Elijah knew that his mother would fuss over the scar, now long-healed, that cut his right eyebrow in two—he'd let a kineta's long reach get the best of him during a scrap on Loeria—and the tattoo that had started as a simple outline on his shoulder of a mountain horizon framing the diamond dust nebula of Amerath 9 but now was extending steadily down his arm as he added more and more memories. At least she wouldn't be able to see the silver bar that he'd allowed Leslie to pierce through his left nipple some months ago. He was pretty sure he could still convince her to make some pancakes.

When the Chimera landed safely on the surface of the planet, Elijah waited at the airlock door beside Leslie while the ship decompressed.

"So, I'm leaving you here this time, right?" the captain teased him, and Elijah scoffed.

"You can't get rid of me."

Leslie stepped close to him and slid one finger through the silver circle that hung from a thin chain to sit just at Elijah's collarbone. The blond had given it to him a few weeks ago in what must have been the most adorable showing of shyness Elijah had ever seen in the older man. He was never going to be the marrying type, he'd said, and any formal showing of commitment could have led to trouble if anyone who meant Leslie harm found out about it. Not to mention the endless ribbing of the crew. So he'd offered Elijah this— something just for them, so they they both knew who belonged to who. It was a compromise that Elijah was happy to make. He had even dared to steal a kiss while Leslie had fastened it around his neck for him.

Leslie tugged the boy a half step closer to him with a smirk on his lips.

"That's the right answer."

True to form, Elijah's mother tutted and scolded him for getting into such trouble on his travels almost the second he walked in the door of his childhood home, and she lifted and twisted his arm to disapprovingly inspect every inch of his inked skin, but she still brought both her son and his guest into the kitchen and plied them with fresh milk and bread and cheeses. She caught him up on all the latest colony gossip—most importantly, that the Federation had appointed his father as the new Administrator—and even offered them beers once they'd filled their bellies with food and listened while Elijah shared some of the less-dangerous stories from his travels.

"You're turning into a scoundrel," his mother said with a sigh as she leaned back in her chair across the dining room table from Elijah and his captain. "I can only assume it's the company you keep—no offence, Captain."

"None taken," Leslie chuckled.

"But you're happy, aren't you?" she pressed in a softer voice. "You feel like you did the right thing?"

Elijah smiled down at the table as he rolled the bottom edge of his beer bottle on the surface. He'd spent a lot of time crossing things off of his list—he'd been to over three dozen different planets now, from desert outposts to cliffside shantytowns and smooth and gleaming space stations, and he still had a lot more to see. Life aboard the Chimera wasn't always easy, and he sometimes ended up bloodied or bruised—and once even sitting next to Harper in a jail cell on Theta Geminus 4—but he wouldn't trade it for anything.

"Yeah," he answered, not needing to look to know the man beside him was smiling faintly at him. "I'm right where I want to be."

ABOUT THE AUTHOR

Tess likes to write about what makes people tick, whether that's deeply-rooted emotional issues, childhood trauma, or just plain hedonism. Throw in a heaping helping of action and violence, a sprinkling of steamy bits, and a whisper of wit (with alliteration optional but preferred), and you have her idea of a perfect novel. She believes in telling stories about real people who live in less-real worlds full of werewolves, witches, demons, vampires, and the occasional alien.

Born and bred in the South, T.S. started writing young, but began writing real novels while working full time as a legal secretary. When she's not writing, she reads other people's books, plays video games, watches movies, and spends time with her husband and daughter. She hopes her daughter grows into a woman who knows what she wants, grabs it, and gets into significantly less trouble than the women in her mother's novels.